Betrayer

Shari Branning

Crazy Cabin Books

Crazy Cabin Books

Cover illustration and design by Tiffany Hilterbrand

Author photo courtesy of Samantha Derrick Photography

Greater love hath no man than this...

1

Poison Arrow

The arrow. Black feathered and stained sickly green, it fled straight and true from the lonely ridge top where a single yeoman crouched with the bow still humming in his hand. It sped fast and hard as though driven not by the tightened string from which it was released, but by the will of a powerful master, arching down over the writhing contortions of battle, unmoved by a thousand screams, or ten thousand clashing swords. In a valley full of war and heaving motion of men and horses it found its single mark. It pierced deep into the chest of the warrior.

Breac woke from the nightmare sweating and chilled. He sat up, rubbing his chest where he had felt the dream arrow enter, and found it sound. Drawing a long breath, he rolled to his feet, lifted the tent flap aside and stepped out to stand swaying in the chill twilight. It was the cold hour before dawn, and the valley was pale with frost. Gray mist crawled under the forest eves and bled out into the hollows of the meadow.

He nodded to a passing sentry. The man had his hands inside his cloak to keep warm, and his hood pulled up close around his face. He returned the nod, still humming to himself.

The dread that had gnawed at Breac when he woke would not go away. It grew to a feeling of impending doom as he stood looking down the valley. He knew the feeling well enough to distrust the peaceful encampment, the silent dim valley. His gaze, half blue-eyed and half brown, searched the shadows. Daring them to yield their secrets. Turning, he ducked back into the tent, buckled on his sword, laced on his riding boots, and donned a black cloak. Last he slipped on a pair of heavy gloves, hiding the milky white scar on his right palm. He left the tent and made his way to where the horses were picketed.

The bay stallion lifted his head at Breac's approach, and raked up earth with a huge hoof. He laid his ears back and tossed his head up, but when the man spoke he stilled, swiveling his ears. Breac whispered to the warhorse while he saddled him.

From behind them a voice spoke. "You will look as old as I soon, if you don't rest."

Breac glanced around at the man who'd spoken, then finished cinching the saddle girth before he replied, "Good morning, Jorah. Our enemy doesn't rest. Neither shall I."

"Our enemy is not a mortal like you and I," Jorah said. He sat on an overturned bucket, smoking a pipe. Bushy white hair stuck out around the rolled up brim of his felt hat, but his short beard was still streaked with black. He had been a general in the King's army for as long as Breac could remember.

"He must be stopped none the less."

Jorah did not reply as Breac paused to look and listen once more. He rested his hands on the stallion's neck under his mane to warm them, studying the valley. In the faint light all appeared still. He glanced to the forested hillsides, and saw nothing amiss.

"Too still," Jorah said.

Breac shook his head. "No.... Just a feeling. I'm going to ride to the top of the ridge and look around."

"Shall I come?"

"No. Rouse the men. Have them ready. And listen for my signal."

Jorah nodded and rose, tapping out his pipe onto the frosty ground. He placed his fist over his heart, bowed slightly, then turned and ambled away.

Breac rode through camp, spoke a quiet password to one of the sentries, and guided the stallion onto a narrow trail out of the valley. The trail slithered through the leafless underbrush, sometimes steep and sometimes switching back and forth. With each step apprehension clawed his stomach. He did not doubt the feeling for an instant. Something was amiss, and already he dreaded finding out what it might be. Near the ridge crest the horse shied, tossing his head up, nostrils flaring. He urged the animal forward until in the trail he saw the body of one of the King's scouts. His throat had been slashed, and dark blood soaked the ground and low bushes. The murderer had not attempted to conceal the body or even his own bloody tracks leading back down the path.

A gust of cold wind pressed Breac's cloak against his body, tousling his sun-bleached hair around his ears. He turned. The trail dropped out of sight a few paces on, heading toward the far valley. Boulders and scraggy saplings lined the ridge, all wind blasted and offering no shield against the rising sun. He slid from the saddle and went forward to the ridge crest on foot. Crouching behind one of the boulders, he looked down into the valley on the other side. Line upon line of battle-ready enemy troops marched in formation south along the base of the mountain. They were already far down the valley, and most of the army had turned east, entering a gorge that would bring them around to his side of the mountain, just a mile south of camp.

"So here we shall meet indeed, Leazor," Breac muttered.

The feeling of unease lifted as he stared down at the mass of troops. The time for apprehension had passed. Now he must act. But as he turned, something struck him as not right about the hillside. Whether it was a sound or a movement from the corner of his eye, he did not know. He crouched by the boulder and scanned the empty forest. Down the path to the right a mountain laurel offered the only cover for an enemy. Even as he thought it, he heard the twang of a bowstring. A black feathered arrow hissed past his shoulder. He lunged toward the laurel, but the enemy scout was already fleeing back toward the cover of dense underbrush. Breac turned and ran back to his horse, swinging into the saddle.

"Fly my friend," he urged. "Do not hold back. We may both die today."

The beast lifted his nose to the wind, swiveled his ears, and sprang away down the path. By some magic he neither stumbled nor lost control of his wild career down the mountain. With a leap they left the path. The stallion stretched out over the dead grass of the valley. The mist was lifting. Breac took the battle horn from his saddle and sounded the call to arms.

The camp came alive in an instant. Shouted orders mingled with shouts of anger, and whinnies of horses. Then the sun rose. It filled the valley with red light and illuminated the endless army marching toward them. As the shadows lifted, the thin mist turned gold, and a bugle sounded from the advancing cavalry. The lines of mounted men began to trot, and then to gallop, and the King's men, now armed and mounted, rushed to meet them.

Breac drew his sword as the line of enemies swept toward him, and his own men came down at his back. He joined the rush, and raised his sword. Jorah galloped along side him, his streaked beard whipping back in the wind, and shouted, "For the High King!"

"For the High King," Breac replied. And then the thunder of battle broke and echoed through the valley like a mighty earthquake.

* * * * *

It was late afternoon when messengers reported that the battle was turning in their favor. Breac reined in the stallion and paused to look around from the top of a knoll. From what he could see the battle was indeed going well. His own men surrounded him. Yet once again he felt the familiar sense of dread. The sense that had warned him of danger since he was a child. His gaze swept over the heaving battlefield to the surrounding hills and lonely ridge tops, then down the valley. Nothing but men and horses and blood and screams. He returned his gaze to one of the ridges, and caught the glint of sunlight on a polished wooden shaft. He turned, and the next instant the arrow sank deep into the muscle of his chest. Black feathered, and stained green, it rocked him back in the saddle. His muscles clenched convulsively, but he felt no pain. Only the growing dread.

The horse threw his head up, high stepping amid another rush of troops. Breac glanced down, pressing his hand against the wound. Blood oozed thick over his gloved fingers. His chest and shoulder felt numb, and his heart labored. He grasped the shaft of the arrow where it entered his chest, but didn't pull. Black feathers meant poison. He was already a dead man. He wondered fleetingly why he was even alive this long. The next thought was for his men. The clash of battle still sounded near, but when he looked up again, he saw his army pushed back from around him by a wedge of enemy Death Riders.

He was alone among the Death Riders, yet none engaged him in battle. The Riders around him sat their mounts, glaring, waiting.

Breac became aware of each breath, the slow sticky beating of his heart, the heaviness that bore down on him. He was also aware of sound and touch, the slick of sweat inside his gloves, the pressure of the saddle gripped in one hand, and the arrow shaft in the other. He saw the faces of his enemies, young and old, all weary and grim, dirtied and bloodied.

The Riders parted for their leader, a tall, black cloaked figure on a white horse. Breac blinked, trying to clear his vision. It seemed to him that the cloaked figure was veiled with red flame and black shadow. All the dread he felt breathed from this creature, washing over him like waves of agony, though most of his body had begun to go numb.

The shrouded figure drew his horse up alongside Breac's stallion. He lifted a gloved hand to push back the hood of his cloak, revealing a white, handsome face and long black hair.

"So we meet at last, Breac—or is it Aindreas? Son of Rajah, man of two nations. You know me?"

"Leazor." The word came out slurred. Breac's tongue felt thick and clumsy. "What do you want?"

A coy smile twisted Leazor's mouth. Narrow, closely set teeth glinted white. "I want to see the High King weeping over your decomposing carcass." His voice poured words like oil "By what power do you conquer my armies? Is it some magic you possess in yourself that makes the King show you friendship? I wish to know."

Breac didn't answer. His breath came hard, his lungs sucking and gurgling.

Leazor breathed a chuckle. "Without you, today will be the King's last victory. A prophecy that's ended almost before it began."

Breac drooped lower in the saddle. Far down the valley a battle horn sounded for a last charge. "Leave me," he gasped.

Without command the white horse stepped closer to Breac's stallion. Gripping Breac's shoulder with one hand, Leazor pulled the arrow out backward from his chest. Blood bubbled out after it.

Leazor threw his head back, raising the bloody arrow toward the sky, and cried, "I salute you, High King, and You, Creator. The battle is yours. But the victory is mine." He clapped spurs to the horse's sides, and the beast reared and leapt away. The Death Riders followed, sounding the horn for retreat.

Breac was alone. He slumped down over the stallion's neck, swayed, and fell. Still he felt no pain as blood spurted thickly from the wound. He felt his heart heave twice, then stop, and the ragged darkness around his mind closed in.

*****

A thousand million bright stars, and the vast darkness of space. Behind is a light, brighter than all the suns in the universe, and a sound—a hundred sounds—a thousand notes—a song that is so far above mere music, more intricately entwined than the most stunning harmony. It is the expression of every purest joy, of victory and glory. He starts to turn, but a hand on his shoulder stops him, and a voice that is at once familiar and strange.

"Not yet, Aindreas, son of Rajah. Not yet."

Utter darkness and stillness reclaim him.

*****

A voice reached into the darkness and dragged him out. He fought it, because as awareness grew, so did pain, and a raging fire in his chest that would try to consume him. He would die again of sheer agony.

His heart beat fast and hard. His eyes rolled back, then forward, coming to focus on the golden sunset sky. The battle clash was gone. A chilly spring wind blasted down the valley, scraping through dry, trampled grass. The cries of wounded men and horses streaked the wind.

"The King commands that you live, Breac."

He turned his head to see the woman who'd spoken. Her low, melodic voice seemed foreign in this place of death. Dressed as a common peasant, she was tall, and very slender, her voice deeper than most women. She was a dryad, a being of the forest. The people of the wood rarely mingled with humans, yet not so infrequently that any but the most foolish could deny their existence.

"You will live," the dryad woman repeated, stretching his cloak over him.

He replied in a hoarse whisper. "I'd rather not."

She smiled. "I was sent here on your behalf, and you would

rather die? Mankind has always been ungrateful."

"I was so close..." he whispered.

"It will be there waiting, when the time is right. Never fear." She laid a slender hand on his chest. "I must help your comrades while I am here," she said. "So rest."

* * * * *

When Breac woke again, he felt as though liquid fire was circulating in his veins.

"Try and relax," someone said. "You won't help yourself clenching up like that. The poison has to work itself out. At least that's what they tell me."

Breac turned his head to see the old man. "Jorah. Still alive."

"There's a few dents in the shield for the smith to hammer out. And these old bones are weary, but all's well. Today the victory is ours... yours."

Breac closed his eyes again. It hurt to talk. Like someone had shoved heated sand down his throat. "Victory." The word came out bitter.

Jorah leaned forward and took the pipe out of his mouth. "Would you rather have lost and seen Leazor take over the whole country with his beastly magic and slavery?"

"No." Breac croaked. "But victory is not mine today. It belongs to the High King, and to Acatra Dahma. Victory is for the men who are celebrating that they will see their wives." He glanced around the makeshift hospital tent. "There is no victory in here."

"There is life!" Jorah jabbed the pipe at him. "Which is saying something, in your case, you ungrateful vagabond."

Breac groaned. "Take care of my horse while I'm here, will you? And enjoy the celebrations. Doubtless you will receive all the honor in my stead."

"You old goat," Jorah snorted. "You know I will. I'll be parading through the streets of Al Acatra on your own horse, drinking all the ale I can hold, feasting at the tables of kings and chieftains, and listening to fair maidens sing my praise. After thirty five years in the service of the High King, I deserve it. More than you, you upstart." He paused, and grew more serious, tucking the pipe back into the corner of his mouth. "Leazor meant to kill you today. He is bound to find out that you're not dead. I'm having guards posted outside this tent."

Breac closed his eyes briefly as Jorah stood, folding his three-legged stool and leaning it against the cot. "So that he will wonder who here is ranked high enough to warrant guards."

The pipe left an arch of smoke as Jorah gestured with it. "Obviously the High King is not ready to release you from service. What his design is I don't know, nor why our enemy is set on your death, but I do know that until you're ready to walk it's my duty to keep you safe."

2

The Henna Knot

Heaven help me, Evie Drake thought as she came out the side door onto the platform and saw the bridesmaids, seven of them all lined up, dressed in lime green. *I've tripped and landed in the nineteen-seventies.* She stepped up to the music stand, conscious of how unsteady she felt in high heels, and adjusted the mic, waiting for the music. Her heart beat fast. A couple hundred strange pairs of eyes stared at her. She ran a sweating hand down her short black skirt, and gripped the microphone with the other, looking down, waiting for the music.

Then the violin started. *Close your eyes. Deep breaths. Count the beats. One-and-two-and...* Forcing the crowded church to disappear from her mind, ignoring her thudding heart. In place of the staring crowd stretched a high, windswept moor overlooking the sea. Instead of the weepy bride, Evie pictured herself, face to the sky, dancing in the strong arms of her lover. And she sang. No matter that she thought the wedding party ridiculous, that she didn't know the bride or the groom, or that she was singing for only a small fee. No matter that the face of her lover was indistinct. She poured into her song all the joy and longing of a wedding of legend, of renown, of proportions larger and nobler than could be contained in the stuffy, crowded little sanctuary.

The song ended. She let the vision go. Reality snapped back into focus, with the bride wiping away a fresh deluge of happy tears. Many in the audience were nodding, looking delighted.

Evie was as familiar with the sudden shrinking, horrified feeling at the end of the song as she was with the initial stage fright. She had come to expect it. She felt as though she'd bared her dreams and sold her soul to a stranger. A whole room full of strangers. Heat flushed her face as she turned and went out the side door through which she'd come.

That's what I get paid for, she thought sourly, *to make strangers happy. To impress mothers-in-law into speechless surprise. They'll go up to the bride afterward and gush over the lovely ceremony, even if the dresses were puke green.* Behind her she could hear the pastor as he recited the familiar words. "Therefore a man shall leave his father and mother, and shall cleave unto his wife." The bride sniffed loudly.

Evie descended narrow stairs into the deserted church basement and found her backpack with a change of clothes, then headed for the ladies room, ignoring the smells of food coming from the kitchen. She did notice the tables, sulking in rows of putrid green, and spangled with lemony accents. Small, multi-colored disco balls hung from the ceiling. *Sheesh.* She shook her head as she pushed open the bathroom door.

She changed quickly into boot-cut jeans and a peasant style blouse, traded the high heels for hiking boots, and tugged the clips out of her dark hair, letting it fall down her back in a mass of gel-stiffened curls. Last she tugged the silver chain and oval locket free of her collar, letting it fall outside her shirt. Washing the makeup off, she studied herself in the mirror, wiped away a black smudge of mascara, and then went out.

James, her date for the day, got out of the car as she crossed the parking lot and opened her door for her.

"Happy birthday," he said, leaning to kiss her cheek as she slid in.

She felt herself blush as he closed the door, and frowned, watching him cross over to the driver's door. Inside the car smelled like a florist shop. She resisted the urge to turn and look in the back seat as James got in.

"How did it go?" he asked, tugging at his seatbelt.

"Alright."

"We don't have to wait around for them to pay you, right? They did that beforehand?"

"Yes, they paid me," she replied, the annoyance creeping into her voice. *Leave it to you to think of the money first thing,* she thought, then, *gosh I'm in a bad mood.*

"Oh, I almost forgot something. You know I never forget things, except when I'm around you." He winked as he unfastened the seatbelt, and leaned into the back. There came a rustle and the clean, sweet scent of fresh cut roses grew stronger. When he drew back and settled in again, he presented a bouquet large enough to make the front seat seem crowded. "For you. Happy birthday."

"They're gorgeous. Thank you."

They were gorgeous. But red roses? Wasn't that taking things a bit fast? They'd only gone out twice, officially. Maybe in his world that constituted a serious relationship, but she was far from feeling anything serious about him. Other than that she seriously did not want to be going to the Renaissance Faire with him today.

"You're welcome," he said. "A little bird told me they're your favorite."

A little bird? For real? The glow of gratification she'd felt about the flowers melted away with her smile as she turned to stare out the window. Discontent and guilt settled in on her heart. *No one's perfect,* she told herself. *Shouldn't be so hard on the poor guy. He's really trying. He's just so...* she glanced over at him as he drove. *Cute. Sweet. Thoughtful... Boring and needy.*

She was in less than a charitable mood at the moment, and the mental berating didn't set well. Did she truly want a guy that had to *really try*? Trying always to please her, but never quite getting things right. Giving her beautiful roses with a bad delivery line. Taking her to a great place, but on the wrong day, and in the wrong way.

Her friends would already be at the Faire, chatting it up, spending money on totally geeky stuff, like hobbit ears or pewter dragon incense burners. Getting lost in a fantasy and pretending for a few hours that the modern world didn't exist. It was almost a sacred ritual for them.

James was no pretender, no dreamer. His feet were so firmly on the ground that she could imagine him growing moss. If he could just not be so... *normal* for the day. She glanced over in time to meet his gaze.

He smiled. "Cheer up. This is going to be fun. You can educate me on all the nuances of being a hippy musician, fantasy lover person."

"A hippy musician?" She raised an eyebrow at him.

"I meant that in a good way. What do they call what you do? Sort of New Age, flower child stuff...?"

She sighed. "Celtic. It's called Celtic music. And I'm not hippy, or New Age."

"Sorry. I really didn't mean that like a bad thing. It's just you always seem so free spirited, you dress like—I don't know. Hippy. Kind of." He glanced sideways at her, and she saw his Adam's apple bob. *Giving a complement, but saying it like an insult...Or was it a complement? Does he really picture me with dreadlocks, smoking weed and strumming my way into a trance so I can communicate with my African violets?* She imagined his look of surprise if he ever sat in on one of her karate classes, or one of her band's jam sessions.

They drove through the fair entrance and a parking attendant waved them on across the muddy field. A second attendant directed James to park at the end of a neat line of vehicles, waving his arms wildly, and scowling as though he might jump through the windshield at them if they parked the merest inch out of line.

It was a long walk from the field to the main gates, and Evie felt over-conscious of James walking beside her. She tried to keep a comfortable distance between them, so he'd know that hand holding was definitely not welcome. No need to start that when she knew she felt nothing for him.

James paid the entrance fee, and they strolled down a short avenue to the central square. The day was October bright, and the fair ablaze with color. So many vendors packed the square that it took a moment to focus on each one. They sold everything from hobbit ears to T-shirts, to fantasy novels, to renaissance history. Outdoor stages were set up with ongoing performances from jugglers, knife throwers, comedy acts, and hypnotists. The smell of food and horses and cigarette smoke made the air seem hot and heavy, until a breeze sent the colorful tent awnings flapping. Some of the people passing by them wore period costumes, peasant gowns, breeches, or pirate outfits.

"They have a jousting match," James said, scanning a pamphlet printed with the schedule. "I assume you'll want to see that?"

"When is it?"

"Just starting, I think. Over there in the grandstand arena."

She pointed to a semi-circular theater stage, half turning to look as they passed it. "Look—Shakespeare's plays."

Squeezing past a group of fake bearded Gandalf look-alikes, they entered the grandstand. Down in the arena a pair of knights were preparing to charge one another. Thick-legged horses stamped, raising dust to coat the bright costumes.

"Hey Evie! James! Over here!"

They spotted the little group waving at them.

"It's your band," James said blandly. "I suppose we'd better go sit with them."

She could read the disappointment in his voice, even though he tried to hide it. Just like the triumph she tried to keep out of hers. "Yep. They'd be hurt if we didn't."

She started climbing up to meet them, with James following.

"Hey guys!"

"Hey hey, look who showed up!" Courtney slapped her arm as she passed. "It's the career lady herself."

"How did it go?" This from Deb.

"It was good. I think they liked it."

"Awesomeness. Next time you take us with you, huh?"

"Sure Anthony. Anyone would be crazy not to want a Celtic rock band in their wedding." She punched his shoulder as she sat down. The teenager pushed glasses up his skinny nose, furrowing shaggy brows at James as he sat down on the other side of her. The kid was a weird one, but he played Irish pennywhistle like an elf, or an angel.

"So what are you two lovebirds up to?" Courtney asked.

"Just got here. Anything new we need to see, besides the Shakespeare?"

"There's a henna artist."

"Sweet. Hey maybe we could hang out with you guys, walk around together." As soon as she said it, Evie felt James shift beside her. Anthony's frown deepened.

"No way! You can't hang out with your groupies on a date! We hereby banish you for the day—as soon as the jousting is over."

Evie laughed. Trying to convince herself she wasn't disappointed.

The day passed slowly, colorful but tedious. James talked too much, and hardly mentioned any of their surroundings. He admitted that he was out of his league among so many fantasy dreamers. Late afternoon deepened into early evening. She pointed to a tent she hadn't seen until then.

"Hey, there's the henna artist." She headed toward it.

James followed. "Henna? What's henna?" he asked.

"It's a plant dye. It lasts two or three weeks on your skin, like a temporary tattoo. It's really cool."

"You're kidding, right? You're into that kind of stuff?"

Well you were the one saying I'm a hippy.

The henna tent was low, and the entrance dark. Panels of deep purple satin hung from tent poles to form walls, and gold banners fluttered from the corners. A wavering line of incense smoke wafted out the entrance. Evie stopped at a plastic folding table set up in front, where the artist displayed a portfolio of designs. She opened the book and flipped through. Pictures and patterns overwhelmed the pages. Dragons, flowers, Chinese characters and Middle-Eastern symbols. Unicorns, skulls, and Celtic crosses.

A young lady stepped out of the tent.

"Can I help you?"

Evie glanced up and smiled. She looked back down at the book.

"Ooh, that's so cool!" she said. She held the book out, tapping one of the symbols. "Can you do it on my palm?"

"Of course. You won't be able to use your hand for a while, though."

"That's okay."

"What is it supposed to be?" James asked, looking over her shoulder.

"It's a Celtic knot."

"Not just any Celtic knot," the henna artist said, smiling. "This is the worlds' traveling symbol. I found it in a book of symbols and spells."

"Really?"

James muttered, "Yeah. Things just got a little dumb."

"I work at an antique bookshop," the young woman explained, taking the portfolio. She tugged the printout free from its plastic slip cover. "That book must be at least two hundred years old. It's beautiful."

"I would love to see it," Evie said.

"It is well worth looking at. Though truthfully, I have seen this pattern in other places too. I don't know if someone in the area owned the book before it came to us, but the travel symbol is carved on a tree on these very grounds."

Evie listened to the woman talk as she followed her into the tent, glancing back long enough to see James ambling off in another direction. The artist motioned her to sit on an overturned crate draped with satin cloth. It was peaceful in there, a little dark, and smelled of sandalwood incense. It reminded Evie of the gypsy fortunetellers' tents she'd always seen in movies. A gray and white cat eyed her from the corner as the artist motioned her to lay her hand on a small card table. The cold henna solution tickled as it went on. She fought the urge to pull her hand away and wipe it down her jeans.

"The legend in the book says that travelers use this symbol to open the door to the other-world," The woman said as she worked. She was attractive, with a blonde pixie cut, and had an air of grace about her. She looked up from her work with a smile. "Careful you don't wander off into Never-Never Land."

"Not much chance of that," Evie said cheerfully, "Though sometimes I wish it was possible. Secretly."

"So do we all," the young woman replied. "Secretly. That's why we come to this place, isn't it? Dress up in ridiculous costumes, and hope that by being just one more nerd no one will suspect how serious this secret longing really is."

Evie gave a dry laugh. The artist seemed to have the ability to pinpoint exactly the truth.

She finished the design and dabbed it with sugar water. "There you are."

"Thanks."

The bright autumn afternoon had faded to dusk when Evie stepped out of the tent and looked around. James had wandered a ways off, deep in conversation with someone, probably from his work. She looked back down at the knot pattern on her hand. It was one of the most intricate patterns of its kind that she had ever seen, and very beautiful. It was her only souvenir from the day, and she felt quite ready to go home.

She started toward James, but a glimpse of something out of the corner of her eye distracted her. She turned aside. Someone had set up a whimsical pair of gateposts for decoration. They led nowhere but toward the forested hillside. Still, she went to them, charmed. They were wrought-iron, with painted vines curling up them. A waist high wrought-iron gate swung open between them, creaking on its hinges. Evie passed through the gate, imagining for a moment that it was a gateway to the land of Fairie, and that the symbol on her hand would let her cross over. She smiled ruefully as she reached the far side, and still heard the noise of the fair behind her. She kept walking. An ancient beech tree stood out from the dusk, its craggy bark reflecting the yellow lantern lights of the fair. Years ago someone had carved into it, leaving a swollen scar. As she drew closer, she looked hard at the carving. It was identical to the mark on her hand. This must be the tree that the henna artist had mentioned. She reached up to trace the lines.

As her hand brushed the carved symbol, her ears rang with a sudden silence. She whirled around. Instead of the fairground, she saw a forest glade, littered with the ruins of decaying stonework. She sucked in a breath of surprise and let it out in a gasp. She spun back and saw only more trees. She was alone.

3
Finding Home

Breac paced through the streets of Al Acatra, the capital. The streets of the lower city were hard packed dirt, and his boots thumped a slow rhythm in the early morning. Thin tendrils of steam rose from the boggy ground at the lower boundaries of the city. He raised his face to the pale morning sky. It was good to feel strength in his limbs again, to breathe deep without pain. Good to greet the morning. Spring had come while he recovered from his wound, painting the world in brilliant, healing green-tones and bringing flocks of birds to fill the new-clothed trees.

Al Acatra was built on a mountainside, and spilled down into the valley, where most of the homes rested on more comfortably flat ground. As Breac walked deeper into the city, the ground began to rise. Some shops and businesses were half dug into the hillside. The street he followed turned sharply and angled upward. At the corner it became a boardwalk, resting on the slope on one side and supported by short posts on the other, so that merchants could push their carts on a level surface. In some places the terrain was gentler, and in those places there would be a cluster of buildings and streets. Some of the alleys and side streets were broad staircases rather than roads. Breac turned up one of these, taking a more strenuous but direct route toward the top. Far up the mountainside the city crawled, crowned at the very top by the High King's palace, under the shadow of a rocky cliff.

It was called The Palace, though no one lived there. Not even the High King. It was a great hall carved out of the mountainside, the rock walls polished till they shone like marble and inlaid with silver tracings that formed words no mortal could read. The single long room opened, doorless, into a pillared courtyard. That place, ancient beyond remembering, served as a gathering for the rulers of the land, where the High King would sit as head.

A little lower down the mountain, below the palace, Breac paused before the doors of the upper stable. Half chiseled into the stony cliff, half built from solid, heavy oak, on either side of it the mountain was sheered off in a series of impossible cliffs, with only a narrow trail leading past it to the palace. Below, he could see all of Al Acatra spread out on the gentler slopes. To stand there, halfway up the mountain with nothing but air on either side was to be one with the sky. A child of the stars.

A vision of vast skies opened before him, ruthless and bitter. Uncaring for humanity, and untamed. A cold emptiness so brutal that to embrace it would be death, yet the tame life of earth would be filthy compared to the starry heaven. And just behind him, he could feel the light.

He turned abruptly and walked through the open doors of the stable, shrugging to settle the bandage more comfortably around his shoulders. The stable hand nodded to him as he entered, and resumed mending harness. Outside the air had been chill, with the sun not yet over the mountain to warm it. Inside, the body heat of the horses kept the chill away. It smelled of dust and hay and horse and leather. Breac took a curry comb and brush from the bin beside the door, and walked down a row of stalls, their doors heavy wood, burnished by sweat and oil until they were smooth and dark.

The stallion put his head out and snorted, indignant and restless. He shoved his muzzle against Breac's chest. The man winced, but he patted the horse's neck and spoke to him.

"Long time, my friend. By your greeting I'd say you missed me."

He let himself into the stall, and ran his hands over the stallion's dark coat.

"You fared better than I. Getting off without a scratch. And rested, and fed the best oats, and hay." He lifted each hoof and checked it in turn. "I've been locked away in the field hospital, with the army surgeon. Living on starvation rations, I'll have you know." Straightening, he gave the horse a pat on the neck, and began brushing. "So next time you think of complaining because we've traveled far and fast, think of me, suffering while you've been living high."

The stallion twisted his head around and gave Breac another shove. Then he perked up, ears alerting, and whinnied toward the door.

"Now, is that any way to treat your master? Who is here, that you give such a welcome to?" He paused in his brushing, listening to the tread of boots coming up the aisle between stalls. A figure stopped in the doorway. Breac looked up, then bowed.

"My Liege."

"My friend," the High King replied. They clasped hands over the stall door, and the King pulled him into a strong, one arm embrace. "You've done very well. How does it suit you, being captain of my armies?"

"I've done many things in your service. It is perhaps more difficult than the others."

"Not the less so, because so few trust you." The High King folded his arms across the top of the stall door, and leaned in, watching him.

Breac looked down, smiling faintly. He pulled the loose horse hair off the curry comb, and ran his thumb over the short prongs. The High King continued, "But they do respect you."

"Yes."

The King took a long breath, studying him. Dust motes danced between them, spreading the scent of hay and hide.

"I have another mission for you. I'm sorry, old friend. I would there was more time for rest, but it is imperative that you take this journey, and no other. It is not because of your many abilities that I send you, though you will need all of them. It is for your heart. Not all the danger will come from your enemies, though they will do everything within their power to thwart."

"What must I do?"

"The town of Darkwood, ten days' journey south of here. You know it?"

"Yes."

"Good. You must start first thing tomorrow, and when you get there, deal with the trouble you will find."

"What trouble, sir?"

"I cannot tell you more than to guarantee that there will always be a way for you, though it will not always seem obvious or desirable. Do you trust me, Breac?"

In answer, Breac held up his right hand, open to show the white scar in his palm. "I swore an oath."

For a moment they searched each other's gaze. Breac would not hesitate to lay down his life for the King he'd sworn service to, yet looking in the other's eyes he saw sadness, and felt a touch of dread.

The High King nodded. "Many nations have now fallen pray to Leazor's tyranny and trickery. They have chosen in following him to reject my authority, so even as High King I cannot interfere. I can but keep our own country safe."

"What of our enemy's movements since his defeat?" Breac asked, averting his two-colored gaze.

"Still terrorizing some of the weaker villages on the borders. I've sent out more riders, but for those who can't or won't use the Kantra, physical protection is limited."

Breac nodded.

"It is not to open war that I send you, where you know your

enemy. Be careful, be true, and remember the laws that keep this country free from oppression." The King smiled as Breac regarded him soberly. "Cheer up, my friend. Soon there will be a time for peace. A time for wandering hearts to find a home. All true servants of the Creator will have their reward. For now, go with my blessing."

Breac placed a fist over his heart and gave him a bow in salute. The King nodded once, then turned and walked away. His footsteps receded down the aisle. There was a flicker of shadow in the doorway, and he was gone. Breac squinted after him, rubbing his knuckles over the blond stubble on his jaw.

Ten day's journey into the wild was no small thing, with enemy soldiers still at large, and with Leazor intent on killing Breac in particular. The Sorcerer had spoken of a prophecy. Breac did not know what he meant, nor did he dwell on it overmuch, though he wished he had asked the High King. Knowledge was always useful, especially when it might concern one's own life or death.

He quickly finished grooming the horse, checked his gear and tack, and left the stable, going down into the city for supplies. Already he ran through the journey in his mind, mapping a course. The fastest route would be mostly through the wilderness, where there were no allies to assist him, should the mission be in peril. And what was the mission? Of such a nature that the King could not tell him? Breac shook his head. He trusted the King, yes. And he would carry out this mission the best that he could. But he was worried, and weary.

* * * * *

Evie spun a slow circle, hand over her mouth, hazel eyes wide. Alone. There should be people. Hundreds of people. Buildings, vendors, and beyond all that the highway. Where had it all gone? Where had *she* gone? Her mind flitted over possibilities. A practical joke? Hallucination? Illusion? She reached a hand out as though the air before her might contain the missing pieces of her world. But it held only air.

The light seemed all wrong here. It had been dusk, hadn't it? Almost dark. Now golden afternoon sunlight tinted the treetops. And another thing. It was mid October. The evening should be chilly, the leaves all turned orange and red and yellow, filling the air with every rattling breeze. Here suddenly everything was fresh and green, like early June.

She had been thinking about entering another world when she went through that gate. Leaving her boring, disappointing life behind... for what? What had she been wishing? To wind up in a strange forest alone, no friends, no idea how to get home?

She stared down at the henna knot on her palm, then looked around for the beech tree with the matching symbol. It had vanished.

She hugged herself as her gut churned. Her numb shock was beginning to resolve itself into a tight, hard core of panic. Her teeth rattled together, and she clamped her jaw shut, forcing her panting breaths to become even and intentional. She marched to the edge of the clearing and lifted aside a curtain of mountain laurel to peer into the gloom under the trees. Dark and hostile. She stifled the urge to run away, and studied the forest. It was draped with vines, muted with moss that hung from branches and crawled across rocks. Boulders and short rock ledges stabbed up through the brown floor, creating a thousand small caves and nooks. Hiding places for the hundreds of eyes she felt were glaring at her. She let the bushes spring back into place and retreated toward the middle of the glade.

As she walked her boot caught on a stone hidden in the tall grass, and she stumbled, striking a shin on the sharp edge.

"Yow!" She propped her foot on the stone and pulled up her

pant-leg to rub the new welt already forming. This whole place looked like an ancient ruin, with long grasses growing around and over squarish blocks of granite. She bent and swept aside the veil of grass at her feet, revealing a slab of black crystal. What had once stood here? A palace perhaps? A temple or pyramid? This could be someplace in her world. Perhaps South America, though the vegetation seemed all wrong.

Listen to yourself! She thought. *As though it could be anywhere other than earth.*

But where on earth? Certainly not Pennsylvania. What if it is another world? Are there such a thing as humans here?

Sheesh. Come on, girl. Don't be silly.

Don't be silly? What is this if not completely, fantastically, insanely silly? How do you explain it away?

Her thoughts were having a tug of war, and she felt like screaming.

"There has to be an explanation," she said aloud. Should she search for that tree with the mark on it? This couldn't be a practical joke, no matter how elaborate. Everything was far too real. The sounds, the smells, the suddenness of the change as she stood still by the beech tree. The world had shifted in an instant, without a noise or a sign. But if not a hoax, then what?

The sound of a wolf cry in the not far distance made her jump. Her heart exploded into a drum roll tempo, and her skin tingled. There definitely weren't any wolves running around the countryside where she lived. She'd never heard one in person before, but this soulful wail was unmistakable. The first cry was answered by a second one even nearer. But was it a wolf cry after all? It sounded like there were words in that awful howl. The voice of a demon perhaps.

"You should not be alone," a voice spoke behind her.

Evie bolted, spinning around a full four feet from where she'd stood. "What?!"

"Where are your companions?"

The person was not human. Either that or this was the best Hollywood grade costume and makeup ever. He was very tall and slender. His golden hair had a greenish caste, plaited together in flat strands that rustled around his ears. Skin sleek and yellow tinted, streaked with faint green and brown lines, like a peeled tree branch. Clad in a simple green tunic and frayed brown trousers, he wore no shoes. His voice startled her. It was deepest bass, but light and resonant, and carried whispery, rippling tones. Like the most exquisite reed instrument ever. It was because of that voice alone that she didn't run screaming into the forest.

Evie stammered, "I—I don't know. Where am I?"

The creature regarded her with round, interested brown eyes, and answered, "In lower Acatra Dahma—what's left of it. The border of the dark land is a mere mile from here. I am Sylvanus, of the dryad people."

Another beast wailed nearby. This time she was almost certain she heard words in the rising and falling of the cry. She tried to imagine one of her friends making that noise to scare her. The conjured image fell flat. That thing sounded evil.

Sylvanus said, "Come. No one should be out here with night coming on. We will talk and walk, yes? Are you hungry?"

"No. Thank you. Do you know how I can get home?"

"Where is home?"

"North Ridge Street?" She said it like a question, as though this creature might have heard of it.

"Ah. You are a traveler," Sylvanus said, looking at her even more curiously than before. "What is it like, this stepping between the worlds?"

"Stepping between *what* worlds? Where am I, and what's going on?" she couldn't keep her voice from rising in desperation.

"You are an accidental worlds' traveler then?" He continued in an aside to himself, "I wonder what will come of this then? A questing soul is called through the Divide without knowledge."

"I was *not* questing."

"But you must have been, or you would not be here. It is the way of things. A soul who is content does not wish to be other than it is."

"I don't know what you're talking about." She said it, and reproached herself because it was a lie. She had been 'vishing. And it made her more afraid, as though her wildest, most fanciful fears were being confirmed. "Can you tell me how to get home?"

"I'm sorry lady, but no."

Evie felt her throat constrict, and the words came out high-pitched. "What do I do?"

4
Darkwood

Sylvanus put a slender hand on her shoulder. "Do not fear," he said. "There is always a way. The human town of Darkwood is but a few miles from here, and there is a chance that the village chieftain will know what to do."

They walked for several hours, as afternoon turned to evening. After a mile the forest opened up a little, and Evie could see further. There were still rocky ledges, but the dark moss seemed less oppressive, and the trees were bigger and further apart. They stopped once and shared travel bread, which tasted like roasted grain and honey, then continued on into the dusk. Sylvanus talked to her about the forest, of roots and rustling winds and deep waters. She found herself comforted in his presence, and felt more at ease than she did with most humans. If she weren't afraid of never getting home again, she'd enjoy this.

Second sunset in one evening, she thought. She'd almost forgotten the wolves while they walked and talked, but now the howling started again, more persistently, and closer. She drew closer to the strange creature called Sylvanus, trying to match his stride, and ever peering into the dark behind them.

"What is that?" she whispered. "Wolves? Or something else. They sound like they're talking to each other... you know, with words."

Sylvanus nodded. "I suspect a few of them are wolves at this moment. I cannot tell what the others might be."

"What?!" She blurted, then lowered her voice again. "Exactly what do you mean by that?"

Sylvanus held a finger to his lips. "Best not to talk about them. They get agitated."

Evie moved closer still to the dryad. It was all she could do to keep from bolting away, maybe climbing a tree. Or at the least grabbing Sylvanus' arm and shaking some answers out of him. The cries ceased suddenly. She could hear the rustle of the creatures behind them and to either side, though it was too dark by now to see more than a passing shadow. Once in awhile the moon would break through the trees above them, and she would catch the glint of eyes. Some low to the ground, others the same height as the dryad.

Sylvanus pulled her to a stop. Holding up his hand, he began to sing. After an instant the moonlight around them seemed to increase. The air took on a faint luminescence, like sunlight beaming through a light fog. Whatever the creatures were, they snarled, and within a minute Evie heard them retreating. Vanishing into the forest.

Sylvanus stopped singing, and the light slowly died away. He started walking again, and the girl hurried to catch up.

"How did you do that?"

"Those who live close to danger must have protection."

"That wasn't what I asked."

Sylvanus just smiled, his faintly striped skin bunching into curious patterns in the moonlight.

More hours passed, and Evie felt her steps slowing. Her thoughts turned toward home. She wanted to be back in her apartment, in bed. Not in some strange land, walking with a strange creature. Her eyes smarted with tears and weariness. Frustration rose up like prison bars around her. Would someone in the town know how she could get home? Would they tell her? What were people like in this place?

It had to be close to midnight or later, and she was starting to think in her exhaustion that this might be a bad dream after all.

The trees opened, and a clearing spread before them, and a

village. It looked strikingly like the imitation wood and plaster of the Renaissance Fair, but so much more real. Faded, flawed, dirty. Bonfires were lit on the main street. Horses and men in cloaks milled around the fires, made into dark silhouettes by the orange glow. Low thatched houses were dark. Unrest and fear came from the town, wafting to them with the stench of burning wood and flesh. Men's voices, boisterous laughter mingled with foul sounding words. A woman somewhere sobbed, and a baby screamed.

Sylvanus stopped at the edge of town, his round eyes flickering over the scene, glinting with starpoint reflections of the fires. Evie asked, "What's going on here?"

"The enemy. We must go."

They turned—and faced two huge men.

"Surely you weren't leaving so soon," one of them said. His voice sounded whiny, spewing out between missing teeth, distorted by a broken and bleeding nose. The accent was unfamiliar.

"Yes—she should do to have some fun with."

Evie shrieked as two others grabbed her arms from behind. She was enveloped in the sharp, mingling odors of liquor, smoke, and unwashed bodies as the men surrounded them. She struggled and kicked, aiming with practiced precision for feet, shins, knees, groins, anything. Many of her blows were met with grunts and curses. A cold knife point pricked her throat, and she stilled.

"Spirited, isn't she?" one of them said.

"Spirited!" another rasped. "I may never breed children again."

The first guffawed. "Brackly, you've got enough. Your wife should thank the girl."

Evie went limp, letting her feet drag, causing the men hauling her to stumble and curse. She jerked away, gave a sharp twist with her arm, allowing her to break free for an instant. A blow between her shoulder blades knocked her flat on her face in the wet grass, gasping to re-inflate her lungs. She was hauled upright again by her hair, still struggling to breathe.

She and Sylvanus were dragged toward the largest of the bonfires. A low wooden platform encircled it.

"This—I don't belong here," she half cried, half gasped.

"Course you do, love. Right here with us." The man holding her gave her a shove, sending her to her knees for the next man to haul upright again.

She almost whispered, "It was a mistake."

They entered the circle of firelight and were greeted by a dozen other dark cloaked men, and the wide eyes of three other prisoners. Evie had the surreal feeling of being plucked up and landed in the middle of a movie set. Cloaks, boots, swords, and bodiced dresses blurred around her.

"Where did you find these two?" one of the men asked.

"Sneaking around the edge of town."

"A dryad, no less. Tie him up and put him with the others. Bring the woman to me."

The man holding her muttered something, but did as he was told. He bound Sylvanus' hands behind him, and shoved him off the side of the platform. The dryad landed in the middle of the huddled prisoners, two women and an older man. The captain, or whatever he was, grabbed a handful of Evie's hair and pulled her head back so he could stare at her face. She got a quick glimpse of dark eyes, a scruffy jaw line and scraggles of oily brown hair before averting her eyes. She would not meet his gaze, instead looking past him to the glittering shroud of stars overhead, sending a silent prayer up there. A dark, winged shape blotted out a small section of stars, the firelight reflecting on glossy feathers.

"Take a look at this." The first man seized her wrist and brought her hand into the firelight.

The captain examined the henna tattoo, and his eyes glittered.

"She's a witch, a worlds-traveler."

"I'm not a witch."

"But you have traveled here from another world."

She didn't answer.

"Tell me. When did you arrive here, in this world?"

She said nothing, and he struck her with the back of his hand.

"Answer when I talk to you!"

She clenched her jaw around the pain, and bared her teeth at him. "Or what?"

He struck again. "Or I'll have you tortured as you've never imagined. I'll hand you over to my men."

There was a cheer of approval from the others.

She snapped out a kick that caught the captain in the side of the knee. He swore and staggered back out of range as she struggled against the hands gripping her. There were too many, and they were too strong for her. She finally subsided.

She said, "You know you'll only do what you like to me, whether I answer or no." The words were ground out through a throat raw from not crying. A shudder wracked her body, a muscle clenching, violent tremor that would not go away.

The captain studied her for a long time. The shudders came harder, preparing for another blow, or something worse, but he only stood and stared through slitted eyes. He turned and began to pace, limping, back and forth in front of her. When he spoke again it was in a gentle tone, calming, like a father or a lover, and his accent became more noticeable. The more she concentrated on the twist of his words, the harder they became to understand. She looked back up at the sky again.

"I misjudged you, lady," he said. "You are a sword maiden, daughter of warriors. Honorable, hard as steel and beautiful as crystal and silver. I am repentant of my rage. I pray you forgive my outburst." His voice remained gentle, but there was something in it—a subtle off-key quality that unnerved her. She remained silent.

He dipped his head. "Very well. I shall smart under your ill favor. More so, as this is obviously your first visit to this land, and you've had a wretched first impression from my men and I. But I beg you, tell me how you come to be traveling with a dryad? For that is a thing not often seen in these days, a human and a dryad walking the forest, sharing conversation."

Evie looked from the captain to Sylvanus, who stared at her with expressionless eyes.

When she still didn't answer the captain said, "He met you in the woods perhaps, when you were newly arrived in this world. Shared with you food and offered protection from wolves. The beasts can be quite nasty in these parts." He paused in his pacing and glanced over at her. "I shall take your silence as a yes, fair lady. Such generosity on his part. He would have introduced himself. Offered you a meal. Scared the beasties away with his meager dryad magic. And then brought you here, to us."

He stopped pacing and stood before her, smiling with all the charm of a tarantula. He touched her face, ran his fingers across her jaw and down her neck, down her chest, spreading goose-bumps with his filthy caress. He stepped in close and dropped his head down to whisper in her ear. Her nose filled with the smell of fish and onions, and tooth decay.

"Would you like to go home? Perhaps we can come to an agreement." Cupping her chin in his hand he turned her face toward his men. "They want you, you know. You can see it in their eyes. Like you could see hunger in the eyes of the wolves."

He forced her head back around to look at him, breathing more of his toxic scent into her face. For a moment she thought he would kiss her. She gagged, and her shaking returned. She clenched her jaw, willing herself not to hurl in his face. Serve him right it would, but she would not be that weak.

"I know how you can get home." Firelight flickered across his face, still so close their noses nearly touched. "But there is a price."

Her heart pounded as he backed away finally. What price?

"I need your help. You see, these dryads, like the one who befriended you, are enemies of my king. I'm under direct orders to kill as many of the creatures as I can. The difficulty is that dryads are immortal, of a sort. There are only two ways to kill them. Either you kill the tree they belong to, which is impossible to tell, or you get one of their friends to turn them over to you. Has to be one of their human friends. So, it's as easy as this. You tell me the dryad here is mine to do as I please to, and I show you the way home and let you go. All of this will go away. Deal?"

Evie trembled. The edges of her world had narrowed down and turned black. Images tipped and bled together. Flames and upturned faces and voices ran in her mind. The captain shook her, rattling her teeth. "Do we have a deal?"

She only whimpered again.

He signaled one of his men forward. "We have a deal, or Nagma here gets his turn first."

As he came leering toward her, Evie felt a shriek rising in her throat, and the instant he laid hands on her, it came out, a scream that made even Nagma hesitate. She lurched away from him, and the captain caught her in a rough embrace, bringing his mouth close to her ear. "Deal?"

She shrieked again, right in his ear. He swore, and struck her, as Nagma grabbed her from behind.

"Deal!" she sobbed.

The captain shoved Nagma away, and signaled for Sylvanus to be brought forward.

"Oh yes, and you have to use his name. Do you know his

name?"

Evie thought she was going to faint. Sylvanus watched her as he was led out. And not him only. The rest of the prisoners' eyes were on her, looking up from the shadows, as well as the men who had gathered around. It seemed every soul in the tiny town, whether citizen or ruffian, was staring at her.

"Just say the words," the captain said. "And it's home again, safe and sound, as though none of this had ever happened. Say, 'I give this dryad—be sure to use his name—into your hands...'"

She closed her eyes, her breath coming in short, frantic gasps. Her face and back throbbed. She wished for the whole scene to just go away. She couldn't betray Sylvanus. No more than should could betray Courtney or any of her other friends. The captain's voice taunted her.

"Just say the words, love, and all this is nothing more than a forgotten nightmare. You owe no loyalties here. Just say it."

Evie clenched her eyes shut. She heard her voice rasping out the words, and something deep inside screamed at her to stop. "I—I give the dryad Sylvanus—over to you." They died to a whisper. She opened her eyes.

A grin twisted the captain's face. "Thank you, my dear." He drew his sword, and for a moment she thought he would run her through. Instead he pointed with it to the edge of the firelight, where an ancient beech stood sentry over the town. "Go on, before I change my mind."

Evie lurched toward the tree, and the crowd of leering men opened before her. Barely visible in the dark, a dim carving scarred the old tree. As she drew close, she saw that it matched the mark on her hand. She cast a last glance back to where Sylvanus stared after her with empty eyes, and then touched the mark.

5

The Price of Betrayal

The town vanished, along with the dark and the firelight and the face of Sylvanus. Evie was surrounded by warm light and soft music. She looked around, still panting with fear. It took her a moment adjusting to the new surroundings to realize she was in someone's house. Her heart surged again with new panic. But no one was in sight. All the lights were on, and a fire burned brightly in the stone fireplace. The sound of running water came to her from somewhere down the hall. Evie put her hand on the back of a sofa to steady herself. She had to get out of here. But where was she? Her thoughts would not focus, her body would not move. Like molten metal the images of the men and the prisoners around the bonfire were seared across her vision. And the eyes of Sylvanus. Once so compassionate, they seemed to stare at her from across the Divide, accusing. What had she done?

What have I done? I'm a murderer!

Guilty! The verdict slammed down on her soul like a gavel, crushing it. Her palms prickled. It had to be a nightmare. All of it. She could never kill anyone, whether by her word, or her hand. It had to be a nightmare.

But then what was she doing in a stranger's house?

The water turned off. She shook herself, and looked around frantically for a fast way out. This room was wide open to the dining room and kitchen beyond. There were no doors within reach, not even for a closet. Too late now. Footsteps in the hall. Evie looked up as another woman turned the corner into the living room. The woman saw her and screamed. Evie screamed as well.

"Who..."

"I'm so sorry... I didn't break in."

"What are you doing in my house?!"

"I... wait... aren't you...?"

"The girl from the fair!"

"Yeah! And you're the henna artist."

"What are you doing in my house?"

Evie's knees went weak. She nearly collapsed onto the floor. "Please—don't call the cops. I don't know how I got here... you won't believe me..."

The henna artist, dressed in a pink bath robe, with a towel wrapped around her head, motioned for Evie to sit down. Her brows crinkled together, her look going from angry to confused, and then for a moment Evie thought she saw understanding, and...triumph? The look came and went so fast it was probably nothing more than Evie's grating nerves, and they stood there staring at each other, mutually perplexed.

"I'm a pretty believing sort," the woman said finally as Evie jerked woodenly toward the couch, melting into its cushiony embrace. "Why don't you give it a try." She scooped up a gray and white cat that had been curled up on the cushions and sat down on the other side of the couch, nestling it in her lap. It stared at Evie with coal black eyes.

Evie searched the room, unconsciously looking for something to steady her. Something that would prove she was not mad. She clenched her hands into fists and pressed them to either side of her head, rocking forward and back. The other woman reached over and gently pulled her hands down, pressing them into Evie's lap before she withdrew.

"Just start anywhere, and we'll sort this out together, ok?" She said gently.

"The Celtic knot symbol you did on my palm."

"Of course. It's my favorite."

"You said it could open the door to the otherworld.... I think you were right."

The woman stroked her cat. She answered slowly, "I see."

"I—I don't know—I guess I'm crazy. I left your tent at the fair, and there was that tree, with the same mark on it, just like you said, and I touched it..."

"And suddenly you were in a different world."

Evie looked up, searching the woman's face for signs that she was baiting her. "Yeah."

"You aren't crazy. I've never been there. But I've heard things... call them legends, rumors. Nothing anyone will admit to openly."

Evie stared at her, the pink robed figure blurring in and out of focus. "So you don't think I'm crazy?"

"No—no I don't. Like I said, I've heard things. Strange stories. Remember how I told you that symbol had been carved on a tree in the fairgrounds? It might not be a random accident. But please tell me what happened to you—what was your name again?"

"Evie."

"Evie. I'm Rachael. Why don't you stay right here and calm down for a little while. You're shaking horribly. I'll go put on some hot chocolate."

Rachael got up, dumping the cat onto the floor. It flicked its tail and stalked over to the fireplace as she went into the kitchen. From the other room came the sound of a cupboard door banging shut, the refrigerator opened and closed, and the microwave hummed. Rachael's cat turned a circle before curling up on the stone hearth. It licked its paws, keeping an eye on Evie as it did. She'd never seen a cat with black eyes before, and decided she didn't like it. She shifted uncomfortably under its stare, and looked about the room, seeing and yet not seeing. Everything looked so normal. Soothing earth tones colored the walls and furniture. Potted plants and touches of wood and pottery left an impression of earth and nature. But it all screamed to her of the other world. A stick of incense smoldered in a holder on top of the mantle. She saw the smoking huts and bonfires of the village. A painting of galloping wild horses brought back the armored war horses tethered in the village square. A photograph of a man in a medieval costume, posing on stage amid painted props only reminded her of the ruffians' leader.

Rachael came back in with two steaming mugs. Evie closed her eyes and wrapped her hands around the mug, taking a long breath. This hot chocolate was the real deal, with a cinnamon stick poking out, and a cap of whipped cream on top. The rich aroma and dark, sultry sweet taste didn't help to wipe the memories from her mind. Here she was, sipping chocolate in a stranger's house, and all she could see gazing at her from the swirling whipped cream were the dryad's eyes, neither sad, nor accusing, nor shocked... just staring at her. She shuddered.

Rachael set her mug down on the coffee table and scooted over so she could rub Evie's shoulder. "We're like sisters now, with a big secret that the rest of the world can never know. Why don't you tell me about it."

Starting from the beginning Evie told her about the dryad, and the town being overrun. She hurried through the part about giving the men Sylvanus' name. "I don't understand," she said. Forgetting about the gel she'd put in her hair for the wedding, she combed her fingers through it until it fell over her face like a veil, "why did I end up back here, instead of at the renaissance fair?"

"I don't really know much about it myself," Rachael said. "But is it possible that the other world parallels ours to a certain extent? The Renaissance Faire is about nine or ten miles from here. Would you say you traveled ten miles with Sylvanus in that world?"

Evie flipped the hair back out of her face and thought about that a second. "Yeah, I guess maybe it was about that."

"There, you see? You cannot leave from different places there, and expect to end up in the same place here. Though I am so glad you did end up here!"

"Me too! But that still doesn't make sense. It's spring there. And it had to have been, oh, I don't know. Two A.M. maybe? What time is it here?"

Rachael glanced at a clock over the fireplace that Evie had mistaken for a wrought iron wall hanging. "Ten P.M."

"See? So they don't parallel each other."

"Ok, so maybe you're right. But think about it like this: if you're in a hotel, and you open a door, you go from the hallway into a bedroom. Then while you're in the bedroom, you open a different door. It's going to take you into maybe a bathroom, or onto a balcony, or someplace else. You wouldn't expect to go through a different door and end up in the same exact place."

"I guess you're right about that. Makes sense." She laughed. "Well, it makes as much sense as any of the rest of this. Another world! I just... don't know what to think about that. It's not exactly something they prepare you for in school."

"It's not that strange, really. Think of all the legends of other worlds, mystical places. Like Tir na nOg, or Asgard, Shangri La, Mount Olympus—all those stories had to come from somewhere."

"I guess."

Rachael smiled. "I'm glad you told me about the town being overrun. I don't know the politics of that world, but I don't think I'll try going there for a long time, even though you have made me quite interested. I had thought about it, you know." She winked at Evie, stirring her chocolate with the cinnamon stick.

"Do you think Sylvanus is alright?"

Rachael smiled, and again the corner of her mouth twisted oddly. "He used magic of some kind to scare the wolves away, right? He probably used it to get away after you were gone."

"I hope so. I'd hate to think that—you know..." She couldn't finish the thought aloud. As though saying it would make it reality. "Don't worry about it now. You're safe, and that's all that matters, right? Just try and think of it as a bad dream. It didn't really happen." Rachael squeezed her shoulder. "Come on. I'll give you a ride home."

* * * * *

Breac rode without stopping through the last night of his journey, and arrived at twilight on the ninth day, to the ashes and soot of Darkwood. Only two buildings remained standing. He dismounted in the street and looked around. Smoke still rose from some of the ruins, and little flames licked along the thick blackened beams of the collapsed stable. The town must have been torched the night before. He walked to the remains of one of the larger buildings, kicking at charred debris, and the stallion followed him, trailing the reigns. A slight breeze picked up the ashes and blew them toward him. The stallion snorted and shied, rolling his eyes. The man saw what the horse had smelled. Blackened bodies, crushed under the collapsed roof.

From the bottom of his soul, Breac groaned. He lifted his face to the sky and shouted a long, wailing note that rose and mourned like a dirge.

"My King, I've failed you!"

Something near panic assaulted him. To have failed the mission, without ever having the chance to fight. He was too late. He bowed his head, gripping his hair with both fists. His nine day journey flashed backward through his mind. The stops he had made, the times he had been waylaid. If he had ridden straight beneath the shadow of Al Kazam, rather than following the coast, if he had not stopped at that farm to fight the band of raiders, if...

He dropped his hands, and sucked a breath. The doubts ceased, as suddenly as they had started. In all his journey he had done the best he knew to do. The High King, in communion with the Creator of all, would know this. And the Creator, the Director of all journeys, would not be surprised by the outcome of this one. The saving of Darkwood, then, was not the object of his mission. He must find out what was. Still, the loss weighed on him, and he wondered that he had not been permitted to stop this slaughter.

The sudden remembrance of what he'd seen the day he lay dying on the battlefield came to him. The light, which he had not quite been able to see the source of, and the music, of which he had caught but a few stanzas. He was comforted, and raising his head, continued through the town. He must figure out what had happened here. Perhaps the deaths of the townspeople would not be in vain.

He made his way past the burned out buildings to where the packed dirt street faded into grassy meadow, walking the town's outmost perimeter. Looking for tracks beyond the churned up confusion of the main thoroughfare. A dozen horses had been ridden into town, and then back out on the southern border. A stone's throw away he found a different pair of tracks coming into town. He stooped to study them. One set he judged to be dryad, or possibly naiad. They were slender and unshod. The other set of prints was strange, not with flat wooden or leather soles. They were small, like those of a woman, or a young boy, and had a blocky pattern of separate shapes pressed into the dirt, altogether forming the print. The pair had been intercepted by booted men, and led into town, where everything became muddled. A bonfire had been lit there. Out of the confusion a glint of silver caught his eye. He bent and picked up an oval locket. Its connecting ring had been bent, letting it fall from the chain. He opened it. There were two color likenesses inside, each of a young woman. Sisters, he guessed, though one was dark, and the other fair. They were both lovely. There was a short inscription on the back which he could not read. He studied the faces a moment, then put the thing in his pocket and continued.

When it grew too dark to see Breac left town, making camp a hundred yards to the north in the shelter of the forest. He was not a superstitious man, but still he had no desire to sleep in a town full of dead bodies. Also, there would be predators tonight.

He made a small fire and set a pot of water on a rock just inside the flames. Then he got out a slab of salted venison and skewered it on a sharpened stick, holding it over the fire to roast it. He did not stare into the flames, and lifted the stick away from the fire so that he would not have to ruin his night vision to check the progress of dinner. He studied the shadows, watchful of enemies, though his mind remained occupied with the puzzle before him. It seemed plain what had happened. The passage of Leazor's men was not subtle. Always they left destruction and death in their wake. But what was he meant to do about it? Hunting them down would do little good at the moment. They were headed south and would have crossed the border into their own evil land long ago.

He had just turned the meat and added tea leaves to the steaming water, when the sharp smell of skunk reached him. First only a whiff, then full force. He set down the stick with the roasting meat and stood, taking up his bow. He searched the shadows for the animal responsible for the smell. Fireflies were thick in the underbrush, and night insects called from the swamp to the east. The bushes rustled.

"Put that down, you mismatched scamp, or I will spray you. Don't think I won't."

"Wha—?!" Breac exclaimed as the skunk waddled into the light. "What are you?"

"A skunk, you idiot. Surely the High King doesn't send ignorant fools on all his missions."

The green, tear-shaped eyes blinked up at him, far too large for such a small creature.

"You're a changer!" Breac said, lowering his bow. "Mykell, of the Green Eyes."

"Fine. A changer if you like." The furry white paws grew large and black, the legs lengthening and the striped back stretching into the sleek form of a panther, gleaming golden black in the firelight. It licked its chops, flattening its whiskers down with a thin pink tongue.

"I hope you have more meat, for a hungry fellow worker," Mykell said.

"Of course, friend."

Mykell stalked into the circle of firelight, every inch of him gleaming as he sniffed first the air, then the ground. He sat on his haunches and blinked at the fire as Breac brought out another hunk of venison.

"Do you fancy your meat raw or cooked?" Breac asked.

Mykell turned his sleek head. "In this form I will take either."

They sat side by side before the fire, and Mykell said, "The High King sent me to watch over your mission. Leazor knows now of your whereabouts, and will do anything within his power to stop you. Also, the High King feared you would not reach the town in time to see what played out there. I took the form of a raven, and flew as fast and straight as the wind, and only just arrived in time to see the betrayal."

Breac looked up sharply. "Betrayal? Tell me you jest."

Mykell shook his head. "I wish I could. It was a girl. A worlds-traveler. She journeyed with a dryad of the southern wood. Leazor's men were here and took them. They tricked the girl—forced her really—into turning him over to be killed, as the law dictates. Apparently he fed her, and saved her from some wolves, likely Ezomrah. They sent her back to wherever she came from, and as soon as she was gone, killed the dryad."

Breac stared at him. "I wish that I could disbelieve you, but I know you speak truth." He turned the sizzling meat over the fire, staring into the flames for the first time. "This is bad."

The panther's ears swiveled backward, and his whiskers flattened. "Of course it's bad. Were you expecting a festival?"

Breac ignored him, talking more to himself as he said, "The dryad helped her, told her his name, and she by her word allowed him to be killed. Betrayal."

Mykell quoted in a soft growl, "Any traitor, betraying to the shedding of blood, must be brought before the High King at Al Acatra, on the Day of Justice, there to be slain by the master of all traitors, Leazor. If the blood debt is not satisfied, the land is forfeit. The King's sovereign law has been distained, and the law of treachery upheld. Leazor will take the throne."

"Blood for blood," Breac said. "It's the law that keeps us free from anarchy and tyranny."

"It's why the neighboring lands are now under Leazor, and no longer have the protection of the High King."

"Quoting the law to ourselves will not make it any better," Breac said. "We both know there's no way around it. You say she returned to her own world?"

"She's gone, yes."

"Would that you had stopped her."

"You know I could not. It was her decision. If she had refused to betray the dryad, I would have done all in my power to help them both. But I am forbidden to interfere in such choices of humans."

Breac sighed "Yes, yes, I know. She must be brought back, so the debt may be fulfilled." He scowled. Better to have gotten here early and fought the entire band of soldiers alone, he thought, than deliver a woman to die at Leazor's hand. Difficult mission indeed. He thought of the difficulty of finding this woman in a strange world, and dismissed it for the moment. More difficult the return to Al Acatra once he had found her. Oh yes. Much more difficult. He had the sudden urge to scold the High King, should he make it back alive. But that would be nearly the same as scolding his Creator, whose purpose he would not question. He sighed again.

"And exactly how do you propose to bring her here?" Mykell said, raising one furry black eyebrow. "You don't know her name, so she can't be summoned—even if you did want to use such dubious methods."

"How did she travel?"

"The Kantra symbol."

"Then we shall do the same."

"*You* shall do the same," Mykell said, shaking his head. "I shall stay here and await your return. Someone must make sure this side is clear when you arrive."

"Very well. Do you know the symbol?"

"I'm a changer, man. That doesn't mean I can read puzzles in the dark. Or memorize them, for that matter. She touched the sentinel beech. I assume it bears the mark."

"Good. I will leave at dawn."

* * * * *

Evie woke in her apartment with a murderous headache, still sprawled in the recliner where she'd passed out the night before. Bright daylight shone through slits in the blinds, striping the room with slivers of light. She groaned. Her neck felt like it would snap in two if she moved. She swatted a strand of hair out of her face and groaned again. There were the images, waiting for her when her mind came alive out of sleep. Eyes open or closed, the nightmare continued, superimposed over her surroundings.

The clutter of sheet music and books scattered about the room, guitar propped against the keyboard, tattered couch—all so familiar—today whispered strange things to her. Questioning her. Who was she really? Someone who could commit murder when she was frightened? Who could betray her friends? Someone who'd gone mad? Dark flames flickered in the recesses of the room. Real only in her mind.

She staggered into the kitchen. She could only handle one goal at a time right now, and at the moment it was to reach the coffee maker. Her fingers fumbled with the filter, spilled the grounds as she tried to measure them out. On the counter her cell phone, half dead, beeped. With coffee on the way, she turned her attention to the phone. Three new voicemails, and several text messages.

Text from Courtney: Howd it go with the new BF yesterday? Kiss you goodnight? ;)

Text from Anthony: Hows the creep.

Evie groaned. She'd forgotten all about James. He must be furious, if he hadn't called the cops and reported her missing. Great. What if this got back to her parents? She popped her knuckles, starting with her thumbs. They would be furious if they found out she'd acted so immature. Especially since they loved James. The voicemail could only be from one person. She put the phone on speaker and keyed in her pin number. The automated voice squawked.

"You have, three, new messages, and, zero, saved messages. To listen to new messages,"

She hit the key, cutting the recording short.

"Hey Eva, where did you go? I just checked the henna tent, and they said you left. Umm. I'm over by the outdoor theatre if you get this."

The next message went along the same line, with James' voice sounding anxious, almost panicked. She deleted it and continued on to the next. This time he sounded resigned, angry.

"Eva, this is James. Hey, I don't know what happened at the fair last night, why you disappeared on me, but... well I guess this means we're through." The speaker crackled where he had let out a sigh. "Look, I just hope you're ok. Call me a sucker, but I'm worried about you. I ran into Anthony, he said you'd probably gone home with Courtney. Look, if you want to dump me, ok, I get it. This relationship has been pretty one-sided. But at least let me know you're ok."

She leaned against the counter and stared blankly at the coffee maker as it perked and gurgled.

Last night was there in her mind, pushing everything else out. Like a toothache that's always harassing, gnawing, making itself known. Only worse. She was not going to get away from it, and now that the panic and trauma were past, she kept thinking of Sylvanus, the dryad. Rachael's reassurance that he was probably fine sounded thin and feeble now. The idea to treat it all as a bad dream sounded pretty feeble too. It had been far too real. No dream had ever frightened her that badly. Or left her feeling this wretchedly guilty. Her elbows thumped onto the counter and she dropped her head into her hands.

The idea must have come sometime in the night. Now as she waited in a daze for the coffee, she remembered the thought that had been nagging her. She wanted to see that book. The one Rachael had gotten the design from in the first place. She had never seen it before, but she wanted to own it, to search it from cover to cover for... for what? What was she hoping to find? *Something.* She admitted to herself. *I don't know what, but there has to be something.* Something that could give her hope.

And what about Rachael? The mysterious henna artist who didn't think Evie was crazy. She had hinted at other strange stories. Evie wondered about those too as she stood there waiting. She had always longed for another place—for the hope that the mundane world around her was not all she could expect to experience. To live and to die here. Now she'd been to another world, and the horror haunted her, while at the same time a strange seduction called to her. How could she ever want to go back to that place? But she did.

She poured her coffee, and nibbled at a slice of toast. Maybe it would be better not to know what had happened to Sylvanus. Then she could still hope. Could make herself believe that he was alright. Could get rid of this *guilt*. Perhaps over time she would come to believe the lie, would push it from her mind and get on with life. But it would always be with her. Wherever she went, whatever happy moments came, it would be there. It would drive her mad.

But then, maybe she could go back and help him. If she did go back, where would she end up? Back in the woods again? In the middle of those men? How would she even find Sylvanus to help him? *Ok, so it was a pretty stupid thought,* she told herself. But she had to think something. She could never go back to normal life. Not after this.

With her appetite now thoroughly gone, she set down the toast and turned to head into the shower. A smudge on her hand caught her eye. One she hadn't noticed last night. She turned her hand over so her palm faced up. A dark red blotch stained her skin. It looked like dried blood. She scratched at it with her fingernail. It didn't come off. Holding her hand closer to her face, she saw that the mark was not just a shapeless blotch. It was a complex, tightly woven pattern of tiny interconnecting lines, even more intricate than the knot pattern on her other hand. Yet this one conveyed no beauty. She squirted dish soap into her hand and stuck it under the faucet, using a scrubby sponge to scour the mark. She turned the water off and stared at her hand. Her skin felt raw, but the mark was just as bright, just as ugly as before.

The back of Evie's neck prickled. She felt she was going to be sick.

6

Searching

In the gray dawn Breac studied the knot pattern on the tree, tracing it with his fingertips. He got quill pen and ink from his saddlebag, and with Mykell watching, got to work copying the lines onto his left palm. Mykell, still in the form of a panther, groomed himself with paws and tongue as he watched.

"Why don't you change to a fish, and take a real bath?" Breac said, breaking a tedious silence.

Mykell paused, one giant black paw suspended in the air. "Fish are slimy," he purred, and continued his stroke. "I hate slimy things."

"But not smelly things," Breac replied.

"A skunk's odor isn't offensive to the skunk."

"Nor can a fish feel that it's slimy."

Mykell stopped grooming himself and watched him, flicking his tail.

"I've one question," Breac said, still drawing with his brows creased together. "If you're a skunk, and you spray something, and then change to something else, does the smell remain?"

Mykell's twitching tail suddenly became much shorter and fuzzier. His big, black paws turned small and white, and the scent of skunk permeated the air.

"Shall I try?" he said.

Breac glanced over at the panther-turned-skunk, and lifted an eyebrow. "Just remember who you have to travel with."

After a pause Mykell said, "That girl. She was something else."

Breac glanced up.

"I've never seen a human woman more beautiful, more *alive*."

"You sound smitten. Though I've never heard of a changer marrying a human."

"I'd be marrying a condemned human, remember. And no, only Ezomrah wed humans. We who are true to the King do not." Mykell sat back on small, furry haunches. Rolls of skin and fat bunched around his middle, making him look round and comical despite his serious expression. "I don't understand why this was allowed to happen. She was courageous. She stood up to the enemy captain, and was abused for it. She spoke with wit, even when faced with death and torture."

"Was she an enchantress?"

"If so, she didn't use her magic, and I know I would have. I tell you—if I *were* a human, and I say *if*, I would not rest until I had found that lady and asked her to be my bride."

"You are smitten."

"I am not smitten. I'm warning you. Be on your guard. I feel there is more in this than unlucky chance."

Breac scowled. His pen strokes had suddenly become much harder, digging into his hand. He lifted the quill and rested it across the top of the inkwell, surveying his work. Nearly finished. He flexed the tension out of his fingers.

Mykell sank down till his belly rested on the ground, chin on paws like a dog. Green eyes stared up at the man. "Have you been in the company of a marked traitor before?"

Breac answered hesitatingly. "Once... a long time ago."

"The High King has sent you to find her. Do not doubt that Leazor will also send forces to claim her before it is time. They have probably already begun to arrive in her world. It is possible they followed her last night even. Or..."

"Or?"

Mykell shook his head, his hide quivering nervously. "Our enemy has sought to take Acatra Dahma for long millennia. Would he stop at trusting our downfall to mere chance? He was of old the Second Immortal, and like the High King, his mind touches on eternity. Who knows what he has foreseen and manipulated to his own ends? Or what he is even now manipulating?"

"He may see glimpses of the future, but only the Creator knows how it will change with the changing wills of men."

"I did not speak to arouse fear," Mykell replied, "only to warn us both. We must not fail."

Breac put down the pen, stopped up the ink bottle, and stood. "It's time."

* * * * *

"She works at an antique store," Evie muttered to herself as she locked the door to her apartment. She tugged her fingerless gloves tighter, overly conscious of the marks they hid. The outer hallway and stairwell of her small apartment building always smelled like cigar smoke and wet dog, but today the foul odor didn't register as she hurried down and out. There were lots of antique dealers in the area, but the one closest to Rachael's house, and the only one Evie could think of that was known for selling books, was Marv's Antique Barn.

As she hurried down the front steps, she caught a movement from the corner of her eye, and glanced to the lilac bush growing beside the stone walkway. An owl had just alighted there. An owl at this time in the morning? With its dark, white speckled back to Evie, its round face was turned almost all the way around. It stared at her with huge black eyes as she passed. A shudder ran through her, and a deep, irrational fear. She broke into a run the last few steps to her car, and slammed the door. The owl dropped from its perch in the lilac and glided to a low branch in the elm tree right above the car. It cocked its head, watching as she turned the key and put the car in gear. A faint cackle of laughter teased her ears, and for an instant her vision warped. She broke off eye contact and hit the gas, swerving out onto the road and nearly hitting another car. *I'm really losing it now. I must be.* Panic rode with her as she hit the country roads leaving town, and hopefully the owl, behind her. *I'll never be able to go home if that thing's still there.*

"I'm losing it," she said out loud, partly to counter her panicked thoughts. "It was only an owl. And I'm gonna be paranoid about it? Really?"

And what about that mark on your hand? What's really happening here?

She rubbed at the stain in her palm, feeling the raw, scrubbed spot under the glove, and bit her lip.

* * * * *

Breac took his sword in his hand. His heart raced, and he braced himself as he reached for the mark, then blinked with the sudden change of surroundings. He dropped to a defensive crouch, sword up. It took an instant to realize he was alone.

He stood in a house, or more likely a small palace, home of a lower king or chieftain. He double checked that there were no people around, and no noises of people. A gentle hum came from another room. He had no idea what could make such a noise, but it didn't seem to be coming any nearer, so he dismissed it for the moment. So many elaborate furnishings filled the room that he had a hard time at first focusing. Unfamiliar details bombarded him. A fireplace, unlit, with a neat little arrangement of half burnt logs inside and no firewood stacked beside it struck him as odd. Framed pictures, potted plants, figurines and furniture. The lavish carpet, couch, and chairs he'd never seen the like of. He ran his hand over the back of the couch, feeling the softness of the fabric. And everything looked spotlessly clean and new. A doorway led into the hall, and another into another room that he couldn't identify. And there was what he was looking for. A travel symbol etched into a stone over the fireplace.

A movement from the hall door. He tensed and looked up, met the coal black eyes of a small cat. It hissed, baring tiny fangs.

He jerked the sword point up. "Ezomrah!"

Surprised, human? The thing spoke into his mind. The next instant it had become a huge white tiger. It leapt at him, knocked him backward into a glassed-in cabinet. Glass cracked at his back as he deflected the claws with his upraised sword, prepared for the battle of his life. But it did not attack farther. Instead it leapt for the window, shattering the glass and taking the screen with it. Breac leapt after it, made a clean dive through the window, rolled, and came upright in time to see the thing shift into a raven and fly off.

For a moment he stood and watched it, before sheathing the sword. If the girl was indeed marked as a traitor, the Ezomrah would be drawn to her. There might be a chance it would lead him to her. Or at least closer to her. He started after it on foot.

The neatly clipped lawn sloped down to meet a road, paved with some solid stone-like material. He stopped in the ditch beside the road and studied the paving, bending down to touch its surface. It didn't quite resemble anything he was used to, but he could see its usefulness right away. A road made of this stuff would never bog a wagon down in mud, or develop ruts. Before he could take another step he heard the *sound.* An object came hurtling down the road toward him. He took a step back as it rushed by, squinting against the wind that blasted him at its passing. Whether the thing was beast or being or a materialization of the wind he couldn't guess at that speed.

He looked warily in both directions before crossing the road and entering the woods. The trees, predictable and safe like old friends, welcomed him into their shade. He set off at a long stride, neither walking nor running, a pace that would eat the miles and never weary him.

* * * * *

Evie pulled into the gravel parking lot at Marv's and breathed a sigh. She had been right. There was Rachael's Blazer sitting beside the building. She eased out of the car, feeling suddenly nervous again. What if the book didn't have the answers she was looking for? What if it wasn't there anymore? What if she really was losing her mind, having a nervous breakdown, hallucinating? Would insanity be better than this constant barrage of emotion? A random image popped into her mind of herself, locked in the embrace of a straitjacket, dark tangled hair over her face and laughing hysterically from the corner of a white padded room. She gave a nervous snort.

A bell above the door jangled as she went in, and a voice called from the back of the store, "Be right with you!"

The place was divided into several rooms. Through one doorway she got a glimpse of old wooden furniture, and through another, stacks of games and toys from decades past. This room looked like any other old bookstore, with the feeling of being cluttered and disorganized, even though the shelves were labeled. It smelled like an antique bookstore, too. Dusty and pungent, with a good dose of old cigar. The walls were lined with books, and rows of shelves marched down one side of the room, stuffed with more books. The other side was taken up with antique bookcases, coffee tables, and nightstands; all staggering under piles of ancient tomes. The light coming in the big show window fell on muted wood and worn carpeting, faded cloth bindings and dancing dust particles. She felt a sneeze building in the back of her nose.

Rachael came from the back room with a stack of musty, dilapidated volumes in one arm, and her gray and white cat in the other. She paused when she saw Evie, then set the books down behind the counter.

"I had a feeling you'd be showing up today."

"Really?" Evie noticed the woman looked a little pale. She seemed agitated, glancing about, but smiled as she set the cat down on the counter and stroked its fur.

"Looking for the book I suppose."

"How did you know?"

"If I had everything happen to me that you did, I would be looking for answers too." She reached under the counter and brought out a thick volume, leather bound and beautifully preserved, and handed it to Evie.

It had no title, just another endless knot stamped into the cover. The pages were thick parchment, hand written in narrow, flowing calligraphy. On the first page was the symbol on Evie's hand, and after it two solid pages of writing.

The page edges were uneven, making it difficult to flip through. They flopped open a dozen pages later, revealing the same mark Evie now bore on her other hand. Her stomach flopped, and her heart suddenly made it hard to hear past the blood rushing in her ears. She squinted at the page for a moment, then bent closer.

"That's the only problem," Rachael said. "You can't read it."

"But..." Evie flipped back to the travel symbol on the first page. She stared for several seconds before the heading became legible. It read "The Wanderer's Key. Be wise, and use it not lightly." She flipped back to the other page. Nothing. Scribbles. She raised confused eyes to the henna artist.

Bitter disappointment tinged through her, like a dentist's drill on raw nerves. The blot in her palm tingled suddenly and horribly. She jerked her hands away from the book and scratched her palm. The cat, sitting a few feet down the counter, hissed, baring its teeth. The small sound made Evie jump. Blood pounded her ears again. Hastily she flipped the book closed and cleared her throat, not daring to meet the other woman's gaze.

"How much is it?"

Before Rachael could answer, the bell above the door jingled. Evie felt her pulse spike even harder as Rachael looked past her at the customer who'd just entered, and she saw the other woman's face go white.

* * * * *

Breac cleared the trees, and stopped. He'd come straight in the direction the Ezomrah had taken, hoping that it had not veered away, and that his hunch was right. Now another road crossed in front of him, and on the far side a gravel lot with a building. A red and gold sign perched at the top of a ten-foot pole at the edge of the gravel. He could not read it.

How far had the Ezomrah come? Had it changed course? He looked both ways down the strange road before hurrying across, then skirted around the edge of the lot, keeping close to the huckleberry and mountain laurel bushes, and out of the open.

Two of the bright objects that he had seen speeding down the road sat near the building. They were both silent now, and did not move or breathe. He had no clearer idea what they might be now than he had had before. No one was in sight out here, but through the front window he could see two women talking. And sitting on the counter between them, the Ezomrah. He edged closer, coming up onto the porch so he could peer in through a corner of the window. The woman behind the counter was tall, her hair cut shorter than his own. The other looked much younger. Rich, dark curls hung loose down her back. He couldn't see much of her face, other than a small, pale nose. She leaned over a book, her hair falling forward to obscure her features. She wore pants like a man, but formfitting ones he had never seen before, and a loose shirt, unbuttoned, with another skin tight one beneath. She carried a small pouch hung crossways from her shoulders.

He dug out the locket, and snapped it open, looked hard at

the likeness of the dark haired girl. They could be the same. He willed her to turn so he could see her face. Finally she did. His heart did something strange then. A sort of jump/stop he had never felt before.

He hurried past the window. Through the door, the cat saw him and hissed. He did not wait to see more.

* * * * *

A shadow fell across the open page. Evie felt, rather than saw, the man who stepped to the counter beside her. He held a huge fist out over the counter and opened it, letting three large coins roll onto the glass. They were all solid gold, and clanked heavily as they landed.

"For the book," he said.

Evie whirled to face him and let out a strangled squeak.

The clothes he wore were no cheap costume from the Renaissance Faire. Knee high leather boots, leather pants, a short woven tunic laced up the front, a steel wrist guard on each arm, each intricately etched, and a thick wool cloak, black. A sword scabbard hung from his belt, displaying the ornate hilt of his sword. Then she got to his face. His skin was deep bronze, his hair straw blond and chopped off raggedly. A week's worth of blond stubble glowed on the lower half of his dark face. His eyes, both shocking and riveting, one deepest brown and the other pure glacier blue. His gaze was locked on her.

Evie's heart stopped, then nearly exploded as it started again. This man was from the other world. He had followed her. He'd been looking for her. She seemed to see justice written across his face as the full weight of that strange night clapped down on her, pressing the air out of her lungs in a horrified gasp. The book dropped from her hands, and she took a single step back.

7
Back to Darkwood

Breac bent and picked up the book. He had recognized it at once as one of the books of the Kantra; sacred, rare, and worth far more in his world than a handful of gold coins. In this world it would be all but worthless except as an artifact. It contained the Songs and the Symbols, the Law, and explained how to use them. But it was the High King's Laws, for the protection of his people, and would only work where his rule was intact. He tucked the book into his belt, then took the girl's arm.

"We have to go," he said, glancing at the woman behind the counter, and the Ezomrah, which had not changed from its cat form. It stared back at him. Neither it nor the woman made any move to stop him. He had the girl halfway to the door before she came out of her shock. Her feet suddenly seemed to grow roots. Her voice took on a tone of defiance.

"Go where? Who are you?"

He turned to face her. Hazel, almost golden eyes cut into him. Her skin would be naturally pale. Now it was white. The strange clothes she wore did nothing to hide her curves. He stared at her, stunned, for a full second. As though he'd never seen a woman before. He remembered Mykell's and the King's warnings. The citizens of Acatra Dahma would be terrorized, killed, and enslaved because of this woman. If she was not killed for her crime other women and children with no blood on their hands would die. But how could she have known that?

He repeated, "We must go back. They are coming for you."

"Who's coming for me?" she cried, voice pitching high as she grabbed the edge of a bookshelf with white fingertips. He ripped the fingerless glove off the hand he gripped, and turned her palm up to reveal the bloodlike stain. He pried her other hand loose from the shelf and pulled that glove off as well, revealing the travel symbol stained into her skin.

"We must go now. They have already begun to arrive."

Breac got a fresh grip on the girl's arm and gave it a yank, though it made him cringe to do so. She stumbled after him to the door. He pulled it open, and they stepped into the sunlight.

They hadn't taken two steps when a blow sent him rocking back. He glanced down at the quivering arrow shaft. It had imbedded itself in the Book of Kantra tucked inside his belt. The shooter was already racing across the gravel toward them.

The girl gasped. He shoved her back through the door behind him and slammed it shut.

"Another way out?" he said, breaking off the shaft of the arrow which he flung to the ground.

The other woman pointed to the back. She fumbled with a set of keys, moving as though to lock the front door, but she was far too slow. And too late. The attacker thrust the door open. She stumbled as it hit her, and fell back against a bookshelf, rocking it, sending a stack of books sliding to the floor.

Breac slammed through the back door, still hauling the girl along with him, and ran across the narrow gravel lane in the back into the cover of the trees. The woods were sparse here, but they plunged in, and Breac at once turned and ran around the side of the building, keeping in the tree line. He dragged the girl back the way he'd come, across the road to the thicker forest beyond. Behind them the enemy crashed through the brush, howling like a slobbering dog. The man must be mad. But he was a good runner, and his wordless cries came closer as he gained ground.

The girl ran now without question or protest, though he still clasped her hand firmly. She was quick on her feet, and though she stumbled over rocks and roots, she kept her balance. Breac neither stumbled nor paused. They ran until the trees opened out, and they came smack up against a stone fence. Breac lifted her over it, then jumped over himself, and they crouched down, panting. They were in a pasture. Half a dozen cows stared at them stupidly, while a dozen others went right on grazing.

He looked over at the girl. She breathed heavily, red lips parted. Her face had taken on a pink tint, her eyes round and startled.

"Stay here," Breac whispered.

He drew his sword and vaulted back over the wall to meet their attacker. Swords clashed and locked, hilt to hilt, and he stared into the glazed eyes of his enemy. Neither spoke. Breac shoved against the sword and leapt back, topping the stone wall in two backward steps. The rocks under his feet tipped, and he staggered. The enemy thrust his sword forward to stab him while he was off guard, but he swept the blade aside with his arm, letting it slide harmlessly off his steel bracer. With the enemy's sword pointed away for an instant, Breac leapt down, and drove his sword through the man's foot. He kicked the weapon out of the man's hand, then leapt back over the wall. The girl was gone.

He grunted in frustration and looked about. He recognized the same shoeprint he'd found outside of Darkwood, pressed into a semi-dried cow pile near the stone wall. A trail of beaten-down grass led down the hill and back across the wall into the woods. He started off in that direction at a dead sprint as the madman howled behind him, attempting to climb the stone wall with a mangled foot. The man wouldn't get far. He had been little more than a distraction, and Breac gave him no more thought. His real enemy was the Ezomrah. If it should catch the girl before he did.... He put on more speed, clearing the stone wall in a leap. His foot landed on a branch, and he made no attempt to catch his fall, rolling with it instead and coming back up still running, ignoring the flare of pain from the wound in his shoulder. She could not have come far. He looked for color or movement ahead of him. There. Her red patterned shirt flickered in and out of the brush. Something else moved off to his side—an owl, flying low through the trees. Ezomrah.

The girl was a fast runner. Breac gained on her, but not fast enough. *Creator, let her stumble,* he thought, as the Ezomrah streaked through the trees, moving ahead of him. It could have caught her by now. It seemed to him as though it toyed with him.

He drew close enough to the girl to hear the brush crackle as she ran. At last the Creator favored him with opportunity. Her foot twisted on a rock, and she crumpled in a pile of dead leaves. The next instant he was on top of her, lifting her to her feet and pulling her along while hardly slowing. She yelped, but ran with him.

* * * * *

Evie couldn't breathe. Her ankle screamed. She wanted to pull away from the man, if only to stop for breath, but the sight of that shadowy owl speeding through the treetops kept her going. For some reason it struck panic in her heart.

They came to the end of the woods, and without pausing the man pulled her toward the road. A horn blared as a speeding car swerved to miss them. That stopped the man. At least for half a second. This time he glanced both ways before he dragged her across. They were at Rachael's house.

Of course Evie had known they would come here. That he must be dragging her back to his own world. And part of her wanted to go. The other part knew that she could never go back and face what might have become of Sylvanus. That his fate might have something to do with the man now dragging her back toward that portal. She threw her weight back and dug her heels into the grass.

Their momentum dragged her forward, but the man swung

around to face her. She shot off a punch that just missed his nose. It landed on his cheek, snapping his head back. She tried to jerk away from him. Finally twisting her wrist suddenly and hard against his thumb, she broke free, and sprinted back toward a neighboring house.

The man tackled her from behind, and they both went rolling in the grass. Evie landed on a fallen branch, drawing blood from her arm.

"We don't have time for this," he said, grunting as she jammed her elbow in his stomach.

"*You* don't have time for this!" she shouted back. "*I* have nothing to do with it."

He rolled her over and pinned her arms to the ground, bringing their faces close. He smelled of pine and horses, dried sweat and leather. Perspiration beaded at his temples, and his breathing sounded hoarse. Their gazes locked, inches apart. A shiver rippled across her skin, and not the type of shiver she would have expected.

"You are most astonishing, my lady," he said, "I have never had to wrestle with a woman before." His Voice! Deep and husky, like a rock singer, but full and warm.

"There's got to be a first for everything, now doesn't there?" She brought her knee up to try and kick him off, but he dodged it, and pinned her legs down with his knees.

"You bring this indignity upon yourself, madam. We are in grave danger here."

What she wouldn't give to hear him sing! "No kidding! I'm being attacked by a crazy man with a sword."

"Not from me!" He actually looked surprised that she would think him a danger to her.

They both caught a movement, and both heads turned in time to see the owl alight on the ground next to them. But it wasn't an owl anymore. Within a second it had morphed into the hugest wolf Evie had ever imagined. She screamed.

The man rolled away from her and up onto his feet in one swift motion, drawing his sword before he was fully upright. The owl-turned-wolf thing snarled. It leapt at them, and the man raised his sword to run it through, but at the last instant it turned back into an owl and flew at his head, talons out. His arms went up to protect his face. Evie snatched up the branch she'd fallen on, wielding it like a baseball bat, and knocked the owl out of the air. It sprawled on the ground, motionless. The man grabbed her hand and pulled her back toward the house.

"Come on!"

This time she ran with him. He didn't give her a chance to climb through the broken window, but picked her up and stepped over the sill with her in his arms. He dropped her feet, keeping one arm tightly about her shoulders, and reached out to the mark in the fireplace. She flinched as he pressed his palm against it.

With the flinch the scene changed. Charred ghosts of the burned out village rose around them. Silence. They stood there, the man looking around, searching for something or someone.

"What is this place?"

"Don't you recognize it?" he replied.

She looked about. The stench of death and smoke hung in the air, not dispelled on the breeze that lifted ashes and swirled them around in tight circles. In the center of what used to be the town square a low wooden platform was the only structure not destroyed. The blackened stone ring in the center was all too familiar. Panic tingled through her.

"Why did you bring me here?"

The man answered, "To fulfill a debt." He did not look at her as he spoke, but glanced around, seeming uncomfortable. He drew his sword and gave a low whistle. Nothing stirred in answer to the call. The trees rustled a little, the late afternoon sun flashed from the leaves, then the wind stilled and there was silence. No birdsong. No insect noise. Her foot and arm throbbed, and her heart pounded a staccato beat in her ears.

The man became more pensive as a moment went by. Watching him made her even more nervous. She cracked her pinky knuckle, the tiny *pop* sounding loud in the stillness. *Anything moves, I'm gonna jump right out of my skin,* she thought. She wanted to ask what was wrong, but his face was drawn so tight, she dared not.

They both jumped at a harsh *caw!* There was a frantic flapping among the tree branches, and a crow somersaulted out of the forest amid a small whirlwind of black feathers. The instant it cleared the trees, it began to change. Evie screamed, then slapped a hand over her mouth as the crow dropped, its body growing too big for the wings. Four legs and hooves took shape, the ruffled feathers smoothed into sleek black hair, and the spindly crow neck grew long, graceful, powerful. The transformation took about a second, so that by the time the creature was low enough, its legs had already fully formed, and met the ground at a full, graceful gallop. The crow-turned-horse was upon them the next instant, rearing and kicking up a cloud of ashes as it stopped.

"The enemy is upon us," the creature cried. "Must fly at once."

"My horse—" the man started.

"No time! I will carry you both. Your charger knows his way home."

Without another word the man turned to Evie and lifted her to the horse's bare back, then leapt up behind her. This time she didn't bother to protest. Cruel images of the men from last night sent new fear pounding in her veins.

* * * * *

Breac sputtered as the girl's long dark hair flew back in his face. He leaned forward over her shoulder as Mykell ran, and shouted into the wind, "How many?"

"Six," Mykell replied.

"So few?"

"The sorcerer Rizann is with them."

"Wonderful. I'd rather fight an entire company."

Mykell did not reply. He was already panting from exertion. Breac could hear their pursuers now, crashing through the brush behind them. He looked back, and saw flashes of movement through the trees. One flickering shape gained quickly, speeding after them as though they stood still.

"Can you go faster?" Breac shouted.

"Are you mad, human?"

"Something's gaining ground, and it's not something I want to meet."

Mykell laid his ears back and surged ahead even faster, straining and gasping.

"Creator defend us, answer my call," Breac muttered, beginning the Song of Protection from the Kantra. More a chant, it came out forcefully through gritted teeth. "Muscle, sinew, steel and claw. Be the strength beneath me, Let me not fall. Fire, tooth, blade and jaw."

"And what can they do for you, Breac?" hissed a reply through the tree branches behind them, cutting the song short. "Think you not that I have power as well?"

Mykell said, "Star Deep Lake."

"Don't stop," Breac replied.

The next second they cleared the trees, and without pause Mykell galloped for the lake, now stumbling through sand and gravel. Breac drew his sword and threw it with all his might over Mykell's head into the water, shouting, "Open, Vivaqua!"

The girl looked back at him, her white face wearing a look of shock. Then her gaze went to the line of trees they'd just left, and her eyes went wide. Breac looked back as well. Five riders emerged from the trees at full gallop, and before them, the sixth rider, Rizann. But not a rider. As Breac looked, rider and horse became one, a creature of grotesque proportions. Wings burst out from its sides, and it leapt into the air, flying toward them fast and straight as an arrow, with talons extended.

Mykell reached the edge of the lake and made a leap out over the water. At the same time the sorcerer descended on them. Breac and the girl both ducked away from the talons. And then Mykell's hooves came down on the surface of the lake.

Instead of splashing into the water and being instantly snatched up by the beast, they were falling. Breac had a dizzying glimpse of a great space, dusky light around them, but growing brighter far, far below. Pillars like great tree trunks, a long staircase. And then Mykell's hooves struck marble stairs, and he was careening downward, unable to stop. Time for a gasp. The girl screamed as Mykell lost his footing and they somersaulted out into the void.

8
The Naiad Queen

Shocking silence followed Evie's scream as they fell. Her stomach wedged itself in her throat. She couldn't have made another sound. The man's arms felt like they'd been turned to rigid steel around her. She gripped fistfuls of the horse's mane, but it wasn't coarse horse's hair anymore. Instead she held handfuls of feathers. Huge wings snapped open on either side of them, and she felt the jolt as the horse-turned-giant eagle pulled out of their freefall. As enormous as he had become in his bird form, the weight of the two humans still bore him down. Muscles strained to keep his wings outstretched, circling downward into the light. Wingtips brushed the pillars, giant columns of swirling water, and sent sprays of droplets raining down. They landed with a whoosh of wings and scuffling of claws on sand. The creature collapsed, wings outspread on the ground, gasping.

In the sudden stillness that followed, Evie could hear blood rushing in her ears. Her hands remained locked around feathers, shaking violently. The man released his hold on her and she started, blinking as her vision swirled and she remembered finally to breathe.

Before them twenty warriors guarded a low dais where a lady sat upon a silken couch. Evie did a double-take on the scene. The warrior nearest had his spear lowered, its double prongs pointed at them. Her eyes met the man's... but he wasn't a man. Darkly blue-flecked eyes, slate gray hair, and fair, almost translucent skin. Her mind scrambled for an explanation. If Sylvanus had been a dryad, a tree creature, and now they were *in* a lake (and she realized suddenly that she was in fact still breathing), then these must be naiads. Water creatures.

She looked beyond the warrior to the naiad lady, who held in her hands the sword that Evie's captor had tossed into the water.

"Welcome, Aindreas, son of Rajah." The creature rose as she spoke, coming down the steps of the dais. Silvery-blue hair rippled with each movement. "Or shall I call you Breac, the Tainted One, as your own people do?" She held out the sword to him. Large clear eyes, with all the changing colors of an opal regarded each of them.

The man took the sword, bowing slightly.

"I cannot say I am glad of your coming," the naiad continued, "Bringing the enemy at your very heels. None the less, you are welcome."

"Thank you, Lady."

So the man's name was Breac. Or Aindreas? Confusing.

The naiad turned and signaled one of the maidens standing by. "Bring refreshment for our guests."

The man—she decided on Breac because it was easier—slid off their horse/eagle's back, and turned to offer her his hand. Their eyes met for an instant, and her stomach flip-flopped. His eyes were so strange, with the two colors, but so *human*. She didn't know any other word for it. Not the eyes of a kidnapper, or bounty hunter, or whatever he was. Not eyes like the thug captain that had forced her into this mess...

Her heart sank. *Sylvanus.*

She jumped and nearly shrieked as the horse-turned-eagle turned again...this time into a sleek black panther.

This is too much!

The queen spoke, seemingly indifferent to the dangerous shape-shifter animal thing that now sat on its haunches, licking huge curved claws. *Of course, why would a naiad think a shape-shifter strange? Silly me.*

"Six men are at this moment churning the shores of my lake searching for you," she said, looking at Breac. "Whatever your mission, it must be of some importance." She turned to the shapeshifter panther and curtsied. "The man's mission must indeed be imperative if you are his companion. We are honored by your presence, Mykell of the green eyes."

The panther, Mykell, inclined his head and replied, "I am in your debt, for providing refuge."

She smiled and turned this time to Evie. "What is your name, worlds' traveler?"

Gawking! Evie snapped her mouth shut and replied, "Eva Drake. Evie."

"And what is your part in this tale?"

She glanced at Breac, who was trying to pry the arrow out of her book of symbols, and gave a slight shrug.

Sylvanus, she thought.

The naiad also looked at Breac. "I am sure it will be made clear soon enough." She turned back to Evie. "Have no fear child. You are in good hands."

At that moment the maid returned with several others, bearing trays of food and pitchers of drink. The three of them sat on the steps of the dais while the food was set out. Evie shrugged out of her outer shirt and examined the cut in her arm where she'd fallen on the branch. She licked her thumb and used it to wipe away some of the dried blood, till one of the naiads brought her a damp cloth and a jar of salve. She sniffed the jar of green gook and wrinkled her nose. Smelled like pond scum. She had serious doubts about smearing the stuff on her skin, bleeding or otherwise. But they were watching. Would she be committing some unknown trespass of this world by refusing what was meant to be kindness? She dabbed a tiny bit onto the edge of the cut, and waited to see if her heart would stop suddenly, or her whole arm fall off. Instead the spot tingled and went numb.

"We have another visitor," the naiad said.

Evie followed the gazes of every other person in the room, to see a man descending the long staircase. He reached the bottom and strode toward them, bowing when he came near. This was the man—or whatever—that had morphed with his horse and flown after them. She hadn't seen his face before, but she recognized his clothing. Boots, trousers, and shirt all black. Black vest with gold embroidery and buttons, gold dagger at his belt.

Breac and Mykell both got to their feet.

"Lady Vivaqua, your beauty has not waned," the stranger said, opening his hands in a gesture of welcome.

"Rizann," the naiad replied. "You are bold to enter here. You must know I will not allow your magic in my palace. Your life is in danger."

The man bowed low. "Majesty, I am placing myself at the mercy of your unfailing hospitality. My life is indeed in your hands. But you are mistaken about your own safety, and the power of the High King, from whom your protection ultimately comes. Even now his rule over this land is in jeopardy."

"I think not," Vivaqua said, raising one silvery blue eyebrow.

"The guests whom you shelter have not told you their mission then," the man said. He pointed straight at Evie. "Yonder sits a betrayer, on her way to be slain, as the Creator's law demands. She is a worlds' traveler, a witch, a seductress, in the hands of a warrior with a tender heart. Can you not see your danger?"

Vivaqua glanced around at those gathered, her gaze resting a moment longer on Breac and Evie. "The King knows his business," she answered lightly. "The truest of hearts must also be tender. But you did not risk your life coming here to tell me that you think the High King's truest servant is in danger of falling in love. What do you want?"

Rizann bowed yet again. "I cannot deceive you. It is my wish that the witch lives, or is killed in a manner not dictated by the law, so that this beautiful country would fall into my master's hands. Alas, that is not my mission. I was sent for the man Breac."

Breac looked at him through narrowed eyes. "For what?"

"I know not. I, like you, do my master's bidding." Rizann turned back to Vivaqua. "Give the man over to me, have one of your own people deliver the girl to the King, and I swear they will be left alone."

Vivaqua chuckled, then laughed, a low, rippling sound. "You jest," she said. "Yes—of course I could hand over the man who came to me for refuge. And then I would be guilty of the same crime as she. Surly you do not take me for such a fool."

"On the contrary, lady. It was you who helped him, not he you. You owe him nothing, and could have refused him shelter, still remaining innocent."

"Could I?" she said. "Could I refuse help to the man who leads the King's armies, and keeps these shores safe from your master? I am already in his debt. You are a conniving magician, Rizann, and your life is in peril. Leave us."

"I could take him," the magician said, drawing himself up and moving toward Breac.

Vivaqua frowned, and the whole room responded. Watery walls and pillars that Evie had hardly had a chance to glance at till now suddenly began to roar and roil, darkening like a violent sea. Gooseflesh raced up her arms and back.

The naiad rose from her couch and advanced toward Rizann, her eyes darkening with the room. Her voice lowered to the rolling tone of a distant thunder storm.

"Leave now, sorcerer."

Rizann did not reply. Instead he rose to his full height, stretching his hands above his head, fingers splayed like talons.

For a moment Evie thought they *were* talons. The shades of darkness around him grew even deeper, while a red glow ignited along his skin and clothing. Could this even be real? The magician looked as though he were about to change into some horrendous monster again. Or perhaps that was in her head as well.

The naiad guards lowered their double pronged spears toward him, and steam hissed from the walls, gathering into a white cloud above them.

The magician paused. His eyes glinted with unreleased power, yet even he apparently dared not attack the naiads in their own watery home. Instead he struck out at Breac, slashing at his face. Half a dozen spears left the guards' hands, but Rizann had already vanished, and they thudded into the sandy floor.

* * * * *

No one in the great hall spoke. Humans, shape-shifter, and naiads all looked around at one another. All safe. The palace walls and pillars became smooth and glassy once again, and the air cleared. Mykell slowly relaxed his silent snarl and licked his whiskers, though his ears remained flattened against his head. Breac let out a sigh, breaking the horrified silence, and gingerly fingered the cuts on his face. Four deep scratches ran from his ear to just under his eye. Evie might have felt sorry for him, if she'd had room left for another emotion. And if she wasn't thinking about killing him herself.

She drew a deep breath, steadied her voice, and spoke softly, looking at the man. "You brought me back here to kill me."

His face got a deer-in-the-headlights expression. But it was Mykell who answered her.

"Surely even in your own world betrayal is wrong."

"But not punishable by death." She took another breath, looking from Breac to Mykell. The shape-shifter had momentarily lost his scariness for her. "I have nothing to do with this world. Let me go home, and I'll never come back."

"Did the dryad Sylvanus deserve death? Did he have anything to do with you? You may not belong in this world, but your actions here have consequences that will destroy this country, and many more lives if they are not set right."

Evie felt her chest constrict. The unrealistic hope that she'd used to hold her guilt at bay unraveled with the certainty of Sylvanus' death. Through another onslaught of panic she managed to attempt a defense. "Those who deserve death certainly don't wish for it. The dryad used magic. I though after I got away perhaps he would be able to escape. If you know your enemy, you must know what they threatened me with." Her voice went squeaky, and she stopped.

The hall was silent in the wake of her protest. Even Mykell seemed reluctant to meet her gaze.

Breac said, "We know the enemy..."

"Peace," said Vivaqua. "What has been done is done. Justice will come, but not tonight. Who can say what the Creator's plans are in all of this? " She signaled one of the maids. "Show Mykell and Breac to our guest chambers, and send for a healer for the man's face. I will talk with Evie Drake awhile longer."

Breac cast her a pitiful look before he followed the naiad maid into a side passage. Mykell rose from his haunches and stalked after them, leaving Evie and the naiad queen alone with the silent guards.

Evie hadn't noticed it getting dark until now, when the great hall had become still. Light no longer streamed in from above. She hadn't bothered to look up before, and wondered if the ceiling, now dark and indistinct, was made of water like the walls and pillars. But water like she had never seen, streaming in constant motion, shot through with thin tendrils of color. Every color. Always moving, always silent, clear as liquid glass, but covered in ornate patterns of swirling water and ribbons of color. Shell brackets held flameless torches, lit with some sort of phosphorescent plant that swayed and moved as though with a current. With the light fading, the colors dimmed one by one into deep purples and blues, with strands of silvery light running through. *The whole palace changes mood with the naiads,* Evie thought. *From bright and beautiful, to angry, to restful, and peaceful.*

She felt suddenly very lonely and out of place here amid the wonder and grandeur of the underwater palace. Very small and insignificant. She'd been accused, found guilty with no argument. A tiny piece of rubbish to be swept away in the grand story of things. Self-loathing assailed her, making her miserable and pitiful. What would these people do with her? Why did the water creature—the naiad, Vivaqua— keep her here? She squeezed her eyes shut, willing the tears not to fall. When she opened them, the naiad stood before her, regarding her with sober opal eyes.

The naiad queen was very beautiful. Her every movement graceful, liquid. Her thick, silver-blue hair flowed with each motion, barely constrained by gravity. An ornate armband encircled her thin arm, just above the elbow. Evie had thought it was made out of silver, but looking closer she saw it was liquid. Water moving constantly in intricate swirls that reflected the light like precious metal. Her dress hung simply from shell fasteners at her shoulders, a green silky material that acted as lively as her hair. Vivaqua took the girl's hand, and they walked, like two sisters. For a long time neither spoke.

"Do you wish to be home?" Vivaqua said finally.

With her first words, she had pinpointed the truth. Evie had fallen from one desperate situation right into another. There seemed no way to escape her own death in this world. Yet with all her heart, this was where she wanted to be.

"No... not really," she replied, running her fingertips along the strange, watery wall. A slight current streamed against her skin, leaving rifts in the watery patterns. She removed her hand, and the wall returned to normal.

Vivaqua smiled. "I rather thought not." She paused, then, "Would you like to tell me?"

Something about the creature inspired trust. Perhaps it was her own guilt and turmoil needing release. A chance to at least partially justify her actions. But when she first tried to speak, her voice broke, and with it her resolve, and she cried.

For a long time the only thing she could get out was, "I was so afraid... I didn't know what to do... I didn't know."

Vivaqua remained silent, letting her cry, leading her through dozens of halls and passages, some small, others grand and empty, still others decorated with fountains or vegetation. Evie had only glimpses through her tears of the glory around her. Vivaqua led her to an ornate stone bench and sat with her. After awhile she calmed down and wiped the tears away.

"All my life I've read stories about places like this," she blurted. Whether it was a good starting point or no, it was the first thing to come clearly to her mind. "I always wished they were real, and that I could come here. I thought all of this didn't exist, and so I would read or sing the stories, and while I was reading or singing, it felt real. Now I'm here, in the middle of all this, and I'm supposed to die. Like wishing for a dream, and it turns into a nightmare. In the most beautiful stories you know the hero is going to overcome everything in the end, no matter what. Or if he or she dies, it's for a noble cause—not as punishment." Evie sniffed, and choked on a suppressed sob. "I guess that must seem silly to you. And it's not even all that, it's just... it's... I don't know. I feel... so very small. And condemned." Her voice grew faint. "And guilty."

Vivaqua just smiled. "All life comes to an end," she said. "Perhaps here we accept that more easily than in other places."

"Death is something that can happen to anyone else," Evie replied. "I guess that's kind of how we look at it. It's never quite a reality until your own heart stops beating."

Vivaqua turned to face her, running slender fingers through Evie's chocolaty hair. "You are a beautiful human child," she said, smiling. "Perhaps I should do well to fear Rizann's words of warning."

"I want to make this right. I don't want to die. What can I do?"

"You can't make it right, child, except by dying. Even in this world we cannot undo the past."

"There has to be a way! Isn't there always a way?" She knew it would sound stupid, even before she said it, but she did anyway, almost whispering, "In the stories there was always a way."

Vivaqua frowned in slow thought. "The High King's own words," she said. "Yet there is only one way, that I know, and it ends in death."

"I don't really have a problem with death," Evie said. "When you die suddenly in a car crash or something. But how can I face it, knowing it's coming, and that it's my own fault?"

"Death is always your own fault," Vivaqua said.

"What do you mean?"

"Have you ever wondered why Sylvanus could not be killed without your consent? It is because at the dawn of the world, when the Creator formed us all, mankind was given rule over the rest of creation, and the High King, the immortal who speaks with the Creator, ruled over all. But it was mankind who first chose to follow Leazor, the Traitor, rather than the King and the Creator. It was similar in your own world."

Evie shrugged, rubbing moisture out of her eyes. "Maybe, I don't know. I've heard things like that before. People don't go around talking about creators much in my world these days."

"Perhaps you do not know then that mankind was cursed.

You who should have lived forever, side by side with the people of wood and water, were made mortal. To this day it continues, the treachery in the hearts of men. Not all crimes must be punished by immediate death, but eventually, death does come to all. It must be so. If mankind were immortal, his crimes would continue to the end of the age, and he would suffer. But he dies, and is renewed again, without the curse."

"That's—beautiful, sort of. But like I said, it's not the dying part. It's the part about knowing when and how I will die that I can't face."

Vivaqua stood and helped Evie to her feet, and they continued walking. The long passage they were in opened into a courtyard. A fountain bubbled in the center, and everything looked white in the moonlight. Evie looked up. The moon shone down, almost at the full, and stars sparkled across the sky. How strange, she thought, in a palace built under the water.

"Do you like it?" Vivaqua said.

"I've never seen anything like this before."

"Moonlight and starlight are in the hearts of the water-people. We treasure them as a rare jewel. Sunlight we can bend and fracture and make into beautiful colors, but moonlight would only be spoiled. We keep the lake surface very thin here. And sometimes," she waved her hand as though parting a curtain, and a thin film of water that Evie hadn't even noticed separating them from the open sky parted. Cool night air flowed down around them. "Sometimes we cannot bear to have anything there at all."

"Oh...!"

Vivaqua smiled. She closed the thin ceiling of water with a motion, and continued across the courtyard. Stopping in front of a doorway curtained by swaying pearlescent strands like a delicate water plant, she said, "No person—human, dryad, naiad, or any other can know the future as we do the present. But sometimes we are given glimpses. I've seen life in your future."

"Life?"

"Life. Whether it bodes good or ill for this country, I do not know. Rest well, Evie Drake. And trust Breac. He is a good man."

Evie brushed aside the rippling curtain and entered a simple room. A real fire burned in a stone hearth, warming the place, making it seem plain and homelike. The glowing water plants and shards of moonlight and sunlight out in the palace were beautiful, but they seemed unearthly and surreal. The fire made her think of home. Of her parents' farmhouse with the woodstove and the country décor. She crossed the room to a driftwood pedestal standing in the corner. It held a basin and pitcher of water. She splashed her face, and tried to rub some of the grime off her hands, lingering over the dark stain in her palm. She rubbed her thumb over it, not really hoping any longer that it would actually come off.

I'm marked for death. I suppose that's what this means.

She ran a wet, shaking hand through her hair. Death. She flopped backwards onto the bed. And she was somehow supposed to miraculously trust this man, this Breac, or was it Aindreas? The man taking her to her death. Not a reasonable suggestion. Yet his voice haunted her. She loved it. She could get lost in it. She could follow a voice like that anywhere, if she wasn't careful. And his eyes. Haunted and sad. In different circumstances she could trust him. Maybe part of her already did. Only a small part.

* * * * *

Breac unfastened his cloak and draped it over the foot of the bed. A fire burned on the hearth, casting flickering yellow shadows across half the room. The living doorway let in moonlight and sent dim, watery reflections over the floor, casting the other half of the room in white. The curtain swayed, sending the light patterns dancing, and Breac looked up to see Mykell poke his panther's head into the room. He saw the man watching him and stalked in.

"What do you think of your mission now?" he said, sitting on his haunches in front of the fireplace.

Breac unbuckled his sword belt and laid it on top of the cloak. He slid the book of the Kantra out of his shirt and placed it next to the sword, then sat on the edge of the bed.

He sighed. "Difficult."

"Did you expect any less?"

"No. But I certainly did not expect this."

"Neither did I, I'm afraid. The girl complicates things, or will, I think."

Breac waved that off. "It's not her... though you are right in that she could make things more difficult. Right now it's our enemy that I'm wondering about."

"Yes. It is a curious development." The panther lifted a paw, studied it, then licked his claws.

"This is the second time Leazor has sought me out to kill me—the first time being in person on the battlefield. He has come to hate me as a personal enemy I believe, and not just as an opposing force. Yet I do not know why. I would speak with the Lady Vivaqua on this. Perhaps she has some insight."

Mykell yawned, his teeth gleaming in the firelight. "If you must go wandering about seeking counsel at all hours of the night, do so. But I am going to sleep while I have the chance."

Breac nodded. "Good night, my friend."

When Mykell had gone, Breac paused to look about the room. He picked up the book of Kantra, running his fingers over the cracked leather binding. The arrow had made quite a hole in the cover, but the damage to the pages inside was minimal. He set the book back down and ducked out through the glimmering curtain into the moonlit courtyard. The fountain sent showers of sparkling white droplets into the warm air, and he wondered in passing what

Evie thought of this place.

He was about to head back to the throne room, when he heard voices coming down one of the side passages. He recognized Vivaqua and Evie, and slipped back to the far side of the fountain before they came into view. Vivaqua's musical voice murmured words he couldn't make out. He felt cool air brush his face, and looked up to see the ceiling of water parted. Stars and moon poured down their silver light. The gap closed, and the girl and the naiad queen drew nearer. Vivaqua spoke again too low to understand, but he heard the girl's reply clearly.

"Life?" she said. Her voice sounded rough like she'd been crying, which, he speculated, he couldn't blame her for.

"Life. Whether it bodes good or ill for this country, I do not know. Rest well, Evie Drake. And trust Breac. He is a good man."

Hearing no more voices, he rose from the stone bench beside the fountain and stepped out to meet Vivaqua.

She walked toward him, smiling as though she had known all along he was there. Perhaps she had.

"I've never known you to give ill advice, Lady. Yet telling the girl to trust me—that was unwise."

"Oh? Are you now untrustworthy?" Vivaqua replied as they walked back across the courtyard toward one of the lighted passages.

"No. But my intention to take her to the King's judgment seat has not changed, and will not."

Vivaqua nodded slowly. "I do not doubt your intentions regarding the High King's law, but we shall see."

Breac frowned. The wise people of wood and water were much like the wise humans he had known. They could be maddening sometimes with their riddle-speak. "As mysterious as ever, I see. If I seek your counsel on a matter, will you be as unclear?"

She laughed. "Perhaps. What is it you wish to know?"

"Rizann's attack today was not the first for me."

"Yes, I know," Vivaqua said. "You refer to the incident on the battlefield."

"Yes. I see you are well informed."

Vivaqua nodded. "I like to hear of all strange happenings."

"Understandable, in this time of darkness. Do you know then that Leazor spoke to me of a certain prophecy? He did not explain what it was. I know only that it seemed to have to do with me, though I do not know what."

"I see." Vivaqua turned a final corner in the passage, which brought them back to the throne room. Instead of sitting on her couch, she motioned for Breac to sit beside her on the stairs of the dais. "And now Rizann is trying not merely to stop your mission, but to capture you."

"Yes. What does it mean? What is the prophecy? Is there a part to play in all this that I do not know?" he spread his hands. "Is there any answer you can give me?"

"Perhaps, in part. You bear the mark of the High King, do you not?"

"Yes," Breac said, pulling off his right glove to reveal the scar burned into his palm.

"That is reason enough for Leazor to fear and hate you," Vivaqua said. "Having sworn yourself to the High King, you are a great threat to him. You are also a mighty leader of men. You use the Kantra against him, and not just your sword. He has not won a single skirmish against you. He fears you. Also you are a friend and if need arose, would be second in command to the King himself, a similar position to that which Leazor held before his treachery. He is jealous of you. Is it a wonder that he wants to kill you?"

Breac shook his head. "No. I have guessed all this before. But I am mortal, he is immortal. He is strong in evil magic. What am I but a passing pebble in his boot?"

"Leazor's downfall was his pride. It has always been pride. And the companion of pride is jealousy. Of course you can never be what he once was, because you are mortal. But he, grasping for the throne that was not his, lost what *was* his. He can never recover his place at the King's side, nor would he choose to. Yet seeing another come close to it vexes him. He hates you with a venom that surpasses human emotion. There may well be more to the tale, but this is the part that I can see."

Breac nodded and sighed, rubbing the backs of his fingers down his jaw. He stared down the length of the great hall, now dim and lit only with the phosphorescent torches.

Vivaqua continued, "As for the prophecy, and what part you play in this present battle for the freedom of Acatra Dahma, I do not know. But," she held up a slender finger, "if it is a prophecy given by the Creator, it is sure and will not fail. And if you wonder about the part you have to fulfill, I say, Aindreas son of Rajah, that in carrying out this mission for the High King, you are already fulfilling it. The Creator's design will not be cheated."

"You are still mysterious, my lady," Breac said, "but encouraging none the less. Thank you." He stood and bowed, fist over heart in salute. "And again, for your hospitality and protection, thank you."

"Good night, Aindreas."

9
Reluctantly Companions

Bright, warm sunlight caressed Evie out of sleep. She lay with her eyes closed, only half awake, imagining she was in her old bedroom at her parents' house, with the light coming in the window on a Saturday morning in July. As she came more awake she knew she was not in the old farmhouse. She thought she must be in her apartment, but that couldn't be either. The smells were all wrong. The air smelled too fresh, as though she'd been sleeping outside, with just a hint of wood smoke. She rolled onto her back and opened her eyes.

She froze. Sucked in a breath and held it, staring up at the ceiling. After a moment she relaxed a bit, rolled out of bed, and stood gaping upward. How many hundreds of feet of water comprised the roof here? It was very clear, allowing sunlight to filter down through, casting shifting light patterns across the room. A school of little silver fish passed overhead, and far above them, a huge red-gold and white koi hovered.

Evie climbed on the bed and reached up, putting her fingers into the cool water. The school shifted in a silvery flash of motion and lingered above her hand for a moment. Dozens of tiny eyes contemplated her fingers, and one fish tried a nibble. She stepped back down grinning.

She did her best to straighten her rumpled clothes and wash up in the basin, scrubbing once again at the dark stain in her palm. It had not changed at all. Fortunately she had managed to hang onto her purse through everything, so she dug in it for her spare stick of deodorant. After that she didn't know what to do. Should she wait until someone came to fetch her? Or go wandering around the palace in hopes that she'd eventually run into Breac or Vivaqua? She certainly had no desire to meet the creature Mykell alone.

Why, oh why, oh why, the horrible fortune that directed her path in this world straight to the executioner? The unfairness of it all made her curse out loud. And what if her next escape attempt failed? What if he came looking for her again? No dawdling around this time. If she ever got back, she'd go straight to the airport and book the first flight to Hawaii.

Her stomach clenched. *And then the only thing chasing you would be your conscience.* Well plenty of people drown that in a bottle of booze. *And in the end, what? A wasted life? Suicide? Might as well stay and die, and give the people their freedom.*

Her heart skipped painfully. She had to get out, find the others, and find out what was truly going on here. Perhaps there was more to it all. Though Vivaqua had seemed quite sure last night that dying was the final answer. Except she had also said she'd seen life in Evie's future. A thin hope that. The word of a non-human being that she'd known only for a few hours. But the only hope she had. Perhaps she would be able to escape then. The naiad hadn't said whether this life included her world or Evie's.

Her thoughts were chasing each other in circles, and feeling she must get away, even if it meant returning to her captors for the time, she left the room, slinging the purse over her shoulders. It felt good to at least have *something* from home.

She poked her head through the curtain to look around before stepping out into the courtyard. The dazzling ceiling of water sent ripples of light flicking and dancing over the sandy floor while the fountain cast white droplets into the sunlit air. Beside the fountain sat a naiad maid, who stood and curtsied, smiling as Evie approached

"Good morning, Evie."

"Morning," Evie said, and then felt awkward, not knowing if she should curtsy in return. In any case she wasn't wearing a skirt.

"Your companions are waiting, if you will come with me."

"Thanks."

Companions? You mean my prison guards.

Evie followed her past the fountain, down a long passage, then another, and finally into the great hall from the night before.

Vivaqua was seated on her couch, and Breac and Mykell sat on the steps of the dais amid packs of supplies, eating a breakfast of honeyed bread and nuts and...

"Is that coffee?!" Evie exclaimed. "I hope there's some left!"

Vivaqua seemed to find the remark amusing. She signaled for more food and drink to be brought.

"It's a royal palace, girl," Mykell said. "Did you honestly think that they just—run out of things?"

Evie blinked. "I don't know," she retorted. "But you could have maybe turned yourself into a camel before I got here, and drunk all the coffee in two palaces."

Mykell stared at her, unblinking. The end of his panther's tail twitched. He said, "Do camels enjoy coffee?"

Vivaqua and Breac chuckled. The man motioned her to join them on the steps. She'd forgotten how startling his eyes were, blue and brown, intense, as though the different colors provided X-ray vision that could see into her soul. His features looked almost part Indian or Arab, his skin darkly tan. He gave her an awkward smile as he passed her a plate of food.

They finished the meal in silence and Breac stood, dusting crumbs from his shirt. He shouldered his pack gingerly, picked up the other and handed it to Evie. She eyed him and the pack. *What, no tying me up? I thought I was a prisoner here.* She took the pack warily, slinging it over her shoulder.

"I cannot provide you with horses, since we do not keep them," Vivaqua said. "But there is money enough in the packs to buy them, if you make it to the next village."

"Thank you," said Breac.

"You must not depart the same way you came," Vivaqua said. "Your enemy has scouts waiting for you there. I will provide you a guide who can lead to you the surface at the northernmost tip of the lake. From there you will have a straight course to the human village of Riverside, fifteen miles north of there."

They bid her farewell, and followed their guide from the hall. Evie took a last, long look at the fountain courtyard as they passed through, and a sudden longing filled her, that she could stay in that place for a long time, drinking in the soul soothing light. If she hadn't been such a weak fool. If she had come to this world a little sooner, or a little later, or arrived in a different place. *If, if, if....* But then, what would have happened if she had not turned over Sylvanus to those men? Goose bumps spread over her body.

The guide took them through many passageways, explaining, "The palace covers the entire lake bottom. It is home to skilled naiad craftsmen and storytellers. They weave their tales deep and wide, sometimes in song. River naiads are the true musicians, though. Have you ever heard them sing? It is said they can cast a spell over any mortal with their voices alone. They can lull humans to sleep, or set them dancing, or seduce them. They would be the most dangerous race, if not for their humor."

They walked for hours, and saw little of anyone else. The passage they were following opened out to a vast, sandy lakebed, strewn with rock and water vegetation that swayed eerily. Light filtered down, greenish, shifting and muted. It was very different from the glory of the palace. Not dreary exactly, but strange and surreal. Evie felt they were trespassing in a realm where they did not belong; strange, and potentially deadly. Also there were no walls or ceiling here to separate water from air. She had the creepy feeling that they were all breathing water... or that the water had been turned to some sort of liquid oxygen, though it did not feel any different as it passed in and out of her lungs. It still gave her a strange, sort of claustrophobic feeling, and she couldn't wait to get out into the world above.

The lakebed valley began to close in, with rocky ledges in some places, and in others merely a gentle sandy slope. They came to another long staircase, ending in a shaft of bright light.

"Farewell," the naiad said. "May the sun be gentle on your back, and thirst never mar your journey."

"Many thanks," Breac replied.

They started up the stairs, and as they climbed, the shaft of light at the top clarified into a patch of bright blue sky. Their heads came even with the surface of the lake, and then they were stepping out onto the shore. Evie looked back and saw only sparkling water.

Breac followed her gaze. "Naiads are the people of the water," he told her. "They are one with it, yet separate, as the dryads are with their trees. It is their life and also their servant. They can manipulate it to their will."

Evie shivered in the sudden breeze. Below the lake surface there had been no air movement. She said, "Did you notice how the plants and stuff swayed down there, like they were under water? Yet we weren't walking through water. How could that be?"

"I noticed," Breac replied. He shook his head. "What mortal can know the secrets of other races? Their way is theirs alone to know, as the way of mankind is for man."

Mykell muttered, "Yes, and try figuring it out some time." He turned and bounded up the rocky bank away from the water, calling back, "Daylight will not wait for us! Neither will Leazor!"

"And neither will Mykell," Breac said with a wink. He grabbed a tree root and swung up the bank after him, then turned and offered his hand to Evie.

At the top of the embankment she paused to look around. Behind them the lake glistened, stretching to a distant forested shore. In front of them, huge trees rose like pillars in a giants' palace. Sparse undergrowth allowed a good view all around, and the moss carpeted ground made for smooth walking.

Fifteen miles of this until the next town? *And then what?* Evie wondered. How many miles or days until they got where they were going? A shudder went through her. She *must* find a way to escape.

Breac started off at a fast walk, and she followed. What else could she do? Mykell stalked along behind them like a nightmare, and she could imagine him staring at her back, morphing into something huge and hideous, fangs dripping. He was not the sort of creature she really wanted following her out of sight. Breac and the naiads trusted him, and she did not sense any of the evil in him that she had in the owl-turned-wolf-turned-owl back in her world. But still, any creature that could change itself into something else on a whim was just...weird. The more she thought about it, the more it creeped her out, so she tried to ignore him.

She watched Breac instead. Broad shouldered and muscled, yet graceful, she found him worth watching. His black cloak had been packed away with the blanket and other supplies, all rolled up and strapped together into a backpack of sorts, just like the one she'd been given. Except he made his look light. His leather pants were stained and scarred, and hung loose, as though made for a slightly larger man. She realized she'd been admiring, and blushed, moving her gaze up to his shaggy blond hair. It looked like he'd cut it himself with his sword, or maybe a butcher knife. He reached to tug at the pack, getting it to a better position on his shoulder. The strap dragged at his shirt, pulling his collar down enough to reveal a strip of white linen underneath. A bandage? Was he wounded?

Evie shifted her own pack. *Maybe that's why his clothes are baggy. Traveling wounded...looking for the betrayer. Looking for me.*

She sighed out loud, and the man turned to glance at her. So many questions. Even if she had the nerve to ask, where would she ever begin?

* * * * *

Breac led them quickly and quietly until the sun was high. He neither saw nor heard any sign of the enemy, and did not feel any of the dread that often warned him of danger. They had come eight miles or so from the lake before they stopped to rest and eat. Mykell at once changed himself, becoming a hawk, and swept up through the trees to circle around in a wide arch. Breac lowered his pack to the ground and stretched his arms. The wound in his shoulder ached already. The thin bandage protecting new skin had bunched under the chafing pack straps, but he didn't feel the skin had torn. He massaged the muscle, trying to ease the tension out of it.

The girl watched Mykell circle above them, and Breac watched her, with her face lifted to the sky, flushed by exercise. Her lips curved faintly in a smile, but her eyes were lost and sad. Sad because she would be slain, and never feel wind in her hair and freedom in her heart. Or perhaps it was regret. She was not the type of girl to give up and be killed, he thought. The confidence in her step demanded respect. Her posture, graceful and strong, declared fight. The depths of her gaze held freedom and defiance. She was proud and beautiful. She would not beg or connive he felt sure. No. She would try to escape.

Why? He silently questioned the Creator of all. He could imagine what they must have threatened her with. Not many things would break a girl like that. But why? She should not have been in that place at that time. Could not her path have been directed elsewhere? Could not Mykell have intervened, just once?

He turned away and began unpacking provisions, food and water, and setting them out. The High King's words echoed through his mind. *"I choose you for your heart. Remember the laws that keep this land free. Be true."*

He turned back abruptly and asked, "Why did you help me fight the Ezomrah?"

She brought her gaze down from the sky to look at him, her eyes sparkling golden-brown in a ray of sunlight that penetrated the forest canopy. "The what?"

"The owl. In your world. You could have fled when it attacked me, but you didn't."

"Oh that." Her face flushed, and she shrugged. "My mistake, I guess. Wasn't thinking." She frowned, becoming more serious. "It just seemed so evil."

Mykell drifted down, pulling up before he landed, and stretching back into a panther.

"What news?" Breac asked.

"No sign of the enemy, as far as I can tell," Mykell said. "No sign of anyone else, either."

"No—I wouldn't expect so."

* * * * *

They ate in silence, and Evie watched her companions. Mykell because she was half afraid of him, and Breac... for some reason she found him fascinating. He looked like a mash-up of nationalities, sort of an East-meets-West exhibit with his blond hair and tawny skin, his two-colored eyes. But he was also strikingly handsome. She felt drawn to him. He had an easy, comfortable way about him, a calm confidence that was both magnetic and, given the circumstances, intimidating. He had winked at her (winked with the brown eye, she remembered), poking fun of Mykell. Had also asked her about the owl—he called it Ezomrah—in her world. He had never yet treated her with hostility, only respect. Perhaps he wasn't eager to drag her off to her death after all?

She took a breath to get her nerve, and said, "Can I ask you something?"

Both heads turned toward her, and her pulse spiked. Not only because she had the full attention of her two very dangerous companions, but there was just something about those eyes...

"Please," the man said, gesturing for her to continue.

"I—I'm not sure how to begin the question." She smiled nervously. "It's about languages I think. And that book that you have."

"The Book of the Kantra."

"Rachael, that's the girl that I was talking to when you came to my world..." she cleared her throat nervously. "She said it was full of symbols and spells, like the travel symbol." She held out her palm with the henna tattoo. "But I couldn't read it."

Breac nodded. He reached for his pack and pulled the book out, handing it to her. "See if you can understand it now."

She took it from him, noticed the size of his hands and imagined their power. It took a moment to focus on the words, and then her heart jumped again, for she could read them. She lifted her eyes to his. "I don't understand."

"It is said that you have many languages in your world. But that it was not always so."

She looked at him curiously. "I guess so. I never studied it, but there are what we call root languages. I suppose it would follow if you went far enough, they would all trace back to a single language. When I was a kid, I heard a story once, sort of a legend or a myth I guess, about people who tried to build a tower into heaven, but God didn't like it, so he made the people unable to understand each other, and they said that's where the different languages come from."

"Communication in this world has not been corrupted as it has in yours, save when men tell lies. Those who travel here from your world understand us, and we them, though we may sound strange to one another." He nodded toward the book. "It is the same with written words. And the travel symbol," he held out his hand with the inked pattern, now badly smudged and faded, "Allowed me to understand while in your world."

"I see—sort of." But she still had so many questions! Question about this world, about him, and Mykell, and the naiads. Questions about magic, and the law, and... she realized she didn't even know enough to know what she didn't know. So how could she even begin to ask the right questions? Frustrating! She realized Breac was watching her. She met his gaze, and forced herself not to look away. "Who are you?"

He smiled, and shrugged, seeming amused. "Men call me Breac, and I am—whatever I need to be."

"And why do they call you Breac?" she asked, remembering Vivaqua's greeting and guessing that though he went by Breac, it was not his true name.

"'Breac' is someone who is speckled, off colored—tainted. Those who do not know me find it hard to trust me. I don't belong in any race, and so they do not know what to do with me."

"But your name is something else. Adrian—or..."

"Aindreas."

"Aindreas." For some reason it gave her a funny feeling to say it, as though using his real name was a very personal thing. She felt Mykell's eyes on her suddenly. She'd forgotten about him.

"Leazor will not wait," the shape-shifter said.

"And neither will daylight. We know." Breac got to his feet, looking tired. He began putting the food packages back into his pack, and hoisted it to his shoulders.

Evie stood as well, and instantly felt the miles that were already behind them. Her body was stiff and tired. She picked up her own pack and slung it over her shoulder, wishing for the broad, comfortable straps of her backpack at home as the thin ropes dug in. She still held the Book of Kantra in her hands, looking at it wistfully. Would there be any help for her in there? Now that she could read it, she wished she might sit down and do just that. Search out its secrets. Holding it gave her a sense of hope for some reason.

"Keep it awhile," Breac said. "But be careful."

"Thank you! But why do I need to be careful?"

He and Mykell had started off again, apparently assuming she would follow, which she did. He turned and waited for her to catch up.

"Words are not to be taken lightly, Evie Drake. Not in this world."

10
Friends and Foes

It was dusk when they arrived in Riverside, and eerily still. Wind gusted down the street, kicking up dirt and blowing it in their faces. Somewhere an open window shutter slapped against the side of a house. Nothing else moved.

"Not even a stray dog abroad tonight," Mykell said.

"The storm will break soon." Breac let his pack slide to the ground, and dug out a pouch of money. Handing Evie two coins out of it, he tied it to his belt. "Get us some rooms. I need to find horses."

Evie looked around sheepishly. "Where?"

"The town chieftain will have extra horses."

"No—I mean the rooms."

Breac hid a smile and pointed down the windswept street to the only two-story building. A swinging sign above the door read: Parrot's Roost Inn and Tavern. The door opened suddenly, letting lavish warm light pour into the street. A man stepped out and staggered away in the opposite direction, never glancing their way.

"Oh," said Evie. Another gust of wind blew hair into her face, and she combed it back with her fingers, looking down at the small coins. "Will this be enough?"

"If it isn't, I'll turn into a skunk and threaten to perfume their dining room," Mykell replied.

Evie laughed. A surprised, musical little sound.

"It might be best for now to conceal yourself," Breac said. "Should anything happen we would have an advantage of surprise."

"Obviously," Mykell replied as he shrunk into the form of a mongrel dog, small and black, and wagged up at them.

"Off with you," Breac said. They started toward the inn, and Evie cast him a look over her shoulder. He watched as they disappeared into the building, and rubbed a hand over his face. The sight of the girl's dark hair whipping in the wind stuck in his mind, and the look she'd given him as she walked away. "Fool," he said aloud to himself.

It had been a single day, and a mostly silent one, but he could feel changes in himself that he did not like to acknowledge. He'd been entertaining feelings he had no business with, and it made him uneasy. This was a bad mission indeed. He questioned the High King inwardly, and then berated himself. He had no business doing that either. His thoughts and feelings were no one's fault but his own, and his alone to deal with.

He slung the pack over his shoulder and turned to the right, skirting around the buildings. The gusts of wind were increasing, first shoving him along from behind, then turning and blowing against him so he had to lean forward as he walked. In a few minutes he came to a meadow, fenced in with a low rock wall. Part of the field had been plowed for crops, and another part consisted of corrals and barns and kennels. The house adjacent was large and well lit. Breac frowned. Something struck him as not right about the place. He'd been here a year before, and remembered it as an unassuming farm, with a few extra horses for travelers or passing scouts. The old house had been torn down, and replaced with this larger one. The same with the barn and stables. New outbuildings now littered the farmyard. A sense of uneasiness touched him.

"Stop where you are," came a command out of the darkness. "Or you'll have an arrow through you."

"Well, I've had enough of that lately," Breac replied, lowering his pack to the ground. He searched the shadows for the man who'd spoken, but saw nothing. "I've come to speak to Darmot. I need horses."

"I know who you are, Breac, favorite of the High King."

The voice held scorn or menace, Breac couldn't decide which.

"Darmot? Have you taken to hiding in the shadows and threatening travelers? You used to be more hospitable."

"Times change. Leazor is on the offensive, if you had not noticed."

"I had. But I'm no servant of the enemy. Will you not sell me two horses? It's a bad night to be standing out here exchanging pleasantries."

Darmot stepped from behind the chicken coop carrying his bow with an arrow nocked to the string. But he held it with one hand, pointed down. At his heels trotted a small dog.

"What is this about, old friend? You act as though you distrust your own shadow," Breac said.

"My town is small, and near the border. The King has not seen fit to send troops to such a small village to protect us. I must see to our protection myself, and would you have me welcome all strangers as sons? Surely you have not become so naïve since you began parading around the capitol with the King."

Breac stiffened, but Darmot continued, "Truly, I'm surprised to see you out in the wild. I thought you had given up scouting and rough living. Though it suited you better than the life of a noble."

"A noble?" Breac said. His hand dropped down near his sword hilt. He could sense something wrong here. His gaze went to Darmot's dog. In the dim light it looked like little more than a dark blot on the grass, but he could feel its eyes on him. Best to get away from here quickly. He said, "I'm not a noble, Darmot, and neither are you. We both serve the High King. Remember that. Now, will you sell me horses, or must I enquire elsewhere?"

* * * * *

Evie stopped outside the inn door and looked down at Mykell.

This seemed all wrong. Wasn't she supposed to be their prisoner? Not the one ordering rooms.... And how did one go about asking for rooms in a place like this?

"Should I knock?" she whispered.

"No," he replied. "And remember. Once inside, you are on your own."

They entered a long room with two fireplaces, a roaring fire in each. To get to the counter separating the kitchen from the dining room, they had to parade past a long table with half a dozen guests already seated. She scanned the faces. *Don't be so skittery*, she told herself. *You're seeing enemies and evil magicians behind every beer glass now. They'll think you stole something if you keep shaking like this.* She rubbed her hands down her jeans, wishing for her gloves back. What if someone spotted the mark in her hand. Or the henna tattoo. Would they know what either meant? Or were such things common here?

A woman wearing a simple, faded blue gown and dirty apron hustled in from the kitchen to stand behind the bar.

"Help you, miss?"

"Uh, yeah." She cleared her throat. "Yes." She stepped over and set the coins down on the rough wood counter, being careful to keep her palms hidden. "Two rooms please."

The woman raised an eyebrow.

"My companion will be along soon."

"Well then," said the woman. "Take a seat there. Dinner's on shortly."

"Thank you."

Evie turned back to face the room. A wave of shyness hit her as she looked over the other guests, most of whom were looking back at her. At the far end of the table sat a man and his wife, and three teenaged sons. At the near end, a trio of rough looking characters laughed and talked loudly. One of them she could see wore a knife on his belt. Their costumes were similar, scarred leather or canvas pants and riding boots, short woven tunics hanging loose or tucked into belts. The woman at the far end smiled kindly at her as she looked about. Her dress was crimson, both brighter and newer looking than the woman's behind the counter, and she wore a lacy bodice over it. Evie returned the smile.

She took a seat halfway down the table, as far from both parties as possible, and slid her pack onto the bench beside her, laying her purse on top of it. Mykell jumped up onto the bench on her other side, and sat. She stroked his fur, wishing she dared talk to him. The other guests just glanced at her now, not with hostility she thought. More out of curiosity. Probably the weird clothes. She rubbed Mykell's head, watching and waiting, sinking into her thoughts.

They returned unbidden to the man, Breac. Or Aindreas. She liked the sound of both names. She like his voice as well. She'd give about anything to hear him sing. And curse the luck that made him her prison guard!

She rubbed her forehead, thinking again of Sylvanus. The two faces had been before her all day. The man Breac, and the dryad Sylvanus. The face of justice, and the face of guilt. It was too much. Too much to think about. Too much to sort out. She'd had all day with her thoughts and feelings, and still they had not come to order. They swirled around, an ugly cauldron of guilt and fear and regret and questions. So many questions!

The door flew open, and she looked up, startled. Two more men came in, an older man with grizzled beard and shapeless felt hat, and a younger, jolly fellow. The old man tossed a coin on the bar, and they took seats near her.

A man, probably the innkeeper, came from the back with a huge animal hide sewn into a bottle, with which he filled the mugs, and then the pitchers at the table. His wife followed with a tray almost as big as she, heaping with bread rolls and roasted meat, and bowls full of savory vegetables, strawberries, and pies. Evie gaped as the food was set out.

"We don't allow dogs to sit at the table."

"Huh?" Evie looked up to see the innkeeper standing over her. He looked apologetic.

"Sorry miss, but we pride ourselves on being a clean, respectable establishment, even though this is a rough area. Your dog will have to sit under the table."

"Oh. Sorry." Evie looked at Mykell, expecting him to jump down. He stared at her stupidly and thumped his tail on the bench, breaking into a panting dog-smile. She snapped her fingers over the floor. "Down, boy."

He wriggled with happiness at the attention, and sidled in closer. *Mykell, I'm gonna kill you.* She scooped him up and dumped him onto the floor. He looked offended.

"Don't you dare look so innocent," she hissed at him as he scooted under the table. He lay down panting on top of her feet.

Everyone had already begun eating when Breac returned. He had his cloak drawn about him, and the hood up, so that his face was half obscured. He hurried over and sat down beside her.

"Everything okay?" she asked.

"Our horses are in the stable," he replied. "Beyond than that, I don't know."

"What do you mean?" Evie felt her skin prickle. Seeing him on edge unnerved her. Mykell had his eyes on him too, peering out from under the table.

Breac shook his head. "Our enemy already has a hold in this town. More than that I can't say at the moment. Still, we will rest now if we are allowed."

The man with the grizzled beard called to them, "Breac, is

that you? You old goat!"

Breac reached up and pushed the hood back from his face. Conversation around them faltered for an instant as his features came into view. Evie couldn't blame them for staring. Startling as he normally looked, the red scratches across his tanned cheek made him even stranger. Strange, but not unattractive. She felt herself flush, and glanced away.

Breac grinned at the old man. "Jorah!"

"What are you doing out in the wild so soon?" the old man, Jorah, said.

"I was going to ask you that. Did you give up victory parades and feasting so soon?"

"Aye. The King's business. It's the same for you, I don't doubt. Though when last I saw you, you were mostly dead."

Breac sighed through his nose. He looked weary as he glanced over at Evie. "It is. Though this is not the time or the place to explain." He lowered his voice and said, "We were pursued from Darkwood to Star Deep Lake by the sorcerer Rizann and his men. I fear they are not far away even now."

"Grave news," Jorah said, also keeping his voice low. "I am but a traveler myself, but if there is anything I can do, I have already fulfilled the mission I was sent on..."

Breac shook his head. "You might do well to spend a few days here and look around. Even in this town trouble is near."

"Aye. I've sensed it too."

Breac settled back in his seat and began filling his plate. The man with the wife and sons at the end of the table pointed a half eaten turkey leg in their direction and said, "You. I know who you are. You're that drifting storyteller." The man tore off a bite of meat and continued, "I heard your mamma was a witch from the North Country. That true?"

Breac shifted and glanced up. He didn't seem perturbed by

the man's blunt question. Uncomfortable and slightly amused perhaps.

Jorah laughed and shook his head. "If the Lady Tyra is a witch, then I'm a toadstool," he muttered. He turned his attention back to his plate, still chuckling.

"Perhaps you have myself and my kin confused with someone else," Breac said to the man.

He grumbled over top of his turkey leg. "That I doubt."

* * * * *

An assortment of low stools, chairs and benches were gathered around the fireplaces, and after the meal the guests seated themselves around, trading news of the towns or regions they'd come from. Breac offered Evie a seat at one of the benches, off to one side, and sat down beside her. Mykell sat on his haunches, leaning against her knees. Her face grew hot from the fire and the day's windburn. She rubbed her eyes and blinked away bleary fatigue.

Jorah and the young man settled down near them, and Jorah leaned in.

"How long have you been in town?" he asked.

"Not long."

"Nor I. I've sensed an unrest here, but why I do not know."

Breac glanced at the young man. Jorah said, "Mergit was sent with me by the High King. He's to be trusted."

Breac nodded and lowering his voice to a murmur said, "I went to Darmot, the town's protector, to buy horses, and was met with an arrow on the string, and harsh words. He knew who I was, and talked of my standing with the High King as if I were a privileged nobleman, leading the life of a courtier. He was both jealous and contemptuous, and his distrust seemed more than what is usually shown me. He has grown his estate in the past year as well."

"Nothing wrong with that," Mergit said lightly.

Evie noticed the way he watched Breac, glancing warily between him and Jorah. *He doesn't trust him either.*

"Nothing indeed," Breac said. "And my congratulations if he was able to gather that much wealth for himself in the past year doing honest work, and paying for honest labor."

"The place is getting that big?" Jorah asked.

"That is a serious accusation," Mergit said, frowning.

Breac replied, "It was not an accusation. You and Jorah will stay and discover the truth of the matter."

Mergit seemed taken aback at the order. Jorah saw the look and laughed. "Yes, my friend," he said, "I'm afraid Breac here outranks me these days. He's been ordering me around like this for the past year, in fact. Not many know of his position."

"There is another reason I question Darmot," Breac said, brushing off the comments about his rank. "I believe he is being influenced by the Ezomrah."

"Grave news indeed," Jorah said.

Mergit turned a little pale.

Evie broke in with, "Wait, what *is* Ezomrah, anyway?"

"I will explain once we are away from this place," Breac replied.

"They're nothing good, lass," Jorah said. "Hope that you never meet one."

"We already have." He glanced at Evie.

Their conversation was interrupted by the innkeeper, who suddenly towered over them.

"Well, friends, I hear we have a bard in our midst," he said, looking around at the group, and then at Breac. His eyes narrowed a bit. "How about a song, if you've an honest tale to sing."

Breac rose and bowed slightly to him. "Always humor a gracious host," he said, smiling. He went to the fireplace, and leaned one arm against the wall beside it, looking into the fire and seeming oblivious that everyone was now staring at him. Evie's heart jumped. She had never thought she'd actually get the chance to hear that voice in song. All thoughts of Ezomrah and curses left her in that moment of pure expectation. He began to sing.

The song started in a near murmur, the notes so low she could feel them vibrate in her ribcage. A shiver went through her. Delight. Pleasure so deep she almost felt guilty. That Voice! It rose a little bit in pitch and volume, chanting. Rough edged, like it had been worn out screaming rock n' roll, yet smooth in its own way, always full and true. It was a complex bouquet. She watched him, savoring it. Entranced.

The song told about ancient days, when the world was free, marred only by the newly traitorous Leazor and a few of his sorcerers. In those days the laws of protection were well known, and the people kept their homes and villages safe without armies or weapons. The land was young, vibrant, and beautiful. Distant fields like green gems, water blue and warm in the merry sunlight. Humans, naiads, dryads, and skin changers all lived in respect and companionship, before the evil grew and the races came to distrust each other.

His voice rose, rolling out a lament more wistful than any Celtic ballad she'd ever heard. Her mind filled with images invoked by the song and the voice. Her heart felt ready to burst with the glory and heartbreak of a time long past. Why must this land be so dark and riddled with danger? Yet it still bore a shadow of the glory. She wondered for the first time if this Leazor character could ever be defeated, and this world restored to what it once was. Then she would never leave this place. Except of course that she was on her way to be killed.

The song ended. She rubbed her eyes. They felt gummy from being in the fresh air all day.

"That's a song that hasn't been sung of late," the innkeeper said. "I've a mind maybe it should be heard more often. How about another?"

Instead of another song, Breac spoke quietly of the lands he had traveled, both West and South and North. All under Leazor's spreading poison. There seemed no way to rid the land of his curse. The other travelers sat and listened, fidgeting, their faces slowly filling with dismay.

Evie stood and excused herself, heading toward the stairs.

"Two doors down on the right," the innkeeper's wife called after her.

"Thanks."

Behind her, someone raised his voice, pleading. "The world's bad enough, at least let us remember better days. Sing another song!"

She paused on the lowest step. She could sit there all night, listening. But she was barely awake, and in her sleepy state her mind was beginning to play tricks on her. The song, and Breac's voice, and his eyes when he glanced at her every so often as he sang were all swirling together and making her stomach do funny things. Or maybe it was her heart. Either way, best to get out of there. Just forget everything and go to bed.

He started singing again, and she almost went back and sat down. Almost. She turned and went upstairs slowly, listening as she went.

* * * * *

Once alone in her room Evie kicked out of her boots and sat cross legged on the bed. She brought out the Book of Kantra and held it, thinking. Part of her was eager, ready to read it from cover to cover. But holding it in her hands with its mysteries still intact, she hesitated. This book for some reason gave her a sense of hope, and though she knew she needed to hurry, she didn't like to start, afraid of proving her hope false.

She opened the book with a sigh, and flipped through some of the pages. The words blurred, and for a moment she saw in their place the eyes of Sylvanus, reproaching her. As if to say, "You killed me, and it is not enough. Still you seek only to save your own life."

She closed her eyes, pressing her fingertips against her temples. *What else can I do? I can't go back and undo it. And I certainly can't help you where you are now.* She looked again at the page, forcing the thoughts away, and began reading the first thing her eyes landed on, whispering it fiercely aloud to drown out the guilt.

Her first whispered words came out as a soft ripple of song. She stopped and stared askance at the offending ballad. Tried again, with the same result. Her voice was singing a tune she had never heard to words she had never read. She continued. She could hardly help herself, and she couldn't imagine it would do any harm. The song appeared to be a story... a love ballad the further she got into it. And somehow, it soothed the hurt in her soul. She lost focus toward the end, and put the book down. She lay back on the bed and stared up at the rough plaster and wood beams of the ceiling. Watching the candle light flicker against them. Wondering about the man whose voice she could hear faintly through the door. Her thoughts became incoherent and faded out.

She started awake to the sound of heavy footfalls inside the room. A dark, cloaked figure stood over the bed.

11
Words with Power

Evie shrieked and dove off the bed to the other side. Adrenaline instantly cleared the disorienting sleep from her mind. The candle on the nightstand still burned brightly. By its light she could see the man in the black cloak as he strode around the bed toward her, and she dove for the bed again, rolled across it, and came up on the other side, knocking her purse to the floor. Its contents spilled across the room.

She landed on her hiking boots, and tripped. The man's sword came down, missing her neck by an inch as she rolled away. She grabbed one of the heavy boots and used it to deflect the next blow, at the same time aiming a kick for the man's groin that sent him staggering back. He was off guard for a moment, and she used it, rockcting to hcr fcct, she grabbed the wrist of his sword hand, and smashed her other hand open-palm into his elbow. She put all her weight behind the blow, turning her body with it, and heard the joint snap.

It was then that Breac burst through the door, with Mykell at his heels.

"What—?!"

The attacker screamed, and so did Evie. She jumped back as he dropped his sword, bumping into the nightstand. The candle tipped over and went out, and the room went dark. Only a faint light from downstairs came through the open door.

There followed an instant of stunned silence, and the harsh breathing of the injured man. Breac said, "They're here." He found Evie's hand, and pulled her toward the door.

"Wait! The book."

She groped back to the bed and found the book, and her

pack, and her purse on the floor. In the dim light from the door she grabbed as much of its contents as she could and shoved them back in the purse, then stomped into her boots. They ran from the bedroom, down the hall, down the stairs to the front room.

The fires were still burning, the guests still seated around them, though now they stared up at the threesome as they raced down the stairs. The front door banged open, and five more men came in, swords drawn. Breac slid to a halt. Evie stopped with him, and Mykell crashed into the backs of their legs. He yelped in surprise.

"Wonderful," Breac muttered. He jerked his sword from the sheath. "Rizann—you've brought only five with you?"

"You are confident for a man who's already been killed once, Breac," the sorcerer replied, glancing at the people seated around the fireplace.

"I've seen death. What else is there to fear?"

"Much!"

With that Rizann and his men charged into the room. Jorah grabbed a fireplace poker, and swung at the soldier's head nearest him as they swept past. The man staggered but kept coming. Breac raised his sword, deflected a blow, and in an instant he was at the core of the fight. Mykell launched himself into the air on hawk's wings, right toward one man's face. An instant before he struck, he curled into a tight ball of porcupine quills. He released the quills stuck in the man's screaming face, and dropped to the floor. Then bit his ankle.

Evie backed away from the fight, watching with horrified fascination. She wished she had a weapon of some kind, and knew how to use it. There. She snatched an oil lamp from its bracket on the wall and pitched it with enough force to smash it across a soldier's back, spattering him with burning oil.

Jorah and Mergit had swords out and joined the battle by that time. The other guests had fled outside or to the kitchen.

Breac knocked one soldier senseless with his sword pummel. Jorah swiped the hand off another. On the balcony above them the man with the broken elbow stumbled into the hall. He would be no further trouble. Breac and Rizann faced off in the center of the floor. Even Jorah backed up warily as quiet eased back into the room. Lightning crackled outside the window, close enough to make their hair stand up.

"What will you do now, Breac?" Rizann said. "You are no longer under the protection of the naiad queen."

"We are protected by the power of the High King, and of the Creator. My friends and I, I place in their care." Here his voice broke into a low chant.

"Creator defend me, answer my call
Muscle, sinew, steel and claw
Be the strength beneath me,
Let me not fall,
Fire, tooth, blade and jaw..."

Rizann swore, lifting his hands, his face turning crimson as he struggled to call down a curse on their heads. The flames rose in the fireplace, and then flattened and snuffed out. The candles in the room did the same. Darkness swept though the inn.

Breac continued, his voice rising into a strong melody.

"Come lightning protect me,
Thunder round all,
Ward from me the evil things
Creator hear my call!"

Lightning struck the inn, and the ground outside. Blue sparks flew out of the fireplace, and electricity sizzled between the iron chandeliers. The candles reignited, casting weird black shadows around the room.

Rizann's lifted hands trembled. His face looked suddenly

misshapen, hollowed and ugly, a screaming scull with skin pulled tight over the bone.

"Come to me, powers unseen, evil, bitterness, edge of cold."

The room turned suddenly painfully frigid. Evie let out a gasp that lingered as a puff of frosty breath. Her lungs ached already. Breac faced the magician, unflinching.

"*Protection I claim; by the passion of flame...*"

Both the fires lighted with a *whump!* and a burst of warmth. Evie backed up another step, and found that Mykell had come to stand beside her, with Jorah and Mergit on the other side. A howl sounded outside in the distance.

"Come to me, despair and death, shriveling of heart and limb."

"*By the depth and joy of many waters,*" Breac flung back. Even as Evie felt her body weaken, strength and hope returned. "*By the healing of greenwood, strength of stone.*"

The magician seemed to have grown larger as well as darker, as though all the shadows cast by the firelight had joined forces with him.

"Silence!" he screamed. The room became deathly silent. Neither the crackle of the fire, nor the drawing of frightened breaths, nor the howling of wind and beast outside reached them. In the silence Evie could not even hear her heart pounding in her ears, though she could feel it beating out a panic rhythm.

Breac opened his mouth as though to speak, and frowned.

It was Rizann's voice that broke through the silence, chanting his curses.

"Despair and darkness, bitterness of cold, bite of flame," he spoke with a smile, his eyes glittering. But the room did not grow as cold this time. And though fire licked the ground at their feet, it did not rise and consume them. Breac, though silenced, still held the magician's gaze without wavering.

Evie sensed something at work here. A battle of wills, and not just words. It flashed through her mind that this man, Breac, was a force to be reckoned. He was much more than a strong man with a sword. He had spoken words, but his resolve held them in place. A new admiration for him rose through her fear.

Rizann had finished chanting his curses, and looked taken aback that his opponents still lived. His expression might have been comical, if his features hadn't been distorted into those of a cadaver.

A movement from the side made Evie turn her head. Mykell had shifted again—into a grizzly bear this time. He rose on his hind legs, and his head brushed the chandelier. Rizann's eyes went to him, with the faintest shadow of fear. He took a step back. Breac sprang forward while the magician's eyes were diverted, and drove his sword through the center of his gold-embroidered vest.

Rizann choked. Sounds came crowding back into the room. The merry snap of the fire, the whistle of wind in the chimney, and the dull thud as he fell face first to the floor, driving the sword blade out through his back. The remaining soldiers, those who were able, fled into the night.

Breac bent and rolled the magician's body, touching it almost reverently as he pulled his sword free and wiped it clean on the black and gold vest.

"Passed into his reward," he commented, then shook himself a bit, and turned to Evie. Taking her hand he pulled her toward the back door. "Come." His voice carried a tone of urgency once again. They ran across the courtyard to the stable, where he began saddling the horses. Jorah, Mergit, and Mykell, back in his panther form, met them there a few minutes later. Jorah handed Breac and Evie their packs, which had been left back in the tavern.

Evie shivered, hugging the pack and her purse to her chest. "Why are we leaving? You killed him."

"Rizann was only one of Leazor's evil magicians." Breac replied. "There are many more, and if Rizann found us, then be sure that the others are on their way. Also there is Darmot. I would not be surprised if he used this as an excuse to turn on us himself. I've felt all evening that evil was near, and I still feel it."

"There are Ezomrah," Mykell said. "I can feel their presence in this town, and they will not be long in getting here. Did you not hear Rizann call evil to himself? Be assured that it is coming."

Jorah nodded. "Aye. Best to be away. Pleasant mess you've left us with though. A dead sorcerer and his cohorts, and whatever else decides to show up now."

"You have my thanks, old friend."

"Mergit and I will deal with the trouble here. We shall try to stall any pursuit, and hope to see you well and soon in Al Acatra."

Jorah and Breac clasped each other by the wrist. "Until then," Breac said. And then he was helping Evie onto a horse, and swinging up onto the other one. From down the street there came a wailing howl, like the wolves Evie had heard that first night in the forest with Sylvanus. A howl with words in it. Mykell hissed. All the fur along his back stood up, and his ears flattened.

"We've stayed too long."

"No longer," Breac replied. He kicked the horse into motion, and Evie's followed on its own. They rode from the courtyard at a fast trot. Evie didn't have much experience with horseback riding, but she was thankful for the little she had. The animals were edgy. They leapt ahead, then balked, flinching and tossing heads. They didn't want to leave the shelter of the stable for the full blast of wind and rain.

They passed through a narrow sheltered lane between the stable and inn, and emerged on the street in a deluge of icy rain. The horses danced. Breac muscled his alongside Evie, and reached out to give her animal a slap on the rump. It bolted, nearly dumping her off. She regained her balance, clenching the reins along with handfuls of wet mane, clinging with her legs to the saddle. Breac caught up with her, and they galloped side by side down the street. She loosed her hold long enough to fling wet hair out of her face. *Where's Mykell? Where are we going?* She wanted to be out of the rain and the cold as much as the frightened horses, but she also wanted to be far away from Rizann's deformed remains, and anything that might be coming in answer to his summons.

Dark movement flashed in the corner of her vision. A black shape separated from the shadows between two buildings. Next second something struck her and the horse with the force of a speeding truck. The beast went down with a squeal. Evie hit the muddy street, sliding and rolling away as the horse crashed onto its side. A feline snarl, and the outline of a huge, square head against lighted windows. The horse screamed in panic. Tried to get to its feet, legs churning. Evie scrambled backward on her rear as it righted itself. Rainwater blurred the huge shape stalking toward her. She tried to blink her vision clear. Where were Breac and Mykell?

The answer came swooping in on a shriek. A hawk shot out of the black sky like an arrow, somersaulted mid-air, and landed on four paws. Claws and teeth. Mykell screamed his fury, and met his opponent, twisting, sliding in the mud in a deadly dance. Evie saw it as she stumbled to her feet, still backing away and ready to run.

A strong hand gripped her shoulder. She spun around, and Breac grabbed her arm, unceremoniously hauling her up in front of him on the horse. She landed with a grunt on her stomach, head off one side and feet off the other. She grabbed the saddle girth with one hand and Breac's leg with the other, and clung for dear life as he reined the horse around and urged it on down the street at a canter. She felt she was sliding off, first backward, then forward. Pain, panic, blinding fear, blinding rain, blinding dark. She could not breathe, could not think. The ground and the hooves pounded under her. Blood pounded her ears.

Finally Breac pulled the horse to a stop and got down, lifting Evie off and then helping her back up the right way. They were still on the road, but in the cover of thick forest. They had left town behind. He mounted up in front of her, and they were moving again, blind and deaf to aught but the storm. She held onto him as shudders rattled her body.

12

Flight

Breac slowed the horse suddenly, and Evie wondered what he could possibly hear or see to make him stop now. Then she heard it. Hooves pounding behind them. Lightning crackled, and a smash of thunder jarred her. An image of a rider-less horse. Black. Another strike of lightning. The horse was Mykell, wild-eyed and frothing. He reared up beside them.

"Must fly! I had to escape. More enemy arriving. Could not fight. Jorah has gone as well." He shook a spray of water from his mane. "I will carry the girl."

It could have been a mile or ten miles that they galloped along the road. Evie could see nothing in the wet, stinging blackness, or hear anything above the frantic, anguished howl of wind racked forest. Nothing to denote the passage of time. Nothing except that gradually her fear was overcome and completely consumed by bone quaking cold. They left the road, slipping and scrambling up a steep embankment into a stand of saplings. She caught glimpses of white bark and thin trunks in the flashes of lightening, and felt their branches lash her face. The storm ruled here with awesome terror. In this place it was an entity, fascinating, ruthless, beautiful. The trees writhed and bowed down before it. Branches over their heads snapped and blew away. Lightning struck a tree nearby. One instant it was dark, and the next their path was lit with flame.

Breac's horse leapt to the side, and tried to bolt. He struggled to hold it back, guiding it in a tight circle to keep from running. Mykell flattened his ears back, glaring at the other animal. It calmed. Though still nervous it bobbed its head meekly.

"Thank you!" Breac had to shout over the roar of fire and

storm. Mykell shook his mane, and they continued.

Evie curled and uncurled her numb fingers, and took a fresh grip on Mykell's mane. *Thank you for what?* She wondered.

* * * * *

The storm had slacked by the time they stopped. The thunder lost itself in the distance, but rain still came down in torrents. Faint gray light replaced the lightning flashes. Morning would come soon. Evie had lost herself in a cold stupor, half dozing on Mykell's back, and barely realized they had stopped. Water dripped in her face from her hair, and her wet clothes stuck, chilling her when she moved. She'd long since ceased thinking of warm fires, hot steaming mugs of coffee or tea, or even dry blankets. Now she just existed.

Mykell didn't wait for her to get off his back. He shrank until her feet hit the ground, shifting into some sort of weasel or ferret, and scampered through the leaves. Evie nearly fell over. Without his body heat keeping at least part of her warm, she started to shake.

"Thank the Creator we did not stop to put our things in the saddlebags," Breac said, letting his pack slide to the ground. "The naiads packed us fresh clothes, and blankets." He nodded to a thick patch of huckleberry bushes. "Get changed if you like, while I tend the horse."

Somehow the clothes inside her pack had stayed dry. She found a light, silky white shirt, and a heavier grey tunic to go over top. The thing came halfway down her thighs, and she could feel the warmth as soon as she put it on. Brown trousers tied with a drawstring. Last she pulled out a wool blanket, cuddling it to her chest as she headed back to find Breac and Mykell.

Breac had changed into similar clothes when she got back. His sword belt hung cocked over his hips, and he'd clasped the steal arm guards back in place. He was just pulling his own blanket out of the pack when she rounded the huckleberry bushes.

"Getting warmer yet?"

"Not really." She blinked blearily. "Are you going to light a fire?"

He shook his head. "I dare not. Besides which," he waved a hand at the dripping forest, "all the wood you see here is wet."

No fire. No warm inn to stop at. Morning coming on. She stood shivering, holding back tears. Breac folded his blanket and laid it at the base of a huge pine. Sitting down on it, he motioned her to join him. He gently pried her blanket away, and wrapped it around the both of them, pulling her close.

"I am sorry, lady."

She only grunted in reply. Her head dropped on his shoulder, and within a minute she had forgotten the cold world. She was dreaming about Rachael's fireplace, homemade hot cocoa, and the black-eyed cat. In her dream the cat had morphed into a hulking black shape that sang to her, calling her to join it as it danced in the flames of the fireplace.

* * * * *

Evie woke when the man shifted beside her. She clawed her way into reality out of yet another nightmare, and opened her eyes on a gray world. Mykell had joined them at some point. Still in his weasel form, he curled between them, sleeping with his nose in his tail. The horse stood a yard off, dozing on three feet and looking dejected. Water dripped from its mane and forelock, and the end of its nose.

Breac stood and stretched, rotating his shoulder and swinging his arm. Evie shivered as her warm nest was ruined. Mykell uncurled, stretching his furry weasel body and yawning hugely. Evie stood slowly, clutching the blanket around her shoulders. She rubbed puffy eyes with dirty fingers, and tried to blink away the irritation. Her neck felt like a thin twig ready to snap.

"Time to move again," Breac said, cinching the saddle girth that he'd loosened the night before. He checked the horse's tack and hooves, and rolled his blanket back up. "Have to eat while we ride."

Mykell shook his damp fur, and with the shake, he took on bird form once again. He flapped into the air, circling above the treetops.

"We'll give him a moment to scout for trouble. Don't want to walk into anything." He rubbed his shoulder.

"What did you do to it?" Evie asked.

"Poison Arrow. Leazor's first assassination attempt."

"Oh." She forced herself to pack the blanket, now pretty well soaked, in with her other wet clothes, and stood shivering, hugging herself. "How long ago?"

"Near two months now."

"Oh." She looked away. She wasn't sure how she felt about having slept the morning away with her head propped on the man's shoulder, huddled under the same blanket. At least he hadn't tried anything. *Give him credit for that. Or does a weasel count as a chaperone?*

They started off again, riding double this time. Breac said, "We'll take turns walking later, but for now we have to get out of the forest."

Mist hung below the trees, soft as the lichen clinging to their branches, and gray as the sky. Evie peered ahead past the man's broad shoulder. She could imagine the ancient trees coming to life and groping toward travelers with stiff limbs and twiggy fingers. Water droplets pattered about them. The horse stepped over the trunk of a huge oak, uprooted in the storm. Its ancient brothers and sisters loomed over them as they passed beneath.

"Are there dryads in this forest?"

Breac swept a shock of wet hair out of his face, and looked

around. "Hard to tell. Good chance of it though." Then, as though sensing her uneasiness, said, "They bear us no ill will."

He fell silent after that. She was coming to find that his frowning silence bothered her. Not that he was much of a talker, but there was silence, and then there was silence. She couldn't have explained it if she tried. After a few moments she got up the nerve to ask him the thing that had been on her mind.

"How many days till we get to... wherever it is."

He sighed. "Eight days at least of travel before we reach the capital." He paused long enough for Evie to measure the beats of the horse's hooves in the wet leaves. "Time is slippery. So short when you wish it was more, so long, when danger is on every side. It takes only an instant for the arrow to fly its course, and a moment for a life to end. A moment is not long enough."

"And neither is eight days," Evie said. "But then, you have eight days, or eight years, or eighty years. In the end it would be just a moment. It would never seem long enough."

"Are you afraid to die?"

"Does it matter?" She sighed heavily, almost missing the soft replay.

"To me."

* * * * *

"We will get back on the road later today, if all goes well," Breac said. He'd pulled the horse to a stop and dismounted. The mist had lifted a little, and less underbrush crowded the forest floor, making travel easier. Evie climbed down long enough to stretch and stomp the feeling back into her feet, then she mounted up again, and they continued with Breac walking and her riding. Mykell stalked along on the other side of the horse.

It began to rain again. Water dripped from her hair into her eyes, and ran down her nose, tickling it. She felt foggy-headed, sleepy, and so cold. She wished she was back home at her apartment, in bed. Or better yet, dozing in the big easy chair in front of the fire in her parents' farmhouse, with the hound dog whining in his sleep at her feet. If ever she got away she swore she'd spend more time there with her family. Time doing nothing but being still. It had been awhile.

Depression and fear were one with the cold. They seeped into her bones and tightened her muscles. Would she ever be able to escape? She knew now how long she had. But what if in that time she never had the chance to slip away? She would be forced to fight and flee, and if she was caught: death. That was after all the whole point of this journey. But would she be able to fight? She looked doubtfully down at the sword on Breac's belt, and the muscled arms under his cloak and tunic, trained to fight and kill. And then there was Mykell, deadlier than any ten wild animals, because he could become any one of them at any time. She sighed. What did Breac think about his mission to bring her to her death?

"Tell me about yourself, lady," he said suddenly.

Evie jumped. She looked down at him. "What?"

"You live in a rich land. Every house is a palace. Does each house require a dozen servants to maintain?"

His question caught her off guard. She stared ahead at the dripping trees, her mind wandering. *Home. A country so rich, so sterile and free of danger. And yet we are afraid of our own shadows. Afraid of death. Not like here. Not like Breac and Mykell.* Finally she said, "Life is so fast. So complicated. We have machines that do our work, they are our servants. They're supposed to make life easier. But they don't. They just make it faster. You get more done, so that you can go do even more. You ride in machines that travel like the wind, and never have time to stop and visit when you get where you're going."

"Are you married?"

"No." She laughed ruefully. "Are you?"

He shook his head.

"Was your mother really a witch?" she asked. "Like that guy at the inn said?"

Mykell snorted. "What you should really be asking about is his father," he muttered.

Breac laughed. "No, she is no witch. She has her ways, though."

"What do you mean?"

"She's a wise lady. She is proficient, and sometimes unconventional in using the Kantra. I would suppose that's why she has the reputation of being a witch."

"And what about your father?" Evie asked, with a glance at Mykell.

"A pirate from the south. A dashing, charming young man by all accounts. He was shipwrecked off the northern coasts, and washed ashore beneath the rocky cliffs of Dragon's Cove."

"And?"

"I never knew him. My mother told me the story, and said it was chance that left him unconscious on the beach where she walked. My aunt told me a different tale—that mother had sung a song in secret, one that she hoped would summon a wealthy prince to ask her hand in marriage. Either the song went wrong, or it was meant to be. She got her man, but no wealthy prince."

Evie laughed. "But why didn't you know him?"

"He was killed when Leazor took control of that country."

"What did your mother do?"

"Fled south with my aunt. They built a small inn. My childhood was spent there."

"Are they still alive?" Evie asked.

"Yes. And still operating a mostly respectable establishment," he said, smiling. "You've told me very little about yourself."

She shrugged, feeling suddenly boring and awkward. "Nothing

as interesting as all that. I guess my life is pretty tame compared to yours."

"You are blessed then. Were—blessed." He ran a hand down his jaw and looked away.

"Some blessing!" A sudden flare of anger bit through her mental fog. Whether she was angry with him, or with the situation, or with the cold and fatigue. "So how many other people have you dragged to their death? Is this how you make your living? You probably have a real reputation." Her hands tightened on the reins. She wished she could gallop away, far away, carve the mark, and then she'd be on her way home. But Mykell would follow. And then they would guard her more carefully. She clamped her mouth shut and glared into the driving raindrops.

Out of the edge of her vision she thought she saw Mykell smirk. The corner of his mouth twisted upward, and a tiny bit of pink tongue protruded from his lips. He looked so odd she forgot to glare for a moment, and watched him.

He looked up at her, and she averted her gaze, glancing over at Breac. He stared straight ahead, his forehead wrinkled in a forlorn expression.

"I am sorry, lady," he said without looking at her.

Me too. Sorry for this whole mess. Rainwater hid the tears slipping down her face. If she could only be alone for a bit. Long enough to sort things out.

The rain slacked off again, turning to a fine, hazy drizzle. Breac grabbed the reins and pulled the horse to a stop. "You will be warmer if you walk for a bit," he said.

They traded places, with him riding and her walking. She did get warmer, but no less tired and miserable. She walked with her head down, not looking beyond the leaves and rocks at her feet.

"When I was a boy, my mother sent me with a traveling merchant." Breac's voice startled her. She looked up, but he wasn't looking at her. He still stared ahead, one gloved hand holding the reins loosely, the other resting on his thigh. His laced up boots were at shoulder height, and she noticed they were worn nearly paper thin.

"The merchant was a master swordsman," he continued. "He taught me to fight with the sword and dagger. When I had learned, I traveled with a hunter, who taught me the bow and staff. I hired on a protection detail for one of the kings of the north, and one of his guards taught me to fight without weapons. Next I learned tracking and woodcraft. I belonged nowhere, and would work for anyone for the right price, until the High King saved my life. He asked if I would work for him. He wanted a guard for his messenger. When the messenger died of a poisoned arrow, I became the messenger."

He paused. Evie reached back and wrung the water out of her hair. The rain began to pick up again. She sighed.

Breac continued. "I've done many things for the High King. Two months ago I led his army into battle against Leazor. The day the army surgeon released me, the King sent me to Darkwood, the village where you betrayed Sylvanus."

Evie scowled at the ground. She didn't want to be reminded.

"He did not tell me what my mission would be, only that I must take care of what I found there."

"Yeah yeah, I know," she snapped, flinging a hand in the air to wave him off. "There's really no need to tell me about that part."

He tugged the horse to a stop and dismounted, handing the reins to Evie. For a moment they faced each other.

"I cannot say how sorry I am of that day. I cannot go against the King's Law. It is everything I have fought for. But..." his gaze flickered away for a second. "If I had traveled faster, and arrived in time to prevent..."

Her angry retort died, and her throat tightened. His gaze came back to her. She closed her eyes. *If only you had.* Flames and dark shapes played through her mind. The still face of Sylvanus. The dark wings of the crow blotting out the stars overhead.

She groped for the stirrup and climbed in to the saddle. *Would you have saved me?*

* * * * *

An hour or more passed in glum silence before Evie got bored enough to say:

"Please tell me about the spell or whatever it was you sang back at the inn."

"A song of protection, from the Kantra."

"How does that work? You sing a song, and nothing bad can happen? Are there other songs?"

Breac smiled. "There are many songs, for many occasions."

"So last night, I started reading that book... and... it sort of started singing itself. I mean, I was singing, but I didn't know the song..."

"Yes. That is how the Book of the Kantra works."

"But..." Eve cast about for the right question among the hundred or so that were dancing through her head. "But...how?"

"People often call what they do not understand magic. So since I don't fully understand it myself, I suppose that is what I would call it. But remember how I told you that communication here is pure. There is only one language, whether written or spoken. When you read *that* book, above all others, you read it as it was intended to be read. You cannot alter it. So if the intent is a song, then you will read it in song."

"But..."

"Words are very powerful. Even more when they are set to music, in the language which spoke creation into existence. It is true the effect of the songs often has something to do with the person singing them, but even those who are weak willed or weak minded can draw some help from them."

"Rachael said they were spells..."

"Not spells. Laws sort of. And Rachael would be disappointed. Unless the laws and the language are the same in your world, they would not work. The Book is useless there. Some of them will not even work in this world."

"Why?"

"The rule of the High King is woven together with the health of the land. Once, he ruled all the countries of the world, but now only this country. The rest have turned to Leazor. Their lands are diseased and cut off from the blessing of the Creator, who honors the songs."

"Uh huh..." She wasn't at all sure she understood everything he'd said, but she had enough to try to wrap her mind around, without asking more.

Breac continued, "Some of the book is history, written as ballads so they can be easily remembered and recited. This is why our country is still free."

"From reciting ballads?"

"From remembering *why* we are free, namely because we keep the laws that ensure protection. Leazor, our enemy, is a powerful dictator. He enslaves those whom he rules. Without the protection of the High King and the power of the Kantra, he would take over the land through evil sorcery. Rejecting the law would be rejecting authority, and without some form of authority, there is no protection. Do you understand?"

"Yes... that's why you're taking me to be killed. So that your country stays free. I'm just another casualty of war."

"No—not just another anything," Breac said. "Every life should be treasured."

Conversation died out. Rain came down hard again. They were all soaked through, and all wore the same miserable expression. They stopped for a few minutes to dig out a handful of jerked meat from the packs, then kept going.

Evie wondered if they would have to spend another night in the wild; if there was any kind of civilization at all between their plodding path and the mysterious city where they were headed. Or if there was, would Breac be willing to stop? She felt she would give almost anything for a hot bath and cup of tea, and a night in a comfortable bed. Besides, most of their clothes and bedding were already soaked.

Dusk threatened to come early to the dripping forest, but the murk receded slightly when they came back onto the road. It was a relief to get out in the open, even though the heavy rain had turned half the road into a stream. Mykell scouted around on wing, and Breac looked long and hard in both directions as they came out into the open.

"This mist makes it near impossible to see," he grumbled.

Mykell turned back into a panther and resumed his sullen stalking beside the horse. "Let's just hope there's nothing *to* see," he muttered, scowling as rain dripped off the ends of his whiskers.

Breac ignored him and began to hum. As he hummed, he began to smile. Mykell gave up on his glowering grump, and bobbed his head in time to the tune. Evie giggled when he changed himself into a duck and flew up to the horse's rump. Breac stopped humming and began to sing to the tune, a ridiculous song about ducks marching in the rain. Mykell quacked a fast marching-beat harmony, swaying back and forth and slapping a webbed foot with the rhythm. Evie nearly rolled off the horse's back, laughing until tears ran with the rainwater down her face. The song ended with Breac rumbling a low bass, and Mykell in his wheezing duck's voice screeched a high, quivering note that ended with a scramble and a flap, and Mykell tumbled head over tail off the back of the horse.

The whole procession came to a halt in gales of laughter. The horse laid his ears back and pranced, but they laughed on. When at last they could breathe again, they continued. Mykell remained a duck, letting the water roll off his back. His mood improved considerably.

A wry smile still twisted the corner of Breac's mouth. It made him look younger. For the first time Evie could see for an instant a glimpse of the man underneath the grime of travel, the weariness of too much responsibility. Breac was a young man. Maybe not that much older than she. Perhaps the same age as James. Without meaning to, she held the mental image of James up next to Breac, this warrior with the riveting eyes. The other seemed bland and weak.

Night came on in force, and the temperature began to drop. Just before dark they changed places, with Evie walking and Breac riding. Evie kept a hand on the horse's neck to keep from stumbling in the dark. She hadn't thought it possible, but it began to rain harder. After half an hour Breac stopped again, and pulled her up onto the horse behind him.

"We're being followed," he said simply, and they rode on.

She looked behind into the dark, but saw nothing. "How do you know?"

He shrugged.

"He is right," Mykell said. He'd changed back into a panther, and stalked invisible in the dark. "The wind is in our direction, and I can smell Ezomrah."

"How many?" Breac asked.

"I don't know."

"What are Ezomrah exactly?" Evie said, remembering their interrupted conversation at the inn, and Jorah's words. Remembering the beast that had attacked her when they fled. Her arms were already covered with goose-bumps from the cold, but now she shivered from dread as well. She had seen these creatures, she thought. The wolves, the owl/tiger, the *beast*. A large part of her didn't want to know anything more.

"I will not speak of them here," Breac said. "We are nearly at our destination for the night."

"Where are we going?"

"There is an inn up ahead."

"Is it safe this time?" She hoped beyond hope that this would turn out better than their stop at the Parrot's Roost.

"This inn is different," Breac replied.

The horse laid its ears back, and pulled at the bit, and Breac loosened the reigns. Despite the extra load the animal was eager to go faster. Beside them, Mykell kept pace.

Evie was already so wet that she almost didn't notice the rain stop, until the moon came out suddenly, and lit the road. She looked up. No stars were visible. Only the moon shining through a gap in the clouds. In the pale light Mykell looked like a black shadow trailing beside them. Behind, scraps of fog filtered through the trees and into the road. Swirling fog that seemed to have eyes and teeth. Evie blinked and looked again, and the vision was gone. Still, she edged up just a little closer to Breac.

"There it is!" he said.

She looked ahead and saw lights, and vague shapes of one or two buildings. The moon vanished again, leaving just the frail lamplight from a few windows to light their road. A gust of wind through the trees brought the sound of falling water droplets in the leaves. Or was it the sound of many light footsteps behind them?

"They are here," Mykell hissed.

Breac kicked the horse into an all out run, and Evie heard distinctly this time the sound of small feet and perhaps wings behind them. She looked back again, could see nothing at all in the dark.

Do not run away, child. You belong with us.

Evie stiffened. It had not been a voice, and it definitely had not been her own thought. The words came from a mind outside of her own. She shook her head. The horse's pounding hooves suddenly sounded like an endless drum roll. A maddening beat, lifting her mind away from her body. She couldn't think past the noise.

A wing brushed her cheek. She flinched away. *Come away with us, Eva. Come taste a betrayer's reward.* Flames ripped across her vision, blotting out the dim night, the silhouette of Breac's head and shoulders in front of her. For a moment she lost the sensation of holding onto him as her awareness tugged upward, out of her physical body. Black wings beat the flames. Heat prickled at her mind.

His voice brought her back. She couldn't follow the words, but knew he was singing. The night around her came back into focus. She had been holding on around his waist, but now he held onto her. She realized he was gripping her clasped fingers to keep her from falling.

Mykell snarled, and then gave a panther's scream, ending somewhere behind them. The horse leapt forward in terror, and in a moment they were in the inn yard, with stone ringing under the horse's hooves. Light from the windows glowed on a weathered signpost for "King's Inn."

Breac muscled the horse to a stop, and all but lifted Evie off, then jumped down himself, letting go the reins. The horse skittered away into the open door of the stable, where there was light, and a woman's melodic voice to meet it. The door of the inn stood open to greet them as well, and the light coming from it was even brighter.

A low stone step led up to the crooked, weathered porch, and thick, rippled glass panes distorted any view of the inside. Breac stopped there on the porch, and turned back to gaze into the night. There was movement beyond the light from the house, and Mykell's shadowy panther shape materialized from beneath the hedge. He seemed unharmed, but the hair along his back stood up, and his ears laid flat.

"Get inside," he hissed. "Do not tarry."

13

Tyra and Ylva

They turned from the dark and fear and stepped into the inn. The door swung shut behind them, and the heavy oak bolt fell into place of its own volition, barring out the night. A raging howl swept around the house, rattling the windows and making flames gutter. Whether it was the wind or their mysterious pursuers Evie didn't know. She hugged herself, shaking. The howl subsided. Peace settled into the house. The travelers were embraced by light and warmth and the smell of baking bread and spicy steam that rose from a black pot hanging in the kitchen fireplace.

Mykell swiveled his ears, sniffing the air. He shook himself like a dog, spraying rainwater across the worn floor, and headed toward a second fireplace at the far end of the long, open room.

Fire, food, warmth, but no people. Evie looked around. Someone must be down in the basement, or root cellar. A trapdoor stood open in the middle of the kitchen floor.

She breathed deeply a few times, taking in the light and the warmth. Thick log walls separated them from the horror outside. The light of the fires and lanterns hung from low ceiling beams were warm and safe; they were not the dark biting flames from her vision. Hunger and aching cold assured her that she was safe in her own body. Slowly her heart calmed its frantic pace.

Breac shrugged off his cloak and hung it on a peg in the wall, then strode over to the trap door and called down, "Is the fair lady of the house in? We're guests who seek shelter."

There was a guffaw from below, and a woman's voice called up "Your flattering of this old woman can only mean you want something, Aindreas."

Breac smiled and stepped back from the opening as the

woman's head, crowned with golden braids, appeared above the floor. She set a cloth-wrapped bundle on the floor, looking up at them with deep merry blue eyes, then climbed up the rest of the way.

She was certainly not an old woman. Perhaps fifty at the most, though she looked several years younger. She lifted her faded brown skirt and stepped around the trap door to give Breac a long embrace. Evie caught the glint of a tear on her weathered face, before she pulled back and flicked it away. She held the man at arm's length.

"We've been expecting you," she said. "The King was here, and seemed to think you would be passing this way, so we've kept the lanterns lit."

"The King was here?" Breac said. He didn't seem the least surprised to hear of the king wandering around the wilderness, staying at wayside inns. "Would that I could have spoken to him. I have many questions."

"Your mission is proving difficult?" she asked.

"Heh. Yes."

She studied his face a moment, and sighed. "All paths are difficult these days. But you are safe here, for as long as you can stay." She turned with a sudden smile toward Evie and Mykell, who had returned from warming himself by the fire. "Now. Who are your companions?"

Breac turned as well and introduced them. "Mykell, and Evie Drake. This is Tyra, my mother."

"Mykell. I think I've heard the name before. A changer, I see."

Mykell inclined his head.

"And Evie. An enchanting road companion for my son. If time does not press you must tell us your story."

"Unfortunately time is pressing," Breac said. "We must leave again in the morning."

"Rest while you can then, and let your hearts be light!" So saying, she spun back toward the kitchen and began pulling things out of cabinets, reaching overhead for a braid of garlic hung from the ceiling, and at the same time taking a kettle hung from a hook in the wall. A pie was slid into the cast iron oven. "Sit by the fire and warm yourselves. When my sister comes in she will pour bath water for you all, and by then dinner will be ready."

Even as she finished speaking, the back door banged open, and another woman came in, along with a gust of damp wind.

"Land sakes!" the woman said, slamming the door behind her. "What a horrid night. I do believe you've brought all the goulies within three leagues screaming to our doorstep, Aindreas." She seemed not the least concerned about the howling voices in the wind, as she set down her two pails of milk and shook the rumples out of her skirt. She continued, "The animals are all in such a bad temper tonight it's a wonder the cows didn't kick the milk pail—or me! And that horse of yours!" She interrupted herself again to jab her foot at the cat that came to investigate the pails of fresh milk. "Shoo Dede!"

The cat, Dede, stretched and sidled up to Evie, purring wickedly.

"Evie, this is my aunt Ylva," Breac said, as she pulled him into a hug. Broad shouldered and muscled as he was, he appeared enveloped as his aunt threw her arms up around him. She was a big-boned woman, though not exactly fat. Her large bosom and flapping red shawl made her seem massive. She wore a green and yellow striped dress that was almost painful to look at. Evie liked her immediately.

"I do think you've grown since last time I held you," she said, releasing Breac.

"I seriously doubt that, Aunty," he replied. He picked up the pails of milk as she was reaching for them, and carried them into the kitchen.

"Perhaps not in height or girth," she said with a twinkle.

"What then?"

"Well, your hair, for one thing! We'll have to cut it for you while you're here, won't we sister," she looked at Tyra. So saying she laughed and headed for the staircase. "I'll have your baths ready in a moment."

* * * * *

Evie followed Ylva up rough-hewn stairs to the second floor, with Breac and Mykell right behind her.

The stairs were thick log, sawn in half, and protruded right out from the log wall. She ran her hand along a banister of peeled pine. It reminded her of a hunting lodge, only no need to fake at being rustic. They turned from the staircase into a wide upper hallway. A blue braided rug ran the length of it, past eight closed doors, four on either side of the hall. Ylva opened the first door to the right and motioned Evie in.

"This is your room, dearie," she said. "Bath's behind the curtain there, and there's a kettle with more hot water. Just come on downstairs when you've finished." She turned and shooed Breac and Mykell back out into the hall. "Get out of here. Let the girl relax in peace. Aindreas, your old bedroom is set up for you. Mykell, yours is right next door here..."

The door closed on Ylva's happy chatter, and the thick log walls cut out the sound of her voice. Evie let out a sigh and slumped against the door. Now what? She felt so very weary. And after their encounter with what she assumed were the Ezomrah, frightened and violated. The privacy of her mind had been breached. And which was worse, having her mind violated, or her body, as the thugs in Darkwood had threatened? Closing her eyes, her hands covered her face. She had the childish urge to crawl into bed with the covers over her head and never come out. But then that wouldn't do much good, since her own mind tortured her.

She crossed the room to the small fireplace, took off her dripping outer tunic, and laid it across the stool next to it. She hooked a finger around the edge of the faded pink curtain in the corner and peeked through. A claw-foot porcelain tub waited there, steaming, and beside it an enormous teakettle sat hissing on the floor. A hot cup of tea snuggled on the folded towel next to a bar of soap. *This must be heaven.*

* * * * *

The kettle was empty, and the bath water had cooled considerably by the time Evie dragged herself out. She wrapped up in a huge towel and plunked down on the stool in front of the fireplace. Her eyes felt bleary, and her head stuffy. She could've fallen asleep right there, savoring the feel of fire heat on her damp skin, but she forced herself to get up and put on the clothes laid out on the bed. There was a loose, cream colored blouse, similar to the style she liked so well at home, but with a bodice of the same color to go over it. She fumbled with it, struggling to get it laced and situated like the one the lady at the Parrot's Roost wore. The long blue skirt also had leather laces, and went on much easier. She lingered, running her hands over the rough, homespun material, suddenly longing for a simpler time, a place like this were she could live in her own world. Safe, quiet, free of the pressure and confusion of pop culture. Someplace where she'd be able to think, to write her songs, work with her hands...

She ran her fingers through her damp, tousled hair. A small, oval mirror hung above the mantel. The glass had waver lines in it, but she stopped a moment anyway to check her appearance. It seemed so odd, seeing her own face here, in a strange world. Who was she, anyway? What was she doing here? Was she merely a prisoner, an insignificant bit player, a wrinkle in someone else's plans? Or could there be a greater purpose? Why was she standing here in a place she didn't belong?

She raised a hand to touch her face, red with windburn, and watched her mirror image copy the motion. Her face, her hand, her thoughts. *For now.* But those eyes. So haunted. Not what she remembered.

She was about to turn away when something reflected in the mirror caught her eye. A mark in the low ceiling beam over her head. It seamed surreal, seeing it here, and she caught her breath, almost expecting it to disappear if she turned around to look. She did turn, and the mark was still there, that familiar travel symbol that had become like a dagger to her whenever she saw it. Hope, pain, and regret, flashed through her. She could go home tonight.

She ran a hand through her hair. She couldn't leave right now. They were expecting her for supper, and she'd already been gone far too long. Yet if she didn't leave at once, would she have the chance later? What if someone came in her room, and saw their mistake? She took a deep breath. Of course they wouldn't. Her hand, as she put it on the door latch to go out, shook. She'd nearly forgotten the marks in her palms. Both the henna tattoo and the dark stain were visible, one on the right and one on the left hand. Perhaps the ladies of the house wouldn't notice, if she kept her hands turned over. Or maybe it didn't really matter here.

Savory, warm smells of dinner met her as she stepped into the hall. She had been locked in her room a long while, she realized, and felt guilty and a little sheepish as she hurried downstairs.

Tyra looked up from stirring the pot over the fire as she came down.

"Oh good. You're just in time." She smiled. "Now if only that son of mine would make an appearance."

Evie smiled. "Well at least now I don't feel bad for being so late."

Tyra laughed. "I would expect nothing less, for all the cold, wet traveling you've been doing."

"It has been pretty miserable," Evie admitted, and then in perfect timing sneezed twice.

Ylva came back into the room as they were speaking, and exclaimed, "You poor child! You're probably half sick, getting drug about in the wild in this chill weather. We must convince Aindreas to stay another day and rest up. It would do you both a bushel of good."

"I'm afraid that won't be possible," Breac said, stepping down from the last stair. He joined them in the kitchen, where they had instinctively grouped around the warmth of the cook fire. "This mission is already hazardous, and delaying will only make the danger worse."

Evie rolled her eyes and turned away, muttering under her breath. *Yeah, with your mysterious "goulies" you refuse to explain. Oh, and did we fail to mention again that your mission is to kill me? Why don't you just get it over with and quit being nice?*

She walked away from the group and stood, staring randomly at the shelves of canned goods on the back wall. Defiance was rising in her again, despite being tired to the bone and foggy headed. For the first time she truly despised him. *Hate that man's guts,* she told herself. True he had never mistreated her in so much as a scowl turned her direction. He defended her like an honored guest on her way to see the king, not a prisoner to be slain. She should hate him. It was the only decent reaction one could have in this situation. He just made it so blasted hard most of the time. She huffed through her nose and scowled.

* * * * *

"If you'll carry this over to the table, Aindreas," Tyra said.

Evie turned from her phony wall studying and tried to cover her grump with a question about the canned peaches. No need to offend the ladies of the house. They were sweet.

Tyra laughed. "No, no, I don't grow the peach trees. Never did have luck with them. We trade with some of our regular guests that come from further down the line. You like peaches?"

"Yeah," Evie said.

"They have always been my son's favorite as well."

They sat down to a meal of thick stew, and fresh, hearty bread. There was fresh milk from the evening's milking, foamy and chilled from the pitcher being set inside a bucket of cold water. There were boiled eggs, pickled in vinegar and garlic. Peach pie was set aside for dessert.

Talking ceased as they ate. The simple meal tasted so good to Evie. Her irritation began easing away with the comfort of a full stomach. She fell to watching Breac, discreetly glancing his way between bites. She hated herself for it. His fault.

He seemed at ease here, laughing with his aunt, asking his mother a question. He and Mykell bantered back and forth. Part of her wished she could join in, but the watching and wishing only made her withdraw farther, as weariness caught up. She was a foreigner here. She did not belong in this friendly conversation. Finally Breac pushed back his plate and glanced around the table.

"Thank you, mother, everything was excellent. You always seem to know exactly what will satisfy."

"It's a mother's gift," she replied with a smile.

"Evie..."

She jumped at her name and realized she'd been dozing. "Huh?"

"You still wish to know about Ezomrah?"

Her heart jolted her awake. Ezomrah. Here it came. She answered hesitantly, "Yeah, I guess." Did she really? It felt like a nightmare thinking about them.

"And well you deserve to know. You've been brought here

against your will, you should at least know what the danger is. And that Mykell and I will do everything in our power to keep you safe until..." he faltered and cleared his throat.

"Ezomrah?" Ylva said in the silent gap. "The poor child is new to this land as it is, and you've already been stirring up Ezomrah?" she clicked her tongue.

"Shh!" Tyra said. "Let him explain. I for one would like to know what the Ezomrah have to do with their mission at all. And Evie, we've seen the travel symbol on your hand. We are now twice as curious to hear your story."

Evie felt her face get hot. Tyra said nothing about the mark in her other hand. But if she knew about the one, she must have seen the other as well.

"The Enemy has dogged our way from the remains of Darkwood, three days ago, till now." Breac replied. "But in answer to Evie's question, the Ezomrah are..." he paused.

"They are changers, like me," Mykell growled. "But twisted and demented, driven mad by forbidden power and Leazor's lies."

The words hummed around in Evie's mind, and sent cold dread through her insides, but she still felt too tired to truly comprehend them.

"Shape-shifters?" she said slowly, over forming the words. "What forbidden power?"

"Certain things are forbidden for us," Mykell said. "Without limit of personal power, there is almost always selfish use of the power, which brings about evil."

"I don't understand. You talk about power, and it's definitely cool to change shapes, but..."

Breac and Mykell glanced at one another.

"Changers are not only how they appear," Breac said. "They exist in more than the physical world."

"So they have a body and a spirit, like humans," she

answered slowly, dreading to hear more.

"Yes, but more than that."

"We have power in the world of the immaterial," Mykell said. "Power over men's spirits, if we choose to exercise it. Power of persuasion, to bend humans' or animals' thoughts where we will."

At Evie's horrified expression, he continued, "I cannot read your mind, Evie Drake, unless you speak it. I could however suggest to you..." his voice drifted off and he seemed to lose interest in the conversation, licking between his claws.

She could feel her face still drawn into a grimace, as she remembered the dark fires, the feeling of leaving her body behind. Slowly a different image took shape in her mind. A mountain crowned with a great sloping field, a standing stone, and the rising sun. In the purple shadow at its base she could just make out the shapes of buildings. A city. Bright blue sky framed the picture with a sense of joy. It reminded her of a hot July day, waking with a feeling of expectation, the start of a vacation, and the city on the mountain was her destination.

Her eyes narrowed. She glanced from Mykell to Breac, and then back. Mykell paused cleaning his claws and looked up. A sly smile curled his lip.

"What's the matter, human? What did you see?"

She hesitated. "A city. Built on a mountainside, with the sunrise behind it."

"Yes? How did you feel about this city?"

She answered grudgingly, "I wanted to go there. It was beautiful."

"Al Acatra," Breac said. "The capital."

"You see? I cannot tell you explicitly to go there, but I can suggest to you that it is desirable."

"And show me a picture of something I've never seen before."

"I could have made the city look to you any way I wanted,"

Mykell said.

Evie cracked her pinkie knuckles under the table. "So what part of that is forbidden?"

"As I said, there is a limit to how far we may go in using our power. We use it to comfort and sometimes to guide, but control is one thing we must never do. Shifters also are not to use their ability to become human. We are what we are, we can take any animal form we please. But some of us became dissatisfied. Leazor lied to them, offering more power, more pleasure in becoming what they weren't meant to be. They used their power to control humans' minds, and turned them to doing evil. They shifted into humans as well, and married humans, breeding a race of demented hybrids."

"So they did become more powerful."

"More powerful?" Mykell said, his ears pivoting backward. "Power is in the book that you carry. In the Creator's laws. We've already explained how that when the King's rule isn't honored, neither are the laws of protection. The Ezomrah are very powerful, yes, but they rely on Leazor's twisted power, not the true power."

"But I don't get it... they can't use the Creator or whatever's magic, yet they do use magic. Or Rizann did."

"Leazor and his minions have learned to control the elements and bend them to their will. But it is not the same as the power the High King wields through his connection with the Creator. The Creator has power over creation because he created it, and his power flows through the King and the land and the air and the sun, and his servants who choose to use it. Leazor's power is dark and twisted, always turning to evil, never to good."

Evie rubbed her ear, taking a minute to digest all that. The High King, apparently immortal, and connected somehow to the Creator. She found that a little easier to accept in this world than she probably would at home. She said, "So the Ezomrah are what have been chasing us." It took all her nerve to ask, "What would they do if they caught us?"

"Who can tell?" Breac said, firelight flickering in his eyes, making them strange and fierce.

Mykell licked his claws, holding each claw up as he spoke, as though counting off a grocery list. "Torture, mind control, mutilation—any number of nasty things." The words belied his easy tone.

The windows rattled, and wind shrieked around the house. Evie jumped. Ylva clicked her tongue. "They've heard you talking about them," she said.

"Is that a bad thing?"

"It drives them a little wild," Breac replied. "Like wine to their heads. That's why I wouldn't speak of them out there." He looked toward the rippled pane glass windows. Evie followed his gaze and thought she saw a shadow flicker across the spattered glass.

"So why are we so safe here, when we weren't at the last inn?" she asked.

Ylva laughed, and Breac smiled. "They know better than to come here."

Evie looked at him dubiously. "What about the hybrid things you talked about?"

"Ugly things," Ylva said. "I once had one come snarl at me while I was drawing water."

"What happened?"

"I sang it mad."

"What?"

Ylva waved her hand. "Never mind that, girlie. They aren't as tough as they let on. Very limited."

"They can only change from human to one other form," Mykell said. "Normally the dominant animal form of their shifter parent. Each shifter has a skin they use the most. Mine is that of a panther."

Evie shivered.

"You're frightening our guest," Tyra said quietly.

"It's not as frightening as being out there," Evie said. She smiled. "I'm just a little cold still I guess."

Tyra rose and began clearing away the dishes. "Sit by the fire awhile, Evie. No sense catching a chill."

"Thank you."

Breac moved one of the benches close to the fire for her. She sat down, and he draped a blanket over her back. His hand rested on her shoulder an instant before he withdrew and sat down on an upturned block of wood. His eyes, one blue, one brown, gleamed in the firelight, studying her.

Dede the cat jumped up on the bench and purred against Evie. She rubbed his ears. Mykell, still in his panther form, sidled over as well. Dede took one look at him, and hissed. The house cat jumped back, spitting and growling and somersaulted off the bench to run under the table. Breac chuckled, but Evie laughed until tears ran down her face. He continued to smile, watching her.

Her laughter finally subsided and she sighed. "I must be really tired."

* * * * *

It might have been a few minutes later, or most of an hour, when Evie excused herself and stumbled upstairs to her room. She collapsed onto the bed and lay there, staring up at the travel symbol above her. It was shadowed and barely visible in the firelight. Her eyes flicked shut. She had to stay awake and go back, but she couldn't do it. She thought she got up at one point and reached up to the mark, but woke a little and realized she was still laying on top of the bed. It was the last thing she remembered for awhile.

Evie started awake. She sat up, heart pounding, panicked,

and for a moment couldn't figure out why. She was still at the inn, in Breac's world. How long had she slept? She had to hurry!

It was still dark, and the fire still burned bright. She must not have been asleep long. That was a relief. Sort of. She dreaded going back, yet she couldn't stay here. She licked her lips, and smoothed her skirt down, wished she had a jacket of some kind, in case it was night at home as well, and chilly. The back of her head throbbed, and her throat felt swollen. She wondered for an instant if she was coming down with a cold. Not that it really mattered.

Why did she hesitate? All it would take was one touch and she would be home. She reached slowly above her head to the carved ceiling beam. Before she could even will it, she had touched the mark.

14

Ezomrah

Breac took down the fireplace poker from its hook on the mantle, and stirred the dying fire. He tossed another piece of wood into the lazy flames. It landed with a soft thump, sending up a spray of sparks like tiny orange fireflies as the logs beneath crumbled into ash. The man leaned back, stretching his feet toward the fire, staring into the flames. Wind groaned around the house, and rain spattered dully against the roof and windows. Inside all was quiet except for the fire, and the purring Dede.

These past nights his sleep had been fitful at best. Mostly he lay awake, staring into the dark. Tonight was no different, except that here they were safe, and he could brood in front of a warm fire. His heart had not known peace since his brief visit to Evie's world. Since he'd looked into her eyes and seen all the fear, the longing, the wonder and defiance. All the conflict that raged there. The girl was turning him upside down, and he had no idea why. He tried to think of her as just another person, an object to be guarded and delivered to their destination, and then forgotten about. He could not.

It was not her physical form. He had seen many other beautiful women in his travels. A few faces he could remember. They were just other people, and faded together with time. Not this girl. He felt a pull when he looked at her. When she spoke her voice nearly cast a spell over him. That was not it either though. He had heard many melodious voices, both male and female, dryad and naiad. Leazor himself was reported to have the most enchanting voice of all.

He could not explain it. Whatever the future might be, he felt their fates were inseparably connected. How, only the Creator could tell.

"I've never known you to be such a storm cloud."

Breac rose and turned to see his aunt Ylva standing at the bottom of the staircase, hands on hips. She wore a long flannel nightshirt, gaudy with yellow and pink flowers, and her red shawl. He couldn't help a small smile. Ylva had not changed much since his childhood. A few more gray hairs and a little more padding under the flamboyant costume, but even those weren't drastic.

"I believe it came with the new position, Aunty."

She raised her eyebrows, gazing narrowly at him. "Is it the position, or the present company?"

He did not reply, having no desire to disclose any of his thoughts about the present company, even to a sympathetic audience.

Ylva came over by the fire, the floorboards creaking under her bare feet, and sat down on an upturned block of wood. She flapped her shawl, waving him to sit down beside her.

"Is it the arrow wound keeping you awake?" she asked.

He shook his head, smiling as he sat back down in the chair beside her.

"It was a curious thing, that day. Your mama had a bad feeling, and spent the morning singing petitions for the Creator to keep you safe. Then the High King came. He told us that our petitions would be granted, that he had plans yet for you, and he winked." She stopped and laughed quietly. "*Winked*! I'll never forget it. Three days later the messenger came saying you'd been wounded. Near death. That was the last we had heard until the King stopped in again to say that you'd be by shortly with two companions."

"And here we are," he said.

"Here you are indeed. I do not question the High King, but it seems he has you out on a dangerous mission very soon after being so near death."

"Too soon for a worried Aunty," he said, smiling. "Do not fear for me for that reason. I am well now."

"Yet you still wear a bandage," she objected, "Though it's been nearly two months. I am doubting the ability of the army surgeons. Surely they know the songs and the herbs that would heal it much faster?"

He laughed quietly. "I don't believe you would be satisfied unless you were able to take care of me yourself. It was not the fault of the care, only of the poison that has made it heal slowly."

Ylva frowned, but said nothing. Breac chuckled inwardly. It had always been a fearful thing to fall ill and be put in the care of aunt Ylva. She had as many remedies as there were days in a year. Most of them worked, but the best ones were the most horrible.

"Tell me something, Aunty."

She looked at him, and he hesitated. "Well?"

"Only if you swear to me you will not make mention of this to my mother."

She chuckled. "Is it to do with your young lady?"

"No."

"No? Well then, ask away. I am curious now."

"To be quite blunt, Leazor is trying to kill me, and I want to know why."

"Ha! That's all? Who isn't he trying to kill, and why ever would he need a reason?"

"He has sent his sorcerers and soldiers to hunt me. The Ezomrah are on our trail as well. It was his assassin's arrow that nearly killed me on the battlefield. You cannot tell me that he has not taken a personal interest in seeing me dead."

"Perhaps." Ylva rocked back and forth on her upturned log, edging it nearer the fire. She pulled the shawl up tighter around her shoulders. "Perhaps he's always wanted you dead. You and your father. Though I can't imagine why."

Breac put another log on the fire, and picked up the blanket Evie had left on the bench, laying it in Ylva's lap. She tucked it in around her legs.

"We've told you the story before."

"Yes. But are there details that you missed? Anything unusual?"

"The pain is in the details, dearie. In the blood and the smoke and the fear."

Breac leaned back in the chair, tipping it back against the end of the table with its front legs in the air, and watched his aunt. She talked into the fire, or looking down at her hands, rocking slowing on her block of wood. Back and forth. *Thump, thump, thump* on the floorboards.

"You know how he came to your cabin, and killed your father, while your mother and I fled with you."

He knew the story well enough. Mother told him over and over of how Rajah made them flee, fighting Leazor so his family could escape. Breac never asked to hear about it, but she told him anyway, saying, 'A man should be courageous, and willing to sacrifice. Your father was a real man. You will grow up never knowing him, but at least you can know he had a hero's heart. You will be like him when you become a man.'

Breac shifted uneasily, and realized Ylva had stopped talking and was watching him. "Go on," he said. "Leazor himself came to our house, and not one of his slaves?"

"Yes. He knew your father somehow. He spoke to him by name."

"You never told me that before."

"Perhaps neither of us thought it important. But now you want to know details. I am trying to remember. It seems so odd. All those years that I tried so hard not to remember, and not to think about the details. Some of it may be lost now."

"What did they say?"

Ylva rubbed the bridge of her nose, frowning. "His soldiers were burning the village. Your mama and I were already putting a few things together, ready to leave, when your father came. He'd been running. He said that our enemy was behind him, that we must flee, and he took a sword from under the mattress. Then Leazor came."

"What did he say?"

"He said... 'Rajah of Carmi-Asriel. You could not hide from me forever.' I think those were the words, or close. He saw us all huddled in the corner. You were barely big enough to walk."

Breac leaned forward suddenly, and the chair legs hit the floor with a thud. Ylva jumped. "Did he say anything then?"

"He looked—puzzled. Or afraid. He tried to walk past your father like he'd forgotten he was there, coming toward us. But your father stopped him. They fought."

"They fought." His chair went back again, the wooden backrest tapping against the table's edge. "They fought," he repeated thoughtfully.

"That is was I said."

"Not many men lift a sword against Leazor."

"Rajah was a brave man."

"No doubt. But not many men *can* lift a sword against Leazor. He is a powerful sorcerer."

"Perhaps."

"Then what did they say?"

"Only Leazor or the Creator can tell you that. Rajah was mortally wounded, but he kept fighting. We ran. Out past your father, down on his knees still deflecting blows, and past the soldiers coming with torches to burn the house. They never saw us or stopped us."

"Yes," he said, thoughtful again. "Because you sang the ancient song." He thought it must be somewhere in the book Evie carried, the song that had made them invisible to their enemy. Even to Leazor, the Chief Sorcerer.

"I think once Leazor realized he'd been tricked, that we were gone, he sent his soldiers after us. We saw them several times riding the highway we traveled. Once they searched an inn we were stopped at for the night, but they took no notice of us. They asked the innkeeper questions, but thank the Creator he told them nothing."

"So..." Breac rubbed the white scar in his palm, staring glassy-eyed into the fire. "What are you playing at, Leazor? What do I have to do with you?"

"I would not be overly concerned about Leazor's plots. They are ever the same: dark and evil. Concern yourself with the Creator's plans instead, and in serving the High King."

"Of course, Aunty. You never fail to remind me of my purpose."

* * * * *

Moonlight, silence, and a frosted October wind. The sudden change made Evie gasp. She hugged herself, hunching her shoulders against the wind, and turned a slow circle. Where was she? Dread knotted in her chest. A black lake stretched out from her feet, its rippled surface seeming heavy, oiled, and silent. Shreds of gray mist hung here and there above the dark water.

Another gust of wind sent dry leaves rattling around her as she turned away from the lake. A few feet away, on the grassy shore rose a finger of standing stone, like a grave marker. In the moonlight she could just make out the travel symbol etched into it. It seemed to be the only marking. A shiver went through her, whether from the cold or from seeing that lonely stone there, looming tall against the forest beyond. Where was this place? She had never seen or heard of anything like it in the area. But what area was she in? How far from home? A mile? Twenty miles? If their position in the other world paralleled where she came out in this world, she must be at least forty miles from the Renaissance Faire. Or was she even in her own world? Could she have traveled to another place entirely?

She shook that thought from her mind. The wind had died down, and she could hear the sound of a distant highway. Of course this was Earth. An orange glow above that hill over there must mean a town. It couldn't be far, yet the thought of walking there in the dark set her on edge. *What happened to the days when you loved going for walks in the dark?*

She started off along the lake shore, muttering as she went, "That was before I got chased by weird shifter creatures and evil magicians and... stuff."

A quiet plunk from the black surface of the lake. She jumped, skittering away from the water. Ripples spread out from the shore directly in front of the standing stone.

Her heart hammered, and she nearly choked on the ball of fear that rose in her throat. She broke into a trot, still talking to herself. "No sense taking my time here. Gotta get warm."

Ahead and to the left a branch snapped. Just in the shadow of the woods. Evie slowed to a walk, and then stopped. This time she didn't speak out loud. *I'm losing it.* A bulky shape emerged from the shadow of the woods to stand in her path. *Oh crap. Now what? Need a weapon.* She glanced around for a tree branch or anything else she could use, but in the instant she looked away, the thing advanced several steps. The outline became clearer. It was a dog, or maybe a coyote or a wolf. *There aren't any wolves in this part of the country!* But what part of the country was she in? Or was this even the United States?

Evie hated meeting any kind of strange animal in the dark—

be it skunks or stray cats. This dog was large, and dark as it was, she could feel it staring at her. *Ezomrah.* It wasn't a question. She knew.

There. A movement from the lake again. The dark water parted for a huge, flat, gleaming head. The serpent rose out of the water on four feet of neck, and then started to slither ashore. It stared with black, unblinking eyes.

There is no escape from us. You are ours.

It's too late to go home. We will always find you, no matter what world you are in.

She looked from the serpent to the dog. Terror paralyzed her. It oozed from the creatures in waves that held her captive.

This is what they want Evie. Run from them.

Run where?

Come back.

Evie took a step back. The serpent lowered its head, ready to move. The dog rose from its haunches, eager, waiting. It tail waved slowly, relishing what was to come.

You can never outrun us, traitor. Your hand is marked, and your heart belongs to us. You know it.

Despair weakened her. She felt there really was no hope. The fear and guilt of that night in Darkwood came back to her as though newly realized.

Sylvanus is dead. Killed by your fear. The serpent bobbed its head, moonlight glinting along the enormous length of it.

Evie! Put them from your mind! Run away! Come back to the inn.

"I'll never make it," she whispered. The dark fire was back. It licked around the edges of her vision. The mark in her hand burned.

Run.

Horror screamed through her mind. There was no room for

thought. She turned and fled.

The stone was too far away. A few paces and she would feel the cold coils of the serpent looped about her, the teeth of the dog in her neck. Or worse. For an instant she felt lifted away, watching herself run, the creatures just a pace behind her, their forms flickering now. Strange. Their animal shapes were there, but underneath lay something more. She could almost see it. She watched, fascinated by them. Waiting to see herself die. Wondering if the pain of it would reach her spirit as she hovered above. Watching.

Suddenly in front of her running body a new shape rose up. A black panther with its lips drawn back in a snarl. Raging green eyes shone out in the dim light, but they weren't looking at her.

Her senses snapped back into place. She skidded to a stop, slipped, and rolled. The panther Mykell leapt over her, landed, and sprang into the air, swatting aside the serpent's head even as it struck. The dog leapt at Mykell, changing at the last instant into a huge white tiger. They slammed into each other, and their screams split the night. Evie scrabbled to her feet, disoriented and cold. She lurched forward, almost fell again. She turned back only once she'd reached the standing stone.

The serpent struck out at Mykell, and he lunged to the side, taking the tiger with him, locked in each other's deadly embrace. Having missed its target, the serpent reared back, shifting into a bull, lowering its horns to charge. Mykell tore away from his dance with the white tiger, and leapt over the horns, landing on the bull's back. The bull shrank and became a wolf.

Evie pressed against the stone, watching as every second brought a new horror. The dark shapes moved and changed so quickly she could hardly follow. How was Mykell not torn apart? In the grasp of the tiger again, he turned into a porcupine, and was dropped. He hit the ground as a skunk, and let out a cloud of sulfurous spray, blinding the wolf. The tiger sprang for him, and just as its claws closed on his furry back, he changed to a sleek serpent. He twisted around in a blur of movement, wrapping his bands of muscle and scale around it. The tiger struggled. It shrank suddenly to the size and form of a cat, but Mykell drew his coils tight once more. There was a snap of bone, and the creature went limp.

The wolf shook its head, recovering from the skunk's spray. It caught sight of Mykell and charged, swatting at his head with a paw. Mykell ducked. He let go the tiger-turned-cat, and became a monkey. In one bound he leapt to the wolf's back, springing from there into a nearby tree. Long monkey arms snaked down and grabbed the wolf, and hurled it against another tree. It's back snapped.

Mykell dropped to the ground, once more a black panther. "More Ezomrah are on their way. I suggest you return to the inn. I may not be able to save you again."

Evie stared at him, her lips parted. She whirled around and slapped the mark on the stone. The next instant she tumbled to the floor in front of the fireplace in her room at the inn. She scrambled up to look around. She was alone. No Ezomrah, no Mykell. She slumped on the edge of the bed and shuddered.

The nightmare had spread. It invaded her own world now too. Everything normal, everything safe, was stripped away. How could she ever go home? Shivering, she crawled under the covers. She hugged the pillow tight, muffling her sobs in its warm, feathery embrace.

* * * * *

When Evie woke there was gray light coming in the window, and rain pounding on the roof. Someone had been in and built the fire up, making the room toasty warm. She rolled over and snuggled deeper into the covers. Her throat felt swollen and scratchy this morning. The thought of getting out of bed seemed overwhelming, let alone traveling all day in the rain, to an end she didn't want to think about. She had to get home.

The memory of the night before hit her like a wall. Real, suffocating. Claustrophobic fear. No hope. No way out. Her only safety was in sticking to Breac and Mykell. And the outcome of that: death.

The travel mark stared down at her from the rafter like a leering face, taunting her. So close, so impossible. They would leave this place today, and when would the next chance be? She would have to make her own mark. Would it be safe to return home in the daytime? If she got there without Mykell or the Ezomrah noticing, would they be able to find her? She gazed for a long time at it, lacking the courage to get out of bed and try again. She seemed to see Mykell's green eyes staring at her, warning.

Evie climbed slowly out of bed and found her own clothes, clean and dry, folded on the stool next to the fire. She dressed even more slowly. The jeans and flannel shirt with the ripped sleeve reminded her painfully of home. As if she could walk down the street and enter her own apartment. Or better yet, her old bedroom in the farmhouse. Her body ached from the days of travel, and her head felt like it might explode. She was a little surprised that no one had come to wake her so they could leave, unless it was earlier than it seemed.

The house was quiet when she opened the door and stepped into the hall. Someone must have come in to fix the fire in her room, but had they gone back to bed? She tiptoed to the stairs and started down silently.

A quiet murmur of conversation drifted up from the kitchen. At mention of her name she stopped. Breac and Mykell were talking in a hush. She could hear them clearly when she stood still, though they were out of sight around the corner. She sat down where she was to listen, her heart pounding suddenly. Was Mykell ratting her out? Were they deciding what should be done with her for trying to run away?

"Do you believe me now, human?" Mykell was saying.

"Yes," Breac answered slowly. "She is very beautiful."

Her heart bounded so hard she put a hand over her chest, as though to keep it from suddenly flying away.

"She is an enchantress without the use of magic," Mykell said. When Breac didn't reply he continued, "Humans are such blind creatures. Can't you see what I am seeing? Your danger is growing."

"Tell me," Breac said. To whether it was a statement or a question his flat tone gave no hint.

Mykell growled, "You have feelings for her."

"I feel pity for her!" He snapped. "She doesn't belong here. It does not mean I cannot do my job."

"No," Mykell said. "I do not question your loyalty to the King. You will fulfill this assignment, no matter the cost. But in the end, she will destroy you."

"In the end she'll be dead."

"Search your heart, human. You know what I say is true. You love her. It has only been three days. We have not yet made even the half of our journey. What of the days to come?"

There was a long silence. Evie felt her world turning upside down. Blood pounded in her ears. *He can't. It's not possible. He's... I'm... a criminal.* But coming from Mykell...?

Breac said at length, "There is another way, you know."

Mykell snarled. The sound was so sharp and so decisive it made Evie jump. "Foolish man! Do not even think it! Put her from your mind! You have no idea what you're saying!"

"The law would be satisfied, and she would go free," Breac pushed.

"*Never*!" Mykell hissed. "It shall not be done!"

15

Trust the Man, Evie

The door banged open suddenly, startling both Evie and the two below. She stood quickly as Tyra came in, followed by Ylva, shaking the raindrops out of her hair. Evie took a few more stairs and paused when Tyra looked her way, as though she was just coming down and saw them standing there.

"Good—" her voice croaked out of a sore throat. She cleared it and tried again. "Good morning."

"Heavens dearie," Ylva said. "You sound like you've swallowed a mouthful of sand. Don't tell me you've caught cold traipsing about in the wilderness."

Evie shrugged as she stepped down. "Maybe a little."

"That settles it!" Tyra said firmly. "You must not continue any further today. You all need rest. The lot of you will be sick if you continue as you've been."

"Beg pardon, m'lady," Mykell said, "but our mission is urgent. We must push on." He cast a sideways look at Breac as he said it.

"I'll hear none of it, so you might as well not talk," Tyra said. "I won't send guests away weary and half sick, no matter who they may be. Mykell, I'm afraid you'll have to consider yourself my prisoner, until the young lady gets feeling better."

Evie felt awash with gratitude, but still looked with apprehension toward Breac. He seemed torn. He glanced her way, then at Mykell, whose whiskers twitched. He sighed.

"Mother is right. Our mission is pressing, but what might we face a mile down the road, or in the dead of night, that will require all of our strength and more to withstand? I would feel better for a full day's rest myself. It wasn't that long ago that I was dying on the battlefield. Perhaps I'm not yet fully recovered, but this journey has me weary."

"Good!" Tyra said. "I'll get breakfast on. And make some tea for the young lady." She addressed Evie, "We'll have you feeling like new by tomorrow."

"So soon?" Evie smiled. "I was hoping to stay here indefinitely."

Tyra laughed.

The morning would have been pleasant, if Evie hadn't felt the need to avoid her two companions. Perhaps they felt the same, for they remained distant from her and from each other. Breac seemed preoccupied and thoughtful. Mykell was silent as well, and about as approachable as a cactus. Evie caught his eye once, as he was staring at her. His expression was unreadable. She feared he would insist she be put in a different room for the night, even though the thought of trying to go back galled her. But so did not having the option to try.

After a quiet breakfast at the small table in the kitchen, Mykell went out to scout around for traces of the Ezomrah. At Ylva's request, Breac followed her to the barn to see about a broken milking stanchion. Evie was left alone with Tyra as she cleaned up the dishes. She offered to help.

"No, no, Evie. I'll take care of these. It won't take but a moment. You sit there and rest and enjoy your tea.

Evie sank back down onto the bench, and wrapped her hands around the steaming mug. "Thank you."

"We all need a chance to recuperate sometimes," Tyra said. "That's why my sister and I put this inn here, in the middle of nowhere."

"I like it here. But I have to ask, the last inn we stopped at, we were attacked, and had to run away. Then when we came here, we were being chased, and this place ended up being safe. Why?"

"The Kantra, of course! We are well protected. Creatures of

evil know they dare not come here."

"But why? What's so different about the magic you use here?"

"Why nothing, only that we use it. The tavern keeper in Riverside is more concerned about the protection he can get from Darmot's band of soldiers, which is very limited indeed, than he is about bothering to use the Kantra. Out here, we would be foolish to think that anyone's soldiers will come to our aid if needed. It's rather a lonely place at times."

Evie played with her mug, running her finger around the rim. "Why did you put me in the room with the travel mark?"

Tyra's hands stilled, resting in the soapy water. "Oh, I really don't know. I suppose to test your heart." She began washing again, pushing her dish rag around a plate long after it was already clean.

"My heart?"

"To find out what it is that Evie Drake really wants. You are still here, I see."

"Not by my choice," Evie said.

"No? But did you really want to leave? You've been called into this world. Does not part of you want to stay?"

Evie looked down at the clear green, steamy liquid in her cup, and sighed. "Yeah, part of me does. But that's not an option, considering the circumstances."

"And what about Breac?"

Evie started, and looked up. Tyra smiled. "There are some things a mother just knows," she said.

"What do you mean?" Evie felt her face getting red.

"You two admire each other very much. It's only a matter of time."

Still red faced, Evie said, "I'm afraid that's impossible as well."

Tyra stopped and turned to look at her, and her blue eyes seemed a little sad in the wrinkles around the corners. "When did true love ever say 'impossible'?"

"True love *is, itself,* impossible," Evie said emphatically.

"Then it isn't true. Trust the man, Evie. He won't let harm come to you."

It's not his choice, Evie thought. She said, "I wasn't called here, you know. I came by accident."

"But of course you were called. Accidents are nothing more than the Creator ordering our lives in ways we don't expect."

"Well I can't say that I'm impressed with his order then."

"I was not impressed either, when my husband was killed. Yet here I am. And who but the Creator could know what might have happened if he had lived? Would worse things have come to be? Would he have been tricked into serving Leazor? Or would my son have turned to evil ways, had we stayed in that country? I certainly would not have built this inn, nor been here to serve you."

Evie frowned.

"My Rajah is not lost. He is simply waiting for me in another place. We will meet again."

Tyra turned back to her chores, and Evie, having lost her appetite for conversation, went into the other room and sat staring into the fire. Outside rain continued to pound, churning up mud in the barnyard. The flowers out in front of the porch drooped from the assault. She watched the gray, wavering forms of Breac and Ylva come out the stable door, and look up toward the roof, shielding eyes from the rain. They went back in.

Evie felt about as sullen as the weather. Sure, they were stopped for the day, and it was warm and cozy, but what about tomorrow? What would they have to face then? More cold rain? More Ezomrah? How many days before they reached Al Acatra? And what if she could never truly go home? *There has to be hope,* she told herself. *I'll keep trying.* Yet she knew there would be no escaping. She might get away from Breac, but the Ezomrah *would* find her. And to stay with Breac would be to die. Maybe.

And what about Tyra's words? Was there a Creator guiding her fate in this world? If so, was there any use in her trying to escape at all? Was there a reason she had stumbled into this place? It would have been easy enough to die in her own world. Was there something particularly special about coming here to be killed? And did the same Creator rule over both?

She picked up the blanket she had snuggled in last night by the fire, and wrapped up in it again, wondering what the possible solution was that Breac had alluded to. Wishing she could forget it all and enjoy the day.

The door banged open again, and Ylva came in, smiling, followed by Breac.

"Well, the garden will be growing fast now," Ylva said. "It's a warm rain, and the horizon is already clearing."

Breac came over by the fireplace and knelt before Evie with his hands cupped. "My lady, I'm afraid the only glimpse you've been given of this world is of the ugly and cruel. May I introduce you to life." He opened his hands to reveal two squirming brown chicks. They peeped and ducked their heads as Evie laughed.

She scooped one of the chicks into her hands and stroked its fuzz with her fingertip. While she was still engrossed in watching the tiny creature, Breac reached his free hand under his cloak. "And beauty," he said, drawing out a tiny red rosebud on its green stem. "Though it cannot match yours."

Evie blushed furiously as she took the flower. "Thank you."

* * * * *

Mykell came in a few minutes later and reported, "I don't see any sign of the Ezomrah. It seems odd they've given up."

"Couldn't they be hiding?" Evie asked.

"They could... but I should be able to sense their presence," he replied. "And I can't."

"They wouldn't give up so easily," Breac said. "I wonder what their purpose is."

"I do not know. I just hope it doesn't mean Leazor has something worse in store for us."

"I wouldn't doubt it," Breac said grimly.

Mykell glanced from Breac to Evie. "Perhaps he's just biding his time."

Breac ignored the insinuation. "Perhaps he is—in order to set a trap. Leazor would not take chances just waiting for opportunity though. He must have something in mind."

* * * * *

The day passed quietly, but too fast for Evie. After lunch Ylva and Tyra were busy in the kitchen, leaving the three traveling companions to sit by the fire and idle away the afternoon. Mykell lay on his belly on the warm hearth stone, licking his claws, or staring at nothing with eyes half shut. Breac and Evie talked, telling stories about their experiences. Breac told about one of the hunters he had traveled with, an old man who had lost an ear in combat with a lion. Evie shared a story about a family vacation ten years ago, the last vacation they'd had together, and the only experience she had ever had with camping. A skunk had gotten in their tent and ruined everything.

The gloom outside deepened, but the rain stopped. Mykell rose and stalked out onto the porch, where he took wing once more to scout the area. Breac watched him go. "You have come to this world in unhappy times, Evie. I wish it were not so. There is much here that I could show you, the likes of which you've never seen."

"I wish that too," Evie said quietly.

"You should see the cities in the south," Breac continued. "Walled in by the desert, yet they are paradise. The flowers that grow there are unforgettable." He smiled. "I once saw a blossom the size of this hearthstone, a purple so deep that it seemed torn from the night sky, growing at the bottom of a clear pool. In the north I've seen creatures of the frost that look like ice and frosted glass that live in the ageless dunes of snow. If there was time, you should see it all. You could write songs about them, and sing, and make them the more beautiful."

Evie gazed at him, wishing for a moment she could read his mind. A lock of blond hair flopped over his face, partially obscuring his brown eye. He seemed so intently focused on her, and his memories. Perhaps creating new memories, events playing in his mind that would never come to be. She knew the scenes flooding her own mind were nothing but impossible wishes. Of seeing the things he had described. Perhaps seeing them with him.

"That can never be," she whispered. "I will leave this world, one way or another, and never come back."

His jaw clenched, and he looked away, staring into the fire.

* * * * *

The next morning Evie woke to a knock at her bedroom door. She jumped and looked around. The fire had not been built up this morning, and only vague gray light came in the window.

"Evie, it's time to leave," Breac called through the door.

For a moment she panicked. Should she touch the mark and run? What if the Ezomrah were still there and it was night again? Would she have another chance? What to do? She listened for Breac's footsteps to head downstairs, and give her a moment to think, but they didn't. He must be waiting for her. She rolled out of bed and opened the door.

"We leave within the hour," he said. He gave her a long look, and smiled before turning to head downstairs.

Evie closed the door and leaned against it for a moment. Tyra's words from yesterday morning ran through her mind. *"Trust the man, Evie. He won't let harm come to you."* She sighed. *It's surely a nice thought. I would give just about anything to be able to believe it.* But then, with the Ezomrah, perhaps believing it was her only option. She sighed and went about getting her things together.

They ate breakfast in the quiet, dim kitchen, and when they were done, Tyra and Ylva hugged each of them. Even Mykell. Their packs and saddlebags had already been filled with provisions, and the water skins with water. When they stepped out onto the porch, Evie saw that they had acquired a second horse from the sisters' stable. That would make the journey easier, but also probably faster, and that she didn't like.

Breac checked the horses' saddle girths one last time, and buckled on the saddlebags. He drew out a pair of gloves and tossed them to Evie. "Forgot about these. Got them from Darmot for you, so you can keep your palms covered. If we get among more people, your marks might be taken the wrong way."

Evie put on the leather gloves, softer and lighter than the ones Breac always wore, and balled her hands. They felt like a second skin. She smiled ruefully down at her hands before turning to the sisters. "Thank you for everything," she said. "I hope...I wish, I could come back some day."

"Perhaps you will some day, dearie," Ylva answered lightly.

Evie gave her a forlorn smile. "Bye."

She went down the stone steps, and mounted up. Breac was already waiting for her. He gave one last wave as they left the yard.

"Who knows when I'll see them again," he said quietly.

The rain had stopped, leaving the scent of damp earth in the still morning air. Light mist hung beneath the trees on either side of the road, and the horses' hooves splashed through puddles of rainwater. The sky was clear though, and especially dazzling right before sunrise, while shadow still covered the rest of the world. Birds of all kinds chatted to each other through the tree branches.

Despite the movement of the horse under her, and beauty all around, Evie kept nodding off toward sleep, and then jerking awake when her body tilted. After about the third time, she looked up to see Breac watching her, laughing.

"What's so funny?"

He shrugged, still smiling. "I should have had Aunt Ylva make coffee."

"That would have been nice."

The sun rose, and the air began to warm up. It felt like one of those spring mornings that turn into a hot afternoon. A few hours passed, and they stopped long enough to shed cloaks and pack them away. Mykell made a quick scan of the area. "No sign of Ezomrah, or anything else," he reported.

Breac shook his head. "I don't like it. They wouldn't just give up."

"Unless Leazor has some other trap set, perhaps," Mykell said.

Evie watched the two of them, and felt a shard of fear pass through her. If the Ezomrah weren't following them here, perhaps there was a chance they wouldn't be watching the portal, either. The thought terrified her, but she must go through with it. Tonight she would carve the mark, and at first light, escape.

16

Night Visions

That night they camped in a wide meadow. Low growing, scrubby huckleberry bushes provided the only wood for a hundred yards in any direction. Evie looked around. There would be no way to put her bedroll near any trees and carve while pretending sleep, as her plan had been. There didn't seem to be any discreet way to carve at all. Dare she wait another night? It didn't seem she had much of a choice. Was their camping here on purpose, to thwart her? Or was it simply because there was a stream here? She glanced at Mykell and wondered if he really was reading her mind, and had suggested to Breac, through telepathy, or whatever it was, to camp where there was no wood. He had said he couldn't read minds, but did she believe him? She swung her leg over the saddle and dropped to the ground. *It wouldn't take that much to figure out how I'm gonna try and get away. No mind reading required.*

Breac tossed her pack at her, starling her out of her thoughts. "Make yourself comfortable."

She swatted away a mosquito. "Yeah right."

Once again Mykell scouted their surroundings. "Nothing."

"I'll make a fire then, for now," Breac said. He walked away, kicking through the brush to dislodge any dead sticks he could use. In a few moments he came back with an armful and began to build the fire. Evie watched.

She silently calculated how many days of travel they had left. Eight, when she'd asked Breac before their stop at the inn. They had lost a day in resting. That would mean six or seven days left. *Six days. That gives me a little time. Provided the bogies don't come kill us all.*

When Breac had the fire going, he got out a tiny leather pouch from among his things, and took out a pinch of something from inside. It looked like plant material, pressed into a stiff green paste. He tossed it on the fire. The wisp of rising smoke took on a greenish tint, and a spicy smell.

"What was that for?" she asked.

"It will drive away the mosquitoes."

He replaced the pouch and then unbuckled his saddlebags, dropping them on the ground near the fire. He unbuckled the saddle girth as well and pulled the saddle from the horse's back. The animal shook itself and dropped to its knees to roll away the sweat and dust of the day's travel. Breac repeated the process with Evie's horse.

"Might as well give them a rest from the saddles," he said, "since there are no enemies near. Who knows what tomorrow night will bring." He slapped the horse on the neck, sending up a puff of dust, and strode away in search of more firewood, calling back, "Mykell, would you be so kind as to convince our animal friends that they need not wander far."

Mykell twitched his ears, looking at the horses with a curled lip and slitted eye.

"So you really can get in their minds and tell them to hang out here," Evie said.

"I can suggest to them that it would be wise to do so, just as I could suggest the same to you," Mykell replied.

Evie frowned. Was that supposed to be some sort of hint? She could imagine, if her ears were as expressive as the ever puzzling changer's were, that they'd be twitching too. She turned away and began digging through the saddlebags. Most of the food they had brought was dehydrated. A few handfuls of carrots, onions, even potatoes and barley. Strips of jerked meat, a few packets of the nutty tasting travel bread, and some hunks of meat wrapped in thick parchment and cured with salt. There was a blackened skillet tied on the outside of the bags, seasoned with a thick layer of grease. The only cooking pot to be found. She wrinkled her nose at it. Why carry something so heavy? The thing must weigh ten pounds or more. Maybe fifteen. She could imagine using it to clobber a few furry Ezomrah heads. Or perhaps to knock some sense into a certain cocky black panther. The thought made her laugh out loud.

Mykell narrowed his eyes at her, but said nothing as she filled the cast iron frying pan with water and added veggies and dried meat and set it on a rock inside the fire. Hopefully she wasn't violating some unspoken no-no about helping with the cooking, or unaware of some secret of how to make this stuff edible. Turning dried nibblets of food into delicacies had not been in her realm of expertise, but why not give it a try? What would be the worst that could happen?

Breac came back carrying an armload of sticks, and dragging a large branch behind him. He saw the pot bubbling by the fire, and Evie caught the half grin that twisted his mouth before he turned away and started cracking sticks over his knee. She gave his back a smug smile, and allowed herself a warm feeling of self-satisfaction as she stirred her creation. Scooping out a spoonful, she watched a half reconstituted carrot swirl around in the steaming liquid, and took a cautious slurp. She sputtered and made a face. Tasted like—water. If she used her imagination she could almost taste a hint of veggie and meat flavor. Surely Breac must carry some spices somewhere! A second search through the luggage brought up nothing. She sat back on her heels and glared at the pot. It did look as though the food was swelling, gaining moisture. Maybe it just needed to boil longer?

"Do we have any salt?"

The evening passed without event, and without mosquitoes. The lack of trouble only seemed to make Breac and Mykell, and in turn Evie, more edgy.

Breac fretted, tapping his spoon against the edge of the tin cup he was using for a bowl. Another humiliating reminder to Evie of her failure as a cook. She hadn't bothered to check if they actually had the proper utensils. "They knew where we were, so they would have no trouble following us." He fell silent, and his hands stilled. He lifted his eyes to the north. "They are waiting, aren't they? Until the most perilous stretch of road.... They may expect us to go around...."

"We don't have time, Mykell said. "They know that."

Breac nodded and sighed. "I know. But what can I do?"

"Be wary," said Mykell, "and travel quickly."

"If we make good time in the next two days, we will camp just within the border. That is when the danger will be greatest."

"The border of what?" Evie broke in.

Breac studied her for a moment. His mismatched eyes looked soft in the twilight. He leaned back against one of the saddles, laying on its side at the edge of his blanket roll, set down his cup and spoon, and put his hands behind his head. She half expected him to start singing. Instead he spoke quietly, half closing his eyes.

"In ancient times, when humans were fewer, and giants and immortals roamed more freely, the High King (who is immortal, if you had not guessed) ruled the whole earth from his mountain, Al Acatra. There is a bond between the King and the land, and it flourished while his reign was complete. Leazor was young then, handsome and bold. He was the King's friend and second in command, appointed by the Creator. He lived in Al Acatra, very close to the palace. But he did not stay friendly toward the King. His hostility grew, until he could not hide it, and he tried to take the throne. He called the King to the top of the mountain, where the immortals communed with the Creator, and stabbed him there. Treachery was unheard of before his uprising, and has earned him the title 'Father of Traitors.'

"Being immortal, the High King did not die, but neither could Leazor be killed. He was banished instead to Al Kazam, the mountain that is cursed. Once every year, on the day of Justice, when criminals are brought before the High King, he is allowed to set foot on Al Acatra. On that day all traitors were, and still are, turned over to him. So for a long time his evil was contained at Al Kazam, and not allowed to spread. But he drew evil to himself. Evil of all kinds, and in all shapes. Meanwhile the ages passed, and the population of men increased. Men who did not remember Leazor, except as a legend.

"Leazor did not stay confined to his mountain fortress. He began to wander far and wide, deceiving whom he could. Through deceit he tricked the first nation into rejecting the King, thus falling subject to Leazor. One by one the nations fell. It's been over a thousand years since the first country became enslaved by him, and now this country is the only one that remains free.

"Al Kazam, the cursed mountain, is only a few days' march from Al Acatra, and the main road runs right past its base. In that way Leazor's actions would never be hidden in some remote place, and his shame would be plainly visible to all. Alas, Leazor no longer needs to hide his troops in the mountain's belly, but can mobilize from anywhere outside our borders."

Evie sat cross-legged on her rolled-out bedding, watching Breac as he spoke. His low voice entranced her. In the growing dusk, the firelight flickered over his face, playing oddly across the slashes Rizann had given him. His aunt Ylva had forgotten her promise to cut his hair, and he'd attempted to tie it back out of the way with a leather thong. Most of it hung jaggedly around his ears, glinting almost white in the firelight and making his tan face seem that much darker. He looked somehow boyish and ancient at the same time.

Her hair must be a wreck as well. At least she'd been able to wash it at the inn. She dug in her purse for the little travel brush she always carried, and set about untangling it.

"So," she said looking dubiously from Breac to Mykell, "we're going right past this mountain where Leazor lives? Is that a good idea?"

"No," Mykell said.

"I'm worried about taking the time to go around," Breac said, watching as she ran the brush through her hair. "Besides, Leazor knows we are coming this way. If he wishes to set a trap, he will have spies waiting for us for miles in every direction. Taking the road right through will be faster, and no more dangerous than going around."

"But you said it was cursed or something, didn't you? What about that?"

"Leazor's mountain fortress is cursed. The land around it is steeped in evil, and bears the marks of his poison, but to innocent passerby it is not dangerous, as long as you keep to the road."

"Innocent passerby, huh?"

Breac removed his gaze from her hair to her face and gave her a rueful smile. "Yes. For us—one can only guess."

"Ha!" Mykell said. "We shall see what kind of devilry the Traitor has in store for us."

"How comforting," Evie muttered. She put away her hairbrush, plaited her hair into a quick braid, and wriggled into her bedroll.

Fireflies blinked in the tall grass around their camp. A mild breeze caressed the meadow, raising a lullaby in the sweet spring air. Breac took the first watch, and Evie fell asleep to the low murmur of his voice softly singing a ballad.

The next day promised to be even warmer than the one before. Their heavy cloaks only lasted long enough to break camp and saddle the horses, then were packed away with the rest of the gear. The good weather seemed to lift everyone's spirits, though Breac and Mykell were still wary. Even Evie, who had drifted in and out of nightmares all night, felt better in the sunshine. Breac still hummed a little as he rode, the same song that she'd fallen asleep to last night. He glanced over at her, looking thoughtful. When she returned his gaze, he smiled.

"You must find this world a strange place," he said.

"I guess. It's like all the myths and superstitions from my world actually live in this one." She laughed. "And they're all chasing us!"

Mykell, who plodded along beside them as a panther, said, "It is not always so. This world is no more evil than any other, though the evil has been growing."

"Maybe evil here is just more visible, more out in the open."

"Perhaps."

Breac said, "If the evil is more visible, then so is the good. You just haven't had the chance to see much of it."

"Oh, I don't know. We don't have naiads and dryads, or shape shifters, good or bad. We don't have any books with magic music—at least if there are any they're most likely the bad kind."

They rode in silence for awhile, until Breac asked abruptly, "Do you like it here, Evie?"

"Ha! Now there's a loaded question." She switched the reins to her other hand and flipped her braid back over her shoulder. "Ever since I've been here we've been that close to death, pursued by all kinds of weird things, and on top of it all, I'm supposed to be on my way to the executioner."

Breac nodded and looked away.

"But," she said, "there is something about this place—almost like a song. It draws you—maybe it's just that pull you feel toward something you've been told you can't have. I don't know. There's just this longing...." She let the thought drift off, listening to the swish of grass around the horse's legs, watching its ears swivel as its head bobbed. An easy, endless motion. "Under different circumstances I think I'd like it here very much." She glanced at Breac, and found him watching her. She gave him a half smile, feeling suddenly shy for some reason. Her heart jumped, and she was relieved when he turned his gaze forward again.

He smiled and nodded. "How far have you read in the Book of Kantra?"

She lifted a shoulder in a shrug. "Just been skipping around I guess, why?"

"I wondered if you had come across any passages that might suggest prophecy."

"I don't think so. I don't know. Why?"

Breac said, "I can't get out of my mind something that Leazor said to me when we met on the battlefield. He spoke of a prophecy from ancient times, ended almost before it began he said... and he tried to kill me."

"That is the point of war," Mykell muttered. "And I'd say he succeeded. If only for a few moments."

"So you're saying there's a prophecy about you?" Evie was intrigued.

He shrugged. "I wish I knew. Perhaps it is of no consequence, but to have information is to have power over your enemies. And if it would give me an inkling as to what Leazor's intentions are, it might help us evade him."

"Right."

Evie cracked her pinkie knuckle with her thumb, shaking her head. "So Leazor is after you for some reason, and the Ezomrah," she glanced at Mykell, "are after me. If I were you, Mykell, I'd hightail it to the farthest place away from the two of us."

Mykell snorted. "Fortunately for you I am duty bound *not* to 'hightail' it."

Breac laughed.

As they were talking the forest began to thin out. Evie had been absorbed in the conversation, but in the pause that followed their discussion she looked around. She'd been distracted the day before, worried about how she was to escape. The thought was still there, niggling her, but in light of the beautiful weather, and the conversation, it didn't seem quite as pressing today. Now she took more notice of where they were riding, and she couldn't stop the goofy grin that kept cracking her face. Why did she feel so happy, talking to Breac like this, just as comfortable and casual as if talking to Courtney back home?

The underbrush they rode through didn't look quite as twiggy now. It was becoming more leafy. Big flamboyant plants swished past them, and wispy moss hung from some of the trees like gray-green veils. There was no more mountain laurel. White birches were replaced by towering ponderosa pines, with their light reddish bark and long brushy needles. Late in the afternoon the forest opened out into another long meadow, a valley between two low foothills. Once again they camped in the open, with no wood nearby to carve the travel mark into.

* * * * *

Evie woke in a cocoon of cold sweat. She felt like she had run a sprint, heart banging against her ribcage. Nightmares again. But so vivid. Her eyes searched the darkness for a light to cling to, an escape from the horror. The moon had not yet risen. Only thin starlight illuminated their camp. Beyond the embers of the dying fire she could just make out the still form of Breac, sleeping with an arm thrown up over his head. Mykell was nowhere to be seen.

She pushed her blankets aside and stood, feeling the coolness of the night sweep over her, raising gooseflesh across her skin. The touch of cold air did nothing to help shake off the feeling of being trapped in a nightmare. Rather, she felt surreal, as though the nightmare had awaked with her. She felt compelled to walk, so she did, stepping quietly through the tall grass, leaving camp behind. Her pulse raced. This was far too real to be a dream, yet she still had that horror, that feeling of being unable to control her own actions, of some Terror coming up behind her. Her wandering steps took her toward the darkly looming eves of the forest, edging the meadow just as it began to slope uphill. The forest. It frightened her. It drew her. She wanted to go back to camp, but her feet would not obey.

The darkness became complete the instant she stepped into the shadow of the trees. A wisp of lichen brushed her face, making her jerk away. Ferns tangled around her feet. She felt like she was walking through one of her nightmares, but she was not. The sweet smell of the ferns and damp earth, the hush of a breeze in the treetops, the rough bark of a tree trunk as she reached out to steady herself, they all told her she must be fully awake.

Evie's eyes popped wide at a sudden glimmer through the trees. The moon must have come out after she entered the forest. It shone brightly in a clearing just ahead. Lifting away a curtain of the hanging moss she stepped into the open. It was a ruin. For just a second she thought she had been taken back to the clearing where she had first come into this world. Moldering stone blocks littered the area, and in the center, a slab of black crystal. No grass or moss grew over it, and here in this place it was not just a black slab of ruin. It was an altar.

The bushes parted on the far side of the clearing, and a figure in white stepped into the moonlight, coming toward Evie, its movement so graceful it seemed to dance rather than walk. As it came closer she could see it was a young girl, perhaps eleven or twelve. Her white dress and yellow hair seemed to glow in the wash of moonlight.

"Hello." The girl sat down on the edge of the altar and looked up at Evie.

"Hey."

"I'll bet you're thinking it's really weird seeing someone like me out here, aren't you?"

Evie shrugged. Weird would be putting it mildly. A shudder went up her back. Maybe she was still dreaming after all. Another nightmare.

"I'm here because you called me."

"Um..."

"In your dreams. You called for help. What are you afraid of, Eva Drake?" Her voice sounded pure and musical.

Evie narrowed her eyes at the girl. "You tell me," she said.

The girl tapped a finger on her chin. "Let me see. You're scared because you're supposed to die soon. You want to go home. It was your fault that that dryad died, and you feel really guilty."

"What do you want?" Evie regretted speaking. She wanted to turn and run back to camp, but again her body would not obey her will. So she stood there, assaulted by images conjured by the girl's words, feeling trapped and even more convinced that she was in a dream.

"I want to help you." The girl hopped off the altar and sashayed up to Evie, taking her hands in her own small white ones. She looked up into her eyes. "It was all a mistake, your coming here. I'll bet you feel like your whole life has been a big mistake, huh? Coming here, getting mixed up with the dryad, then coming back again with Breac."

"Not exactly my choice," Evie muttered.

"Of course it wasn't." The girl pulled her back toward the altar. "But it *was* your fault. You must feel really guilty, huh?"

"What kind of a helper are you?" Evie swallowed against an assault of emotions. Guilt, fear, anger. Everything that had plagued her since she came here. "You're supposed to make me feel better, not worse."

"Am I?" The girl looked up at her, eyes bluish white in the moonlight. The faintest breeze stirred the golden curls around her face. "I can't change how you feel about yourself, you know, or what you did."

It seemed every wrong thing Evie had done in the last several years rushed back to her. She *had* felt like her life was one big mistake, or a whole series of mistakes strung together. Her parents had wanted her to go to college; she said no. They wanted her to get established at her new job before she moved out. She didn't wait. Then the job fell through, leaving her with a six month lease, no income, and $600 in the bank. She pushed her friends to form a band so they could make a few dollars playing at bars and a handful of parties. Enough money to buy some groceries till she found a waitress job. She had ignored her family's calls and offers of help. Then they wanted her to go out with James, and partly out of guilt she did. Leading him along when she had no desire for a relationship with him. Great life.

Then more memories came, from further back. Always the ugly, hateful memories. Being mean to her sister, screaming at her parents....

"What are you doing to me?" She jerked her hands away from the girl, balling them into fists. She felt the ineffective rage she had felt in the dreams. The self-loathing. Feeling like she'd been forced to do all those things. But she shouldn't have. They were wrong. Sylvanus' eyes coalesced in the white light, hovering before her, pleading with her. She saw the captain's sword raised. Firelight gleamed darkly along the edge. Then a spreading stain of blood. Shimmering blood, as though it had been mixed with shards of crystal. She looked down, and her hands were covered with it.

Evie screamed, but her voice fell muted with the scattering

leaves around her. She leapt away, pitching backward over leaden feet, and landed in the crumbling rocky remains of a statue. Her hand flailed against the stone face, painting a bloody grin.

The girl laughed lightly.

"This—it's just a dream," Evie gasped.

"Is it? Or is all of it a dream? This whole world. You could wake up back in your apartment with no memory of this place. No more blood on your hands." The girl stood over her, the moonlight glinting silver in her eyes.

Evie sat up, turning her hands to look at them. They were clean, but the decapitated statue's smeared grin remained. Black hollows of eyes stared up at her. She whimpered. "Help me."

"That's why I'm here," the girl said.

"High King, Creator, whoever you are. Please." She turned her face up to the white moon.

"I said *I'm* here to help you!" The girl grabbed her arm with unnatural strength and hauled her to her feet, leading her back toward the crystal altar. "You can make all of this go away. Just lay down on the crystal. You'll go to sleep, and when you wake, you'll be home."

Evie stared at the black altar. Tiny fissures in it caught the moonlight in traces of silver. Her mind clouded. Visions of her own world filled her sight, so real she could hear the beat of the music as her friends played one of her songs.

Touch it! Embrace it! It is your salvation.

Her hand was moving. She watched it reach out toward the black altar.

A screech shredded the night. A dark bird-shape plummeted toward them out of the sky, at the same instant Evie was jerked backward and shoved to the side. Breac leapt onto the altar, sword raised. The girl shrieked, but she was no longer a little girl. Her smooth face melted away, her head shrinking into the curved beak and brown feathers of an eagle. Breac brought his sword point down in the center of the altar. It embedded in the crystal with a crack that echoed through the glade.

Mykell screeched again, talons out to meet the Ezomrah, but the creature flapped into the air. It vanished shrieking into the trees.

The altar cracked again. More fissures opened up, making the dark crystal into a sparkling field of scattered moonlight. Breac leapt free as it splintered apart. His sword clattered onto the rocky ground as crystal chimed around it.

A curtain lifted from Evie's mind. The dreamlike feeling dissipated. She gazed around the ruins and at the shattered remains of the altar. Real terror weakened her. She felt she would start screaming and never stop.

17

'Ware the Naiad Song

"Where were you?" Breac demanded, glaring at Mykell.

For the first time since they had been traveling together, Mykell looked frightened and apologetic.

"I sensed Ezomrah near. They were not close to camp. They lured me away. I thought..." he shook his head. "I have failed you."

"You should have woken me," Breac said.

"I am sorry. I didn't sense an immediate threat, and thought to investigate without disturbing you." Mykell shook his head. "It must have been their plan."

Breac turned to Evie, still scowling. The girl looked scared nearly senseless, so he tried to gentle his voice. "What happened, Evie?"

She ignored his question, hugging herself. "Would I have gone home if I had laid down on that altar?" she asked.

"No. Your spirit would have been taken over by the Ezomrah. Because of the curse, you are open to them."

Her knees hit the ground before he could catch her. She bent double, her face to the earth, and screamed. A long wail that transformed into sobs. Her whole body shook, the cries coming from so deep it sounded like she might be torn apart from within.

Breac gave Mykell a helpless look.

"She is a brave lady," the changer said. "But she is far from all she has known, and cannot go back. Sing to her."

Breac touched her shoulder. Her cries did not stop. He lowered himself onto the ground beside her and put his hand on her back. He could feel the warmth of her skin through the thin layers of material, the ridge of her spine. Unaccustomed to handling women, the familiarity of the touch had him blushing in the dark. Yet he wished he dared pull her closer. Her body heaved in another sob, and his heart broke.

His voice cracked as he started the lullaby his mother used to sing.

"When shadows fall the trees will sway,
The night-wind calls,
Between the dark
And the day.
The twilight gleams, a light will fall
From pale moonbeams, A voice will call."

She sniffed, and her body relaxed, leaning into him a little. He stroked her back. She'd almost been lost a few moments ago. She had been so close to climbing up onto that altar, and the Ezomrah would have had her. The thought of guarding her, under the Ezomrah's control, all the way to Al Acatra made cold sweat break out on his temples. Seeing her pretty face distorted by an evil expression, hearing the Ezomrah's words in her sweet voice. Never being able to speak with her again before she died.

He closed his eyes. Tried to focus on the song.

"A silver light that flees away
To falling night
Between the dark
And the day."

The girl slumped against him, still whimpering. It was not until he tried to help her up that he realized she had either fallen asleep or passed out as he sang. And she still moaned in her sleep, like a lost kitten. He lifted her up and turned to head back to the campsite. Mykell followed silently.

* * * * *

The next morning was a silent one. The bright sunlight did nothing to disperse Evie's gloom, and Breac and Mykell didn't seem much more cheerful than she. Mykell shifted into a weasel and perched between her horse's ears, chattering to himself. Now and then he would bare tiny white fangs, growling and turning in nervous circles. Breac wore a permanent worried frown. He kept glancing over at her. She avoided catching his eye.

For probably the tenth time she rubbed her hands on her pant legs. They felt dry inside the gloves. No blood. She was beginning to question her sanity. She felt ashamed for being so weak and stupid last night. But what could she have done? She had not been in control of herself. The whole thing felt like a dream, remembered like a dream. Until Breac came. She shot him a sideways look, and found he was looking back. He opened his mouth like he was going to say something, then closed it, looking away.

She stared blankly ahead, sinking deeper into misery, knowing she would never go home again. She wished she could die right then and be done with it all. People died suddenly all the time in accidents, or slowly from cancer... why did it hang so heavy over her?

All life comes to an end, Vivaqua had said.

Evie just wanted to scream and gallop away. Keep going and going and never stop. If she rode fast enough could she outrun the Ezomrah? Could she outrun her own mind? Is this what it would feel like to go crazy? She could hardly breathe.

Another memory spoke to her, unbidden. Tyra's voice: *Trust the man, Evie. He won't let harm come to you.* And then Vivaqua: *I've seen life in your future.*

It was like someone had shined a flashlight into her darkness. Breaking the spell of madness that hung over her. Could it be true? Was there any hope?

She sneaked another sideways glance at Breac. He still wore a scowl. Sweat beaded and rolled down the side of his face. He palmed it away with a gloved hand.

Perhaps it wasn't much of a hope, but it was the only hope she had, and she clung to it. Mentally inching out of her despair. Still, Breac was bound to the law. What could he do?

By midday they were back into forest. Cool green shade relieved the scorching sunlight. A deep gurgle of water and strengthening of light ahead signaled a river coming up. Glimpses through the trees showed steep banks and smoothly flowing water.

They drew up atop the bank and looked around. Willows dipped trailing fingers into the water, shading still hollows where yellow leaves collected on the surface, and tree roots hung out from the broken edges of the bank. Far up river the current was swifter, foaming around rocks. Below them the bank sloped down gently, covered in tall grass and gravel. Sun glinted from the water's rippling surface, and a fish darted away as their shadows fell over it. They stared down into clear, shallow water.

Breac shook his head. "I am surrounded by mysteries. "I've traveled all through these lands, yet can't remember there being a ford between the capital and the town of Riverside."

"And we've been trusting you to lead us?" Mykell said. He scampered down the horse's neck and over Evie's thigh to perch behind her on the rump, where he shifted into a hawk.

She and Breac urged the unwilling animals forward down the bank. Hooves slipping on dead leaves, they jumped down into the shallow water. Except that it was not shallow.

Evie gasped as the cold water rose to her knees, then her waist. Even seated on the horse she could feel the current that pulled at them, unearthly fierce. The horses frantically tried to stay above water, muscles strained as they kicked, but were dragged downward toward the river bottom. They were being forced under. She tried to hang on to the saddle, but the current seemed to have a mind of its own, ripping her free from the horse completely. Churning, icy water slapped her face. She took a gasping breath before it closed over her.

She opened her eyes underwater. For a moment all she saw was blurry brown, streaked with filtering sunlight. Then there were other colors, blue and green and yellow and red, ripping through the water like blurred Christmas lights. The ponderous gurgle of underwater was laced with tones, like voices, touching every note on the musical scale with beautiful, terrifying resonance. She was disoriented, terrified. She kicked and flailed, grabbing at the spears of sunlight like tow lines. The colors circled closer.

Suddenly the weight of the water was gone. Evie gasped, and afterward was shocked that she had not sucked water into her lungs. She breathed air, but still the blurred confusion of colors spiraled all around. Her ears popped from relief of pressure, and she heard the music more clearly. It was voices. Hundreds, or perhaps thousands of unearthly voices. All seemed to be singing something different, but they were all in harmony. She put out her hands, and felt nothing. No sign of her horse. Her feet touched earth, but it was constantly shifting and giving way, making her lose her footing.

Someone grabbed her around the waist from behind. She screamed, turned, and came face to face with Breac.

"River naiads," he said.

"Are they trying to kill us?!" She could feel the strain in his arm around her middle, and resisted the urge to cling to him.

"No."

"What do they want?"

He looked around at the fleeting colors. "What do you want of us?" he called.

The voices hushed, though the swirling motion never ceased. Suddenly there was a face before them. Breac and Evie both jumped. The creature's body remained indistinct, though the face strangely angled and pointy, floated only a foot away. The naiad stared at them with huge, lidless gray eyes. Gray-green hair streamed back from its steep forehead. Whether it was male or female was impossible to tell. When it spoke, its deep voice crashed and echoed over each syllable, like river rapids echoing off canyon walls.

"Aindreas, son of Rajah, we have long desired to meet you," it said, and as soon as it had spoken, it shot past them in a gray-green rush.

A chorus of voices rose around them again, and a few spoke to them. Another face paused before them, this time with the hands visible, webbed and moving constantly like a water plant. The eyes and hair were burgundy, the voice light and lisping.

"Aindreas, who is your companion?"

"Yes, who?" said another, not visible as more than a brown rush.

"A beautiful human."

"Aindreas, child of two nations, now a feared warrior."

"Feared among humans, yet all alone. What is your weakness, Aindreas?"

Sometimes they got glimpses of the naiads speaking, sometimes not.

Breac said quietly, "They are playing with us." But Evie felt his arm tighten around her.

The air rippled with laughter, and the voices began a new song. This time they sang all together, with one intent. A chill shot up Evie's back, fear and unknown delight. Whatever was happening, she was powerless to stop it. Nor did she want to. The hair on her arms lifted. Emotions swirled around her chest like the colors swirling through the water. Some were familiar, joy, ecstasy, longing. Some were not. Feelings that she couldn't describe or name, they were the strongest of all. Wild, sensual music whirled around them, the words sometimes sung, and sometimes spoken or chanted, like nothing she had ever heard before.

Could this be? What have we found?
Duty bound, your heart was sleeping
Blows the moon-wind through her hair
Wakes your heart, her voice of satin
In her presence you fear yourself.

Come, child, smell the springtime,
Earth and life and warm sweet wind
New living, the world is cloaked in green-bright
Hear the Waking whisper his name.
Why so sad, human children?

Touch of skin, brush of hand
Sound of voice that kindles flame
Be free, your hearts, to love each other
Heed our song, you know it's true.
Hidden, the desire that grows in you...

Evie found herself, still held tight in Breac's arms, looking up into his eyes. Love and pain. And a hunger that almost scared her. Almost. Except that she felt it too. The naiads' song invoked images of their few days together, somehow infused with new meaning. The first time she saw him, like a figure stepped out of a dream. Then the nearness of him later, when he tackled her, and they went rolling in the lawn. The smell of grass and earth and horse and sweat. His eyes. Gazing at her so intensely. How many times in the past few days had he looked at her like that?

The song continued. Breac dropped his head down till their faces were inches apart. Her gaze flitted back and forth between his eyes, unsure whether to settle on the blue or the brown. As though the different colors held different meanings, and gazing long into one or the other could somehow change her feelings, change the moment. The brown, that made her think of warmth and passion, aware of his body pressed close, breath warm on her face. Her heart pounded. Back to the blue, and her heart missed its beat, for there she saw power, loyalty, leadership, struggle. A man torn. Fighting his feelings, fighting this spell that the naiads held them under, fighting himself. And in both eyes, incredible pain.

She slid her hand up his shoulder to the back of his neck. Fingertips trembling against his skin. Suddenly she was fighting as well. Desire raged for an instant, to draw his head down the rest of the way, to...

She snatched her hand away.

If she gave in, would he have enough strength for the both of them? Not likely. And the consequences? Perhaps he would help her escape. But perhaps his loyalty to the King would hold true, and he would deliver her to be killed regardless. Either way, he would be broken.

Nor would she *ever* tangle with a man on a river-bottom in front of a hundred naiads.

On that thought she jerked back and gave him a shove. He looked startled for an instant, breathing hard.

A ripple went through the air around them. A pause in the song...

Another voice broke into the silence. Mykell.

"What is this madness?" he demanded.

Evie spotted him swimming toward them as a salmon. Silvery laughter tingled around them.

"Behold! Mykell of the Green Eyes has turned water creature like us. Such a thing has not been heard of since days of old!" they sang. A whirl of swirling colors surrounded him. "Come to rescue your friends from our enchantment?"

Mykell turned piranha and snapped at them. There was a great rumble, and the atmosphere around them trembled. Evie thought sure Mykell had brought down the naiads' wrath on them. But no... they were laughing. Laughing even harder than before.

"No fear, Mykell," they said. "We will release your friends to you. It's not often though, that travelers with such reputations as yourselves cross our river. We should be ashamed if we did not show our hospitality."

"Hospitality my fin," Mykell said. "And you certainly picked the worst two people possible to seduce. I really cannot stress enough the severity of the mistake you may have just made."

"Tell us, oh wise one," they chorused.

"Breac absolutely cannot be allowed to fall in love with this woman."

This brought a veritable thunder of laughter. If Mykell had had ears at the time, they would have been flattened back. As it was he gnashed his piranha teeth at them.

"But have you become blind, Mykell? Can you not see it? They already are in love!"

The river naiads continued to laugh, but they relented. Evie found herself and Breac standing dripping wet in the middle of the river, in water no deeper than their knees. They looked around in bewilderment. Mykell bobbed to the surface as a duck, scolding loudly and ruffling his feathers.

One of the river naiads rose from the water to stand before them. It looked not unlike the lake naiads, but fiercer, more angular, and taller. It had grayish brown hair and eyes, a voice like a clear rippling stream, and was clothed scantily in waterweeds. It was laughing, but bowed to them grandly.

"Friends," it said. "We have delayed your mission and had our fun. What can we now do to help you?"

"What do you know of the enemy's movements in this area?"

The naiad's face grew somber. "Not many of his troops have passed here in the last few days. Fewer even than normal. But Leazor's evil presence is powerful. It runs like a poison in the river, down from Al Kazam."

"That is the path we have to take. We must make it to the capital, and cannot delay to skirt far around the mountain."

"Beware then! I fear Leazor has some new evil he's brought to the mountain. Three nights ago I saw the forest in flames, and now smoke rests over the land across this river."

Breac said, "There are strange things happening these days. What do you know about ancient prophecy?"

The naiad laughed. "More than you mortals can ever hope to. But please, you must be more specific."

"I'm afraid I cannot. Leazor has been trying to kill me."

"I fail to see how that would be unusual."

"I met him on the battlefield, and he referenced a prophecy. Several days ago he sent his servant Rizann to thwart our mission, I thought. But the magician seemed less interested in failing the mission, than in seeing me dead."

"Would not killing you thwart the mission?" the naiad said. "Still. Perhaps there is more to his actions. I do not know." The creature paused, troubled, and shook its head, sending water droplets sparkling in all directions. "No, I cannot say I know for sure. There may be... no.... No, I cannot say."

"You know nothing?" Breac pushed.

"Nothing that will help you."

The horses were waiting for them, calm and unharmed on the far riverbank when they left the naiads. Breac checked their supplies, and found their food and water had been replenished. They rode out in silence, released from the naiad's spell. Or had it truly been a spell that could be cast and released so easily? What had been lurking as a vague wish, a might-have-been, was now a glaring, impossible, burning desire. Evie glanced at Breac, met his eye, and they both looked away. Mykell watched them in glowering silence. None of them spoke more than a few words the rest of the day.

As Evie's mind wandered she imagined sitting on the couch at home, guitar in hand, with Courtney sitting next to her.

So wait a sec, Courtney would say, *you're telling me you think you might like this guy, like as in love like?*

I don't know, she replied to the imaginary Courtney. *I'm so confused! Every time I leave him, bad things happen.*

That doesn't mean you're in love with him. That only means he's protecting you.

Fortunately in her imagination Courtney seemed to know all about what was happening, so Evie didn't have to explain it all. She said, *I know. Just sayin'. But you haven't seen him, either. You haven't seen the way he looks at me, the way he talks to me.*

So he's in love with you now? That's still not a good reason to like this guy.

That's not what you said about James.

But that's different. James is a hottie. Not to mention he actually lives in your own world.

Since when is that a requirement of love? Isn't love something that can't be explained, something that doesn't really abide by reason? Naming a person's good traits won't make you fall in love with them. Not that Breac doesn't have good traits...

Evie sighed in exasperation, waving off the mental debate like an annoying bug. She scowled at her horse's ears.

Midway through the afternoon she noticed a smell of smoke in the air, as the naiad had told them. A gray-orange haze covered the sun even before the road dipped down into the lowland. High cliffs rose on either side of the travelers, facing Al Kazam and running at right angles to the road. Once they were past, Evie looked back and could see that they stretched for miles, a natural barrier between this cursed place and the green world beyond. She wrinkled her nose at the smell and the dread that crept up from the smoldering ground. *The cursed land,* she thought. *How fitting.*

The trees beneath the cliffs were charred, and the ground reeked with the recent burning. The reek and the smoke made their noses wrinkle and itch, but after a mile they had left the burnt forest behind. The blackened trees ended abruptly at the edge of a swamp. They paused, drawing the horses up, and looked at the ugly land ahead of them.

"I think this is worse than the burnt forest," Breac said.

"Yes," Mykell agreed, his black tail twitching. "Much worse."

Evie had thought the burnt land smelled bad. This was way worse. The stringy, sparse vegetation that grew out of the water was coated in yellowish-orange sludge. The water itself was clear, but only about six inches deep. Underneath, more of the yellow sediment layered the swamp bottom, and it was anyone's guess how deep that was. Steam rose in places from boiling, sulfurous infections in the ground. There were tree stumps out there, shriveled and spongy, sticking up like rotted teeth.

The road ahead still looked solid, so they urged the horses on. At once they were engulfed in sulfur fumes. Even Mykell made a face, huffing his displeasure through curled lips.

"We have to keep going now," Breac said. "This is just a narrow belt of the swamp, so we should have solid ground for camping within a few miles."

"If we don't get eaten alive first," Evie said, swatting at a swarm of bloodthirsty insects. She hadn't noticed them until now. There were clouds of them here and there all over the swamp, usually hovering over the boiling steam vents. Sulfuric haze obscured the sun.

Evie thought she would choke by the time the sulfur swamp came to an end, dwindling out into the occasional pool of tepid water. The ground rose a little, and the trees got a little thicker. They passed huge stone ruins, crumbling and mossy.

"Leazor's temples of old," Mykell said.

Evie shuddered. Had the ruin in the clearing been a temple as well? The altar a place of sacrifice to the king of sorcerers?

The swamp behind them, they rode through a sparse forest almost as depressing as the swamp had been. Though it was green and alive, it just didn't seem *right*. The stunted, twisted trees were hung with dark moss like vast, heavy curtains. The lush, big-leaved vegetation that grew on the other side of the naiad river was nowhere in sight here. Gnarled laurels, spotted with disease and bug infestation lined the road. Rocks were covered in gray, moldy looking moss.

"We have to spend the night here?"

"And soon," Breac replied.

18
An Evil Dawn

They made camp a little way from the road, each working or resting in silence until after dinner, when Mykell sidled up to Breac. "The King did well to warn you of the peril of this mission."

Breac unrolled his bedroll. He nodded slowly. "Yes. I cannot question the laws, or the King's purpose in sending me, but..."

Mykell growled deep in his throat. "You must not falter now!"

Evie watched them from the corner of her eye as she laid out her own bedding at the foot of a twisted old oak, smoothing the wrinkles out of the blankets. Breac bowed his head. He spoke so low she almost missed the words. "I would like a word with the lady."

Mykell took to owl's wings and swooped into the darkening sky.

Evie turned her back, still patting down creases, pretending she hadn't heard, though her heartbeat suddenly faltered. She felt the blankets shift under her knees as Breac knelt behind her. She turned and at once met his gaze.

"Evie."

"Yes?"

He took her hand. "Dare I speak what both of us are thinking?"

"Breac...I..." She shook her head and laughed a little. "It's impossible I think."

"I know. I've been trying to speak to you all day. Even before the naiads—but I find I do not know what to say, any more than I know what to do. My lady, I am not the same man who came seeking you in your world. Yet I am the same. Still bound to the Law." He let go her hand, and she looked up, watching as he slowly removed the glove from his right hand and held his palm out to her, displaying a white oval scar. "I swore an oath to the High King, and sealed it with fire. As long as he serves the Creator, I must serve him. But now my heart is divided. I love you."

There it was. No longer a secret.

She wanted to kiss him, throw her arms around him, tell him she loved him as well. But she remained staring down at the mark in his hand and said, "So you would bring me to Leazor to be slain."

"I would as soon die."

"Then come back to my world with me."

"I cannot! I would be the worst traitor of all. How could I live, even in another world, knowing the destruction I had caused?"

She looked down at her hands, whispered, "You couldn't. It's not in you. You'd be better off not loving me."

Breac gave a broken laugh.

"I wish we hadn't crossed that river," she said.

"This was no fault of the naiads. They merely brought to light what has been there since the beginning of this quest. How could I but see you, and not be moved? And now I am betrayed by my own heart."

She raised a trembling hand and placed it on his chest. His heart beat fast. The heat of his body warmed her palm. "What hope have we then?"

His eyes dropped, and his face went pale, but he did not speak.

"Betrayal is rewarded with death. No matter the outcome of all this, it's your treacherous heart that will suffer." She dropped her hand and looked away. "I think mine died already."

* * * * *

Evie lay awake, curled in her blanket at the foot of the old oak. Mykell was on watch, and he occasionally glanced her direction. She had taken the pocket knife out of her purse before crawling into bed, and now held it awkwardly in her left hand, squinting in the faint moonlight at her henna tattoo.

She had already fallen asleep once, and had such hideous nightmares that once again she woke in a cold sweat. Her brain felt mangled as she pressed the knife point into the tree. Should she really be doing this? There seemed little hope in trying to escape. Even thinking about home didn't feel the same as it used to, though not because of the Ezomrah. She couldn't escape. Did she want to? Dare she try? It all made her head hurt.

Twice she dozed off, and the tiny pocket knife fell from her hand. Each time she woke in terror. Blood and fire soaked her dreams. Even in sleep she could not escape. Dread weighted her hand, weakening the lines she carved. By the time she finished, dawn was softening the darkness. She lay exhausted, staring at the crooked design through scratchy eyes. In a different time and place she would have laughed. Her carving looked so horrible it might not work.

If she was going to try, she should do it before sunrise came to reveal her absence. Her dread transformed into terror as she considered it.

Breac sat not far off, humming softly, watching the shadows. She stared at the silhouette of his back for a long time. Finally she turned her face back to the tree, and reached out to it. But she didn't touch it. Not yet. The horses nickered, stamping nervously. There was a soft rustle as Breac got to his feet. She froze.

Behind her, and beyond where Breac stood, there came a crackle of brush. She raised her head ever so slightly so she could hear. Mykell snuffled in his sleep, and tucked his nose farther under his paw. A whisper of metal on leather as Breac drew his sword made her tense up, feeling suddenly queasy. *Please, no more trouble. Not here.*

A crash echoed through the forest. Mykell jerked to his feet, blinking, fangs bared as he blinked away sleep. *Now,* Evie thought. *Go now!* There was another rumbling crash, followed by a blast of foul air. She rolled over and sat up. The skin on the back of her neck prickled. It was still too dark to see far into the trees. Breac and Mykell were distracted. She could slip away. Still she dared not. What if the mark didn't work after all? What if she got away, and something happened to him?

Crash! Evie jumped. More wood smashed. Maybe a hundred yards into the forest. Silence. They all waited, tense and still. Then the trees right over their heads cracked, crashed, and were ripped away. A huge shape blotted out the gray sky. Borne up on canopied wings, air swirled around it, thick with decay. It descended, landing before them, plowing up dirt and rocks and bushes that were in its path. Evie jerked back, slamming into the tree. A scream stuck in her throat. Mykell crouched, staring up at the monster, his snarl frozen in place. The horses bolted.

Breac stood, face lifted, sword in hand. The dragon curved its neck down, bringing it face to face with the man. Its head was as big as he, each of its teeth the length of an arm. For a moment man and beast were both still. It lifted one clawed forefoot, the size of a boulder. Breac crouched, sword raised. The dragon paused again. Its head and raised foot twitched oddly, for an instant giving the impression of a robot or marionette. There was something wrong with its eyes as well, but the light was still too weak to tell what. It gnashed its huge teeth, then struck.

Breac threw himself backward, as his sword went spinning into the brush. Mykell leapt over him, turned hawk, and flew at the dragon's eye. He was swatted out of the air, and went tumbling after the sword. Breac wriggled backward on his elbows, rolled, and got to his feet. The dragon knocked him flying. He landed hard, smashed into a briar bush and rolled away.

Evie screamed, then slapped a hand over her mouth, shrinking back against the tree. The dragon took no notice.

Breac groaned and rolled to his side, pushing himself half up. "What do you want?" He was enveloped in black, sulfurous smoke as the monster chugged out a laugh.

"You!"

It reached out again, and this time locked its claws around him as he was still trying to rise. It opened its wings and shoved off from the ground, carrying the man with it. Evie could just see him in the dim light, struggling to loosen the dragon's strangle hold around his chest. To no avail.

Mykell flapped out of the brush, somersaulted mid air, and plowed headlong into the ground. He lay still for a moment, slowly morphing back into his panther form, then got up and shook his head, looking about for the dragon. Evie pointed silently into the air. Still dazed, he leapt after it, fell back, and stared at the ground stupidly.

"A bird, Mykell! Or something that can fly."

He snarled at her, shifted into a hawk, and shot straight up into the air, then changed to a giant eagle. But still only a quarter the dragon's size. Streaking upward, talons out, he went for the monster's face. They grappled in the air for a moment, wings half drawn in, clawing and spinning, high enough to catch the first rays of light over the horizon. The dragon's scales glittered as they spun, faster and faster, losing altitude, now light, now shadow, dropping toward the earth. The dragon snorted a stream of fire, and Mykell spiraled away. A thrust of his wings brought him face to face with it again, and he aimed his curved beak at the thing's eye.

The rising sun shot up over the edge of the world, making the two winged figures into black cutouts against the sky. Evie squinted, and put her hands up to her eyes like binoculars, but they were spinning now before the face of the sun, and she could not see. Mykell gave the high, rasping screech of the eagle, and came plunging down, end over end, leaving a black trail of smoke. He caught himself with open wings just above the trees, faltered, and crashed down. The dragon rose high in the air again, hovering for just an instant before it turned and sped away.

Evie ran to Mykell. He had shifted back into a panther and lay still, breathing shallowly. Two deep gashes ran across his side, baring his ribs. Most of the fur was gone from that side of his body, leaving blackened hide. Evie's stomach flip-flopped as she put her hands under his head.

"What can I do Mykell? Tell me what to do!"

His opened his eyes for an instant. "All is lost now." His eyes closed, and his grimace relaxed. His breathing settled into a shallow rhythm.

Evie sat back, hugging her legs and resting her head on her knees, hiding her eyes from this hideous place. The dragon's reek still hung in the air. Foul insects chattered from the underbrush. Mykell was dying, Breac was gone. What could she do? Her tired mind slogged through options. There must be some kind of first aid supplies among their things. She pushed herself off the ground and headed back to camp. Maybe.... Wait, the *book!* She started running.

She dropped to her knees by her bed and almost fell over reaching for her pack. The book lay on top. Forgetting all about the first aid supplies, she grabbed it and ran back to Mykell.

She sat cross-legged on the ground beside him, and suddenly felt terrified that she would open the book and find nothing. Its reassuring leather cover stared up at her, looking worn and wise. She put her hand on Mykell's head and stroked his fur. His breathing was still regular. She opened the book in her lap, and began scanning through some of the pages she had already read.

Most of it was ballads of history, which she'd discovered when read out loud turned the reader's voice to song. And once sung, they clung in her memory with the tenacity of nursery rhymes. The melodies were haunting, and the stories they told, though sometimes sad, sometimes happy, all had a beauty to them, a calm order. Would the adventure they were in now be anything like the old ballads? It certainly seemed hopeless enough.

None of the pieces had titles, though some did have short introductions. As she got past the part of the book that she had already read she slowed down, scanning the first few lines of each piece. There was a blessing to be sung over one's crops or livestock, a song that would impart peace, another story of ancient valor, and the design of a brand that warriors of old would have marked in their palm, if they were sworn servants of the King. She recognized it as the mark Breac bore in his hand. 'Sealed with fire,' he had said. A brand. She made a face.

At last she paused over one song, scanning through it. Her heart beat faster. She began to read aloud, and as usual, the melody overtook her. Her voice trembled, even sustained as it was by the magic of the book.

Weary and broken,
Rest here for awhile.
Peace I have spoken,
Creator grant.
Brightness of sunlight,
Music of water,
Starlight and wind's might
Fill you with strength.

Tho' faith be shaken,
Soul lost in trouble,
Hope will awaken,

Hear and believe.

I hold in my song

Creation's blessings

Make failing heart strong

Hear and be well

Evie sang, holding the book, and stroking Mykell's fur with her other hand. The glory of the newly risen sun shone all around them, like a tangible thing that she could reach out and touch. Or reach out and grasp with her voice, and the words of her song. She felt strength flowing through her, and an unfamiliar power. The words of the song ended, but Evie didn't stop singing. There was a song on the very next page that seemed to be a continuation almost, with a similar melody. It was a song about the glory of nature, the foundations of the mountains, even the very molecules in the air, all praising their Maker, how they had been blessed at the beginning of the world.

As she sang she continued to stroke Mykell's side. His breathing deepened, and a gentle purr vibrated up through her fingers. She looked down in surprise.

The gashes in his side had closed, smoothed together under new skin. He purred in deep sleep, like a huge cat.

The song drifted to an end. "Mykell?" she called softly.

One of his ears twitched.

"Mykell, wake up!"

He stretched and yawned, and blinked up at her for an instant before reality returned to him. He leapt up, ears flattened back, looking about frantically.

"They've taken Breac!" He stopped, and turned his head to inspect the gashes on his side. Only a patch of missing fur remained. "You've healed me." His nose wrinkled and twitched. "I'm bald. How unbecoming."

An insane little giggle escaped her as she dropped the book

and threw her arms around his neck. "What do we do?" she cried.

He twisted his head away, looked at her strangely. "I should think you would be trying to escape."

"I should be, but how could I leave you and Breac? How can I leave him now? I love him, Mykell. It might be the death of me, but I do."

Mykell looked toward the north where the dragon had disappeared. "Al Kazam. Our enemy's cursed mountain. There is no hope for the man now." He looked at her with tears in his green eyes. "He's already dead. To go after him would be to die in vain. And if you die here, all our mission is in vain."

Anger flared through her. "You honestly think I'm going to let you take me to your King now? I will not. I will fight you to the death, Mykell." She pointed after the dragon with a shaking finger. "Either kill me now, or let me go after him."

Mykell looked at her, startled, then toward the mountain, just barely visible above the treetops. "There is no hope that way," he said.

"Then there is no hope at all. Where are your laws, if we leave him now? Where is justice in that? Is it your King's will that you leave your friend, his most loyal servant, to die? Don't tell me there isn't hope. I have not seen Breac dead, and until I do, I *must* hope!"

Mykell paced. "Perhaps you are right. How can I tell? This is an evil day... an evil mission from the beginning."

"Well I'm telling you what's right. Are you going to help me, or not?"

Mykell stopped pacing. "We can't just walk in there."

"Tell me."

"We do not know the way. And any way we choose will be guarded. This is a fortress."

"It's a mountain," Eve said, looking toward the jagged peak, black against the sky. "How do you get inside a mountain?"

"You don't"

"We have to get to it, first," she said.

"You'd better have a rope."

They went back to the campsite, and Evie found a rope among Breac's things, which she slung over her shoulders, and a long knife that she fastened to her belt. She took one of the water bottles and a few packages of food, then went carefully through her purse. She'd never been inside a mountain before, let alone a cursed mountain fortress. What would they need? Definitely not a cell phone. She tossed the long dead phone into the bushes, along with key ring and pocketbook, though she thought twice about those. Next went her sunglasses. She kept the folding pocket tool with its pliers and knives and screwdrivers. The small amount of food went in the purse, along with a few other things she had chosen, then she lengthened the strap to make it a shoulder bag.

Mykell went sniffing about in the brush and came back with Breac's sword in his teeth. Evie wrinkled her nose at it. "How exactly am I supposed to carry that? That thing weighs like forty pounds."

Mykell carried it the few yards to the road, and stuck it point first in the dirt, pressing it down with his paws until it stood up like Excalibur sticking out of the rock. "Perhaps it will come home to him."

With their horses gone, Evie and Mykell set off on foot toward Al Kazam. Within an hour the trees had thinned, and they stood at the foot of the mountain. Evie looked up at the steep slope, rising to sheer rock cliffs hundreds of feet above their heads, and repeated her question. "How do you get inside a mountain?"

Mykell lifted his paw, pointing toward the ruins of a temple. "Look." It rose from the side of the mountain, its foundation a stepped pyramid, with the top forming a broad, open courtyard rimmed with massive stone columns. The columns supported what was left of a dome roof. Crumbling megaliths shaped a half circle on the slope beneath the temple.

Evie eyed the ruins, scowling as though she could stare them down. She huffed a breath. "We can start there—I guess." She popped her knuckles, hitched the coil of rope up her shoulder, and started walking, feeling like a bug as they passed under the shadow of the megaliths. Mykell stalked after her, all the fur standing up along his back. She paused, winded, at the foot of the pyramid, and looked up. From this angle she couldn't see the top.

"Best to keep moving. The longer we linger here, the more likely we will be spotted. Leazor is bound to have lookouts somewhere."

Evie's skin prickled. "What about the Ezomrah?" she said quietly.

Mykell looked pained as he said, "They will not be long in finding us. They are drawn to you."

"And when they do?"

"Then our fate is at the mercy of a gracious Creator. I suggest, human, that you sing whatever songs you remember from the Book of Kantra. Sing them softly, or to yourself, but have them always in your mind. That is your only shield."

Evie touched her face with her fingertips. Her skin had gone suddenly cold. Her mind scrambled to recall any of the songs. She started mumbling the first one she could remember as she began to climb.

The steps leading to the top of the temple were moss covered and crumbling. Their edges broke away under her feet as she scrambled up, forcing her to use her hands. Mykell leapt up after her. Finally they stood at the top, looking out over the valley. To the north another mountain faced them across a great expanse. It stood black against the bright morning sky.

"The King's mountain," Mykell said. "We are close."

Evie turned and looked back the way they had come. She could see the swamp, yellowish and steaming in the cool morning, and the burnt forest, with smoke still rising in places. Beyond, the dark cliffs drew a line separating this place from the good land full of blessing. Most of the naiad river was hidden in the lowlands on the other side of the cliffs, but to the east a bend brought it back into view, twinkling faintly before it was lost to sight behind Al Kazam. Off in the blue distance she imagined a little inn, where two sisters kept evil away with their songs. *Sing for us today, Tyra and Ylva. Your Aindreas needs you.*

She turned and walked through the rubble of the fallen roof, stepping around mossy blocks the size of a washing machine.

"Look."

Another altar sat in the center of the courtyard, a single huge block of polished black crystal. Panic, and dank, cold air swirled around her as she circled it. In the daylight the crystal did not appear beautiful at all. Only evil. Or perhaps that was her perception. On the far side of it a black hole opened before her feet, and foul air blasted up into her face. She flinched as Mykell leapt up onto the altar. From there he peered down into the hole.

"You don't want to go down there," he said.

"I have to. That's probably the only way to get in without knocking on their door."

"That is where they cast their victims, after they were sacrificed. And there could well be sentries below."

Her hands shook as she took the coil of rope from around her shoulders. "It's a good thing we brought this then."

19

Into Al Kazam

Mykell shook his head, muttering, as Evie piled her things onto the crystal altar. She selected one of the ruined pillars that looked like it would hold her weight without crumbling and secured the rope around it, then tested it. She tossed the rest of the coiled rope into the hole and watched it flip and twist down into the darkness.

"Can you turn into something and fly down there, just to see how far it is, and if anything is waiting at the bottom?"

Mykell muttered something under his breath.

"Mykell, wait."

"What now, human?"

She nodded at the altar where she'd dumped their gear. "If I touch it, will something bad happen?"

"No. Not unless there are Ezomrah near. Regardless, you will be protected if you keep the Kantra always in your mind and on your lips. Do not forget that. They cannot stand their Creator's songs."

"Okay."

"May I proceed now?"

"Um, sure."

Grumbling, he jumped up on leathery bat wings, flapped crazily for a moment, and then vanished down in. A moment later he came back, squeaking and chirping.

"I hope you're not saying words, 'cause I can't understand you."

He stretched down, and grew, and was a panther again. "It isn't extremely deep. About fifty feet. But..."

"But what?"

"I couldn't tell where the floor actually started."

Evie looked at him, her forehead wrinkling as her eyebrows went up. "I'll be able to make it that far," she said, afraid to ask. "You want to come back up here and untie the rope once I'm down so I can take it with me?"

"Fine."

"Okay." She looked at him, and the fear she'd been trying to squelch rose up and nearly choked her. "What's gonna happen in there?"

Mykell sat on his haunches and lifted one sleek black paw to touch her hand. "Only what the Creator allows," he said. "This is a strange journey we are on. Who can say what the purpose is? I was very sure at the beginning. But now even I question if there may be more in it than we can see. Does that comfort you?"

The corner of her mouth lifted in a halfhearted smile. "I'm not sure."

"It does me," he said. "And perhaps you were right about going after Breac. Here has been provided a way when I thought there was no way, and that is most encouraging to me. But we should go. If there is any hope for either of you it is in speed."

"Yeah."

Evie slung the purse and the water skin back around her shoulders and grabbed the rope. The long knife at her belt clanked against stone as she sat on the edge of the pit. The cold air coming up at her smelled stale. It stank like mold and decay, though judging by the ruined temple, no sacrifice could have been tossed down for thousands of years. She tucked the book of Kantra in her waistband behind her back, squirming until it felt comfortable. She looped the rope around one foot, holding it tight with the other to help take some of the pressure off her arms. Tightening her grip on the rope, she began to lower herself down. Her head dropped below the floor. Mykell, once again a bat, followed her, his squeaks echoing off the narrow walls as they descended. He swooped past her face, and she jerked back, making the rope sway. Her foot slipped, and for a moment she hung on only with her hands. Her arms and hands burned. For a desperate moment she struggled to get the rope looped around her foot again. Finally she succeeded, and hung there for a few seconds, trembling.

"Don't do that!"

She took a deep breath, and began inching her way downward again. How far had she come? She looked up and was surprised how far away the patch of light appeared already. Her feet scraped against something, and she held on with her hands again, trying to feel the floor. Whatever was under her crunched and shifted. She could find no solid footing, yet could go no further.

"Tell me that isn't bones," she whispered. "Please tell me."

Mykell flapped around, squeaking unintelligibly. She lowered herself further, feeling the bones, or whatever they were, shifting and giving way around her legs until she was up to her knees. Her arms ached, and her hands, even with gloves on, felt raw. She tried to lower herself more, and her hands slipped, plunging her to the chest in scraping, shifting skeletons. She could feel a scream trying to rise in her throat. The whole mass began to shift with her weight, sliding, rolling, pulling her along with it. The pit ended in a steep slope, falling down a passage that led deeper and further into the mountain. Thousands of skeletons had been piled at the bottom of the pit, settling down on top of each other. Now with Evie's weight on top, everything gave way, cascading down the steep tunnel, carrying her along, helpless.

Further into the mountain she slid. Being heavier than the bones, she kept sinking down in the pile. Ribs, and pieces of arms and legs rattled around her face. Little things like fingers bumped along underneath, and around and over top rolled the skulls. One struck the top of her head, drawing a yelp. As everything picked up speed, the bones bounded past her. Her rear end connected with earth, slowing her progress. She rolled, tucked into a fetal position, scraping arms, hands, hips and knees until finally she skidded to a stop. She lay curled up still covering her head as the cascade continued around her, bones smacking into her back.

The horrible rush subsided finally, though echoes still rumbled up and down the tunnel. Mykell swooped down, fluttered around her head, and landed, growing back to his panther form. She put her arms around his neck and buried her face in his fur.

"Are you hurt?" he asked.

"No."

He sighed. "That was not good."

She shook her head without taking her face out of his fur. The smell of sunlight and dragon smoke lingered on him.

"Let's not wait to find out what might have just been awakened, shall we? When I said there could be sentries at the bottom, I did not mean that they had to be human."

She pulled her face away from his side. "What about the rope?"

"I will get it. Remember, keep the Kantra in your mind. Especially now."

He swooped up the tunnel again, and disappeared. Evie shivered. She looked around, and could see no more than a few feet farther along. She tried to think of the words to one of the songs, any of the songs. But echoes from her tumble still rippled back to her, sounding like a whispering army on the march. She curled up tighter, and imagined what kinds of horrible beasts could be lurking down here, guarding the pit. An instant later she heard wings flapping down the tunnel, to be replaced in a moment with soft footfalls. Mykell appeared out of the gloom with the end of the rope in his teeth. She took it and silently began to coil it up again.

"We should go," Mykell said.

Evie slung the rope over her shoulder and stood. They continued down the tunnel, stumbling over scattered bones as the weak light faded to black.

* * * * *

Breac had stared into the dragon's eyes, and realized the beast was being controlled, assumedly by Leazor. The eyes were glassed over, and a white film distorted the black slit of a pupil. So this had been their enemy's plan.

He thought of that day on the battlefield, when he had looked beyond the edge of death, and found his heart's desire. He had expected to die there, and he expected to die here, bitten in half, or burnt. His whole body throbbed from the dragon's blow, but instead of dispatching him right then, the monster extended its talons and grabbed him up. He felt ribs crack in the clawed grip, and pain knifed through his chest. He struggled to loosen the claws, knowing it was no use. His breath came short, and for an instant he panicked, but then lack of air robbed him even of that, and he hung senseless.

He was vaguely aware when the dragon landed and released him. Air flooded back into his lungs, and he gasped, coming fully awake. He'd been dropped on his side on a flat stone. His chest felt like fire, and his head throbbed. He rolled onto his belly, his face pressed against the cold floor, and focused on breathing.

Claws scratched against stone, and hot, foul air puffed against his back. He pushed up and got his knees under him, then stayed there, bent over panting, waiting for the dragon to strike. There would be more pain, and then, hopefully, death. Nothing happened.

He straightened up slowly, and turned his head to see the monster crouched a few yards away, eyeing him with one glazed orb. He saw that they were in a cave, the ceiling barely high enough to accommodate the dragon's hunched form. As he watched, the white film over its eye disappeared, revealing the pupil, shaped like an elongated diamond, rimmed in orange. It blinked, and shuffled backward toward the cave entrance, huffing a small jet of flame before it turned and dropped away out of sight.

Breac was alone for the moment. He staggered to his feet and shuffled to the edge of the cave. The floor ended abruptly in a sheer cliff. He leaned against the wall, holding his ribs, looking out over Leazor's reeking lands.

"And the Faire Land must wait for another day, or another hour," he said.

What was Evie doing now? Had she escaped? Perhaps gone back to her own world? Or perhaps Mykell lived, and was taking her on to Al Acatra alone. He groaned. *Evie, oh Evie. I cannot help you now. I would have tried. I would have given everything for you...*

A low rumble signaled the opening of a door in the back of the cave. He turned to see half a dozen soldiers file through. They crowded around him, grabbing him, lashing his wrists together behind his back. He winced as they shoved him toward the door.

They descended a long, sloping tunnel, burrowing far down into this mountain that had been cursed of old. The High King had relinquished his power here, and Breac knew that no magic could now save him.

He could hardly breathe as they led him for hours through the tunnels, some lit with torches, some utterly dark. He reeled, drunk on pain, bumping into his guards and drawing curses. One struck him in the face, and he went to his knees and was drug for awhile. At last the tunnel leveled out. It ended in a barred iron door. One of the soldiers lifted aside the bolt, and they entered a low stone room lit with a single guttering torch on the far wall. Shackles hung from the walls, and in the center of the room, a familiar slab of black crystal, stained reddish-brown.

A soldier cut the rope from his hands, to be replaced with iron cuffs and chain. They took his cloak and left him there alone.

He slumped back against the damp, cold wall. His whole body ached, and he struggled to breathe with his hands shackled above his head, even though they were loose. He could smell burning grease from the torch above his head, and from all around, the stench of putrefying blood. His stomach rolled in protest, and his vision spun.

He let his head fall forward, muttering.

"Failed. Evie, the King, Acatra Dahma. My Creator, I have tried. Was there no other way? Will you raise up another to finish my work? A protector for Evie who would do for her what I would have done?" He groaned, his pain complete.

"You see now why I have no need to torture my prisoners," a voice said.

Breac lifted his head to see Leazor standing by the door, though he hadn't heard him enter.

The Traitor was not alone. On his shoulder sat a brown song sparrow, and a cat came purring around the side of the altar, rubbing itself against the corners. Other shadowy creatures slunk into the corners. They all had black, bottomless eyes, all fastened on Breac. Ezomrah.

"Each man is tormented with his own guilt or failure," Leazor said. He gave a low, melodic laugh as he came around the altar. He wore a black cloak over a tight fitting white shirt, an ornate sword, with matching scabbard and belt, and high laced boots over blue trousers. With his hair slicked back he looked younger than Breac. "You seem especially tormented. To be sent on a mission that was, shall I say, painful to begin with. And now there is no way out for you. Either you see the woman you love killed, or your country handed over to me."

Leazor sat on the edge of the altar, folded his arms, and crossed his feet. The cat leapt up beside him. "Would it be so bad? Really? Serving me? You wouldn't be in this position right now, that's certain. Torn between two loves." He smiled. "Poor Breac. You could just love her you know. Run away with her to her own world, and forget about all this."

"We both know that's a lie," Breac said.

Leazor shrugged. "Very well." He pushed himself from the altar and paced, appearing deep in thought. There was something hypnotic about the Traitor. He looked young and handsome, regal even. Like a prince. He certainly did not seem evil now. There were no dark flames about him, as Breac had seen, or imagined he had seen, on the battlefield. Even in a crowd he would be hard not to watch. But watching him was making Breac even dizzier, so he gave up and let his head hang down again. The Traitor wanted him dead. Why could he not hurry and get it over with? Must he toy with Breac like a child?

"Has the King ever mentioned to you what happens to the victims of his justice?"

Breac made no reply.

"I take it he has not. Well, it's only fair you should know, since it is your lady love that's condemned to die. You see, his servants are under the illusion that when they die, they will go to some mystical, wonderful place. I don't know much about that. I've not been on speaking terms with your King in well over three thousand years."

Breac said without looking up, "I've been there... almost. Thanks to you. Even you, Leazor, cannot imagine it."

Leazor waved him off. "Fine, fine. That's wonderful for you. Unfortunately, your lady love can never hope to go there. Not if she dies the death of a traitor, as your precious law demands." He shook his head sadly. "No... I'm afraid to be slain on the Altar of

Justice means far more than a quick death. It means that you die with a curse on you. Ask the King if you like, or perhaps I can show you. Either way, it's not very pretty. To be forever in darkness, fully aware of the Fire Worms that gnaw your flesh, and can never consume you, because you're already dead."

Breac lifted his head slowly. His shaggy hair hung over his face, dark with sweat. He stared past it at the Traitor and wheezed, "You lie."

Leazor shook his head. "No, this time I am telling you the truth. Come, I'll show you. Those who are accursed from the Creator, Breac, are in my power. And here, in this place that is cursed, you are in my power too."

"Only as long as I'm alive."

"True. I admit I can do nothing to you after you're dead, even here. But I can still create for you a living death. Come," he curled his finger, as though to summon Breac, though he was still chained to the wall. Breac felt himself lift away from the wall and the ground, but the chains tugged him to a halt.

"None of that," Leazor said. "Let him go."

The shackles released, and Breac slammed down on top of the altar. He grunted and tried to roll away, but the pain in his chest and head nearly blinded him. Chains at the corners snaked out of their own accord to fasten his wrists and ankles down.

"I'm disappointed, Breac," Leazor said. "I thought you would have asked by now why you are here, why I have singled you out to show hospitality in my home."

"It doesn't matter."

"Ha! You are right. It doesn't." He paced beside the altar. "I will kill you, and prophesies will no longer matter. No one will be able to defeat me. Your girl will die in her own world at the hands of my servants, and I will have the rule, unchallenged. Or even if justice is done on the girl, better to have this land go free a little longer, than have you free to be fulfilling prophecy. It pains me to kill you and send you to your rest. So for comfort, I will first give you a sample of what Eva Drake will be going through for all eternity."

Leazor stopped by Breac's head, and glanced around at the Ezomrah. "Friends," he said. Every last creature of them vanished. Leazor stretched out his hand over the man's face. Breac was at once plunged into darkness.

20

Leazor's Altar

There came a moment, even with her eyes adjusted, that there simply was no more light. Not the merest shadow or hint of gray. Evie stopped and waved her hand in front of her face.

"Can you see anything?" she asked Mykell.

"No."

She took a cautious step forward—and smashed her head off a low hanging rock.

"Ow!"

"Shh!"

"What if I step in a hole like that?"

"Maybe I should go first," Mykell said.

"Maybe you should. At least you can fly if you have to."

They started again, and this time Evie went forward with her hand in front of her face. She found that the rock she'd banged her head off of was not alone. The whole tunnel roof started getting lower, and the walls closed in. She brushed slick rock on one side, and bounced off a jagged outcropping on the other.

"Ow. Is it just gonna get narrower till it ends?" she wondered out loud.

"We shall see."

"Maybe that's why nothing was guarding the hole. 'Cause it really doesn't lead into the mountain."

After awhile she began to wonder if it had been a few minutes, or a few hours that they had been in the tunnel. She was forced to creep along, holding one hand above her head to feel for rocks. Her shoulders and hips scraped against the walls, and still the tunnel sloped down and down. Her skin crawled, and her chest constricted. Her breaths came hard and fast.

"Calm yourself, human. Your panic will not help Breac."

"I hate small places that I can't get out of," she replied. "What if I get stuck, or the tunnel stops, and I have to crawl out backward, uphill, all this distance? I'd never make it."

"You have me to pull you out," Mykell said. "This tunnel is the very least of my concerns, and the least threat to you."

Eventually she noticed that they were no longer going downhill. And that she no longer brushed against the walls and roof. Within a few minutes she was able to walk upright again. They passed an opening on the right, and then one on the left. Passages became more frequent, and they could always feel air moving out of them, sometimes freezing cold, sometimes hot like the blast from a furnace. Mykell stopped and sniffed at each one, but he gave no hint at what he might have learned. Every time they passed an opening she feared they should have taken it. But they kept on.

"This is madness," Mykell hissed. "We have no idea where we're going."

Evie sniffed in the dark, and stopped. "I don't know. We have to be getting somewhere. You're the one smelling the way."

"And I assure you, I have not smelled anything promising. I wonder we haven't heard any noise of people or animals. Leazor must keep troops here."

They continued walking for what seemed like hours, until Mykell stopped short. Evie almost fell over him

"What?" she asked. "Why'd you stop?"

"Listen."

They both held their breaths. A slight tap reached them, from the rock all around, then another and another. Evie put her ear against the wall.

"It's a rhythm," she breathed.

She could hear Mykell sniffing, the sound moving up the

tunnel as he took a few more steps.

"Is it safe to keep going?" Evie asked.

Mykell laughed shortly. "Safe? You jest."

"You knew what I meant."

"Did I? You humans can be insufferable. If you meant: 'Is this threat an immediate one', then why did you not ask that?" He let out a growly sigh and continued muttering to himself, his voice moving further up the tunnel, leaving Evie to follow.

"Always saying one thing and meaning another. It is no great wonder mankind is the most disagreeable, argumentative, violent race of sentient beings in the created universe. Even when they aren't lying, they seem all but incapable of expressing any kind of coherent communication. Do they ever truly understand one another? Creator knows there are times when they are beyond my comprehension...."

He stopped again, and as if she hadn't learned from the last time, Evie fell over him, sprawling on her belly across his back, while her head and flailing arms struck the floor. She rolled off and hit the wall.

"Ow! Mykell! Stop doing that!" She sat up, rubbing her elbow and forehead.

"Quiet! Can't you hear that?"

"Hear what?"

"Hush up and listen."

Evie listened, trying to tune out the pounding in her head, but could hear nothing. She wanted to strangle Mykell. "I don't hear anything."

"Put your ear to the wall."

"Oh good grief!" But she put her head to the wall, and this time could hear a faint, eerie melody.

After another hour or so of creeping forward, she said, "There's a light."

"I see it," Mykell hissed.

The tunnel ended suddenly in an iron door. The merest crack of light came from underneath it, but in that utter darkness it seemed like a brilliant sun. Evie and Mykell looked around. They could hear men's voices from the other side of the door, laughing, singing, cursing. Mykell sniffed at the crack of light, and shrank down to a mouse so he could peer under, though even as a mouse he couldn't fit through. He turned back to a panther.

"What's there?" Evie whispered.

"A dozen soldiers, off duty. It's a bunkhouse."

"Does it go anywhere?"

"You mean maybe to another door?"

"I mean does it look promising?"

"Not especially."

Evie groaned. "This is hopeless."

The door swung open suddenly, letting out a blinding flood of torchlight. She and Mykell both jumped back. A soldier stood framed in the light, sword in hand. His fellows crowded behind.

"How did you get here?" the soldier said.

Mykell leapt forward. "Run! I'll find you!"

Evie didn't wait to hear more. She turned and fled back the way they'd come. She could see the tunnel faintly in the light from the open door. There was a split ahead that she did not remember passing, one passage going left, the other right. She ran left, and the tunnel turned sharply, leaving her once again in pitch dark. She stopped, panting, and listened. She could hear shouts far away, and a panther's scream that made her breath catch. It was colder here. Cold enough to make her shiver. Crouching, she felt ahead with her hands, and found that the ground sloped down. It was littered with rubble. This was not the way they had come. Should she continue, or go back? They couldn't go farther the way they had been going anyway, and surely Mykell would be able to smell her out, and if the worst came, smell their way back. If he lived.

She walked a few more paces and stopped. She was utterly alone here, yet had the crawly feeling that she was not alone. She couldn't see anything at all, and heard nothing more than the distant commotion. Was Mykell still alive? If not she would never be able to find her own way out. One might wander these tunnels forever, until they died of hunger, or fell in a hole, or were captured by Leazor. She continued walking. *Don't want to think about that. Not yet.*

Evie didn't know what it was that made her stop. Nothing had changed about the tunnel, she heard no noise, yet her skin crawled. She could feel something. A *presence.*

She turned back. "Mykell?"

There might have been the faintest hiss of breath through fangs.

"Is that you?"

No reply.

She took a step backward and waited, her mind scrambling for any of the songs of the Kantra. In the silence there came a faint footfall, not three yards away. Cold panic spread through her veins like poison. She wanted to scream, but dared not. She wanted to run, but what exactly might pursue? What lay further on in the tunnel that she had been traveling? Her hand gripped the hilt of the knife in her belt, ready to pull it out, shaking. "*Creator defend me, answer my call,*" her mind fumbled with the words. "*Muscle, sinew, steel and claw...*"

She took another step backwards, further into the tunnel, and her foot turned on a rock. Her hand shot out to steady herself against the wall, but there was no wall. She pitched sideways, and fell, felt rocks grind under her as she slid down another few feet. She heard a slobbering hiss, and felt a puff of hot air across her face. She screamed. Sliding still further down the slope, now very steep, her feet shot out over the edge of a drop off of some kind. How far of a drop? What was at the bottom? She scrabbled desperately at the ground, trying to get up and get her knees under her. The effort took her further down, until most of her weight was over the edge. Hot breath followed her, and a close hiss. She slid down, and felt sharp claws reach out for her, tearing her gloves and the backs of her fingers. The ground slipped away, and she fell with a shriek.

The shriek was cut short when she plunged into deep, frigid water.

Her head broke the surface, and she gasped, cried out, and sank again. Again she came up, fighting to swim against the deathly cold. Her eyes popped out for any light, any hope to grasp for. There came a splash not four feet away. Something heavy bumped against her legs, swirling the water around her. She yelped, but the movement turned her, and she caught sight of a light. Her eyes fastened on it like a lifeline, and she struck out toward it, floundering as her muscles refused to work in the freezing water. The yellow light reflected faintly off the surface, glinting on the ripples she was making. Hers were the only movements in the still, cold lake. But she was not alone.

Come down, Evie. Come down to me. Down, down into the deep.

Ezomrah! They had found her. She tried to swim faster. The cold made her clumsy and slow. Her chin sank, and she paddled furiously to stay up. The light was close. Just above her.

You cannot fight the cold and the darkness. You are the darkness! Your soul is cursed and cold and lifeless. So come down to me.

The light from the tunnel above ended as she swam into the shadow of a sheer blank wall. She leapt up to grab the edge, but came at least a foot short. The creature bumped her legs again, spinning her back away from the wall. Unbearable laughter rippled through her mind like madness. She tasted blood. Saw the flames. It was going to take her.

A dull pain in her ankle barely registered until she felt herself being pulled under. She flailed. Her hand slapped the knife at her side, and she struggled to pull it free as water closed over her head. Her whole body went numb. Gurgling filled her ears, and insane laughter. A pinch in her arm, pulling her down further. She held the long knife in her other hand, and thrust with it, felt resistance as it met flesh, and stabbed deeper, twisting the blade with all her strength. A squeal of pain enveloped her as warm blood saturated the water. Her head shot up out of the water, and she gasped horrible choking breaths. With an effort she unlocked her hand from the knife. So cold. She could barely move. She let herself sink down, down.

Come lightning protect me,
Thunder round all
Ward from me the evil things,
Creator hear my call.

She surged upward. Her arm struck the edge of the tunnel above, and her fingers caught hold. Her body slammed into the wall, and she hung there, shaking violently, her face pressed against the cold rock. She gasped and sobbed and thought she would fall again and be lost. She grasped the edge with her other hand and heaved upward a few inches. Her fingers found purchase in a groove in the tunnel floor. She got an elbow over the edge and rested there an instant. Then wriggling, straining, got her belly over the edge, then her knee. She rolled onto the hard stone floor, and curled up. Her mind was shutting down. Sounds of dripping water and hard breathing melding with flickering light of torches. She knew not whether she was awake or unconscious. All she knew was that she was shaking, and could not stop.

Get up!

She swatted feebly at the annoying thought.

Evie Drake, get up now, or as I live, I will knock you senseless when I find you.

She stirred. "Mykell?" Her soft question went unanswered in the empty corridor.

Sing songs of the Kantra. Think of Breac.

She murmured the first line of the healing song. The healing would not work here in Leazor's dungeons, but the tune was there for her. Somehow the words reached through the fog in her mind. She knew suddenly that she must get up and move. She must get warm. She pushed herself off the ground, and looked down. She'd been lying in a puddle of watery blood. Her sleeve and one shoe were soaked with it. She felt too weak to stand, but got to her knees and started crawling. Her purse and water skin dragged the floor beside her, elongating the pattern of blood. Still she muttered the song.

The light grew stronger. She pushed herself upright, leaning against the wall, took a torch out of one of the brackets. Kneeling, she held it between her knees, warming her hands over its flame until her fingers would work. Stumbling to her feet again, she clumsily replaced the torch and kept going, pressing a hand around the growing pain in her arm. The thing must have bitten her. She'd been too cold and numb hardly to feel it. Her ankle stung now too, but at least she could still walk.

This tunnel was much smoother than the one on the other side of the lake, the rock under her feet polished with use. Stronger light came from an opening up ahead. When she reached it she looked down a passage lit with torches. No signs of life here. She followed the light, every second looking over her shoulder, expecting there to be soldiers coming up behind. Or there might be more Ezomrah. But it might mean she was closer to Breac.

The passage split into two, and she stopped and looked around again. One direction it sloped up into a shadow of growing darkness. The other direction it bent down and away into growing light. She turned toward the light. She would not go back into darkness, and if she stopped, the cold would overcome her. Turning a last corner she found that the tunnel ended abruptly at a barred iron door.

Evie eased back and leaned against the wall. A door barred on the outside could mean a dungeon. And what would a dungeon mean? Breac might be there, or he might be dead. There would probably be soldiers, or worse things. She should wait for Mykell. But was Mykell still alive? Would he be able to find her after her fall into the lake? She closed her eyes, squeezing her arm. Blood slicked her fingers. Real blood this time, and pain to go with it.

The door taunted her. She must open it, but dared not. After another long look around she moved over to it, and stood with her ear against the rough metal, listening. There might have been a moan, or it could have been the ancient, shifting mountain. A fit of recklessness seized her. It was only a matter of time before she was dead anyway. If she could see Breac one last time, if he was behind that door, then she would try. She eased the bar up with one hand and lifted it away, leaning it against the wall, careful to make no sound. She pushed the door with her fingertips, and it opened silently inward. Yet another crystal altar sat in the center of the room and shackles hung from thick chains on the wall. The door kept swinging, revealing the man chained to the altar. And it was indeed Breac.

* * * * *

Leazor's hand covered Breac's face, and a deep, involuntary shudder went through him. He felt his eyes roll back, and darkness surrounded him, a darkness that he could feel. He lost the sensation of Leazor's hand, of the shackles that bound him, and of the cold altar under him. He was falling. He jerked, but it didn't stop. Then the first bite of fiery pain assaulted him, like white hot teeth tearing off his skin. He recoiled, writhing, but shackles still held him, though he could not feel them. Another sting of pain, and another, until his whole body burned. He felt his flesh was being eaten, torn away, igniting with unseen flame that would not cease. He screamed a raw, desperate scream of agony, and could not stop, though the sound was lost in an utter void. He could not endure. His heart would stop, and he would die, and all would be over. But it did not stop.

* * * * *

Evie froze, gaping in horror. She looked around the room and back down the tunnel, and saw no one. She rushed to the altar, but shied back from touching Breac. His eyes were rolled back in the sockets, open and unseeing, his jaw clenched, lips peeled back against grinding white teeth. His whole body was rigid, back arched and arms straining up against the chains.

She touched his hand, and felt his skin fiery hot, almost too hot to touch, and not sweating, but dry as ash. He showed no acknowledgement of her touch. She put her hands on his face, ran her fingers through his hair, uncaring that she was smearing her blood on him. "Breac," she whispered. "Come back! Pease come back. What can I do?"

She took a deep breath, recalled one of the songs of the Kantra to keep in her mind, and hoisted herself up onto the altar beside him. "Looks like we'll be dying here together now, doesn't it?" she muttered, pulling the Book of Kantra from her belt. She laid it on his chest, watching for any change. When none came she continued, shrugging her purse off, and then carefully peeling out of her dripping outer shirt. Underneath she still wore her black tank top. She sucked air through her teeth as the cloth pulled free of her arm. The sight of so much of her own blood made her queasy. Her hands were already covered in it, but they had been torn up by the Ezomrah's claws before she fell in the lake, and still oozed. A double row of puncture wounds ringed her arm just below the elbow. *That thing must've had one massive mouthful of teeth,* she thought, wrapping the shirt around her arm the best she could. Nothing more she could do about it now. Probably wouldn't live too much longer down in this hole anyhow.

Evie opened the book. Soggy on the outside, the text seemed undamaged by the water. She murmured the song of healing, already knowing that it would do nothing. Once again the words and melody came to her, but there was no coursing power. No blessed healing remained in the air of this cursed mountain. Frustration burned in her, warming her a little.

"No! Don't do this to me!" Forgetting the need for silence, she screamed the words at the crystal veined ceiling. "If you're so powerful, why don't you help him, High King! Is this how you take care of your friends?" she threw the book against the wall with all her strength. "What do I do?!"

21

The Kantra

Another long moment of horror passed. Watching the man on the altar. Watching the door. Icy panic shuddered through her. Her scalp prickled with the feeling of an unearthly gaze resting on her. She could barely breathe past the scream building in her chest. She wanted *out*. Weak, wounded, cold, and alone, she slumped over Breac's body. Too frightened to cry. She could never find her way out alone. Mykell was probably dead. Breac was held in some sort of spell. The torches on the wall guttered with a wind she could not feel.

Alone.

She still had the feeling of being watched, and remembering Mykell's warning, muttered a few lines of song, not even hearing the words. She felt suddenly that she must have the book back. Sliding off the altar, she went to pick it up, almost panicked that something would happen before it was in her hands.

The damp leather cover felt reassuring, and holding it she felt a little less alone. It had fallen near the door, and as she straightened, she saw a ring of keys hanging on a peg just outside. She stared at them in disbelief for a moment, then reached for them, taking another look down the tunnel. It still appeared deserted, and no sound echoed down the walls.

It took several tries, kneeling on the altar with the heavy iron keys shaking in her hands before finally the shackles released. No way would she be able to get Breac down from the altar without dropping him, so she sat down cross-legged and lifted his head to rest in her lap. She laid the book on the altar beside them and flipped it open. It fell open somewhere in the middle, and she began to read or to sing whatever was before her.

Feeling tired and sick, she read several pages without even trying to comprehend the words. They might have been an introduction, but her only thought was that she must read. So she read on, while the unnatural heat from Breac's body slowly seeped into her, easing a little of her chill and bringing her strength back. She came to a song. It covered the page that lay open, and continued, how far she didn't know, for she wouldn't flip ahead. She started reading without hesitation, and halfway through the first line, the words had turned to notes. She sang.

Like the first morning of creation,
Cool sunlight on sparkling dew,
Perfect song, rising from the garden.
All is bright, everything new.

With the dawn man goes to his labor
To work until the day is done.
Praising his Maker for each blessing,
Then rests till rising of the sun.

The sun is setting, moon is rising,
Night, for beasts to seek their prey.
The constellations spread above him
Guide a traveler on his way.

Creation flows in perfect rhythm,
Day and night, season and year,
This song of the master Creator,
Sung for all His works to hear.

Whatever evil spell hung over this place, stifling the power of the Kantra, it could not touch the enchantment of the book itself. Evie sang as she never had before, without restraint or hesitation.

Without even the restrictions of humanity, for she sang both deep and high without straining, though her voice cracked a few times with emotion.

She looked up at a sudden movement. A cat crouched before her, staring with bottomless black eyes. It had appeared from nowhere, just on the other side of Breac's body. She jumped, and her heart thudded, but the song had hold of her voice, and she could not stop singing. The cat bared its razor teeth at her, its ears back flat. A murmur of evil passed through her mind, but the words were lost to the song. She and the cat stared at one another with huge eyes. After another moment of singing though, it jumped off the altar and ran from the room.

She looked down at Breac again, and his face had relaxed just a little. He looked like he was listening. She touched his face, and ran her hands through his hair, but she could not have stopped singing if she had wanted to.

It happened again. This time it was a sparrow, with the same menacing black eyes. Four more times as the song progressed. The Ezomrah appeared out of nowhere, only to run away down the tunnel.

By the end of the second verse Breac's whole body had begun to relax. At the third his jaw unclenched, and he heaved a ragged sigh. His eyes closed, and sweat broke out on his face. He breathed hard now, almost crying, shuddering, but he was back.

Finally the song drew to a stop and released her voice. She set the book down, and bent over Breac.

"Wake up!" she begged. "Please! Wake up... Breac. I love you."

He opened his eyes and stared at her. There was not a hint of confusion in his gaze. He knew exactly who she was, where they were, and why, but his look was full of unutterable despair. He moved an arm, found it free, and pulled her down to him. He clung to her and sobbed.

For a long time they held each other, neither moving. When Breac spoke, his voice was broken and rasping.

"I'm so sorry, Evie. I love you..."

* * * * *

Mykell found them like that a few minutes later. He appeared in the door like a black shadow, nose to the ground smelling the way. He raised his head, his whiskers and ears drooping with relief.

"You're alive." He looked back over his shoulder before coming to stand before the altar, head lowered. "Forgive me. I had no hope of finding you alive, and would have gone on, but for Evie. I have done you wrong friend, servant of my King."

Breac drew a shuddering breath and sat up, hugging an arm around his ribs as he eased himself off the altar. Evie slid down and stood beside him. He put his other arm around her.

"There is nothing to forgive," Breac said. "You would have carried on the mission, and the future of this country is far more important than my life. Still, I thank you."

Mykell opened his mouth to respond, but stopped, listening. His ears and whiskers flattened back, and his hide quivered.

"He is coming," he hissed.

Breac closed his eyes for just an instant. "No..."

They all looked to the doorway, where a shadow loomed, flickering on the wall outside. The next instant the enemy, Leazor, stood in the door. He surveyed them all with a small smile.

"Very good."

Breac tightened his arm around Evie, pulling her back until they stopped against the altar. She gripped the edge, and felt the book brush her hand. Grabbing it, she clung to it with both hands, holding it like a shield before her. Leazor took two huge steps and slapped it away.

"I don't like that book," he said. "And do not think that it will be any use to you here."

Evie felt as though everything had been turned to slow motion. She watched in horrible detail Leazor's handsome face distort in a snarl. She watched the book fall. Watched it land on its spine. Naturally it came open in the middle where it had been a moment ago. One page wavered in the air, undecided. Slowly it drooped over, covering the passage she had just read, and revealing the next two pages. She scanned the words.

Breac pushed her back against the altar as Leazor drew his sword. He stepped in front of her, and Mykell stood at his side, facing the enemy. Evie remembered the confrontation at the *Parrot's Roost* between Breac and Rizann, the battle of wills. Would there be a similar struggle here? But no. No protection, no healing, no blessing remained in this place. They would all be chopped in pieces by Leazor's sword, or fried by lightning. They had come to it at last.

Leazor smiled, his eyes flickering between their faces, delighting in the moment. He raised his sword, drawing lazy circles with it in the air. The air throbbed with power. Dread like she had never known choked Evie, the feeling that hell had come to earth. This time Breac was powerless against it.

She looked back down at the book, her gaze drawn to it. It had no power here, but it still felt like a comfort. The only comfort. The only speck of hope. She didn't dare pick it up, but from where it lay she read, and whispered the words. The whisper became hushed singing.

From depths of sorrow I have cried
My voice in anguish raised.
Terrors surround on every side;
To You my cry is raised.

Leazor began to laugh, his voice covering her frail song.

"Come to me, fear," he said.

Blinding panic surged through Evie. Mykell crouched, cowering, and Breac winced. He glanced back at her and she saw a tear tracking down his face. She would have stopped singing then, and started screaming, but once again the song had hold of her voice, and she was as powerless against it as she was against Leazor's sorcery.

> *Starlight and sunlight have failed me*
> *Darkness swallows my sight.*
> *Yet darkness cannot hide from Thee,*
> *Creator of day and night.*
> *Though in despair, I will wait for You*
> *More than watchmen at the wall,*
> *Waiting for dawn to break anew,*
> *You will hear and answer my call.*

"Come to me, weakness," Leazor said.

Even before she could feel the full effect of the curse, her knees hit the floor. Breac slumped against the altar beside her. Her heart labored, its beat painfully slow as she bowed over, staring down at the open page before her. She struggled to fill her lungs enough to stay alive. The song would not let her go. It stole each precious breath. Her vision swam with dark splotches, but the words stayed focused, and the song kept on. She could no longer control the volume. The melody poured out with force, loud, fierce, strong and piercing. It set the altar vibrating at her back. Breac reached a shaking hand to the book and slid it to where they could both see. His voice joined with hers, not singing in unison, but chanting deep and low. Goosebumps raced up her arms, and her heart leapt with new power. The song rose, unbearable in the tiny room.

> *The Creator of all, he heard me*
> *Delivered me from my fears.*
> *Death is swallowed in victory*

Out of darkness my hope appears.

Leazor glared at them, his rage strong enough to shake the mountain.

"Come to me, death."

My enemies' power He subdued
At His command, all is well.
He restored my soul, my strength renewed
He spoke and the mountains fell.

At the final note, power exploded through the room. A force like lightning snapped through the air, blasting them back against the altar. Leazor slammed into the wall. Another, deeper sound replaced the music. The underground lake, held back by the wall behind them, raged with the vibrations carried through the veins of crystal in the rock. Like an earthquake sweeping through the mountain, the water sent back shockwaves that shattered the crystal seams. Cracks multiplied through the altar. The ground trembled. A huge slab of stone shook loose from the ceiling and crashed down, rocking the earth. Breac took Evie's hand, grabbed the book, and together they ran from the room, following Mykell. Just behind them the altar shattered. A wave of splintered crystal showered around them as they raced back down the tunnel, and turned, following the way that Evie and Mykell had taken. Behind them Leazor roused, screaming his rage. A boulder fell from the roof, blocking the tunnel and their view of the enemy.

They kept running. Before they had turned the final corner they were already splashing through icy lake water. The tunnel was awash in it, laboring their steps. Breac grabbed a torch from the wall. They turned the corner and were almost swept away by the rush of water. Mykell was lifted off his feet, paddling furiously until the swell dropped him.

"The lake is overflowing," he cried. "We can't go this way."

In the torchlight, Evie caught sight of a sleek silver body, carried by the flood. Jaws hung open lifeless, revealing double rows of razor teeth.

They turned the other direction, and looked up onto darkness.

Breac took another torch from the wall, and handed it to her.

"Come on."

22

Through the Tunnels

They ran, leaving the lake behind. Ahead, the tunnel dipped down, the torchlight danced on black water, and they plunged in once again up to the waist. Evie stumbled with the icy shock. Mykell shifted into his bat form and swooped up into the darkness ahead of them. He flew back in a moment, squeaking.

"What?"

He turned back into a panther and landed a few yards in front of them. "The tunnel goes up after this."

After a few wallowing steps the water released them, sloshing around their ankles. The ground rolled, and Evie went to her knees in the shallow water. Her chest ached, felt ready to explode, whether from cold, fear, or pain she didn't know. Breac hauled her to her feet, and she stumbled after him. Behind them a boulder broke loose from the quaking ceiling and crashed into the water where she'd been a moment ago.

The tunnel sloped upward, taking them out of the water, but debris still continued to fall all around them. Dirt rained down, dimming the torchlight in dusty curtains. A rock struck Breac's shoulder. He grunted.

Again the ground heaved. As if dynamite had been set off behind them the tunnel exploded.

Choking dust, thunder in her head and chest. Pain. Her body convulsed. The first thing she truly became aware of was that she was crawling, scrabbling on her hands and knees while the world cracked and rained and thudded around her. She could see nothing.

A hand touched her arm, then gripped it. Her eyes fastened on a tiny red ember in the darkness. One of the torches. She reached toward it, her fingers touched wood, and her hand closed around it even as she was hauled upright and dragged forward, staggering.

"It's not over! Run!" Breac's voice sounded raw and guttural. Laced with pain. More dust and chunks of rock spewed around them.

She forced one foot forward, then the other. Couldn't find a rhythm. Fell again. A wet nose pressed against her face.

"I will carry you, human. Hold onto my fur."

She found Mykell's neck, and wrapped her arms around it. Only for a second. The next second his neck was too thick for her to reach around, and Breac was shoving her onto his back, taking the torch from her hand, and heaving himself up behind her. Mykell, in horse form, surged ahead up the tunnel.

* * * * *

Gradually the rain of debris slowed, then ceased altogether. Mykell eased back into a trot, and then a walk, panting. Breac spoke. "We need to stop."

"There will be pursuit."

"Just for a moment."

Mykell stopped and knelt, and Breac slid off his back, helping Evie gently after him. She was dazed still, and leaned heavily against him. Pain shot through his chest and ribcage as he fumbled in the dark. His boot struck the tunnel wall, and together they sat, leaning their backs against it.

He felt in his pockets for his tiny flint and struck a spark, relighting the torch. Mykell, back in panther form for the moment, held it in his paws while Breac turned to examine the girl.

"Do you know where we are?" she asked, holding a hand against her head, and blinking in the torchlight.

"Only that we are in the tunnels still." He examined first the growing knot on her head, turned her face toward him to see her eyes. They looked normal, as far as he could tell in the dim light. Her arm and ankle were much worse. They still bled freely. He rewrapped her shirt around her arm, tightening it until she gasped, and tied it off. Next he grasped his shirtsleeve and gave it a yank, tearing it off at the shoulder. He wound it around her ankle, shoe and all. She pulled away.

"I'm so cold."

He put his arm around her waist, pulling her close. "What happened?"

"It was Ezomrah, I think. I fell in the lake, and it came after me. It's dead."

"You are fortunate to be alive yourself. Or perhaps your life has a purpose that is not yet fulfilled. The Creator's rule is still intact, even in this place of darkness."

"And that is a comforting thought," Mykell broke in. "But if you wish to keep both of you alive, we had best continue."

She nearly fell when they stood again, and her face scrunched with pain.

"I guess it hurts worse when you're not running for your life." She tried to force a laugh, but managed only a whimper.

Mykell morphed back into his horse form. "We will go faster if you ride."

The ground no longer bucked under them as they continued down the tunnel, Evie riding, Breac walking alongside with the torch. They heard no noise above their own footfalls. The passage curved to the right, branching off into several wider passages. At each one they passed Mykell paused and lowered his head, sniffing first the ground, then the air that breathed out of the openings. He lingered a long time at the last, sniffing, cocking his horse head and looking like an enormous dog as his ears swiveled and his nose twitched.

The tunnel in question was much narrower, the ceiling lower

than the others they had passed, and the one they were following. The torch cast jagged shadows over the floor. The light was too dim to see far, but from what Breac could make out, it seemed to curve up and to the left.

"It's strange," Mykell said. "I smell more outdoor air flowing down this way, but very little scent of humans. I believe this is most likely our shortest way out of the mountain, but why so little used?"

"Unless..." Breac let his voice trail off. Mykell was perking his ears backward now, looking back over his rump down the tunnel.

"We are followed.".

"By what?"

His eyes caught the torchlight, gleaming green. "It's a were-creature of some sort." His form shrank rapidly, back into a panther. Breac caught the girl before her feet touched the ground. "Do not wait for me." He turned and stalked back the way they'd come, vanishing into the dim twilight beyond the torchlight's reach.

With Evie leaning against him they limped into the narrow tunnel, going up around the bend, out of sight of where Mykell had left them, then continued on a little way. He paused to listen, and Evie sank down onto the floor, wincing as she stretched her leg out. He sat painfully beside her.

"How do you feel?"

"I'd say I've been worse, but... I actually don't think I have." She did manage a little laugh this time. "I broke my arm once before, but I don't remember it hurting this bad. At any rate I didn't have to walk on it."

"If Mykell is right, that there is fresh air here, then hopefully we will be out soon. And then perhaps the Book of Kantra will be some help to us."

"Instant healing—I could go for that."

"Perhaps. But more likely a simple renewing of our strength."

She gave him a curious look, but said nothing.

He wanted to offer some kind of encouragement, but the words died before they were ever fully thought of. Hope seemed a ridiculous sentiment in this place of darkness. Still, they had come this far, and that alone was a miracle. The Creator's hand must indeed be on them. He sighed, sending pain shooting through his ribcage.

"Where's Mykell gotten off to?" she muttered.

Breac grimaced as he shifted. He switched the torch from his right hand to his left, making the flame puff and sputter softly.

"He is back there somewhere in the dark, waiting. I would rather have him with us on this mission than a whole company of warriors."

She leaned back against the wall, eyes bright. "Why won't the healing song work here, when the other two did?"

"An excellent question. I've been thinking about that."

"Wait, how could you know I tried to sing the healing song to you? You were unconscious."

"I heard you. Very, very far away your voice came into the void..." his voice trailed off as he remembered the hell she'd pulled him out of. The hell she was bound for herself. He wanted to weep. With an effort he tried to continue. His voice cracked. He cleared his throat and tried again. "There is no blessing in the air of this place. Leazor rules here, and has perverted the mountain so that his poison seeps into the land around. The sulfur, the diseased forest, all come out of this place. However, even though the songs have not their intended effect, they still are unbearable to the Ezomrah, who held my mind. The music forced them to flee."

"And the Altar exploding and everything?"

"That, I believe, was a matter of the sound itself. Sound can be a powerful thing. An energy, a..." he fumbled. "A force."

Her expression cleared with sudden understanding. "Right. I think I get it. Like a sonic boom, or a singer who can shatter glass, or old time crystal radios." Her mind off her pain for a moment, she leaned forward, eyes crinkling with an almost smile. "And the whole dungeon back there was lined with some kind of crystal veins. Maybe that could've carried the sounds to the lake, 'cause that would have been somewhere right behind us. And... oh I don't know."

"You might not be far from the truth. But I know the music, that song, was too big for Leazor's cave. It is meant to be sung in great outdoor amphitheaters, where it will roll like thunder from the hills and whisper through the grasses. That song cannot be confined.

"I think there is more to it than that though. I think that even in this place, singing the Creator's praise ruined Leazor's power. In his pride, he thinks he is very powerful, but he can never be stronger than the One who made him."

Evie leaned back again. In the torchlight her blood looked black, staining the crude bandages like ink. The sight pained him. Without all of her blood being spilled, his country would fall. Was it worth the cost? Was he loyal to his king and his Creator to the point of turning over the woman he loved? He wondered how much of his feeling she shared. Surely she felt something for him. She had said she loved him after their encounter with the river naiads, and she had risked her life to rescue him. But many would risk their life without a thought, for the tiniest thread of hope, as she had done. Risking one's life and laying it down without question were two different matters. Would she follow him to the place of justice?

Did she trust him?

Should it matter? It would not change his decision in the end, yet it did matter to him very much. He couldn't say why. He must know.

"Evie...?"

She looked up and met his gaze.

"Evie, do you trust me?"

Her dark eyebrows drew together in confusion for an instant. She gazed at him steadily, then her eyes lost focus, looking inward.

"Oh Breac..." Her face wrinkled and she covered it with a bloodied hand, crying.

Hearing his name from her lips made his heart twist. But if this was his answer, what did it mean? He thought he knew, and it felt like having the wind kicked out of him.

Should never have asked.

He pushed himself away from the wall and shuffled over to her on his knees. Held her. Felt her cold cheek pressed into his neck, her body convulsing with sobs.

A panther scream made them jerk apart, staring wide eyed. The scream came again, blasting up out of the darkness. Mykell's battle shriek. Then came an eerie wail, the howl of a deranged beast in pain, a scuffle of rolling bodies and ripping hide. A moment later Mykell appeared out of the tunnel, a black shape with blood gleaming like oil on his snout and whiskers.

"Eeeeyugh." The girl shuddered. "Like a monster in a horror movie."

"Werewolf," he said, licking his whiskers.

Breac got to his feet and helped the girl up. "Let's go. You made enough noise back there to draw a whole pack of werewolves down on us."

Mykell bristled. "I didn't see you back there defending the mission."

* * * * *

The passage they followed leveled out, and began sloping down. Evie was walking again. The downward angle made it easier, but she kept picturing them descending once again into Leazor's dungeons, never to find their way out.

Her eyes lost focus. There wasn't much to focus on in that hole anyway. Rock and more rock. This tunnel ran straight, with no opening on either side. Her thoughts kept drifting in and out. Her pain and weakness, and images from their days of travel muddled together. Breac's face. His look the last time he held her, and his question: *Do you trust me?*

She trusted him to do what he thought was right. To be true to his king, and his Creator. *God* was the word her mind used. Real? Imaginary? What kind of God did he believe had created this world? A pagan deity, one of many? A single all powerful being like the God of the Jews or Christians? But her mind was wandering. She had been thinking of his question... he had meant did she trust him with her life. Did she? Did she truly love him as he claimed to love her? She had come back for him. Was that love? It didn't feel warm and fuzzy. Or thrilling, or exciting. It felt more like determination. Like stepping into a black hole of terror and pain to bring back the only thing that made sense any more. The only person who could reach into her madness.

Mykell stopped in front of them. "Listen."

The sweet sound of water splashing on stone had filled the silence so gradually she hadn't noticed when it began. A few more minutes brought them to a thin stream spurting from a crevasse in the tunnel wall. It sparkled orange and golden in the torchlight. She eyed the miniature waterfall, feeling suddenly thirsty.

"Don't drink it," Breac said. "I wouldn't trust anything in this mountain."

Another fissure a ways down the tunnel spouted more water. Then there was another. Soon they were splashing through a swiftly flowing stream. The roar of more powerful water echoed up to meet them. Evie didn't give much heed to the water. It numbed her feet, and its voice crashed through the underground, echoing the throb in her head.

The passage continued to slope downward, and grew ever brighter. The roar of a subterranean river came louder each moment, until finally they could see it ahead. The tunnel they were following ran into another, larger way, joining it at right angles. Their stream and the river converged in a deafening thunder. The stone around them seemed to tremble with the force of it.

Their tunnel ended in a two food drop-off, where the small stream spilled into the river. Strong daylight washed in from this new passage, and the roar of the water reverberated in Evie's chest. She felt both blinded and deafened, stunned into near oblivion. Ice cold water pushed against their legs, trying to topple her into the river, deadening the pain in her ankle and leaving a bone deep ache in its place. They stopped, staring down at the mighty rush of water.

Mykell peered around the corner, then, changing into hawk form, rose above the water and disappeared. He flew back a moment later and resumed his panther shape. He started to speak, but the sound was obliterated by the river echoing through the mountain.

Breac shook his head. Mykell's black brows scrunched downward and his ears swiveled back, giving him an offended look.

I dislike using mind-speak, humans.

Breac lifted a shoulder in a shrug.

The opening is just around the corner. An image intruded itself into Evie's mind, and she assumed Breac's as well. Blindingly blue sky framed in black stone. The river shot out the tunnel mouth and was lost beyond.

There is a path.

The image turned downward, looking at the rushing river. To one side a narrow ledge ran just below the water's surface. Perhaps a foot wide.

Breac nodded, frowning in thought.

The Sky Falls.

Evie wondered what that meant. Judging by Breac's look, it was nothing good.

Another image invaded her mind's eye, still in bird's-eye view, of water cascading out into an empty sky. Then, far below, a blur of green, and a thin sliver of reflected sunlight. Farther away a sparkle, and an expanse of blue on the horizon. Then they were wheeling back toward the mountain, and the waterfall came in view again, this time on a level with Mykell's flight. The mighty cascade looked thin, white, and broken against the solid rock face. But the rock wasn't solid. First a shadow, then as they looked closer, a long, zigzagging staircase appeared behind the water, carved into the rock. The stairs were steep, and seemed to go on forever.

Their present surroundings snapped back into place. Already Breac was headed for the corner where their tunnel joined the river tunnel. He steadied himself with a hand on the wall, and looked down. Evie watched the water eddy around his boots and then tumble over the edge into the river. Her stomach butterflied. He took a cautious step down, then turned, shuffling, and held out his hand for her to join him.

She sloshed over to the wall, and then followed it, setting each step carefully until she reached the corner and looked down to where he stood. As Mykell had shown them, the ledge was maybe a foot wide, and stood a few inches below the surface of the water. She looked past him to the opening, and blinked, dazzled. Not far now. And then would come the stairs.

The swift current pushed at Evie's feet as they shuffled along, so powerful that even at a depth of only a few inches it threatened to sweep her off the ledge. She walked behind Mykell, keeping a hand on the rock wall, and Breac, coming behind her, held onto her belt. When at last they made it to the edge and looked out they had a dizzy glimpse of green below them, an entirely different world than the cursed land of shadow on the far side of the mountain. A spray of rainbowed water rose from the base of the falls, lingering halfway between heaven and earth. Below that, a green pool and ribbon of river that vanished into jungle. Then far away beyond the green strip of jungle there was a twinkling expanse of water. It all looked so far away. Farther even than Mykell's vision of it that he had given them.

Carved stairs descended across the face of the cliff, disappearing behind the waterfall, only to emerge on the other side, then reverse and come back a hundred feet below them. Evie reeled. She put her hand on the tunnel wall while her empty stomach flip-flopped, threatening to make her dry-heave over the edge.

Breac maneuvered past her and stepped out onto the first stair. He grasped the handrail, a set of parallel grooves chiseled into the rock face at waist level, and held his hand out for Evie.

When she hesitated, he scuffed his boot on the stone, indicating that the steps were not slippery. She swallowed. She still felt like hurling.

She concentrated on the first water pocked, rounded step. It could have been a mile down. She tried to block out visions of pitching headlong into the void as she reached her foot down and set it on the narrow stone. The world started to tip. The height, or her weakness? She took another wavering step, then another, and put her hand on the rock wall. It felt slick with growing algae, but fortunately the stairs were clean and rough, as Breac had shown her.

Breac descended the stairs facing partly outward, holding Evie's hand or elbow at all times. His face bore a grimace, and she figured she didn't look much better. Her wounds started to bleed again, in response to her panicked heart rate. She could feel the warmth of it filling her already wet shoe.

The roar of the river all but ceased once they were out of the cave. They made the first pass between the rock and the water, spilling silently into the void. Sunlight sparked through it in slivers of rainbow and diamond. They could have reached out their hands and filled them with the plummeting droplets. For just an instant Evie felt her fear ease a little as she paused, staring.

Ahead of her Breac stopped. He let go her arm, and turned to face the cliff, putting both hands against the rock. He stepped backwards and down onto a stair step right below the one he'd been on. As soon as he moved she could see that they had come to the first switchback. The stairway seemed to end, and she stared out into a whole lot of nothing. Breac took the next step, now headed the opposite direction, with his face at waist level. He clung to the stairs above him, right at her feet, struggling for balance.

Evie's chest tightened with the same feeling of claustrophobia she'd felt in the cave tunnel with Mykell. Only here they were surrounded with inescapable air, instead of solid rock. She stood on the last step and looked an inch past her feet into a blotchy green faraway-ness. Again the world started spinning. Her fingers whitened on the handrail.

"Just look at the next step," Breac said, the first words any of them had spoken since the tunnels, when the noise became too much.

She shuffled around, putting her back to the cliff face, and looked down at that next stair—just a little ledge cut in the rock right below her. She decided she didn't like that view, and turned to face the cliff, grasping the carved rail with all her might and reaching a foot behind her, down, down—*Where'd that step go?* Her toe brushed it. She let go the rail and grabbed the steps they'd just come down, like Breac had done.

She felt strong hands grasp her arms, helping her down to the next step, and the next. She came face to face with Breac, and he smiled.

"You did fine. Every turn brings us closer to the bottom, and we can make good time in between, so be comforted."

Above them Mykell surveyed the turn. He must have decided he didn't like it, for he took wing and leapt off the rock, gliding down in a slow spiral until he disappeared into the spray.

"I really hate him right now." She eased down to sit on the stairs, fighting not to burst into tears. Breac joined her. They rested for a few minutes on the wet rock, heedless of the green slime that smeared their arms from the wall. Evie put her head in her hands and closed her eyes. Her world was still spinning. She tried to mutter a few stanzas of the healing song, but felt too out of breath to sing out loud. The air seemed thinner up here. Or perhaps it was just her. Her ankle throbbed even worse when she stopped moving, and again she struggled not to cry, to keep her panic in check.

Breac touched her shoulder. She looked up to see him standing, offering his hand. "We will make it," he said quietly.

One step at a time the pool and river drew closer. They made another turn, and passed into the cloud of spray. Within minutes they were soaked to the skin with the warm mist. When they emerged they were much closer to the bottom. A hundred feet or so separated them from the moss covered boulders at the pool's edge.

Suddenly Evie's ankle buckled. She pitched sideways. Before she had time to scream Breac had caught the back of her shirt. For an instant she hung there, staring straight down at the rocks while her flimsy tank top stretched further and further. Breac grunted in pain. For a moment she thought they would both fall over the edge, and Mykell was circling high above now, too far away to catch them. Then he pulled her back. His arms went around her waist, and held her tight against him. She could feel him panting, could hear the deep wheeze in his chest. The world seemed very bright all of a sudden. Starbursts of adrenaline popped behind her eyes, for a moment erasing the pain in her ankle and arm. She shook. He pulled her even tighter in his arms, standing there, leaning against the cliff face. His hand moved to the back of her head and pressed her face into his neck.

"Evie, Evie. How many times must I come so close to losing you?" he whispered, panting.

At last she drew a shaking breath. "The ground isn't getting any closer with us standing here."

He nodded. She took a step, with him holding tight to her shoulder, and stopped again.

"It's no good. My knees might as well be so much strawberry jelly. And my ankle..." She sat down, and took a few steps sliding on her rear, then looked back at him. "Hey. At least this is progress, right?"

A small smile twisted his mouth, but he had a queer expression, as though his feelings were so mixed up his face couldn't keep up with them.

Mykell met them as they came down off the last stair, alighting on a mossy boulder beside the pool. The cataract ended in a cloud of mist and rainbows, the sound of it echoing off the cliff face like a mighty thunder of applause. Evie sat back down right away on a mossy boulder beside the water, and Breac lowered himself down beside her. Mykell hopped over to them, still a hawk. He squawked. Breac cupped his hand behind his ear, a silent "What?"

Mykell spoke louder this time, his raspy bird voice barely understandable over the noise of the water. "There is a ship in the channels of the swamp. It hides in the thick of the mangroves, and has no flag. I saw no one on deck."

"And along the river?"

"I could see nothing, however... I can sense someone is near."

Breac sighed wearily. "We cannot race our enemies all the way to the capital. We have no horses, no weapons, we are both hurt and tired."

"Stating the obvious will not bring us the help we need." Mykell ruffled his feathers and flexed his wings. "The girl should sing the healing song. That might help at least one of the items in your list of complaints." So saying he took flight, circled once around their heads, and disappeared into the jungle.

Evie felt suddenly shy as Breac looked at her.

"It can't hurt," he said, "Even if it only serves to renew our courage."

He doesn't actually believe the healing song will heal, she thought. *Why? Was it an accident that it worked on Mykell? A fluke? Or does it work really well for shape-shifters?*

She fidgeted, feeling put on the spot and expected to perform. She was used to performing, but not like this. She had been desperate when she sang the song over Mykell. Looking at Breac, she suddenly felt it was a very intimate thing to put her hands on someone's wounds and sing over them. And singing over the man she desired... she was afraid.

"What is wrong?"

"I—"she cleared her throat. "Uh, nothing. Give me your hands."

They held hands, and Evie closed her eyes, as much because the song felt like a prayer as because she was afraid to meet Breac's gaze.

"*Weary and broken, rest here for awhile...*" she began. At once she could feel the power. She opened her eyes, and for an instant caught a shimmer in the air around the man, who gazed at her wide-eyed. It felt like being connected to a battery, a power source outside of herself, energizing, renewing, healing. The pain in her ankle vanished, along with the aches and soreness, even the fear.

The song ended, and still they held hands. He had felt it all too. She could see it in his eyes, in the twist of his lips as he leaned toward her. She felt no longer fear, but desire, such as had overtaken them with the river naiads' song. Yet there was still a bashfulness, as though body and soul had been uncovered before him. A shiver went through her. He released one of her hands and put his behind her neck, pulling her closer, till they were staring inches from each other's eyes.

He kissed her so softly at first. Like flower petals. Like petals with a jolt of lightning behind, as the fire ignited. Not merely a kiss. All the words unspoken. All the desires felt in secret. All the pain and the should-have-beens.

Breac pulled away abruptly. The hunger in his eyes almost scared her, but her own must reflect the same expression.

"Perhaps that song worked a little too well?" he said.

She felt heat wash over her face.

At that moment Mykell dropped out of the sky, slowed enough not to kill himself, and morphed back into a panther before he hit the ground. He raised a sleek eyebrow at them. "All well, I see."

"Yes," Breac said, a little breathless, which only made Mykell's dubious expression deepen. "What did you see?"

"Nothing more."

Breac sat back. "Good." He tugged off a boot and set it beside him on the rock, followed by the other. Then pulled the book of the Kantra out of his belt and laid it down beside the boots.

Evie untied her shirt from around her arm. Even though it was healed, the blood remained, making her feel a bit squeamish. She took Breac's sleeve off her ankle as well, and then dunked her shirt in the pool, trying to clean it. The shirt bled, staining the water around it, but the cloud of dirt and blood were quickly swept away downstream.

"Humans. Have you forgotten that we could be pursued at any moment?"

"No," said Breac, testing the water with his toe. He stuck both feet in. "Healed we may be, but we've come a long way wounded, and have a long way to go. I for one could use a rest still. Besides, I must think."

Mykell twitched his tail impatiently. "Perhaps so. But do you really think sitting around splashing in the water is a good idea? We should get as far away from this mountain as possible."

Breac stared into the deep water. "Where have we to run to for shelter?" he said after a moment. "We can't race an army on horseback all the way to the capital. We have no horses, no weapons, no provisions. Our only hope for protection is in the Book of Kantra."

"We can at least travel for some way under shelter of the jungle. Or, now that we are almost there, do you propose that we sit down and give up?"

"Heh..." Breac sighed. He looked up at the cliff above them. Nothing moved along its face. The tiny black opening from which they'd come stared like an eyeless socket. "Who keeps the stairs scraped clean?" he said suddenly.

Mykell shot a look up at the stone stairway. "I don't know."

Across the pool a dragonfly landed on one of the mossy rocks and sat motionless. The pool spilled out into a wide, cool river that passed into dappled green jungle light.

"I don't either. Perhaps we shall meet him. Or them."

"Do you suppose it to be friend or foe?"

"I don't suppose anything. But one can hope," Breac said. He bent over the water and scooped a handful up, watching it drip back into the pool. Hundreds of tiny fish swam in the clear water.

He pointed them out to Evie. "See, they keep the river pure from Leazor's poison. They thrive eating the filth off the bottom of the pool, and make the water safe to drink."

Evie bent over to get a clearer view of the bright little fish... a small tidal wave hit her in the face. She sat up spluttering, and looked at Breac. His face wore a smirk.

"Did you just... you didn't..." she leaned over with cupped hands and splashed him back. In an instant the water was flying, until SPLASH! Evie slipped off the mossy rock and into the water with a squeal. She bobbed to the surface spitting water. "You just... you...." That was it. She grabbed his ankle and pulled him in after her. Their laughter rang against the cliff. Mykell lay on his belly on the shore, one black paw resting crossed over the other, watching them. Evie clung to the rocks with one arm, and tugged off her boots, setting them beside Breac's. Then she lay back and floated, arms outspread. The water was cool, but not cold like the underground lake. Warm sunlight felt like a welcome embrace.

Breac dove to the bottom of the pool, picked up a small object, and resurfaced to dunk Evie under again.

"Are you two humans done with your playtime?"

Breac swam to the rock and heaved himself up. Evie followed. The air was warm enough here that she didn't feel chilled coming out of the water, only refreshed.

Breac held up the object he had pulled from the bottom of the pool. It glinted dully in the light, a many pointed silver star, with a milk white gem set in the middle. A piece of broken cord was knotted around a loop in one of the points.

"What is it?"

"A pendant. The seal of Carmi-Asriel," he replied. "It has not been here long." He fingered the braided sinew cord. The ends were just beginning to unravel. It could have been in the water twenty minutes and received that much damage. He tucked it into a pocket, surveying the jungle around them.

Evie sat back on her heels to wring the water out of her hair. Breac sat beside her, tugging on his boots. He knotted the laces and stood. "Mykell is right, as always. We should go. I don't know what came over me."

Evie wrung out her shirt and put it back on wet. She felt conspicuous in only the wet tank top. She had to dump water out of her boots before she could put them on again. Breac paced, frowning, and glancing from the cliff to the jungle.

"I feel danger close."

A screeching, hissing wail descended on the peaceful world, punctuating Breac's words with sudden terror. Evie jumped up, her boot laces half tied, Mykell crouched, hissing, and Breac's hand went to his side, where his sword no longer hung.

23

The Son of Rajah

"The Kantra," Breac muttered. He turned and grasped Evie's shoulder. "Sing!"

She looked at him stupidly, paralyzed.

He started the first line of the protecting song, the authority of the command for help ringing in his voice. She joined in. Even as they sang, a shadow passed over them. Breac did not look up. His eyes remained closed as though in prayer. Fear crawled up the back of her neck. She wanted to look up, watch their doom circling ever closer to the ground. But she dared not. Some instinct told her that the power of the song would only be weakened by watching their enemy. With an effort she closed her eyes as well and directed the song as a prayer, begging the Creator and whatever strange laws governed this world to hear them and honor the song.

She felt the impact through her feet when the dragon settled to earth. Her eyes flew open. Like a living tree the neck stretched and curved over toward them from across the pool. Milky eyes seemed blind to the world, yet the beast knew exactly where to find its prey. The monster inhaled, and it felt as though all the warmth was drawn out of the air around them.

Breac shoved her suddenly, and for the second time that afternoon she toppled into the pool. From underwater she sensed a shadow pass over the pool. And then, in the instant before her head broke the surface, she felt *them* as well.

Evie! You can never run from us!

Bubbles escaped her mouth in an underwater exclamation. *Oh no, you can't have me that easy!* Her head flew up out of the water, the song of protection already on her lips. Black eyes stared at her from the rocks at the pools edge. Claws out and teeth bared, ready to mutilate the instant she came within reach. If she did not move, it would shift into some water creature and come after her in the pool. She met the creature's gaze and sang. The black eyes wavered, the thing took a step back.

* * * * *

Beyond where the Ezomrah crouched at the pool's edge, Breac dodged another jet of flame from the dragon's maw. He'd been a fool to linger here by the pool. Should have considered that a song of the Kantra could have the potential to affect his judgment. Now with no weapons and nowhere to hide, he faced the monster. And Creator only knew what was happening to Evie and Mykell right now. He sent up a silent petition for their safety, even as he dropped to the ground, smashing and rolling through vegetation. He slapped at his flaming pant-let. Pain and the smell of burnt skin felt like a rude wakening from a pleasant dream, where he had been healed completely and pain free. The dragon snorted black smoke.

No one escapes from me!

"Wrong!" Breac replied out loud. He shuffled on his elbows backward in the brush, facing up at the monster. "I have escaped you many times. You deceive yourself as well as others."

The mighty head reared back, but then Mykell was between them, wings outstretched, eagle eyes glittering.

* * * * *

The Ezomrah retreated, backing further away from the pool and Evie, who paddled toward it, still singing between pants. It was there, staring back at her, and then it was on the ground, paws flailing in the air and howling. She gawked at it in confusion. What...? Then she saw the white feathered arrow in its side. She swam to the rock and hoisted herself out of the water. The dragon had its back to her now. The gleaming scaled tale swept the ground, its tip passing a yard from her feet. She got a glimpse of Breac, down in the brush on the other side of it. Smoke rose at intervals all around him. Mykell had just alighted in his eagle form, wings spread.

"No, no, Breac, Mykell..." She had no weapon. None of them had, except Mykell. But they'd already found that his claws and beak were no good against the dragon's scales and fire. She had to do *something.* The arrow. Regardless where it had come from, it was a weapon. *And probably no better than Mykell's claws.* She dashed to the Ezomrah's still twitching corps and yanked the arrow from between its ribs. It came out smeared in blood and fur, but as she held it up, the tip of the head caught the light, twinkling as though crusted in jewels. She clenched the shaft in her fist, and looked to the dragon. It had reared onto its hind legs, neck extended and head curved down, high as a telephone pole.

Again it seemed to her as though something was wrong with it. It should have struck, or breathed out more flame, but it seemed to be having a disagreement with itself. The tail lay still, and the head twitched, neck bulging with strain. Was Leazor losing his hold on the thing? And why? Could it be because of the song?

She started forward, her lips spilling another song from the book of Kantra, though she was oblivious to the words. So long as it was a song of power.

The monster jerked and shuddered, roaring a blast of flames as Evie ran up beside the length of tail. Mykell flapped in one direction and Breac rolled in the other. The mass of the dragon's body surged forward, wings canopied to support its weight as it reached for the man with flames and claws.

Evie shrieked, dove after it and stabbed the arrow through a massive hind leg, staring as the fragile arrowhead penetrated between the bone and tendon and stuck out the far side. For an eon long millisecond she gaped at her work. Surprise. That should not have worked. Panic. The beast roared again and swung to face her.

I'm dead.

She flung herself to the side, landed, and somersaulted behind a boulder. She flattened to the ground beneath a stream of fire. The dragon roared, and her world was obliterated by black smoke. She scrabbled to get away, anywhere. Which direction? She banged into another rock. Her heart stopped.

I'm dead.

It roared again. She blinked through the dissipating smoke, expecting a blast of flames in her face. Instead, the dragon had backed away, gnashing at its side, where two more arrows, and as she looked, a third, had appeared. It shrieked, a harsh, teakettle, nails-on-chalkboard screech. The white eyes were quickly darkening. The slitted pupil and orange iris clarifying behind the milky glaze. It flapped backward, struck the cliff face, and screamed again, writhing like a serpent on its hind legs. The foul smelling wings churned, lifting it over their heads. Evie flattened her back against the rock, staring as it passed over, higher and higher, hissing, head bobbing and weaving as though still struggling with itself. The tail jerked, throwing its flight off kilter. It slammed into the mountain again, and tumbled a hundred feet or so before righting itself and putting on speed. In a moment it disappeared behind the hills.

Evie slumped against the rock, and started to release her held breath, when a figure stepped out of the jungle before her. A man with a bow in his hand, an arrow nocked to the string. She sucked the air right back in again. The man motioned for her to get up, so she did, turning to see four others, all with bows and arrows at the ready, step out of the trees. She scanned the area. Blackened ground, burnt off vegetation, charred rocks. Mykell morphed into his panther form, and crouched, watching the men. Breac sat up slowly, wincing. One leather pant leg had been badly charred, with a hole burnt in a part of it. He gripped his knee below the burn and propped himself up with his other hand on the ground as the men approached. She walked to him, stopped, and turned to face the strangers who had closed the distance and stood in a semi-circle six feet away.

One man took a step forward, studying the travelers. His gaze rested longest on Breac, measuring the wounded warrior and his guardians, a shifter and an unarmed woman.

"Good afternoon, travelers," the man said.

Breac nodded, a sly smile twisting his lips. "I've certainly had worse afternoons, though I can't speak as well for this morning. What can we do for you?"

"My name is Kuruk. I've a proposition for you and your companions." He nodded in turn at Evie and Mykell, then continued. "Be coming back with us to our ship. You will be safer there than in the jungle. Tell your story to the captain, with whatever news you have, and let him decide whether you are friend or foe. Anyone who comes out of Al Kazam alive is either a very great threat, or a very great warrior. If you are for the High King, we would assist you. If you are spies and traitors, we shall know your mission. That or have our arrows in you now, for we cannot let you go free to tell of us without knowing your purpose. Neither of us, I think, want that."

"We will come," Breac replied. "We are indebted to you for our lives."

"Better that than fighting off whatever else Leazor sends after us," Mykell muttered.

Kuruk bowed toward Evie. "M'lady." He turned back to Breac. "We have been watching you, and had thought that the lady was wounded and might require our aid. I see now I was mistaken. Perhaps it is yourself who requires aid."

"Help me up."

Two of the men shouldered their bows, slipping the arrows back into the quiver. They got on either side of Breac and hoisted him to his feet. He limped a few paces and turned. "It'll do for now. Shall we go?"

Kuruk jerked his head toward the jungle, signaling the others to march. Breac and Evie fell into step, while Mykell paced behind, with four of the men fanned out behind them, and Kuruk leading. Breac walked haltingly, scowling as his pants rubbed the burn on his leg. He said nothing about having Evie sing the healing song again, and she didn't volunteer, though she reached out to touch his hand. Their fingers entwined, and he gave her hand a squeeze.

They walked in silence for over an hour, during which her heart finally slowed to its normal rhythm. The pounding, panicky fear she'd felt after the attack was slowly replaced by a weight of cold dread. She kept glancing up and over her shoulder. Mykell did the same. Breac simply marched, his expression blank as though asleep on his feet. Ahead of them, Kuruk slid through the jungle, ducking, slipping around, through, over and under every obstacle like a dancer. Evie felt like an ox, bulldozing her way through their leafy surroundings. Her feet started catching on unseen rocks and sticks, and her legs and back felt so weary. The sun had sunk below the treetops, but what should have been cool evening felt muggy and oppressive. Her wet clothing stuck to her body, dragging at her weary limbs even more.

She'd been this tired on the night Sylvanus died. Her heart sank even lower. She let go Breac's hand and hugged herself, staring at the ground as she walked. She had been so tired. What would have happened if she had not met the dryad? Or if they had not stopped at that village? Or if the village had not been occupied? Would she have gotten safe home? Would she have met Breac, perhaps in some other way? She squirmed with the thought. *If only all of this had been different.* But he was a hunted man also. It was not only she whom the enemy pursued. Would she have been better able to help him without the curse? Or at least free to love him...

Her eyes burned suddenly, and she blinked, looking up and taking a deep breath to clear away the tears.

* * * * *

Breac lifted aside a tangled curtain of hanging vines for the girl. "What would you do if you could go home right now?" He felt like a fool the second he asked. He had disturbed an unbroken silence. Besides that, he should already know the answer. Women always hated danger. Evie was used to a comfortable, secure life. She must hate this place.

But she didn't answer right away. Finally she said, "I... don't know."

"Would you go?" he pushed.

She looked up into his eyes. "I don't know."

Dear Creator, she was so beautiful. He couldn't imagine a more perfect creature existing in his world or hers. And he'd nearly gotten her killed. Was taking her to be killed. But no... he couldn't let that happen. His lungs refused to work for a full minute while his legs kept going, and her eyes remained on his. He drew breath with a gulp, saw the puzzlement that flickered across her face. He suddenly felt desperate to know her mind.

"Do you trust me?"

Her dark brows came together. Her eyes looked panicked. "I... does it matter?"

"To me. You are taking me apart, piece by piece, and you don't even know it. I need your trust." There. He'd said it. He, the warrior uncaring for anyone's ridicule or anyone's praise save his King's. He was desperate for this woman's trust. He was asking the impossible.

"I love you," she offered.

"But do you trust me?"

Kuruk was looking back at them. Mykell's green eyes sliced into him from behind. He swiped his sleeve across his face.

She looked away. This time his feet quit working. His toe caught in a root, and he stumbled to his knees, staring up at her. He must look completely stupefied. Evie's eyes went wide. She put a hand over her mouth and giggled. Breac felt his ears heating up as Mykell walked past, ears thrown back. The scouts behind them came to a halt.

Breac stumbled to his feet. He and Evie hurried to catch up, but Kuruk had stopped. They had left the river a few minutes ago, and now came to a smaller channel, its still water sitting low between sharp banks. A rowboat nestled close between the banks, almost touching them. Grass and tree roots brushed its sides. It must have been as far as they could take it.

Kuruk untied the rope securing the boat to a tree, and shook it loose. One by one they climbed in, all except Mykell, who paused, one paw suspended over the water. With a soft plash he slipped in, and a silvery fish body disappeared into the shadowed stream. One of the scouts frowned after him.

"Let him go," Kuruk said. "He'll follow."

There was no way to row in the tight passage. Instead they pushed and pulled their way along using tree roots and rocks that stuck out of the banks, until in a few minutes the channel broadened, and suddenly they were confronted by a confusion of natural waterways, separating bits of boggy land. Mangroves rose out of the water on fingery pedestals and towered over them. Kuruk and his men picked up the oars, and the boat zipped through the darkening water.

"Have to get to the ship before nightfall," Kuruk said. "Even the best of us would be lost here in the dark. And then you've got the beasties following you."

Breac stretched his leg out in the bottom of the boat, and sighed heavily. Evie reached out, her hand hovering over the wound for a moment as their eyes met in the dusky light. He tilted his head only faintly, and she touched his leg, her fingertips sliding through the burn hole. He winced. She chewed her lips for a moment, hesitant. Afraid. She started to sing softly, and the healing song took on new character in the twilight. Gentle and soothing as a lullaby. The scouts rowed and listened, and one hummed along a little. There were no emotional fireworks this time, just a calm peace, both restful and renewing.

He felt relief, both from the pain and that his emotions and judgment were left intact. He checked the burn, found not even a scar, and relaxed back on the bench.

"There's a pretty trick," one of the scouts said. "I dare say we should keep the lady in any event."

Breac let the wave of annoyance come and go, remaining silent. He would not declare their purpose, nor invoke the High King's authority unless he must. And that would depend on the captain.

The boat shot out of the channel and into a much larger waterway, though still dissected by towering mangroves and strips of marshy ground. The light strengthened now that they were out of the close jungle, from purple dusk to evening blue. The ship lay before them.

* * * * *

Evie stared. The only ship she'd ever been on was a replica of the Mayflower, and she had wondered how so many people could have crowded there for so many months. This boat was no bigger, but from their vantage point, it loomed high over them as they drew near, into its shadow. A dozen men watched their approach, and she wished she could hide somewhere. But Leazor's fortress had been much worse than this. The *dragon* had been much worse than this.

That's me, Eva Drake—dragon fighter. And I'm scared cause of a few dudes on a boat?

A rope ladder was tossed over to them, along with ropes to hoist up the landing boat. Kuruk climbed up first, and offered her a hand, half hoisting her from the ladder to the deck. She tugged her tank-top and shirt straight, and waited for Breac, ignoring the stares. A pigeon startled her, circling her head, then landed on her shoulder. Mykell of course. She raised her hand to him, and he nibbled her finger with his beak, a little gesture of reassurance.

Evie expected a rush of activity, like she'd always seen on the movies when a ship turned tail and sailed away. Granted there was no wind to sail by in the swamp. Instead the men gathered around them like they were some kind of curious exhibit. She took a step closer to Breac, and Mykell, perched on her shoulder, ruffled his feathers. None of the sailors wore a uniform of any kind, but their clothes were far from ragged. Bright colors and jewels abounded in the crowd, but the adornments were simple. Nothing that would get in the way of a day's work.

The crowd parted for a man to pass. He was a head taller than most of the other sailors, and solidly built. At once Evie thought of him as the captain. He had a presence about him that proclaimed him a leader who would take no question and no hesitation to his orders. His black hair and beard were streaked with white, and there were lines in his sun darkened face. He sized them up briefly, and then turned to the leader of the scouts.

"What have you brought me, Kuruk?"

Kuruk gave a sloppy, fist over heart bow. "Escapees from Leazor's mountain. They were pursued by a dragon, and several of the Ezomrah, which are now dead or fled away. They are knowing something about Leazor's recent movements, I think. They claim to be on their way to Al Acatra on a mission for the High King. Sir."

The captain nodded, and turned to Breac. "My name is Byrne, and this is my ship. Please. Convince me that you are not spies."

A wry smile twisted Breac's face. He put a fist over his heart and bowed in salute, much more gracefully than Kuruk had, then spread out his hand and offered his scarred palm to the captain for inspection. "I am called Breac, servant to the High King. My companions and I travel on his business."

"Servant? I think rather warrior or messenger from the look of you."

"I serve the High King in whatever matter he assigns. With our enemy on the move there has been fighting."

Byrne rocked back on his heels, stroking his beard, studying the travelers. "You are not very free in explaining yourself and your mission. Who are you companions?"

"Just as you must find out about myself and my companions, and choose whether to trust us, I must make the same judgment of you, or become a fool." Breac eyed him for a moment, then turned to Evie and Mykell. "The lady Eva Drake, and Mykell."

Mykell hopped off Evie's shoulder and dropped to the deck in his panther form. He curled a lip, showing a glint of white fangs.

Breac continued, "Our mission I will not speak of openly here, but we were on our way to Al Acatra when I was captured by the enemy. My friends rescued me, and we were able to escape the mountain, which is when your men picked us up."

"I see. I find it hard to believe that you got out of the mountain without Leazor's consent."

"But we were pursued," Breac began, when someone called from the crowd.

"Wait!"

One of the sailors laughed. "Watch it, capt'n. The boss is here."

Byrne looked mildly disgusted as two men pushed through to where they stood. One, tall and fair, looked very young. He was dressed in black silk trousers, and a red silk shirt, with gold earrings. The other was very old, but tough and spry. He stepped up close to Breac, and gave him a thorough inspection. His blue eyes, whitening over with cataracts, still somehow maintained their sharpness. He pointed a gnarled finger at Breac, then swung it over and aimed it at the captain.

"This is the man. And you're standing here questioning him like a common thief. Shame on you, sir."

Byrne gestured toward the young man, and then the old. "My first mate, Lance. And the other is Tarek. We keep him for decoration, and because he knows the currents, and certain other useful things."

Tarek bowed to Breac, not the customary half bow salute, but a full bow that one would give a king, ending on one knee with his face toward the ground. He straightened up. "Seven days ago we had stopped in the harbor at Southpoint. I happened to run into the High King while we were there, or perhaps he sought me out. One can never be sure in these matters. And he said that we should stop off here if we wanted to know of Leazor's movements, and that certain travelers would be along who would need help. He told me that one of them would be the son of prophecy, the man called by a name others had given him, whose eyes were of two nations. Tell me, you who are called Breac—what is your real name?"

Breac flushed. "My name is Aindreas, son of Rajah of Carmi-Asriel."

At that a murmur went up from some of the older crew members. Tarek dropped to his knees, while the captain blanched and stuttered. "Rajah!"

24

Answers

Breac frowned. "What does the name mean to you?"

"Rajah is dead. I watched him die, childless," Byrne said.

"Then it was not the same man."

"There is only one Rajah of Carmi-Asriel."

Breac raised an eyebrow.

"Do you not know? He was prince of that land."

From his knees, Tarek spoke up. "Please, tell us of him."

"He's dead."

Another murmur went up. Breac shot Evie a glance. She realized she had her mouth hanging open and shut it with a click. He looked as bewildered as she. Mykell took everything in, sitting placidly on his haunches. He flicked his tail when Breac looked at him.

Breac drew himself up. A muscle in his jaw jumped. Before the captain could speak again, he said, "Is it then safe to presume that you will offer aid for my companions and I?"

"It is, and we shall. Though I would know your full story, and any news of the enemy that you can provide."

"You will have both, but need I remind you that we were pursued from Al Kazam, and while the first attack is over, there will be others. We are in danger staying here."

Lance, the first mate, spoke for the first time. "We have other scouts we must wait for. They won't come back until they know more of your pursuit."

"Nightfall is already upon us," Byrne said. "Even Tarek and I cannot maneuver these swamps after sundown. We will spend the night here regardless."

Evie saw Breac's expression fall. He looked suddenly tired and worried. She turned away with an ache in her heart and looked out over the shadowed waters. Trees rose up with spreading roots and branches like creepy wooden nets. No wonder the captain would not navigate here after dark.

"There is relative safety here," Byrne said. "Very few know the channels through this swamp, which you must navigate with a ship of any size. There are many places that are so thick even a rowboat cannot pass, and unless Leazor's men know this place by heart, daylight or dark, we will be safe."

"It isn't so much men that I was thinking of," Breac said.

"I see. You fear Ezomrah, or another dragon. That is what we have Tarek for. He knows the ancient ways."

Tarek bowed.

Mykell twitched his tail and rose from his haunches. "You also have me. Leazor's dragon was wounded and out of his control. He cannot find another to replace it so soon. I believe the captain. We should be safe here for the night."

Breac nodded. "Very well."

The captain smiled for the first time, and his face creased with dozens of squint and laugh lines. "Tonight, we will celebrate. The son of our lost brother has returned to fulfill ancient prophesy—if you will believe old Tarek here—escaping the cursed mountain. Tomorrow we sail for Al Acatra. Or the town of Ravenport, since that is as close as we can get to it by sea."

Breac nodded again. "Thank you. The Creator bless you, and the High King reward you."

"Come with me," Byrne said, putting his hand on Breac's shoulder. "We have just come from the southern coasts, and our stores are full. You and the lady need clothes and weapons, and I dare say a bath and a good meal."

Evie put a hand over her stomach. How long *had* it been since their last meal? At least twenty four hours. She had been so scared out of her mind for most of that time she had hardly noticed, and then the healing had given them strength. Now at the mention of food her insides twisted and rumbled.

The captain let them pick a fresh change of clothes, and for Breac a new sword and bow. Evie declined any kind of weapon, until Byrne brought out a jeweled dagger.

"Every lady should carry one of these," he said. "Especially one as beautiful as yourself."

She took the dagger, sliding it part way out of the sheath. The blade shone with her reflected image. Hardly what she would recognize as her own face, dirt streaked, tanned, and more thoughtful than last time she'd looked at her reflection. The edge of the blade glittered, as the arrowhead had. She peered closer.

"Diamond chips," Byrne answered her unspoken question. "The only weapon that will pierce dragon hide."

Her mouth formed an O. That would explain some things.

Next Byrne led them to his cabin, where a corner had been curtained off with a steaming bathtub.

"I'm sorry accommodations are not better. This is the only tub we have aboard, and that only because I've a buyer for it in Cliff Bay. You'll have to take turns. I'm sorry for the inconvenience, lady."

Evie felt her face turning crimson. "That's... uh, ok I guess." At this point, the only really important thing was that it was a bath.

"We will leave the room of course."

Her face got even redder. "Of course." *Why am I blushing like a schoolgirl?*

* * * * *

When Evie stepped out of the cabin it was nearly dark, but a big full moon hung low over the swamp. Breac was waiting outside the door. He smiled at her, and she caught a glint of something in his eyes. She couldn't be sure what it was, but in the cool light she thought he had looked over her figure ever so briefly. She ran her hands over her folded arms, feeling suddenly awkward in the silk dress. It had been the simplest one she could find among the things Byrne offered her, but it occurred to her that it also did very well to show off her curves.

"Cold, my lady?' Breac asked, putting a hand on her arm.

"Not really. Just... well, maybe a little chilly. I'll be fine."

"Evie."

"Yes?"

"You have a great gift."

She looked up at him. The moon made his hair gleam whitish. "What?"

"The healing today."

She flushed, thinking about that moment. That feeling of her soul being completely exposed to him. Of being, for just a moment, one with him. She stammered, "It—it was the song. Not me."

"The song is for healing, but how well it works depends on the person singing it. For most mortals it helps calm and sooth. Even most dryads, who have the gift of healing, cannot do what you have done. I felt the power coming through you."

"You didn't know the song, so how do you know so much about it?"

"When I walked with death on the battlefield the High King sent a dryad to help me. She sang this song, and it still took me weeks to recover."

She looked down at her hands. They looked and felt normal enough, though they were scratched now from pushing through the brush. They didn't look like they held any special gift. And had he felt more than just the healing? Had he felt the same as she?

A breeze lifted the damp hair off her neck, and rippled the hem of her dress. She met his eyes again, and found his gaze even more intense.

"I am certainly glad it didn't take us weeks to recover this time," she said softly. "That would have been... inconvenient."

"It would."

She smiled and dropped a curtsy. "I'll see you later." She turned and headed toward the main deck, where Mykell perched on the rail, watching the moonrise through owl eyes.

"Evie," Breac called after her.

She turned—and found that he had followed, and stood right behind her. He put his hand to her cheek, ran his fingers through her hair until his hand was behind her head, and drew her face close to his. Heat washed up her neck as he kissed her for the second time that day. It was a long moment before he released her.

"Thank you," he said.

She ran her tongue over her swollen lips. "You're welcome."

He bowed slightly before he turned away, stepping into the cabin and closing the door. Evie rubbed at the goose bumps on her arms. *Fool!*

* * * * *

"My scouts have found no signs of pursuit," Byrne said. He, Lance, and Tarek were seated at the desk in the captain's cabin with Breac and Evie. Mykell paced about sniffing the corners of the room. The dishes and what remained of supper had been cleared away, replaced with a chart of Acatra Dahma's coast.

"Leazor would never give up," Breac replied. He felt the burden of the mission and their safety weighing on him once again as he fingered the hilt of his new sword. "I guess that he is setting a trap, sending his servants to cut us off before we reach Al Acatra."

"That is my thought too." Byrne tapped his finger on the chart. "The way along the coast by ship and then inland on foot will be longer than the straight route he will take, though if the winds are favorable we may cut much time off the journey. Still, I do not think it wise to assume we will outrun him."

"May the High King protect us then."

Mykell prowled over and jumped up onto one of the chairs like a huge cat. "He has so far."

Tarek said, "Do not forget the prophecy. It is you who will break Leazor's power."

Breac turned his gaze to the old man. "Please, tell me what prophecy you speak of, and how you come to know about it. I have been seeking the answer to this riddle for some time."

"The prophecy is etched in the very stone of Leazor's fortress. I know of it because it was my great-grandfather's great-grandfather, a stonemason, who carved it there. He was an evil man, but even evil must serve the Creator's purpose. He was given the prophecy and driven mad until he put the words there, reminding Leazor through the long years that his power will not always be strong."

"And what does the prophecy say?"

"That in a time of great darkness, a servant of the King will rise, with the light of two nations in his eyes, called by a name others have given him. He will wrest control from the Sorcerer's grasp." Tarek grinned, showing missing teeth. "That prophecy has been passed down in my family through all those years. Each child was made to memorize it. I never did have much of an interest in it when I was young. Don't remember the exact words, but I know sure enough what it was talking about."

Breac stared out the cabin windows to the darkening swamp. He felt lost. Who was he to meddle in ancient prophesy? And how could this possibly be fulfilled through him? He remembered the words of the Lady Vivaqua, now many days ago: *'If you wonder about the part you have to fulfill, I say, Aindreas son of Rajah, that in carrying out this mission for the High King, you are already fulfilling it. The Creator's design will not be cheated.'* He drummed his fingers on the sword hilt. The room had become very still. Which path would he walk? The one that had been laid out for him for centuries past, or the other dark way that he now looked down. Or were they indeed somehow the same?

"Tell me about my father," he said finally. "He died before I could talk, and I think even my mother didn't fully know his past. She told me that he was a pirate."

"Rajah was the only prince of Carmi-Asriel," Tarek began. "Thirty years ago, or was it thirty-one? Leazor took over that country."

"It was thirty-two or three," Byrne interrupted.

Tarek nodded toward him. "Right you are. I lose count. Leazor tricked the king into harboring a traitor, and so when the Day of Justice had come and gone, rule of the land was turned over to Leazor. He forced the royal family into service to him, making them deny the High King. All except for Prince Rajah, who would not deny the true King or the Creator. He escaped and fled to the sea, where he took a position on my ship, the *Laughing Widow*. In all my years at sea, I don't ever remember a time when there was peace between Leazor's fleet of war, and the merchant vessels of both free and enslaved countries. We attack each other freely. It was information that your father provided which allowed us to surprise and overcome two of the enemy's ships. The next day Leazor's warships overtook us far to the north. Leazor, who was on board one of the vessels, was more interested in reclaiming Rajah than in taking the rest of us. He offered to let us go if we gave him up. Now, that would have been deemed treachery, and so we could not, nor would we have anyway. But Rajah, he went anyway, all on his own. We watched them hang him from the bowsprit. When they cut the rope, and he went under, that was the last we ever saw of him. But we've not forgotten, those who still sail under the blue sky, and the rest have heard the story."

Breac resumed drumming his fingers. From the deck he could hear one of the sailors playing a tune on a harmonica. Another piped in with a reed pipe, or a flute, and still another with a deep voiced fiddle. The song was a lullaby his mother used to sing, of which he couldn't remember the words. The music set his heart to aching. Evie, the prophecy, and now the news about his father. It all circled through his mind, colored dark by the song and the night.

Enough. He would consider things when he was alone. For now he felt me must get away from them. From the expectations and dread, and thoughts of an unknown future.

He pushed his chair back away from the table and stood. Reaching a hand to Evie, he pulled her to her feet.

"My lady, would you dance with me?"

Evie's face flushed. She had been doing a lot of that tonight, and he had to suppress a grin each time. He led her onto the deck, and the others followed. They stepped out into moonlight. Silver white light essence glowed over the worn wood of the ship, making the trees and rigging into silhouettes. In the trees and all along the surface of the water fireflies winked like stars rained down into the world of men.

"Ohh," Evie breathed. She lifted her eyes to the dance of the living lanterns, the starlight reflecting softly off her skin. Her eyes shone with delight. Could he ever forsake her to death, on the chance that he could defeat Leazor, and knowing that there was also a chance to save her life?

Breac twirled her around to face him. The trio of musicians, seated on upturned buckets, stopped and applauded as they took position in the middle of an open place on the deck.

"What'll it be, soldier?" the fiddle player called.

"Play something from the south."

The musicians laughed and conferred among themselves. They started a jaunty tune from Carmi-Asriel. Breac smiled, and swept Evie into the dance. She stepped awkwardly at first, but picked up the simple step fast. From that song they dove right into another, and another, and the moonlight and fireflies blurred around them with the rising mist. At last they both stumbled, laughing and panting. They stood against the railing, staring out into the swamp, and the thousands of tiny winking lights. When the music came to a stop, Breac turned to her.

"One last dance?"

"Sure."

He called to the musicians, "Play the lullaby again."

The fiddle player tapped out a beat, and they began. Breac took her hand, and led her back out slowly this time. He twirled her around, and caught her in his arms, watching her dark hair swirl around her shoulders. Her face turned up, pale in the moonlight, watching him with an expression he'd rarely seen in a woman's eyes, and never directed toward him. He forgot everything in that instant, everything in the world but her.

They stepped back, swaying to the music, and he put his foot on a bolt in the deck. He staggered and crashed over backward into a pile of coiled rope, taking Evie down with him. The music ended in guffaws from the musicians. Sprawled awkwardly on top of him, the girl laughed as she rolled off. She sat up and smoothed the skirt over her knees.

Breac disengaged his arm from the coil of rope and reached over, pulling her back down with him. He kissed her lips and her eyelids, desire rising again with her body against his. He swallowed and whispered, so the others who were still laughing could not hear, "What are you doing to me?"

She gave him a long look, her joy slowly dissolving into uncertainty. She stood swiftly, putting on a smile for the others as she curtsied. "Glad you find us so entertaining," she called lightly as she turned and helped haul him to his feet.

He stood and came face to face with Mykell, perched on the railing in owl form. The changer stared at him with huge, unblinking eyes.

Fool!

25

Game of Hearts

Evie woke to a gentle rocking motion, and sat up. She'd been given the first mate's tiny cabin to sleep in, and had been so exhausted last night that she hadn't given it a second glance. Now she looked around, sniffing the air. It smelled of stale sweat and exotic cologne. Quite the combination. Pushing the blanket off, she sat up, feeling the motion of the boat become more pronounced. It took a moment's getting used to.

Last night she had hung her old clothes from pegs in the wall, hoping to dry them. This morning they were still a little damp, so she donned the dress again, smoothing wrinkles out of the clinging silk. Light from a small window brightened the cabin enough to see clearly the maps and charts tacked to the wall, along with a pencil sketch of a young lady. Her fingertips traced the unfamiliar contours of the land. Where were they on this map? Or was this someplace foreign? Could Acatra Dahma be on one of these other charts? Strange to be in a place where she couldn't even recognize a map.

She rolled her head, popping her neck, and then twisted to pop her back. Too much sleeping on hard surfaces. Still she felt good this morning. She smiled as she headed out to find the others.

On deck she realized why the ship was rocking. They were under way. The entire crew save Byrne, Lance, and Tarek were below deck rowing. Already the swamp trees were thinning out, and more and more open water was becoming visible. Salty wind swept through her hair, sending goose bumps up her arms.

Breac joined her at the rail as they left the last of the swamp trees behind, and the crew were called up from the oars. They raised the sails, and the salt wind had them moving in moments.

The wind tousled Breac's hair, and tugged at the embroidered cloak Byrne had given him, flapping the edges back. He stood straight, resting a hand on the railing and looking out to sea. With his face turned and only his blue eye visible, he looked regal. Favored by the High King, the son of royalty, a man whose future held endless potential.

Evie ran her hands through her hair, holding it back from her face for a moment. She let go, and the wind whipped it instantly into a dark brown mess around her head. Her good mood slowly dissolved as she watched him. It seemed of late that every hour she spent with the man made her that much more miserable. She had never wanted anyone, anything, more than she wanted him. Ever. Not even her music could compare. She had rescued him, had been rescued by him, had healed him, kissed him, fallen to pieces in front of him. A part of her felt sure that she would lay down her life for him, if she had to. But then, she had given in to cowardice before...

But what of his heart? What would her death do to him? What was this journey, bringing her to her death, doing to him right now? It would be better if he felt nothing for her. Far better. Then the only broken heart would be the one that was to die. But she couldn't undo his feelings any more than she could undo Sylvanus' death.

She turned to go back inside.

"Do you trust me, Evie?" His voice caught her before she could take a step.

She stopped breathing for a moment. Without turning she said, "Why is it so important to you?"

He stepped up behind her, putting a hand on her shoulder. She could feel the warmth of his light grip through the thin material. Did he have any idea how his touch affected her?

"I have to know. I am a shattered man. You've stripped me of who I thought I was, and thrown it to the wind. What I desire can never be, yet I am driven to know. Evie, have you recovered from the naiad's enchantment? Was it a passing whim?"

"No!" she said. "It was not."

"Then if you were not forced to be here, would you stay? If you lived, would you offer your life to me, to be my wife?"

Her face went cold, then hot, and her eyes stung. Head down, she ran for the cabin, covering her mouth to hold back a cry.

* * * * *

Breac felt the air leave him like he'd been gut punched. Some of the crewmembers gave him scowling glances after the cabin door slammed behind the girl. Mykell was nowhere in sight, thank the Creator. He retreated until he ran out of deck, then sank down in a coil of rope. The same rope he and Evie had landed on last night when they danced. He put his head in his hands, and shuddered.

"Trouble with your lady love?"

He looked up to see Tarek standing over him, his fingers teasing the fringe on a green scarf he wore. Breac grunted in reply, wishing he could pull the cloak over his head and hide. Or jump overboard. Why must they always pester him. Always giving advice, or questions, or plans.

"You had better go after her."

"Had I?" he looked up onto the smoky blue-white eyes.

"When women run away, that generally means they want us to chase after them."

"I am afraid it is not so simple this time."

"No?" Tarek aimed that soulful gaze right through Breac's heart.

He winced. "No. It's been my experience that people run when they want to get away from something. From me." He scowled.

"So you're going to sit there like a stupid ox and let her cry her pretty eyes dry alone."

Breac's scowl turned into a glare.

Tarek chortled. "You are a good judge of men. I can tell that because I am too." He grasped the rail, and leaned down until his flat nose, speckled from too much sun, was an inch from Breac's. "But you're a bad judge of women." He straightened up, looking triumphant as though he'd delivered some great bit of wisdom, and strode off. The end of his scarf flapped over his shoulder as though waving at Breac, taunting him.

He scowled after the old man. "No one who's been aboard a ship that long can be such a great judge of women either," he muttered. Still, the thought of Evie crying alone, with no one to comfort her, was more than he could endure. He wanted to be near her. Even if only to catch her tears. He stood and headed for the cabin.

Lance looked up from his charts on the captain's desk when Breac came in. He said nothing but jerked his chin toward the first mate's cabin. Breac felt his face flush as he strode to the door. He put his hand on the latch, then hesitated. He let go the latch and raised his hand to knock, and hesitated again. Lance was watching him. The other man shook his head, and turned back to his work.

Scratching a non-existent itch on his forehead, he raised his hand again, and knocked. She didn't answer, so he opened the door, peering in cautiously, ready to slam it shut if need be. The girl sat cross legged in the bunk, clutching a pillow to her chest. Her skirt splayed out in disarray around her knees, showing off her lower legs and bare feet. His heart lost rhythm for a moment.

She watched him, her eyes red, lips pressed tight together. She looked as though she had been waiting for him, and he felt a shred of annoyance toward Tarek, that he may have been right.

"Is this how you torture all your prisoners?" she whispered. "Make them fall in love with you before they're executed?"

"All my prisoners until now have been men," he stated. He knew it was the wrong thing to say, but what the right thing would have been escaped him. He felt like a hunted squirrel. The hunter's arrows were aimed at his heart, and he braced himself for further rebuke.

An insane little giggle escaped her. At once the giggle turned into a quiet sob. She dropped the pillow and raised a tear streaked, twisted face to him. He left the door hanging open and sat down beside her, pulling her into his lap to hold her tight.

* * * * *

It was early evening when Byrne joined them where they stood at the bow, looking out at the shore passing swiftly. The swamp and jungle were far behind them, replaced by low sandstone cliffs. And beyond those, rolling grassland. A flock of birds rose from the tall grass and chased a current of wind, their cries lost in the flapping canvas and rush of water under the prow.

"We will be in the harbor at Ravenport by nightfall," Byrne said. "We have not spoken of what we will do when we reach it."

Breac nodded. "I am listening, if you have a plan."

"If it is agreeable to you, I will send my men into the village tonight to find horses and supplies, and have them waiting at the docks before dawn. We will spend the night here on the ship, as it will be safer than any of the inns. In the morning you will leave for Al Acatra. I will have Kuruk and seven others accompany you. It is the most I can spare. You should reach the city before the evening if you hurry, and do not run into trouble."

Breac saluted him with a bow. "I thank you. May the Creator reward you richly for your kindness."

Byrne strode away, leaving them alone with the rush of wind in their ears. Evie felt dread tightening in her again. If it was a day's march from Ravenport to Al Acatra, then tonight would be their last. Breac had not asked her again whether she trusted him.

Part of her was happy to put off the conversation as long as possible. The other part was afraid. Afraid that he had given up. That in not answering he would assume the answer was no. Did it truly matter?

Would she escape tonight, or would she stay? The Ezomrah had not haunted her dreams while on board the ship, and after her victory in the dungeon and by the pool she gave them little thought as she considered the possibility of going back. Leaving this world. Leaving Breac. Keeping the guilt that was her companion, and the dread that she would never truly be free, and trying to move on in her world with a life that seemed distant and unimportant. Perhaps it would have been better if she had died inside Al Kazam. Perhaps she should just kill herself and get it over with.

The ship nosed into the water, sending cold spray into their faces. She shuddered. She became aware suddenly that Breac was staring at her. The colors of his eyes seemed to take on a life of their own in the crimson sunset, the brown one gleaming nearly red, and the blue one sparkling clear, almost white. She felt awkward in his presence. Unworthy. Guilty.

"You are beautiful Eva."

She felt pressure building behind her eyes. Tears threatening to spill again.

The far, watery horizon glowed with sun fire as the evening deepened. The sun turned the sky and water to blood. A flock of gulls circled the mast, and landed in the water, bobbing on the scarlet waves. Even their white feathers looked pink. *Like blood.*

Breac was still watching her. He looked lost.

The sun went down, and the air took on a chill. By the time it was dark enough to see them, they spotted lights on shore. The ship entered a tiny, rocky harbor, and dropped anchor. In the gloom they could just make out the shoreline, littered with boulders and broken fishing huts, and a little father in, more lights. Docks reached out into the oily looking water, lined with small dark boats. Lance and two others climbed into the landing boat, and called for it to be lowered. Evie heard the splash as it hit the water below them, and the scrape and creak of the oars as the men rowed toward the docks. Her eyes went buggy trying to follow their progress in the gloom.

"Now what?" she murmured.

Breac put his hand on hers. "We wait. It is safer for them to go ashore than any of us. Leazor must know which way we plan to come, and have an ambush set. We have no idea where it may be."

She withdrew her hand and squeezed his arm.

It was two hours before the landing boat reappeared out of the darkness. The lantern hanging from the ship's bow did little to illuminate it. It looked like a black shadow crawling toward them over the water. Lance hailed the ship, and they hauled him up.

"How do things look?" Byrne asked.

The first mate shrugged. "Calm. Our horses are in the livery, with the rest of the supplies, and the others are guarding them, in case of incident. I saw nothing suspicious there, and no ill will toward us."

"I hope that it remains so till morning," Byrne replied.

* * * * *

Evie lay awake in her bunk. A lamp burned, swaying gently from a hook above the bed, casting shadows back and forth. And in her hands, the jeweled dagger Byrne had given her.

There were two things she could see to use the dagger for: ending her life at once, or making one more attempt to go home. She dismissed the first idea. If she were to die, let it at least be for a good cause, to satisfy the law and let Breac's people stay free.

The second idea was the one she had rehearsed over and over. Thinking about it made her break out in a cold sweat. The same feeling she imagined she'd have if she tried to rob a bank, or assassinate the president. Guilty. Afraid. Traitor.

She shook her head, muttering to herself, "Have to make a choice. I hate choices."

She set the dagger point against a wooden beam over her head, pressing upward with both hands, leaving a line in the rough wood.

Home. Even to think about it, it didn't feel like home anymore. The Ezomrah would find her eventually of course. Perhaps she could fend them off with the songs of the Kantra. If not, they would take her mind and drive her mad. Not that she wasn't already there.

The second line appeared behind the tip of the blade. She still had not answered Breac's question. *Do I trust him?* She trusted him to be loyal. He was nothing, if not that. Unlike her. And what would his loyalty mean for her life? Could she bear to trust him, and then have him turn her over in the end? It would not change anything, other than dying with a shattered heart.

A third line stretched across the other two. The knot was taking shape.

26

Breac's Oath

Breac twisted around in the hammock strung for him in the captain's cabin. Byrne snored from the bunk, and Mykell, laying on the floor, slept with a paw over his face as though to ward off the noise. Moonlight coming in through the windows made a checker block pattern across the floor. Breac sighed and rolled out of the hammock, making no sound as his feet hit the floor. He stepped out onto the deck and stood in the chill white night. The rigging stood up against the moon like twisted demon shapes. A dank, dead fish smell rose in the still air. Dawn was a few hours away yet. He glanced around for the sentry that must be on duty, and saw the man asleep, propped in a coil of rope. He shook his head. Good thing Leazor had broken off pursuit. They'd be having their throats slit while they slept. He walked over and leaned against the railing. His heart beat heavily, laboring like that day on the battlefield as he stared at the decision before him. Cold sweat broke out on his body.

He did not fear death. But the death of the accursed? That was something different altogether. That he did fear. That hideous, dark place where the Ezomrah in disembodied form gnawed his flesh. His soul recoiled. The memory made him choke. Never had he questioned anything he was asked to do, whether suffer or die, or do the impossible task for his King. But now he questioned his strength. If he gave it any thought, he could never go through with his plan. Never though, could he let Evie face that fate. Never.

From his soul, he groaned. His knees faltered, and he dropped to the deck, kneeling with his head against the railing, gasping until his whole body heaved with silent sobs.

"Creator, what would you have me do?"

Only the sound of the creaking boat and water licking hungrily against its sides met his plea. Resolution strengthened in his heart. He made his choice.

"By the Faire Land, I swear I will take her place, if it is permitted."

The white moonlight swirled around him, as with a heavy fog rolling in, though it remained clear. A form became visible beside him on the deck, and solidified, washed in moonlight. Breac shuffled to his feet and bowed low. "My Liege."

"You have sworn, Aindreas, son of Rajah. The Creator permits. As do I," the High King said.

Breac felt his heart constrict. Dread filled him. He bowed again. "So be it. I will take her mark upon my hand."

The High King touched his left palm, and he watched the ugly blot spread across his skin. He lifted his other hand, expecting the mark of loyalty to the High King to disappear. Instead it glowed with a slight radiance of its own.

"You are no less my servant now than you have been all your life," the High King said.

Breac bowed his head. "I am comforted then."

The High King put his hand on his head. "Courage," he said. When Breac looked up, he was gone.

The cabin door creaked softly, and looking that way, he saw a low black shape slink on deck. Mykell was at his side before he had time to hide the mark on his palm.

"What have you done human?" Mykell hissed so loudly that the sleeping sentry stirred.

"The only thing I can do," Breac replied.

Mykell snarled, showing gleaming fangs. "You could have handed her over to be killed, as was the plan."

"I could not! And neither could you."

"Stupid, stupid fool!" Mykell cried, forsaking all semblance of quiet. "This thing cannot be done!"

The sentry started awake and jumped up, sword out, searching about for what had woken him.

"Do you have any idea what will be done to you?" Mykell continued, ears back, baring all his teeth now.

"The same as would be done to her."

"You are not merely exchanging your body to be killed. You are giving away your soul! Do you not understand? Your eternal soul in the hands of the Enemy. What have you done?!"

Breac bowed his head, nearly choking. "I know. I have given my word."

"You've committed no crime!" Mykell raged on. "I would not see her put to death, but she was meant to go, and I cannot stop it. You... you on the other hand....What have you done?" The last word ended in a shriek, followed by a panther's soul-stopping wail. Mykell leapt into the air, screaming his rage as an eagle, a hawk, a great owl, and a panther again, changing so rapidly that his form blurred. He hit the deck as a panther and continued changing, voicing his fury in animal screams that blurred together and became a continuous, hideous sound of horror and fear. Even Breac took a step back as men came stumbling up out of the hatch and the cabin to see what was attacking them.

With a final, piercing shriek, Mykell fled into the night.

Breac watched him go, then turned to the crowd gathered and asking questions. He mumbled that it was nothing, and hiding the new mark on his hand, ducked back into the cabin. Leaning heavily on the door, he took a deep breath, and strode to the other end of the room, to the tiny door that opened into the first mate's cabin, where Evie was asleep. He cracked the door to make sure she was alright. A lantern burned above the bunk, illuminating rumpled blankets and an empty bed. She was gone.

* * * * *

Evie went from dim lantern light to complete darkness. She tensed, afraid to move. Stillness made her ears ring. Her own breathing sounded loud, and she could tell from the sound that she was completely surrounded by—something. She put her hands out and felt cloth and plywood. She felt around and found more of the same, in all shapes. She was surrounded by the stuff. It smelled of dust and paint and old cloth. And the darkness wasn't getting any less dark. There was a little more space to the left, and she tried shoving her way in that direction. She bumped into something, heard it rock, and reached out for it just in time to hear it crash into a bunch of other somethings. The other somethings scattered before it, hitting the floor. Evie froze, waiting for shouts and lights. When nothing happened she continued more slowly, a step at a time, until her outstretched hand felt velvety cloth before her, hanging down in a rippling curtain. She turned and walked along beside it. It was long, and tall, farther than she could reach above her head. It ended finally in a wall.

She lifted aside the edge of the curtain, putting her hand out and feeling nothing beyond it. She put her foot out, and stepped into a vast space. That much she could feel and hear. Finally some light here. Red exit signs glowed at intervals around the huge room. Row upon row of shadowy seats stretched up and away from the edge of the platform where she stood.

"A theatre," she whispered. "What am I doing here?"

A sudden noise at the door. Her heart slammed in her chest. The sound of rushing traffic entered with the opening door, along with a vague form. The door chinked shut, and the lights flicked on. Evie cringed.

"Evie? What on earth!"

It was Rachael.

"Rachael? What are you doing here? Where am I?" She squinted in the harsh light.

"Getting ready for tonight's rehearsal." Rachael held up her violin case. "How did you get in here?" she said, walking toward the stage.

"The mark."

"Of course." Rachael snapped her fingers. "The sets. I forgot I used the mark to decorate one of the tapestries. The one you used to escape must have lined up closest to this one. Did anyone follow you? Does that man know you escaped?"

"Not yet."

Evie felt bewildered, out of place. With her eyes adjusting to the light, everything looked so strange, like images out of a remembered dream.

"We have to get you out of here then. You'll need all the head start you can get."

"Where are we?"

"At the Willow River Center for the Performing Arts."

"But that's, like, a hundred miles from home. What are you doing all the way out here?"

"Hey, beggars can't be choosers, right? If I want to perform I have to go where opportunity takes me. There aren't many theatres around our area, if you haven't noticed." She let herself into the orchestra pit, and walked over to the stage. "We need to get you out of here before they come looking for you."

"Wait."

"Wait?"

This felt all wrong. Evie's left palm tingled, and she scratched it absently, staring about her.

"Why did you ask if I was followed? How did you know about Breac?"

"Is that his name? Last time I saw you, some strange man was dragging you out of the antique shop. I got home and my house was broken into. Of course I assumed you had been kidnapped." She put her hand on Evie's shoe, which was shoulder level with her in the orchestra pit. "What was it all about? Are you sure they didn't follow you?"

Evie sat down on the edge of the stage. "It's night there. Everyone is asleep. I have time."

Rachael boosted herself up next to Evie, laying her violin case beside her on the stage. "What's all this about?" she asked again.

Evie rubbed her palm. "Without my death, their whole world will crumble," she recited. Something still did not seem right here. She felt disoriented. And why were there no Ezomrah closing in on her?

"So what? That's their problem, hon. You got dragged into it. It's really not your fault. They'll figure something out."

"No, they won't. It's how things work in that world. There will be no safe countries for the people to flee to."

Rachael stroked her back. "I know you feel bad, but you can't honestly be thinking of sacrificing yourself for people you don't even know. I'm sure it will turn out all right for them. They have magic, after all."

"The High King's magic. It only works if the King's rule is intact. Without my death, there is no magic." A whimsical smile tugged at her mouth. "Kind of funny, isn't it? Mykell, the naiads, Tyra and Ylva, they will all suffer because I was a coward. And Breac..."

"That horrible man who kidnapped you? He's the one that deserves to die! Think! He kidnapped you!"

Evie rubbed her temples. She had come here to think. Rachael's prattle was not making that easy.

"You can't be serious. You fell for him didn't you?"

She didn't reply. Why was Rachael here anyway? And at the very moment that Evie arrived back in this world?

"He's playing games with you! Can't you see that? It's a

common thing for a girl who's been kidnapped to fall in love with her captor. It's a mental illness. You have to trust me, hon."

Evie looked at her steadily, until Rachael rolled her eyes. "What?"

"It's not like that. I know what you're talking about, but you don't know Breac. He treats me as his equal. He's never touched me, has never kept me tied up or locked up. I love him."

"Listen to yourself!" Rachael mimicked her tone, "*I love him. He's trying to kill you!*"

"No... he isn't," she said absently.

Do you trust me? Breac's question still rang in her ears. She thought about how the naiad queen had counseled her do just that.

"I didn't come here to run away."

"What?" Rachael's expression hardened.

"I came to think. And to say goodbye. I love him. I trust him. Even if it is nothing more than a delusion. What do I have to live for here? I'll never be able to forget that world, and him, and everything that's happened. Even if I could, the Ezomrah would find me and drive me mad. I may as well die anyway as live like that. I will give my life for him, if that's what it takes."

"What about your boyfriend here?" Rachael changed tactics.

"James isn't my boyfriend. He never was."

"What about your family?"

"Please tell them...I don't know what you could tell them. Maybe I could write a letter for you to deliver..."

"You're making a very big mistake," Rachael said. A fierce scowl distorted her pretty face. "A *very* big one."

"Am I?" Evie stared down at her hands. *Am I?*

It took a moment to realize that she was only looking at the faded henna tattoo. The curse mark was gone. *What?* She stared, lips parting as her heart hammered out a new rhythm. What did it mean?

"What's the matter?" Rachael asked.

Evie clenched her fist shut

"I have to go back. Now!"

She stood and turned back toward the stage curtain. Behind her, Rachael spoke. "I can't let you do that."

"What?" Evie turned. She caught a flash glimpse of Rachael with her arms raised, just an instant before the violin case slammed into the side of her head. Her body jerked sideways, and she sprawled across the stage. "What was that for?!" she screamed.

Rachael strode toward her. "I can't let you leave."

"Why?" Evie looked at her, bewildered, holding her pounding head. Had the woman gone mad? Or was she really that committed to making sure Evie didn't throw her life away? Of all people she had thought that Rachael would understand. Unless...

The woman reached into her jacket and pulled out a pistol. A tiny brown creature clung to her hand as she withdrew it. It ran up her arm and perched on her shoulder. Evie ignored the gun, squinting through her headache at the creature. The overlarge, pit black eyes stared at her as the tiny body morphed into that of an eagle. *You've made a very foolish decision, Eva Drake.*

27
The Tables are Turned

Evie stared into the Ezomrah's bottomless eyes, heard the words it spoke into her mind, and quietly panicked. The creature spread its wings and took air. It landed on the stage before her and became a leopard. The lips curled back to show yellowed fangs, as though grinning at her. In that instant of silence, a boot struck the wood floor. The stage curtain parted, and the leopard's gaze turned, along with Evie's and Rachael's.

"Breac!"

He stepped onto the stage, his sword out, point drooping downward. Every inch of him spoke of great weariness. His face looked strained. The Ezomrah stared at him, and he stared back, neither moving. The leopard's lips curled into a gleaming smile. For an instant the man seemed frozen, face twisting with fear. The leopard took a single step toward him. Breac sprang forward, closing the gap within a second, and plunged his sword into the creature. The thing screamed and leapt at him. He let go the sword hilt and grabbed its head with both hands as it crashed into his chest, sending them both rolling. With a quick twist he snapped its neck.

Rachael shrieked. She leveled the pistol at Breac. Evie, still sprawled on the ground, kicked at her feet. She stumbled, and the gun cracked. Overhead the ornate plaster ceiling fractured, raining dust on them. Rachael jumped off the stage, landing in the orchestra pit. She crashed into the rows of chairs and music stands and scrambled away, running for the exit.

Breac stood slowly, and pulled his sword from the creature's chest, then wiped it on his boot. He came and sat next to Evie, surveying the dead beast. It was no longer a leopard, but didn't resemble anything else, either.

"It was changing when I killed it," he said.

"Into what?"

He shrugged. "A snake perhaps?"

Evie stared at the deformed body, then looked away. "I'm sorry," she said. "For everything."

He laid the sword in his lap and drew her in close, rubbing a gloved finger up and down her cheek. "I understand."

"No—no you don't. I—"

His voice rasped as he cut her off. "I didn't come here to take you captive."

"And I didn't come here to run away."

He said nothing as his mismatched eyes flickered over her face.

"I came... to sort things out," she said. "And to say goodbye."

"And I have come to see if you will return with me. As a companion instead of a captive. I cannot find the strength to finish this journey alone."

She smiled. "I will. Whatever the end is. I trust you, Breac. And I love you. I'll come."

He let out a breath, and seemed to relax, as though he'd been straining to hear those words.

"But look." She held out her palm to him. "The mark is gone. What does that mean?"

Pain flashed over his face for the briefest instant. "I have spoken to the High King. It means that we have an agreement."

"What sort of agreement? And when did you see the King?"

He smiled and kissed her palm where the stain used to be. "It means..." he paused, stared up at the gilded ceiling for a moment. "It means that the Ezomrah will no longer be seeking to destroy you. When we reach Al Acatra all of this will be resolved. The High King will explain it fully."

"Oh." She frowned, unsatisfied with his answer. She should be leaping for joy, singing and shouting. But he did not seem joyful. He seemed sad and distant, and all she could feel was dread.

Taking her hand, he kissed it again and helped her to her feet. "Shall we be going?"

She groaned and put a hand to her head as she stood up, remembering too late that she'd been hit. Her headache exploded into colorful starbursts behind her eyes.

"Are you hurt?"

"She hit me with the violin case."

* * * * *

Byrne was waiting for them, brooding in the light of a single candle on the desk when they stepped into the captain's cabin. "My men are worried," he said simply.

"There is nothing to fear," Breac replied. "Save the danger of a sleeping sentry."

Byrne nodded, and ran a hand over his face. He blinked wearily. "Dawn is approaching. It is time for you to be on your way." He rose and strode toward the door, pausing as he was going out to let Mykell enter. "I will be waiting on deck."

The door swung closed, and the three were left alone in the candle light. Mykell padded forward on silent paws, and bowed his head. "Forgive me, my friend. I was in the wrong."

Breac bowed in return. "I have nothing to forgive."

Evie cast a glance between the two, but didn't ask. They packed their things quickly, and Evie changed back into her old clothes, with the addition of a warm cloak. Before she left the first mate's cabin she tucked the dagger Byrne had given her into her belt. They joined the captain and Lance on deck, along with the group of men who were to travel with them. In the group was Kuruk, the scout, and another of the scouts whose name Evie hadn't heard. The other scout took their packs and loaded them in the landing boat.

Breac saluted the captain. "Again, thank you for your kindness." He drew from his pocket the broken pendant he'd found in the pool beneath Al Kazam. "I found this when we fled the mountain. I assume it must belong to one of your company."

"The seal of Carmi-Asriel," Byrne said, picking it up to study it in the dim light.

"It's mine," Kuruk said. The captain passed it to him, but he waved it off. "Keep it. It's suited more to you than me."

They boarded the landing boat, and waited as it was lowered, listening to the creak of the pulleys and smelling the salty dawn. Waves lapped the ship's hull, now towering over them.

The oars slipped in and out of the black water with only a soft plunk, no louder than the groan of wood on wood as their handles rubbed the sides of the boat. Kuruk threw a line over the pier as the oars were brought in, and the boat nosed up against the dock. The two men left to guard their supplies the night before waited for them on shore with the horses and provisions. Few words were exchanged as the guards took the boat, and their party took the horses. Breac and Kuruk went over everything, checking the horses and gear one last time before they mounted up. Evie stood shivering, watching the eastern sky go from black to deep blue, and the stars begin to fade. Mykell perched on her shoulder as an owl, cooing softly to himself and swiveling his head around, looking beyond the men and horses to the shadows under the docks and between the buildings. His feathers tickled her cheek as he shifted, repositioning his feet.

"If our journey goes well, we should be in Al Acatra this evening," he said. He shook out his feathers. "Tomorrow is the Day of Justice. There is no time now for delay."

A shiver went through Evie. The Day of Justice. So they had

come to it at last, or almost had. Would her life truly be spared? Why had Breac not spoken of another way before? Was the cost so great? She watched him, rubbing her palm where the mark had been. Why had it disappeared at all? Fear rose in her stomach. A new kind of fear. She dare not give shape to her dread, even in thoughts.

In the village a door banged, and voices called. A lantern bobbed down toward the shore.

"Time to be going," Kuruk said.

Breac seemed not to have heard. His face was toward the village. That much she could make out by the light of their single lantern, and the dawn's dim glow. He seemed different somehow, suddenly. Distant. Like his mind was literally somewhere else.

"Wait here," he mumbled, already striding up the dock toward the village.

The others looked at each other, puzzled, but waited.

* * * * *

Breac was no stranger to fear, but he had never been a servant to it, either. This Fear was something new altogether.

He had not been right since he swore his oath, and took Evie's mark to himself. It was not so noticeable on the ship, but when he had gone to her world and faced the Ezomrah there, then he felt it. The creature had known, and thought that he was under its power, which he assumed was how he'd been able to surprise and kill it.

Now he wrestled against the silent command: *Go.*

He felt his body moving, and could not stop, heard himself tell the others to wait, while his mind screamed at them for help. Even Mykell watched him blankly, giving no indication that he realized what was happening.

The village loomed darkly around him. He heard a startled question, and a light flared several houses down.

"Creator help me!" he gasped, coming to a stop between two houses. Wisps of predawn sea fog hung low in the alley. He pressed his back against a wall, struggling against the command to continue. And the fear like he had never known choked him.

How had Evie coped with this for so long? Or was it his knowledge that strengthened the horror? He searched his mind for the words of a song of the Kantra. Any song. His frantic lips spilled words, at first jumbled, then solidified into the melody of the healing song, now neither soothing nor arousing, but plaintive, pensive.

The song finished, he let out a long, shaking breath. Now more in his own mind, he pushed back the fear, and considered. He had been brought here alone for a reason, and doubtless he would soon know what it was. He wiped sweat from his face, imagining what could be stalking him even now. The Ezomrah no doubt were near, waiting for him to draw his last breath. Then they would carry his spirit away.

He took a long breath and shoved off from the wall, stepped to the edge of the building. The street was empty. Rounded sea stones crunched under his boots as he left the alley. A breath of wind lifted the corners of his cloak and dried the cold sweat on his face. It stank of saltwater and rotten fish, and something more. The scent of decay.

He stopped dead at a shadowy movement from the corner of his eye. He looked, and saw only darkness between two buildings. But something was there. He ceased breathing as his nose caught a whiff of smoke.

Breeeeeac.

Breac started, and with the start he was already running. He ducked between two buildings, panting the words of the song of protection under his breath. He flattened himself against a wall.

The building in whose shadow he hid was a tavern, and

across from him, the livery stable. The end of the alley should have given him a view of the sea, gray and still in the predawn. He looked that way and instead saw a moving wall of darkness. He blinked.

Breeeeeac. You cannot hide from me now. You swore an oath. I will pay my vow when the time is right.

The air rumbled, and the scent of smoke grew stronger. Still he watched that strange dark mass sliding past the opening. Here and there it gleamed dully, reflecting the slowly brightening sky. Then it was gone. The gray sea beckoned him to flee. A movement from the street side. He turned his head. A great yellow eye, big as the tavern door, winked at him. He bolted away, racing down the alley toward the sea. A black object fell across the opening, barring his way. He stared in confusion for an instant. Was the creature big enough to loop round the stable and wink at him, while blocking his escape the opposite direction with its tail? It appeared so. This then, was not the same dragon that Leazor had partially possessed before. No. This creature was far bigger, and without the haze over its eye, which would mean that it was willingly working with the Sorcerer, instead of being controlled by him.

He'd never known panic before. Now it froze him to the spot. Insane laughter ripped through his mind. His thoughts were going to pieces in all directions. He thought he could taste blood. Had he been killed already, without feeling it, and this was the beginning of his torment?

"Creator help me!" He cried aloud. No, this was not the end. Not yet. He sprinted the few yards between buildings, stopped with his hand on the stable wall, and turned to face the two story tavern. The great glowing eye was turning, the scaled nostrils coming into view around the corner. He sprang away from the stable. Two running paces brought him back to the tavern wall. He leapt at it, planted one boot on it, then the other, reached for the overhanging eves. His fingers caught hold even as he fell away from the wall. For an instant he dangled above the alley by one hand. Only an instant. He grabbed on with the other hand, and swung himself up, a full half second before fire blasted between the two buildings.

Breac was already running up the slanted roof and down the far side. The distance to the next building was less. He leapt across, boots thudding loudly on the wooden shingles, competing with his wild heartbeat. People were already running into the street, screaming.

He took one more roof, three buildings now separating him from the burning alley, and dropped down into another dark corner. He crouched by the wall, panting. A figure ran round the side of the building and nearly fell over him.

"There you are." The figure dropped down beside him. In the lightening twilight Breac could make out the face of Kuruk.

"I'm sorry," he replied. "Its—"

"Don't be minding that. Mykell spoke with me. I know not all is what it seems." The sailor-scout gripped his shoulder, shaking him a little. "Courage up, friend. We are in the hands of the Master Creator, whose purpose will not fail."

"I am in your debt."

"Aye, you are. Now come. We must not let them destroy the village on our account."

"Right."

Breac followed him into the street, where they were nearly knocked over by a wild eyed woman with a baby. She shoved him out of the way as if he were a stray goat and kept running. A bearded seaman followed three paces behind, running with his sword in his hand. Another jet of flame roared across in front of them, lighting the blacksmith shop ablaze. As soon as the fire settled, they bolted back toward the docks, and the road out of town. The beast saw them. The great head rose above the burning rooftops, turning as it followed their progress. It rumbled out a cloud of smoke, but they raced on. Behind them timber cracked and splintered in the wake of the monstrous thrashing tail. They sped past the docks, saw that the ship had already passed beyond the rocky mouth of the bay and was out of sight. The rest of their party had disappeared as well. They kept running, following the road toward Al Acatra as behind them the monster reared up, spreading wings that nearly overshadowed the entire village. It gave a ponderous flap, landing on a house, crushing it.

Breac felt, rather than saw the Ezomrah. He had a sense of lifting away from his body, for a moment hovering over, watching himself run. The image seemed distorted, sounds replaced by the guttural roar of fire and laughter. A pair of green eyes suddenly filled his vision, and fleeting notes of song. Normal vision and the sensation of his own body running hit him so hard he stumbled. Kuruk hauled him up by the collar and shoved him forward as smoke billowed past them. Mykell's black panther form sprang up out of the shadows by the road. From the tail of his vision Breac saw him rear up, his Ezomrah opponent becoming visible as their bodies crashed together.

"It's not for looking good, mate," Kuruk panted, glancing over his shoulder. "At least we've drawn it out of town."

They topped a rise in the road and stopped. Below, their companions were huddled in a tight circle, back to back fighting a score of Leazor's Death riders. Behind, the dragon rose into the sky, a nightmare on black wings.

"Curses!"

"You said it."

28

Evie Does Battle

Evie had watched Breac's form disappear into the darkness, and frowned. He did not seem right this morning. And why on earth would he leave suddenly to go into the village? She popped her pinkie knuckle, glancing back at the ship. She could see its black bulk against the gray sea and lighter sky. It had already turned and was gliding toward open waters. Mykell startled her when he dropped from her shoulder and alighted on Kuruk. The sailor-scout jumped and just stopped himself from swatting at Mykell. He tilted his head, listening perhaps to words the shifter spoke only into his mind. Then he roused himself suddenly, swung down from the horse, and handed the reins to Winneth, an older man, short and wiry. "Time to start."

"But Breac..." Evie began.

"I'll find him." Then to Winneth, "Don't be waiting for us." He turned and started toward the village, and Mykell flew in the opposite direction, leaving the rest of them staring at each other in confusion.

Evie fell in with the group reluctantly, glancing back toward Ravenport, with its growing number of lighted windows. She felt suddenly alone, and wondered if the Ezomrah would attack again while her guardians were away. But no... the mark was gone, and Breac had said that she needn't worry any more. Her scalp prickled. Again she felt that dread, a fear that she dare not name.

Their horses started up the road, laboring through sand, their hooves clinking dully against rocks and driftwood. The sand grew hard packed and gave way gradually to dirt as they topped a knoll and left the twinkling village behind.

Dawn had begun, easing back the darkness. Evie could see

her companions' faces vaguely now, though they hadn't been riding for more than a minute or two. Suddenly the dusk behind them lit up. They heard a crack of timber from the village. As one they stopped the horses and looked back.

"Ezra," Winneth said, jerking his head back toward the village. The other man, Evie recognized him as the harmonica player, though she hadn't known his name before, turned his horse and galloped to the top of the knoll.

"Ravenport is under attack!"

Winneth turned his horse, and the others followed, but at that moment the dusk came alive. The attack did not begin as an attack so much as a quickening of shadows. They were turning their horses back toward Ravenport, alone on the road, and suddenly a dark mass separated itself from the trees and brambles and moved toward them. The shadows were almost upon then before she recognized them as riders cloaked in black, on dark steeds. Instantly she was surrounded by the sailor guard, circling around her, swords hissing as they left sheaths. The dark riders made a circle around them, riding round and round, hemming them in tighter. Evie's mare snorted, stepping nervously as the other horses pressed in against her. The riders passed before the noses of the sailor's horses, until the group became a mass of tense animals, with the circle of dark riders revolving around the perimeter.

It all happened so fast Evie barely had time to comprehend the situation in the growing half light. The riders all held weapons, swords or short spears. She had a fleeting moment imagining being struck by one of the spears, and wondered how it would feel to have her ribs split apart.

A battle shriek sounded from the top of the hill. She jerked her head around to see Ezra galloping down toward them, screaming his wrath all the way. Gone the twinkling-eyed musician. The attention of the riders diverted as well. They stopped their circling. Again before she had time to process it all, the sailors struck, using the instant's distraction to kick their animals forward. After that she didn't have a clear view of anything.

She pulled out her own little dagger, heart racing as she looked around. There were no openings to flee through, no escape. A dark body loomed in front of her. A black gloved hand stretched out to take her reins. She struck it with the dagger, hardly aware that she was screaming. She had a glimpse of her attacker's eyes, angry and pained. Instinct more than clear sight made her jerk sideways away from the man's sword blade. The motion nearly cost her seat. One foot swung loose of the stirrup, and the other began slipping as she listed to the side, clinging one-handed to the horse's mane. She raised her tiny weapon, and by some miracle caught the sword as it was coming down a second time. The attacker's blade caught on the dagger's hand guard, and her weak defense redirected the blow. Both blades hacked into the saddle pommel an inch from her leg as she hung crooked from the opposite side. The tip of her dagger dug into the horse's neck. The animal reared, and Evie slid off into a world of dust and flying hooves.

* * * * *

Breac looked back to see a massive shadow, nearly blotting out the gray sky, circle over them.

"*Today will I die*," he muttered, quoting a lyric from the Book of Kantra. "*May the Creator weep for me. Blood of my heart, tears of my eye, Offered to Him in loyalty.*" So saying he drew his sword.

Kuruk snatched the bow and quiver from his back. He struggled for an instant to restring the bow, then nocked an arrow to the string. "I'm not for dying till we've brought the beast down."

"Then let us do so."

The dragon made a sweep over the fighting, flying high

enough to catch the first rays of sunrise light. The blackish wings glowed pink for a moment as light shone through, and the scales glinted with mottled purple and brown. Kuruk's arrow vanished from the string. Breac could not see where it had struck, but he knew it had. The beast roared, faltered for an instant, and came speeding toward them. He and Kuruk leapt away, rolling into the berry brambles on either side of the road as Leazor's host tore through.

Breac felt his skin and shirt being shredded as he disengaged from the prickers. The dragon already had its huge yellow eye fastened on him. From the beast's far side came Kuruk's yell, sounding small and far away. The beast flinched and whipped its head to the other side, sweeping the area with a jet of flame, which was followed by a yelp of pain from the sailor. Breac ran up alongside the crouching body, praying that he could reach the head as it was turning back, and be able to stab it through the eye before it saw him. It didn't work. The head jerked about suddenly, searching back along its body till it spotted him. Its sides expanded, drawing breath for another blast of fire.

* * * * *

Evie stumbled to her feet, crying out as a hoof caught her arm. It went numb to the hand, and the dagger fell from her grasp. She stared down at the weapon for perhaps a full second as a decade's worth of thoughts flashed through her mind. She dare not bend down for it and risk getting kicked in the head. But that could happen anyway. What was she doing in this place? Useless and afraid, a woman without a weapon in a man's battle. One of the horses knocked into her, nearly sending her sprawling again. She stumbled backward, tripped and fell over something lying in the road. It was Ezra.

For an instant she stared into his eyes, a few feet from her own face. They blinked slowly, and opened. Across their glassy surface she thought she saw something flicker for a moment, an image like a reflection of light. A light that had shape and moved, filling the sightless eyes until they flashed golden for a moment, and then was gone, leaving behind the glass green stare of a dead man, his lips frozen in a faint smile.

She wanted to scream, but couldn't, because she wasn't breathing. She gulped a breath, and wriggled backward away from the corpse, then staggering once more to her feet, realized that she had escaped the crush of battle, or that it had moved on without her. Her dagger lay a few feet way, half buried in sand and dirt. She grabbed it and looked first to the knot of men fighting on horseback, then to the hill crest, where a huge shape had alighted. A dragon. Or perhaps a grandfather of dragons. Its bulk overflowed the road.

"Breac is there."

She spun to see Mykell alight, shifting into his panther form. He panted through a snarl.

"Help him. I will come to you when I can." He turned and leapt into the battle, landing on the back of a horse, just behind the rider. His paws circled, like a person using two hands to open a pickle jar, and the man's head flopped aside, dangling. Mykell leapt over the body, now spurting blood like a garden fountain, and disappeared.

Evie turned and sprinted up the hill toward Breac and the dragon. *What am I doing? I can't fight a dragon!* But her feet kept going. She gripped the dagger now in her left hand, her right hanging useless.

Again she sang the song of protection, like a mantra, like a shield going before her this bloody dawn. She felt a quiver of power in the still air. Perhaps Breac was right. Perhaps they were not alone.

With that thought she topped the hill and stopped, blasted by the power of the new risen sun. Ahead in the road crouched the dragon. It had its head twisted back toward her, but not looking at her. It had eyes for Breac only. She had a sickening sense of déjà vu as for a second time she ran up alongside a dragon's tail, this time ducking under it between the hind legs. She stopped, crouched under the steaming belly, and threw up a last prayer for success. She thrust the dagger upward with all her strength. It flew from her hand ahead of a gush of scalding blood, and her scaly ceiling heaved upward. The blast of fire that was meant for Breac came out suddenly without aim in a howl of pain. She saw him hit the ground as flames roared over his head. He was up and running the instant the air was clear. Evie rolled out from under the beast, away from the flow of steaming blood. Now the dragon's eye was on her and not Breac. She stared into the yellow slit, and stopped breathing.

* * * * *

Breac knew not who or what had attacked the dragon and saved his life, and he didn't stop to think about it. He swatted cinders out of his hair and was up and running at the same time. The long snaky neck shot upward, higher than the treetops, then the head began to descend, curving down and back, its great yellow eye fixed on a target behind him. Breac stopped and turned. He stood now in the tightening crook of the dragon's neck, as it dropped lower and drew in closer. He could feel the heat radiating from the creature's body, see the horned back of its head. Another second and it would be low enough. He glanced past it to whatever had caught its attention. Evie.

His heart squeezed painfully as he watched her lips move, reciting the song of protection. And then for just an instant the world seemed to still, as if time had stopped, giving him a unique sort of clarity. The air felt alive. He met the girl's eyes, and they were bright with knowing. Knowing the same thing that he was knowing. That they were not alone. Once again the Sorcerer's evil power had been matched by a girl singing a song. Leazor had fixed on her, seeming to forget for a moment about Breac. A grim smile twisted his lips.

He flipped his sword around to hold it in a stabbing position, his fist backward on the hilt like an impossibly long knife, and leapt forward. Two running steps and he sprang up, caught hold of one of the short spikes of horns on the dragon's head, and in the same motion sank the sword to the hilt in the yellow eye.

Breac dropped to the ground as the head shot skyward, spewing a geyser of flame into the sunrise. He rolled to his feet, grabbed Evie, and together they ran as the dragon's body began a convulsive dance of death.

Breac!

He stumbled as the Sorcerer's disembodied rage enveloped them.

You are marked! You are mine! You cannot escape me!

His body fell away, his spirit embraced by a fiery presence. He sensed a Void. A great, heavy, endlessly black nothing that was at once bitter and burning. Sounds beyond the range of human hearing pressed him. Inaudible screams.

And then...

He was lying crumpled half on his side. A slender arm encircled his neck and shoulder as soft dark hair hung over his face. Her voice fell over him like sweet cool water. Another presence flickered into his mind. Mykell.

The Sorcerer tried to take you before the appointed time. He was denied.

Breac's whole body shuddered. The girl stopped singing, loosening her hold enough to look in his face. She looked as though she was trying to speak, and couldn't. He closed his eyes, fighting back a scream or a sob, one of the two. Again his body shook.

* * * * *

Evie heard her name called, softly but urgently. She felt numb, sitting there holding his shaking body. *Too much,* her mind kept protesting, refusing to sort through everything. Blood, death, an unseen power, and now this horror as Breac did battle with himself silently in her arms. She had seen. Oh, yes, she had seen. The curse she had born in her hand now marred his. So she sat, simply existing for the moment, and each emotion rose unbearably, to be replaced instantly by another, and another. Too much. She was numb and cold, but lava boiled beneath.

"Evie!" The call was sharp this time. She looked up to see Mykell at eye level, giving her a stare. She stared back.

"Your gift is needed."

My gift?

"Kuruk is dying. Others will be close behind."

Breac must have heard. He rolled away from her and knelt facing away. She rose, and with a touch to his shoulder, followed Mykell. She refused to look at the dragon as they passed its still body lying in the road.

Kuruk lay on his back in a tangle of blackberry brambles. He trembled, breathing in short gasps through melted lips. Evie blanched.

"What if I can't help him?" she whispered.

Mykell actually snarled at her. "It is not you helping him, it is the song of the Creator. Order your mind, human, and get to it."

She knelt and laid her own hand, blistered by the dragon's blood, over Kuruk's blackened one. She closed her eyes to shut out her fear, and began the song.

Weary and Broken,
Rest here for awhile.
Peace I have spoken,

Creator grant.

Brightness of sunlight,

Music of water,

Starlight and wind's might

Fill you with strength...

As many times as she had sung the healing song in the last few days, she could not weary of it. It seemed to change on its own with each recitation, and its effect on her changed as well. When she turned from the last wounded man she felt both weary and refreshed, emptied and filled. Her own injuries were long gone. She sat on a boulder alongside the road, still dazed, and watched the small group gather, greet one another, and then begin tending the three fallen. One of the men rode into Ravenport for shovels, and returned with two others from the village to assist with the digging and return the equipment once they were done.

Evie tried not to stare at the bodies, yet her eyes kept straying that way. It wasn't the blood and gore that held her attention, but the vacant eyes, staring glassy and greenish at nothing. The lack of life. Like puppets waiting for someone to come and animate them. Death.

Kuruk went quickly through the pockets of the deceased before they were laid in the shallow hole and covered over. Passing close by her boulder, he dropped something into her hands. She looked down at Ezra's harmonica, and saw instead the creature of light reflected in his dying gaze, then the same gaze, twinkling and full of mirth as he played and stamped his foot to the music. Mykell separated from the others and sat beside her.

"They are but shells now," he said. "Still, we do well to respect them. Their spirits have fled away, and found true life, and perfected bodies in their new home."

"And where is their new home?"

Mykell lifted his face to the sky, and tested the wind with a quivering nose. "The Faire Land. The hope of every true servant of the Creator. Even I do not know where to find it, or whether it is a country, a place across the sea, or in the sky, or just on the other side of our next breath."

"In my world we would call that heaven," she said, picking up the harmonica gingerly. She blew a soft note on it. It had a sweet, mellow tone. "But how do you know it's really out there, if you know so little about it?"

"Ha *ha!*" Mykell lashed himself with his tail, his eyes sparkling. "I know. Because in my heart, I am homesick for that land. And because I know the King, and the Creator. The Faire Land is very real, Evie. You can hazard your life on it."

Evie looked at him quizzically, but no more explanation was forthcoming. "What about Sylvanus?"

"Doubtless joined in the Great Song even now. Dancing with his Creator."

"And when Breac...?"

Mykell gazed at her without reply. His green eyes grew even brighter for a moment before he turned away. His great shining black body shrank till it was tiny and brown, and he spread his new sparrows' wings and flew off.

The sobs came as Evie slipped to the ground, and would not cease.

29

Traitor's Death

Most of the country they now rode through was farmland. Rolling hills, wooded valleys, and little streams as far as the travelers could see, if they had been looking. The five who remained from the ship seemed mostly impassive and distant. Kuruk, Orran, and Sanrik, the three over whom she had sung the healing song, had each thanked her, and now and then cast her a curious glance. They were glancing at Breac as well, and their eyes held dread as well as curiosity, as if they too began to guess the outcome of this last journey.

Evie rode as if in a trance. The clop of the horses' hooves, creak of leather, rush of wind in her ears as it blew in off the sea smelling of salt and endless open spaces—all seemed to whisper a song to her. Like something from the Kantra, something she had not yet learned. It dried the tears on her face and lulled her into a shaky peace, a brittle kind of numbness. She could not look at Breac. She could not speak to him.

Miles stretched long and silent behind them. No one offered to stop for a meal. The battle outside of Ravenport had changed everything. Leazor had been rebuffed. Refused a victory before his time. Yet he knew his victory was assured. The unspoken feeling in the group was that he would not attack again. So they traveled openly without fear or watching for ambush. Even Mykell seemed content to ride along, perched on Breac's shoulder in sparrow form. Now and again he twittered in the man's ear.

As midday passed, Evie began to notice the birds. Flocks of crows had been sweeping overhead for some time, giving her an uncomfortable feeling as their dense formations blocked the sun. But until then she didn't comprehend that they were keeping up with the travelers. A great cloud of them would go sailing overhead to land in a field, coating it like thick black snow. When she and her companions came even with them, they would sweep into the air again, only to land in another field or tree. And the number was growing. Instead of one flock, there were three or four. Perhaps several thousand birds. One alighted for a moment on her horse's head between its ears. It cocked a beady black eye at her. Ezomrah.

Her horse spooked. It took off, carrying them far ahead of the others, into a swirling vortex of black wings and eyes. She tugged the reins, pulling the animal around in a tight circle. The air felt cold and had a bitter edge in here. An acrid taste coated her mouth. She slapped her heals against the mare's sides, urging her back the way they'd come. They emerged from the whirlwind, nearly colliding with the rest of the group.

Kuruk asked, "All well?"

She spit off to the side. "Yes." Then added, "It's not me they're after now."

The whirlwind of black bodies dispersed as they rode through it, the myriad of rasping caws sounding very much like the evil laughter Evie had heard so many times in her mind.

Breac shifted in the saddle and looked up. His face had all the expression of a mask, but his eyes...so intense. Tortured. Evie put a hand over her heart, sure that it was screaming the pain her mouth could not release.

* * * * *

The sun went down. As if it had been her only energy source, Evie felt fatigue grip her.

They stopped for a while to let the horses rest, and she nibbled some jerky and travel bread, watching Breac. He sat away from the others, his knees drawn up and arms draped across them. Blond hair hung over his eyes. He seemed a stranger, slumped beside the road, weary and burdened. She had only known him a few days. In her own world, under normal circumstances, he would be almost a stranger. Merely an interesting acquaintance. But here, now...

She looked down. Took another tiny bite of the honeyed bread. It nearly choked her. She tossed the rest of it into the bushes and turned away.

She walked across the road, stepping over deep ruts carved into the sandy dirt by passing wagon wheels. Long, coarse grass grew on either side, tugging at her legs. The road here ran parallel with the coast, and a few strides brought her to a sea cliff overlooking the water. Twenty feet below, the high tide bashed against rocks and nipped the base of the precipice. Salt wind rushed in her ears, the waves churned deep, timeless notes, and grass rustled around her feet. Again she had the feeling of a vast, eternal Song. A lyric too grand to be understood all at once. Like a great, unseen Composer stooped to play in her ear just a little bit, a stanza or so, of His masterpiece.

She coughed, choking on sudden tears. The pain in her heart had changed a bit, as though the Song was whispering words to it that her mind could not grasp.

An aching love for Breac opened in her chest. She struggled against another onslaught of tears as she peeked over her shoulder at him. He sat still, head bowed over his knees.

What comfort could she offer him? She who was the cause of his pain?

She turned back toward the sea, looking down at her hands. Healed from all their scratches and burns, but filthy with travel and death. She scratched at a spot of dried blood with her fingernail. Looked back at Breac again. Then to the sea.

Be still, it seemed to say. *Be still. His Creator and yours is not weak nor blind. Be still.*

She pulled a deep breath through her mouth, and sniffed, running a sleeve under her nose.

"Lady Evie?"

She jumped, swiping quickly at the tears as she turned to face Kuruk. "Yes?"

"We must be going."

"I'm—" Her voice broke, so she cleared her throat and tried again. "I'm ready."

* * * * *

It was well past noon when Evie woke the next day. They had ridden into Al Acatra in the middle of the night and taken rooms at an inn. Their ride through the city still felt vague, shadowed by fatigue and sorrow. She remembered the steep climb, and street lamps casting islands of yellow light over darkened shops and wood planked streets.

She remembered that Breac had tried to bid her good night, standing in the hallway between their rooms. He took her hand and pressed it against his cheek, meeting her eyes for the first time since the dragon attack. His look sliced into her, and again she fought tears, knowing that if she started to cry she would never stop.

"Tomorrow..." he began, and grimaced as though the word was poisonous. "Tomorrow...I...I will speak with you." He kissed her hand. "Until then."

She stopped him before he could pull away. "Until then," she had said, choking on the words, and kissed him softly.

Evie sat up slowly, feeling like her entire person, body and soul, had been replaced with one massive ache this morning. Or rather this afternoon, judging by the light coming in the window. She wanted to sink back on the feather stuffed mattress and retreat into oblivion. Instead she rose with a sigh and straightened her clothes, now filthy and torn. *Just like the rest of me.*

A large mirror with an ornate oval frame hung above a basin of water on the dresser. She splashed her face and rubbed it dry on the little hand towel. She looked rough. Her mouth had turned thin and hard, her eyes dull and rimmed in purple shadows. Her hair hung in clumpy spirals. How long since she'd brushed it? She couldn't even begin to remember. Sunburn colored her cheekbones and brought out a mess of freckles, and her nose was beginning to peel. She noticed it all without a flicker of caring. Today either she or Breac would die. Strange, after running from inevitable death all week, how she suddenly wished for it. Breac purposed to give his life for her. She could not let him.

The inn's common room was mostly empty when she went down. Orran and Winneth occupied a small table in the corner. No one else was in sight. She sat down with them, noticing that they looked like they had just woken up as well.

"Where're Breac and Mykell?" she asked.

Winneth shook his head. "Not here."

She started to rise, and he grabbed her wrist, pulling her back gently.

"Best stay and have a meal with us, lass. No sense in passing out from hunger later. Besides, they are with the King."

"I have to talk to them!" She tried to rise again, and Winneth pulled her down.

"Leave it, lass. He will find you when he's ready to speak. You will see him before the end."

"The end..." she echoed, feeling the blood drain out of her face.

Winneth and Orran exchanged an uncomfortable look, but just then a maid came out of the back with a tray of food, and a stack of plates. Evie's stomach growled in spite of herself. They had a plate loaded in front of her in three seconds flat, and Orran pressed a fork into her hand.

"Eat."

She stared at the plate. *The end* kept running through her head. The end. No more kisses in the moonlight, no more dances, no more songs. No more hope.

She bolted from the table and ran. She yanked open the door, and was moving too fast to avoid a startled Mykell. She went over top of him, head first, and landed on the boardwalk.

"Mykell!"

He blinked down at her, ears back. "Really. Was that necessary?"

"Where's Breac?" She sat up, rubbing her shoulder.

"I was coming to find you. He awaits."

* * * * *

Evie followed Mykell higher into the city. They turned from the boardwalk onto a side street and up a natural staircase formed of rocks and roots. Alders lined the way, offering a flickering shade as they climbed. Children's laughter and glimpses of houses came through the screen of branches, until finally their lane leveled out into a grassy open area like a small park, with a spring cascading out of a rocky rift at the base of a short ledge. On the park's opposite side, across from the ledge, a row of gnarled apple trees guarded a drop off. Evie stopped, huffing for breath.

"Come human, we have not reached our destination."

Several women stood in line, waiting to fill pitchers and buckets from the spring, while their children chased each other in the grass. They all stopped and stared as Evie and Mykell passed.

Beyond the park the lane merged with a larger, dusty road leading past a stable, and then a marble courtyard.

"The High King's palace," Mykell said, glancing beyond the courtyard. Cut into the mountainside, marble melded with stone to form a grand entrance. Vines swirled up the front until it was hard to tell where the mountain ended and the building began. "He doesn't live there of course. It is a hall of meetings and judgment."

"Judgment?" Evie squeaked.

"Yes."

She popped her knuckles, squinting at the dark entrance. "Is Breac there?"

"No."

The city ended abruptly, the road dwindling into a footpath after they passed the palace. It took a steep turn up the mountain, turning into more of a hiking trail, lined with boulders and more alders. Beyond these she could see nothing but sky. Whether they traveled beside a gorge, a valley, or an open meadow she couldn't tell until they came out into a great, sloping field, and she saw that the whole mountain sheared off a few yards from the path.

She was so intent on the climb, putting one foot in front of the other, trying to breathe, that she didn't notice the ring of boulders until they were right on it. They had come nearly to the top of the meadow, walking along the edge of the cliff. Mykell stopped in front of her, and she looked up to see the circle of boulders, right at the edge. In the center rose a standing stone shaped like a tall, thin cone, carved with symbols and words in a continuous jumble. Breac sat with his back resting against the base of the stone. He was alone.

"I will leave you," Mykell said. He padded to the cliff's edge and leapt over. An instant later he reappeared as an eagle, gliding upward in a slow spiral.

Evie stepped over to the circle, and stopped, resting her hand on a boulder. Breac sat with his legs drawn up, forearms resting on knees, his head bowed. He seemed unaware of her. Her gaze went from him to the stone, and fixed for a moment on one of the symbols etched there. She realized it was her travel symbol. Some of the others looked familiar as well, taken from the Book of the Kantra. Or perhaps the Book of Kantra was taken from this stone.

It felt both ancient and powerful.

"Leazor was banished from this place," Breac said suddenly, without looking up. "Along with the Ezomrah. They cannot enter here, nor do they like to come near."

"What is this place?"

"It is where the High King comes each dawn to speak with the Creator. All the power in this world, all the good, it begins here." He raised his head, swiping the hair out of his face, and looked at her. "Thoughts flow the clearest here, and the lies we tell ourselves grow thin."

"It sounds... dangerous."

He smiled and reached a hand toward her. "For some."

She paused an instant before stepping into the circle, but made it to the stone and took his hand without having any crises of disillusionment, which she supposed was a good thing. She sat down and leaned her head on his shoulder.

"So what have you been using all this clarity to think about?"

"You." He smiled and brushed a curl out of her face.

She frowned. "Breac, I have to talk to you about something..." he cut her off with a finger on her lips.

"I know. What you seek cannot be."

"But..."

"I swore an oath. It is final."

"No! You can't! I won't let you! Please! Just let me die."

He leaned in and kissed her. A hard, possessive kiss that left her lips throbbing. When he finally pulled away, she started to protest again, and he silenced her with another kiss.

"Breac!" she gasped finally.

"Yes?"

"You're making it worse!"

"Well if you would be still."

"Fine."

"Fine."

He leaned back and looked at her for a long moment. "Can you hear it?"

"What am I supposed to be hearing?" she asked, her heart throbbing painfully.

"The Creator's Song. You must be still."

She looked at him curiously, then out over the cliff's edge. From here she couldn't see the valley or whatever lay below the mountain. All she could see were more mountains, purple in the distance, and a glimmer of sea. Cloud formations hugged the horizon. A rush of wind sounded loud in her ears.

"And what is the song telling you?" she asked.

"That my love for you was meant to be. All of Creation, its seasons and cycles, evenings and mornings, endings and beginnings, are ordered by the Creator. It is the rhythm of the Song. As long as He cannot fail, they cannot fail. That my life, short and hard as it has been, is part of the song. It has a purpose—that I could be here, loving, living, and dying for you."

He kissed her again—on the forehead this time. "That is what I came up here for. To listen and to think. And it has brought me peace, of a sort. Though—it is no easier."

She groaned, a cry of desperation that started away down in her soul. "Breac, no..." Again with the finger on her lips. She tried to speak around his finger. "Please..."

He replaced his finger with his lips, killing her protest, then moved to whisper in her ear. "You're not listening very well."

Tears welled up. "Neither are you! I can't do this! Dying I can do. But I'm not strong enough to lose you."

"I'm sorry, Evie."

A voice broke in above them, making her jump. A low, lilting voice.

"It is time."

Breac pulled away, his eyes suddenly full of trouble. Evie looked up to see a man standing over them, looking down. He wore simple clothing; brown trousers, a short, faded green tunic, and leather moccasins. He had short black hair, startling blue eyes, and a wide mouth. The man nodded to her. "Eva Drake. Well met."

Breac scrambled to his feet and bowed in salute. "Sire."

"You're... you're the King!" Evie stammered as she got up. "You have to stop him!" her eyes stung, and she ducked her head. "Please."

The High King's face softened. "I cannot, lady. He swore an oath. Your death would no longer satisfy the law. It is he who must die."

"No!"

"Peace," he said, laying a hand on her shoulder. At once the scream she'd been holding back died in her throat, and a brittle peace settled in her, like she had felt on the road after Ravenport. She hated the feeling. She wanted to fight, to save Breac. But... she was overwhelmed with a feeling of purpose, of rightness, even though her mind struggled against it. So she followed them back down the mountainside, letting the tears fall silently.

* * * * *

They entered the stony coolness of the Judgment Hall, footsteps echoing off the high vaulted ceiling. The room really was like a great hall, delving into the mountain. Evie traced her fingers along the wall, over spidery words carved in the polished rock. White veins of quartz looked like lightning bolts zigzagging down from the shadowy heights.

They stopped before a semi-circle of people seated on thrones at the far end of the room. Evie turned at a whisper of sound, and found that a small crowd was filing in behind them. She swallowed around a knot of panic.

"Greetings, Aindreas, and Lady Eva Drake. We meet again,"

said one of the seated dignitaries.

Evie turned back around to face forward, and saw that it was Vivaqua, the naiad queen, who addressed them. She looked around at the other faces as the High King took his seat in the middle. Some were human, and some were not. On one throne sat a red-gold lion, his body turned catty-corner in the seat, one paw draped over the arm rest. He regarded her with eyes the same color as his fiery fur. Was he truly a lion? Or another shape shifter like Mykell?

She spotted a dryad as well, and another jolt of panic went through her. She was beginning to feel dizzy.

"Other matters have already been put to rest," the High King began. "One thing yet remains for this Day of Justice. The betrayal of the dryad Sylvanus by this woman, Eva Drake."

Evie's gaze skipped to the dryad ruler, who remained impassive, and back to the King.

"Leazor," the King said. "Come here."

The air shimmered, and Leazor appeared before the King. He gave an exaggerated bow, his black cloak sweeping the floor. "Your Highness."

Evie was breathing so hard she was seeing spots. She gripped Breac's arm, suddenly afraid she would pass out. He bent toward her, his breath tickling her ear as he whispered, his voice urgent, raw.

"I love you, Evie. Remember that. Do not think that I or the Creator have forsaken you."

She shot him a terrified glance. His face was the only thing she could really see clearly. Everything else had become shadowy and blurred.

"Leazor, Father of Traitors," the High King said. "It is your right to claim all who betray the blood of a friend." He nodded toward Evie.

"It has always been my one pleasure in serving you. But I was given to understand that the lady is not mine any longer to claim." The Sorcerer's eyes turned to Breac, gleaming. "It is a far greater prize that I come to claim today."

Silence. Evie scanned the faces before her. Some watched the King, others Leazor. Most were looking fierce and wary. Except Vivaqua. The naiad queen met her gaze, her expression unruffled. *I have seen life in your future, Eva Drake.* An echo of that long ago conversation whispered to her. *Is this what you saw?* Evie wanted to ask. The faintest of smiles curved Vivaqua's pale lips. Evie's runaway heartbeat stopped cold, and then kicked in like bongo drums in her ears. Leazor spoke again, reclaiming her attention.

"You must be loath, your *highness* to give up your most favored servant in exchange for this...traitor."

Evie felt like she'd been stabbed. There it was. Breac squeezed her shoulder tight enough to hurt, while the King's face remained hard, creased with tension. Sweat trickled down his cheek, and he ran a hand through his black hair.

"Enough, Sorcerer. My servant Aindreas has sworn an oath, that he will take the lady Eva's place, and give himself into your hands. Do you accept?"

"Oh I do indeed."

30
The Standing Stone

"NO!" Evie screamed, her voice echoing from the vault above. All eyes in the room turned to her. "I am the traitor. Take me."

"I do not accept," Leazor said, frowning, though his eyes glinted with wicked merriment.

Evie took a step toward the Sorcerer, putting herself between him and Breac. The moment had come. Her heart pummeled her from the inside, and her breath burned. Her vision had gone spotty again. The room seemed to be so much more crowded than before. She glanced around. The people who had come in behind them were huddled together, and surrounding them, creeping close to where Evie and Breac stood, were the Ezomrah. Thousands of bottomless black eyes focused on them, creatures in all shapes and forms. She whirled back to Leazor.

"Please! He has done nothing. You would have innocent blood on your hands? Take me instead!"

"*Please.*" Leazor mocked, stepping toward her. He touched her face, sending cold like electricity jolting through her. "You have no idea what you are saying child." He leaned close, brushing his face against her hair. "But since you say please..."

Evie felt something press into her hand. She looked down and saw a knife. She went to drop it, but Leazor's fist closed over hers, crushing her fingers against the leather wrapped grip. He spun her around to face Breac, holding her against his chest with an arm that may as well have been solid steel, while his other hand remained clenched around her hand and the knife.

Breac stared back at her. The blue and brown of his gaze had been replaced by bottomless black.

"As you can see," Leazor said in her ear, "you are too late."

Air stuck in her throat. Those black eyes pressed on her.

Leazor raised the knife, with her hand firmly locked around it. With a quick jerk he slid it across Breac's throat. Evie's vision filled with spraying blood. Leazor's chest expanded against her back in a sigh.

And then he was gone.

Breac's knees hit the floor, and he fell sideways at Evie's feet. His eyes remained just as black and empty as before, yet they still seemed to stare up at her. She opened her hand, and the knife clattered onto the floor. The only sound in a world that had stopped turning. She lifted her hand to touch her face, coated with blood. His blood.

* * * * *

When Evie knew anything again, she knew that the world had ended, and for a few merciful seconds, she couldn't remember why.

She sat up. She was in a bed. Her room at the inn. A black shadow moved from the corner, and she turned to see Mykell, a cat, leap up beside her. He stared at her with wide green eyes, and she stared back. The only light in the room was from a stumpy candle. Had she blacked out? Or had she simply ceased to exist for awhile? Breac was dead.

She looked down at her hands. In the candlelight they seemed clean. No blood. Her clothes were new. A gray gown. Or maybe it was blue. She looked back up at Mykell. Just looked. She couldn't speak. Had nothing to say.

There were no words to put it into context. Words were safe, with boundaries... neat little ways to express oneself. What she felt was far beyond the realm of words. No boundaries. No expression for remorse or guilt or anguish. Words were dust. Words and tears.

Mykell watched her, green eyes far too bright in the dim room.

She looked down at her hands again, rubbing them on the

blankets. "Breac..."

Mykell spoke. "Your debt is paid, human. There is no blood on your hands."

"Then why can I still feel it?"

Mykell's ears rotated backward, and he gazed at her, head cocked to the side for a moment. "Perhaps if you speak with the King.... He's requested you to meet him in the palace before sunrise."

"Why? Will he kill me now?"

The shifter pinned his ears back and narrowed his eyes. "I doubt it."

Evie pushed the blankets away and stood, feeling shaky and wooden. Mykell jumped down with her, taking his panther shape.

Downstairs, the kitchen was already alive and bustling. A girl came out of the back with a plate in her hands, offering it to Evie with a look of sympathy. Evie shook her head. Mykell, however, barred her way.

"First, eat," he said.

She looked at the plate of food, and her stomach growled. Treacherous organ! How could it? Mykell head-butted her into a chair, and the girl set the plate in front of her.

"But sunrise!" Evie protested.

"Is far off yet. We have time."

She thought the food would gag her, but again her hunger betrayed her. She downed the whole plate without tasting a thing. Only then would Mykell let her out the door, and together they made the trek to the palace in the dark.

The High King waited for them in the shadow of one of the marble pillars outside the palace. She didn't see him until he stepped out into the gray twilight and took her hand. She jumped.

"Thank you for coming. It would not have seemed right without your presence this dawn."

Evie gave him a blank look. *More words.* Perhaps words and sounds held power here, but no voice could change death.

The King pulled her into the great hall, where a torch burned at each side of the doorway. Beyond the torches stretched shadowy emptiness, but along the walls a glimmer of silver caught her eye. The words she had noticed carved there yesterday seemed to glow with a slight radiance of their own.

"Where is he?" she whispered as they passed by the torches and entered the black midnight of the hall.

"We will go to him soon." The King led her along the wall, brushing his hand over the etchings until they had left the torchlight behind, and only the spidery silver words were visible. "From the dawn of time this day had been written in the stars. There are other days as well, but this one has always been my favorite."

Evie listened to the words. Meaningless words. But what else could she do? Still, a part of her wondered, why this day of all days? Was it truly the end of the world?

"Leazor was once my friend, the second most powerful being in this world, as the Creator granted us power. We ruled and cared for our people together. But his wisdom was turned to cruelty. Now, no longer a friend to the Creator who gave him being, he thinks he is still powerful. But he has forgotten what true power is."

Evie hugged herself, staring into the darkness, letting her eyes lose focus. *Stop! Oh please stop talking. Breac is dead. And you go on as if anything else matters. Did he mean as little to you as all that?*

The King grasped her shoulders in the dark, gently but firmly. "Words have power in this world, Eva Drake. Do you believe that?"

She looked up at him, seeing only the dim circle of his face, and the gleam of his eyes. She didn't reply.

"They are sacred in fact," he went on. Had he heard her thoughts? "Powerful and sacred as blood in this world. And I think in yours as well. Is it not written in one of your great books, 'The Word was made flesh'?"

"I don't know," she whispered miserably. *First Leazor and writing in the stars, now blood and words. What is the point in all this?*

"Breac gave his sacred word that he would take your place yesterday. That was why neither you nor I could stop it. Believe me. Words are very powerful. And blood."

Mykell, whom Evie had not heard following them, said, "The dark is giving way. Dawn will be upon us soon."

"Good! We must be going then."

The King turned her gently, still with a hand on her shoulder, and began guiding her back toward the torches and the growing light of dawn, when a sound reached faintly through the silent morning. Light but shrill, it stopped them all for a moment.

"What was it?" Mykell asked, his voice gone wary.

The King said, "Leazor's battle horn. He's brought his army." Then he actually laughed. "Now I will not have to summon him as far."

Evie's stomach turned and she sucked a breath, letting it out in a moan. "No..."

They left the palace, turning onto the path up the mountain. Evie was soon panting, scrambling to keep up. Mykell bounded past her. As they crossed the meadow she could see the standing stone in the distance, but it was not until they drew close that she could make out the ring of boulders through the long grass.

Flowers were strewn about the circle, on and around the boulders, at the base of the standing stone, and over Breac's body where it lay on a bed of hemlock and alder boughs. His eyes had been closed, and his skin was gray-white, like the standing stone, except for the gash across his throat. Evie dropped to her knees.

The sight of Breac lying there banished every other thought. She needed to hold him, to have him back, warm and breathing, in her arms. But his face was cold as the night.

The King stood over them, resting a hand on the standing stone while he gazed out across the dark valley to the mountains flashing golden far away.

"Stand up," he said quietly. "The sun is coming, and we have no time for tears."

Evie hardly heard him, but got slowly to her feet, compelled to do so. Mykell sat on his haunches beside her.

The High King winked at her. Winked! Again her body rebelled against her, for her heart gave a great, hopeful leap as he turned and shouted, "Leazor! Come here!"

The sorcerer appeared like an unwilling vision on the mountaintop, standing just outside the ring of stones. Evie cringed.

Leazor looked around, then at the High King. He sneered. "And what do you require of me today, oh highest of wretched, deposed kings? Do you wish to beg for the lives of your subjects? Perhaps you would like a small, filthy cave for your exile, like the one you gave me?"

"Silence!"

Leazor's mouth shut with a click and he glared.

The High King returned his gaze, looking sad and stern, but also a little amused. Or perhaps Evie's mind was finally giving out after all. Mykell shifted closer, leaning against her leg, and she dropped a hand to rest on his head.

"You are arrogant, Leazor. In all your trickery and deceit, have you also deceived yourself? Do you fancy that you are now king over all the land, and that the Creator will overlook your crimes and favor you once again?"

Leazor barked a laugh. "My army stands ready to sweep over this mountain and subdue it like a rebellious child. Where will the kingship be then? No, your *highness*, I certainly have not forgotten how things stand. But have you? Surely you remember the stonemason sent to carve my doom on the very portal of my lair. You seemed insistent enough that *I* be forced to remember it. It was concerning the warrior, called by a name that others gave him, with the light of two nations in his eyes, the man who would bring my defeat." Leazor paused and spat toward Breac's body. Evie's eye twitched as he continued. "Perhaps the Creator has gone to sleep since then, and cares not any more. Perhaps this world has become so corrupt that he no longer cares what becomes of it, for now that man is dead. The prophecy is void. Not even you can stop me."

The King gazed at him for a moment, then threw his head back and laughed. Not a rueful or arrogant laugh, but a merry one, as though Leazor had told a brilliant joke. Evie and Mykell looked at each other. What was this madness? Breac's body lay a few feet away, and here was the High King, laughing, while Leazor glared his fury. Yet the King's laughter was so joyous, so infectious, that once again Evie's heart rebelled, leaping with hope. When Mykell glanced at her again there was a light in his green eyes.

The King's laughter subsided to a last, gentle chuckle, and he straightened, raising piercing eyes to his enemy.

"But you have already been defeated, Leazor. By your own hand."

Leazor's face darkened. "The man is dead. His soul is in the hands of my servants. Not even the naiad healers could bring him back now."

"And in dying he has condemned you."

"What?" Leazor's face turned horrible. Evie quivered as a dark aura spread around him.

"For long centuries it has been your right and your duty to deal out punishment to those who shed innocent blood. And this duty you have abused to your own gain, the while you have shed gallons of innocent blood, and never felt justice."

"Who will demand justice on me? Your Creator, who hides his face? It was he who made it my right to claim all traitors' lives. Can I claim my own? Can I punish myself?"

The High King tipped his head in assent. "Hardly."

"Who then will claim this justice? The dead? Those whom I have killed?" Leazor waved his hand over the mountaintop. "I don't see many ghosts walking about, do you? Again, your Creator keeps the spirits of the dead well away from this world. So if I, the Creator's instrument of justice, can do nothing to myself, and those innocent whom I have killed, who would have the right, can also do nothing, then why should I fear? The dead stay dead. There is a certain beauty to that, *I* think."

"It was not always so, nor is it still," the King said. "A few souls the Creator has granted be returned to my service. Those who swore allegiance to me and took my mark. Those souls I command."

Leazor looked like he had just eaten something rotten. "You have your soul mark, as do I," he said. "But I dare guess that you have not had people lining up to be branded in recent years. Not with most of the habited world in my control."

"Still, I have a few sworn servants."

Leazor did not reply, and in the silence came a gust of wind, blowing the hair back from Evie's face. She looked around. The light was strong, the horizon fiery white. In a second the sun's edge would split sky and sea.

The King said, "In answer to your question, Leazor, it is the innocent dead who shall claim justice."

Leazor, face gone waxy and rigid, stepped back. Evie looked to the High King as he raised his face to the sky. A blinding sliver of light pierced the horizon, and she felt the air and earth tremble.

"Creator!" the King cried, "Hear me this dawn. Grant the life of my servant, grant justice that has been denied."

Evie stepped back, her gaze jumping between Breac's body and the High King. She went suddenly dizzy as the gash across Breac's throat sealed shut, and his skin changed from chalky gray to deep tan. Her knees wavered, then hit the ground, sending a shock up to her skull.

"Aindreas, son of Rajah, wake up."

And his chest expanded.

His eyes opened. Clear blue and brown, with no hint of blackness nor emptiness. He sat up, saw Evie, and a slow smile spread over his face.

Breac. The word didn't quite reach her lips the first time.

"Breac..." she whispered it. Then suddenly she was screaming his name. She launched herself at him, and they rolled backward off the funeral bed of branches and into the grass. His laugh filled her ear, warm and full of life. His arms around her were warm and strong. His kisses the warmest of all. She tucked her face into the crook of his neck, and breathed the scent of pine and horse and ozone that always clung to him. And still she couldn't stop saying his name, sobbing.

The High King spoke softly. "We have unfinished business."

Evie pulled back, her hands lingering on him, touching him, clutching handfuls of his shirt. Not ready to give him up yet. His eyes met hers, sending her heart somersaulting. He hugged her tight before rolling to his feet to stand before the King. Evie got up more slowly, waiting with a hand on Mykell's head.

The King turned back to Leazor. "Look, Traitor. One who was dead stands before you. An innocent man whom you killed. It is he who will claim justice."

Despite the newly risen sun, the mountaintop seemed to be growing darker. Ghostly flames licked down Leazor's arms and played about his hands.

"And what sort of justice might that be?" the Sorcerer said. "Have you forgotten that I am just as immortal as you are? Even with your trickery I cannot be killed, even by one who is, unfortunately, back from the dead."

"You will not be killed. But this man stands before you to claim what is due on behalf of all the innocents."

"And what might that be?"

Breac spoke for the first time. "I do not strip away your life, Leazor, but your power. Your duty to punish traitors will remain just that, a duty. No more will you let them live and, through the Law, enslave a nation. Henceforth you *will* fulfill your obligation to slay any traitor, unless they swear fealty to the High King, and take his mark upon them.

"The nations you have enslaved, whose innocent lives you have taken, will rise up against you. Your rule will be overthrown as the kings remember their Creator and swear fealty to the High King. You will still be cunning and powerful, but never again will your hand be raised against an innocent life, for though your spirit wanders the land, your flesh will never leave Al Kazam unless summoned. This is the justice I claim. This will be your curse."

Leazor growled deep in his throat, the savage sound of a beast. Lightening crackled over the mountaintop, striking outside the ring of boulders. He drew his sword and lunged toward Breac, but reaching the boulders, he was thrown back, repelled as though by a force field. The sword flew out of his hand. He got to his feet again, his rage palpable.

A black shadow passed over them. Mykell looked up and snarled as thousands of the Ezomrah in raven form swirled around their refuge, their wings blotting out the sun. They parted as

Leazor drew near once again. This time he stopped just outside the ring of stones. He held out his hand, and his sword flew back to his grasp.

"Fight me, son of Rajah. I will bleed you once again. Just like your father died on his knees before me. Come out and face me."

Breac and the High King exchanged a look, and Evie squeaked as Breac stepped away from her, leaving the protection of the ring. Leazor's eyes turned wild with triumph. He raised his sword, and brought it down at Breac's head, a move that should have cut the man in two. Instead the sword passed through him like mist.

"You've killed me twice now, Leazor. Is that not enough? You have no power here. Already you are losing your physical form."

The Ezomrah circled upward as the High King stepped up behind Breac.

Leazor's eyes, still wild, flashed with insanity. But his voice was low and eerily calm. "Spirit I may be, bound to Al Kazam. But I will never cease pursuing you. My servants will haunt you, they will seek out the ones you love and destroy them. They will never stop until they have corrupted your children, and destroyed your faith in your King and your Creator."

The High King broke in. "You have no power over my servant now. You may hunt him and seek to destroy him, but his life and the lives of his loved ones are in the hands of the Creator, where they have always been. Now. Leave us."

Leazor vanished.

The Ezomrah circled upward now even faster. Soon they were a blot in the sky high above. They passed over the city toward Al Kazam and were gone.

"And his army?" Mykell asked.

The King squinted at the sky, his eyes momentarily distant. "Scattering," he said finally. "For now. Leazor's hold on his men is shaken. As Breac said, he will still have power, but he will be limited. And it will be more difficult for him now." His gaze returned to the immediate surroundings, and he smiled and clapped Breac on the back. "You've done it, my friend."

"I supposed I have."

"You did not expect the prophecy to play out as it did?"

"Truthfully, I had given up thinking about it. I thought the prophecy must take care of itself, because I had other matters."

The King smiled. "Well. That's the way of most prophesies. I've seen many fulfilled, and I can tell you, they usually are unexpected. But now that that's taken care of—I think we may have another bit of business to attend to."

Mykell slipped away from Evie's side. He padded over to the High King, inclined his head, and sat, smirking. And suddenly Breac stood before her, filling her entire vision.

"Lady Evie, you'll remember on the ship I asked you a question which you never answered."

Her face flamed. "Would that be the, uh, the one about...about...?"

"You are now free to stay in this world. You have been given life, and, it seems, so have I. So what is your answer?"

Apparently her face wasn't done turning up the heat yet. "Ye...es. Yes."

Suddenly she was caught up, suffocating in an embrace so tight she felt her back pop.

"Thank the Creator," he whispered. "You scared me for a moment."

She laughed. "So....When?"

"Tonight!"

"Tonight?! Wow. That's... that's... tonight."

"Need we wait?"

"Well, that doesn't leave a girl much time to prepare."

The King broke in with "It shall be done!" They both turned to see him grinning, eyes twinkling. "On my word, you two are painful to watch. Well I say, let the pain end. Tonight it shall be."

* * * * *

It was dusk, and paper lanterns lined the path, from the door of the inn where Evie had spent the day preparing, up and around the bend that led to the palace. Lanterns and fireflies. Evie waited, fidgeting, by the door as Rilla, one of the girls who had helped with her hair, watched out the window. The girl let out a little squeal. "They're coming!"

Evie closed her eyes and breathed deep. After the rush of emotions over the past week, she felt surprisingly calm. This is what she had waited for. The tears and the blood that had flowed freely, the fear and the hope, the long road... it was the Creator leading them to this moment. She knew that now as surely as she knew she was not the same person who, fearful and dissatisfied, had first stumbled into this world. She was no longer a betrayer.

Her hand went to her hair, braided into a crown and studded with white flowers. Her gown, white lace over midnight blue silk, rustled as she bounced lightly on her toes.

"How do I look?" It was probably the tenth time she'd asked, but she couldn't help it.

"Perfect," Rilla said. "He will forget how to walk when he sees you." She peeked out the window again. "Almost here!" Then she turned, brushed a kiss across Evie's cheek, and scurried away. Evie was left alone in the empty common room of the inn. She stole another deep breath. The butterflies were catching up with her now. She could hear voices approaching from the other side of the door. She put her hand on the latch and opened it, her heart beating a drumroll as she closed her eyes for just an instant.

She opened them to see Breac standing before her.

Aindreas.

Tall, broad, and clean shaven, his hair finally trimmed and tied back in a short tail. She barely recognized him without the burden and grime of their journey. He wore black trousers and a white shirt, belted with a blue sash. He looked so much younger. She giggled at the thought that she didn't know her soon-to-be husband's age, then blushed. He looked very handsome. And—she allowed herself to think it—hot. Very hot.

She looked down, suddenly bashful. Breac cupped her chin in his hand and lifted her face so he could look in her eyes. He said nothing, just smiled, and her heart raced.

Music started somewhere. A fiddle, a flute, a harmonica. For the first time Evie looked past Breac, noticing the crowd of people that had followed, waiting to escort them to the palace for the ceremony. The High King was there, and Queen Vivaqua. Mykell, Kuruk, Winneth and Orran, Jorah and Mergit. Even Tyra and Ylva had somehow made it. She gave them a little wave. Then her eyes went back to Breac, and met his. For just a moment, surrounded by people and lights and music, they were alone.

"My Evie," he said softly, smiling. "You were more than worth it. All of it."

She smiled up at him, a smile so big it probably looked goofy, with her heart too full to respond.

"It seems I've finally found my way home," he said.

"Me too."

He thrust his hand into his pocket and came out with a chain and pendant that flashed silvery in the light. "May I?"

She turned her back to him while he clasped the chain around her neck, then turned, lifting the pendant to look at it. "My locket!" she flicked it open to see the tiny photos of her and her sister still in place. "When did you find this?"

"In a past lifetime."

Her breath caught, and then she laughed. "Thank you."

He offered his arm, and she took it. Together, with the people trailing behind, they walked to the palace. Only Evie thought they were floating on soft lights and a breeze scented with jasmine and spice.

They made their vows in the pillared courtyard, under an arbor of silvery ribbons of water, commanded by Vivaqua. Vows to never depart from one another in spirit or in loyalty, and as they spoke them she looked into his eyes. One brown, one blue.

Epilogue

Fourteen days later they stood in a forest clearing, where grass and vines obscured crumbling ruins. Breac handed Evie his reins and stepped toward the ruins.

"Where was it?"

Evie studied the clearing, the brush growing around the edge, and the half buried slabs of rock. "To the left," she said finally. "There! Right there."

He stooped and brushed grass away from a huge stone, moss covered, slanting up out of the ground at an angle. He worked his way upward, peeling away the thick layers of moss and matted leaves, and at last stepped back. "There it is."

She led the horses to where he stood. "If only I had known."

Breac shook his head. "I cannot say what would have happened if you had found the mark and gone right back the moment you came. But I cannot bear the thought of never standing here with you now, my wife."

"Sylvanus would be alive."

"Perhaps."

"And you wouldn't have had to die."

"One can never tell. It was the only way Leazor could be stopped."

"I still can't forgive myself though."

The look he gave her heated her right down to the toes. "We've had this discussion before, and you'll remember how it ended."

Evie felt blood creeping into her face, and glanced back at the caravan, the soldiers and their families who had traveled with them, and were to await their return, keeping the portal safe. "Was that a threat, Son of Rajah?"

His lips quirked. "Take it as you will."

"I will choose to ignore it then, shameless man." She laughed.

Breac signaled, and one of the soldiers came and took their horses. He offered Evie his arm. "What will your family say to your bringing home a stranger to whom you are married?"

"I have no idea."

"Then I suppose it's time to find out."

She squeezed his arm, and together they touched the mark.

A Note from the Author

...To you my reader! Thank you for picking up my book! You are the reason I write (of course there's the other reason—that I would go crazy with all those characters and stories trapped in my head!). You took time out of your busy life, and from the millions of books clamoring for your attention, you chose Betrayer. For this I am truly honored. Thank you!

As a writer my biggest inspiration comes from the Greatest Story ever told—the Gospel. That epic Fairy Tale that is also true, and has a place in history. It's to God alone I must humbly credit any skill or success I have.

With that in mind, this story is not meant to be an allegory. If anything, it is merely a dim echo of the sacrificial love Christ has given us. The story began long ago on a firefly lit night in East Texas, with a character named Breac, in a spiral bound notebook that my friend and I took turns writing in. From Texas, on a long train ride to Pennsylvania, and then an even longer road trip to Alaska, Breac and his world continued to develop. Evie didn't come along until several years later. It's been ten years from that Texas night to this writing. What a journey!

I'd like to give a shout out to the people who made this all possible. First to my muse and Breac's co-creator, Tiffany. You've been there through it all, quite literally from cover to cover. I'm truly grateful for the time, insight, and talent you put into doing the artwork, not to mention all the hours of listening to me bounce ideas around!

To Brett, my one and only, the heart of my love story.

To my folks. Because without Dad's crazy writing games and story creating antics I most definitely wouldn't be creating worlds. And without Mom's prayer support and patient interest in my dream (even though she didn't always understand it) I would have given up long ago.

Finally to the friends and relations who have not only encouraged, listened, and prayed, but have shaped who I am, whom I don't have the space to acknowledge properly, a big thanks. You are not forgotten!

Made in the USA
Charleston, SC
21 December 2014